DARK ROVER'S SHIRE

THE CHILDREN OF THE GODS
BOOK NINETY-SEVEN

I. T. LUCAS

Copyright © 2025 by I. T. Lucas

All rights reserved.

No part of this book may be reproduced in any form or by any electronic or mechanical means, including information storage and retrieval systems, without written permission from the author, except for the use of brief quotations in a book review.

Published by Evening Star Press, LLC.

EveningStarPress.com

ISBN: 978-1-962067-80-5

KIAN

ifty-three hours had passed since the raids, and forty-nine since it had been confirmed that there was no fifth terror nest lurking somewhere in Los Angeles. Now was the time for a deeper dive, but as Kian observed the prisoner through the two-way mirror in the interrogation room, he wasn't sure they would be able to get anything coherent out of the Doomer.

The deterioration in his condition was remarkable.

"How long has he been twitching like that?" Kian asked Theo, who was in charge of the dungeon in Max's absence.

"About fifteen hours." Theo rose to his feet. "Julian says he's suffering withdrawal symptoms. Even the sedatives are not helping. All the Doomers we captured this time have been twitching like that, some worse than others, and they don't sleep unless we sedate them. Soras here seems more affected than the others, but he also seems to be more intelligent than average, which is uncommon for rank-and-file Doomers."

That was why Kian had chosen to interrogate this specific Doomer again, but it might be necessary to wait until he stabilized.

The prisoner was shackled to a metal chair that was bolted down, which was the only reason he was still seated and not sprawled and twitching on the floor. His head was lolling forward, sweat beaded on his forehead, and his bare feet kept tapping manically on the concrete. The same compulsive movement was happening with his hands, which he was fisting and relaxing just as obsessively.

"What is he on?" Toven asked. "Did Julian find out?"

The doctor had taken blood samples shortly after the prisoners had been delivered to the keep, so he'd had enough time to analyze the results, but some were so bizarre that Julian needed help from Kaia to decipher them, and they were still working on that.

"The blood work came back." Kian pulled out his phone and started scrolling until he found the email from the doctor. "The drug cocktail is powerful, designed for immortal physiology. I don't understand half of what Julian wrote here, but there is something about amphetamine derivatives at doses that would kill a human. We're talking twenty times the lethal threshold. He also mentions synthetic adrenaline compounds that resist our naturally accelerated metabolism, along with neural enhancers that should cause permanent damage but somehow don't." He looked up. "There were several compounds Julian couldn't identify at all because the molecular structures don't exist in any database. Kaia is working on that."

Toven rubbed a hand over his jaw. "They must have a specialist working for them."

"Obviously." Kian pocketed his phone. "Shall we have a chat with the prisoner about who that mystery scientist is?"

Toven nodded. "That could shed some light on what we are dealing with, but given the state the guy is in, I'm not sure we will get anything useful out of him."

As they entered the cell, the Doomer's head snapped up, his eyes struggling to focus. The twitching intensified, muscles spasming beneath his skin as if they were trying to escape.

"Withdrawal is hitting you hard," Kian said, taking a seat at a safe distance from the metal chair. "How long since your last dose?"

"Too long." The Doomer's lips pulled back from his teeth—not quite a smile, not quite a snarl. "Worth it. The gifts... bestowed only on the select who... who…" His voice came out rough, breaking on certain words. "The chemist. You couldn't... couldn't understand. Weak. All of you are weak. Weak—"

A violent convulsion cut off his words, his body straining against the shackles hard enough to make the bolts groan and welts rise on his skin.

The drugs must have impaired Soras's mind, or maybe it was the withdrawal, but either way, Kian had a feeling he wouldn't be much use to them. Not until his body adjusted to the lack of stimulants.

"You mentioned the chemist." Toven's tone was

commanding but without that special resonance that carried compulsion. "Tell us about him. Or is it a her?"

The Doomer laughed or tried to. It came out as more of a wheeze. "Females are vapid and incapable of scientific thought. No female could... Brilliant. He's so brilliant. Making us... better. Stronger. The Brother-hood's future."

So far, the Doomer hadn't tried to resist direct questions, so Toven hadn't used compulsion on him, and Kian wondered if the drugs were responsible for the guy's loose tongue.

"What's his name?" Toven asked.

"No!" The Doomer's head twisted side to side, muscles straining as if against invisible bonds.

"Look into my eyes," Toven commanded, this time using compulsion.

The Doomer kept shaking his head.

"Interesting," Toven murmured. "He's managing to resist."

"I said, look at me." The god increased the pressure.

The Doomer's head snapped forward, eyes locking with Toven's, pupils so dilated that they were black pools in bloodshot whites.

"That is much better," Toven said. "What is the chemist's name?"

"Zhao. Dr. Marcus Zhao." The words came out less halting and flat, as if the compulsion had managed to overcome the withdrawal jitters.

Kian typed a message to Roni to start researching the name.

"How long has he been working for the Brother-hood?" Toven asked.

"A year and a half, maybe more."

Kian was starting to suspect that the Doomer had been exaggerating his withdrawal symptoms before Toven's compulsion forced him to drop the act. If so, it was clever on his part, and Kian regarded the guy with renewed interest.

According to Soras, only a select few had been chosen for enhancement. Since recently Navuh had been valuing Doomers based on smarts rather than brawn and cruelty, it made sense that Soras was more intelligent than his average brethren.

At the sound of an incoming text, Kian looked down at his phone and read the text from Roni.

Dr. Zhao disappeared about a year ago from a confer-ence in Hong Kong. His lab at Berkeley specialized in neuro-chemistry. Kaia is going over his published papers. She'll send you a summary.

Kian typed back a thank you before returning his attention to the prisoner.

"I assume that Dr. Zhao was taken against his will?"

The Doomer actually smiled. "He was promised all the beautiful females he could handle if he cooperated and threatened with harm to family members if he did not. This method never fails."

Kian found it curious that this time, Soras had volunteered the information without being compelled.

"What is Dr. Zhao creating?" Toven asked.

"Enhancement formulas." The Doomer shivered, the twitching intensifying for some reason. "Volunteers only. Those who want... want to be better. Many failures."

"Define failures," Kian commanded.

Soras's body convulsed again, and Toven repeated the question using compulsion to force him to answer.

"First batch was twenty volunteers. Fifteen couldn't tolerate it. Seizures. Psychotic breaks. Five survived, became Level One. Stronger, faster, more resilient."

So, there were different levels. That was interesting.

"What level are you?" Toven asked.

"Two." Pride crept into the Doomer's voice. "Twice baseline strength. Reaction time... significantly improved. Can go weeks without sleep."

Kian exchanged a glance with Toven. Weeks without sleep? That alone would be a significant tactical advantage, but there was a chance that the Doomer was boasting.

No one could go for so long without sleep, not even gods.

Sleep was critical to the body, and if the guy had gone so long without, it was no wonder he was psychotic.

"How many enhanced warriors have been made so far?" Toven asked.

"Eighty-seven stable. Twenty more in... in process-ing. Different levels. Level Three still... problematic."

"Problematic how?" Kian asked.

The Doomer didn't answer until Toven used compulsion to force him to talk.

The guy's face contorted. "They break. Their mind. Mohdes was Three, but he killed four Level Ones before he was stopped. Tore their hearts right out of their bodies."

"What's the goal of this enhancement program?" Toven asked.

Wasn't that obvious? Navuh had discovered a way to expedite the realization of his objective of global domination.

The Doomer's eyes shone with manic glee. "Unstoppable army. Eventually, all fighters...The strong ascending. Lord Navuh's vision..." Another convulsion racked Soras's body.

An entire army of enhanced warriors, stronger and faster than normal immortals, capable of functioning without sleep for days or even weeks at a time, was a nightmare.

Kian took a deep breath.

Could he get one damn break and some good news for a change?

How much more did the cruel Fates think he could take?

"Is Dr. Zhao working on your island?" Toven asked.

"Of course. Lord Navuh had a fancy laboratory built for him."

A rescue would be impossible. They'd managed to extract Carol, but that was because the harem was located in an isolated and convenient spot on the island, and she'd been ready for them. Storming through Navuh's army of misfits would be suicidal.

The only way to obliterate the island was to nuke it, but there were too many innocents living there for Kian to do that. His aunt was one of them.

If only Areana could be convinced to leave her deranged mate and let them extract her straight from the harem like they had Carol, the decision to destroy the island would be much easier.

Well, not really.

There were still thousands of people living on that island who'd been abducted and brought there as slave labor, either as sex providers or maids, builders, gardeners, and any other type of work that was needed on the *Pleasure* side of the island—the side known to the rich and depraved around the world.

"How often do you need the drugs?" Toven continued his questioning.

"Every day for maintenance. Every three days minimum or..." Another convulsion. "The shaking never stops. Some couldn't take it. Begged for death."

"And yet you volunteered," Toven said. "Why?"

"To be more. To help bring Lord Navuh's vision to life. To honor Mortdh with the deaths of his enemies. Mark my words. Your time will come." He bared his fangs at them. "You are all dead already."

Kian kept his expression neutral despite the flare of anger. Mere months ago, he would have laughed off the delusions of grandeur, but now he was taking them more seriously.

After his impassioned monologue, the Doomer's twitching and jerking intensified, so much so that his wrists started bleeding from how forcefully he was tugging on his restraints. When his eyes rolled back in his head, and drool slithered down his jaw, it was clear that the session was over.

They weren't going to extract anything more from him.

Kian stood, motioning for Toven to follow him out.

It occurred to him that the enhancement operation had been ongoing for a long time, and yet he hadn't heard about it from Lokan. Kian had already suspected that Navuh was keeping Lokan in the dark, but that proved it beyond a shadow of a doubt.

Lokan needed to jump ship yesterday. They had known this day was coming and had prepared for it, but Lokan had always maintained that he would know when the time was right.

Evidently, he didn't have a clue, and what's more, the information that Lokan had been supplying to Kian about the Brotherhood had been misleading. It was one of the reasons he'd been complacent and hadn't suspected what Navuh was building. Kian had been sure that Navuh was working on creating a smart army of immortals, which wouldn't be ready for a while because the children born from his new breeding program needed to grow up first. But clearly that hadn't been the only thing Navuh had been working on.

Far from it.

"Lokan and Carol are in danger," he told Toven when they were alone in the corridor. "They need to leave China right now."

Toven nodded. "I agree."

"I'm going to call Kalugal first. Perhaps he's heard from his brother recently." Kian selected Kalugal's number.

"Hello, cousin," Kalugal answered. "I'm making final arrangements for the trip to Egypt. We should be ready to leave on Tuesday."

"That's not what I'm calling about. Toven and I just finished interrogating one of the Doomers we caught in the raids, and we learned that your father has abducted a chemist to the island who's creating enhancement drugs for the Brotherhood. This has been going on for about a year and a half, and yet Lokan remains unaware. Navuh is definitely keeping him in the dark on purpose and instructing his adopted sons not to share anything with him. There is no longer doubt in my mind that he suspects Lokan."

"He needs to evacuate immediately," Kalugal said.

"My thoughts exactly. I called you first to check if you've heard from him recently."

"I haven't," Kalugal said. "I don't call Lokan because I don't want to risk compromising him, and he rarely calls."

Kian nodded. "Same here. I just wanted to share with you what I found out, so if he contacts you, you'd know what's going on. I will send the pre-agreed signal to Carol just in case their communications are compromised."

Both Lokan and Carol had clan phones, but when they were in company, it was better to send an encrypted signal that didn't reveal the sender's identity.

"Thank you. Let me know if you need anything from me. The trip to Egypt can wait."

"They have a pre-agreed route that will make

following them difficult. Lokan and Carol know what to do."

After ending the call, Kian pulled out Carol's contact, chose the application that would deliver the message anonymously, and typed the single emoji they'd agreed on during the cruise, when they'd planned for just such a scenario.

It was a sailboat, and it meant dropping everything and activating emergency protocols.

When his phone rang only a few moments later, Kian was surprised to see the call was from Lokan.

"That was fast," he answered. "I just sent Carol the pre-agreed signal a moment ago. I didn't want to call in case you were compromised in any way."

"We are not, and she's already packing. What triggered this?"

"There have been several developments that made me wonder if your father was keeping you in the dark on purpose, but now I'm convinced of it. Turns out that Navuh has been enhancing warriors for over a year and a half, and you had no clue. He's creating a chemically augmented army of stronger and faster Doomers."

"No one told me anything." Lokan sounded grim. "I have a couple of trusted sources, and now I worry that they have been compromised."

It was a valid concern and proof that one should never rely solely on snitches. "They were probably scared to share what they knew," Kian said. "Navuh also planned a massive terror attack on Los Angeles." He gave Lokan a succinct version of the events.

"Fuck." Lokan rarely cursed, but this development deserved it. "Bombing a Lasusa concert full of kids? My father has lost the last shreds of his humanity."

If Navuh ever had them, he'd lost them a very long time ago, but Kian didn't say that. "You need to get going," he told Lokan instead.

"We're moving now."

"Be careful."

"Always."

As Lokan ended the call, Kian slipped his phone into his pocket and let out a breath.

A brilliant scientist creating monster Doomers, Navuh establishing nests of vipers all over the world, and now Kian's most valuable intelligence asset was running for his life.

What else could go wrong?

Theo walked over to where Kian was standing with Toven. "Julian called. He wants more blood samples from all the enhanced Doomers. He thinks he might be able to create a counteragent, something to neutralize the enhancements and ease their suffering."

Kian didn't care about their pain, but he wanted them to be more coherent so Toven could get more reliable information out of them.

"Get Julian what he needs." He turned to Toven. "Shall we?"

The god nodded.

Inside the elevator, Kian leaned against the wall. "We're about to face an enemy unlike anything we've dealt with before. Stronger, faster, able to operate without rest."

Even the Kra-ell couldn't match that because they needed sleep even more than immortals, and they didn't heal as fast.

"You need a cyborg army," Toven said. "And the sooner the better."

Kian shook his head. "I never intended for the new version of Odus to be anything other than butlers and gardeners."

"I know." Toven regarded him with a small smile playing on his lips. "But you can't count only on the exoskeletons to give you an edge. You need more Guardians, and there are no more to be had. You have no choice. Be thankful that the option even exists."

"I know." He let out a breath. "And I am."

The problem was that the Odus wouldn't be ready anytime soon. They didn't even have a working prototype yet.

The only way to stop the enhancement program from expanding was to extract Dr. Zhao from the island, alive or dead, and destroy the laboratory, but assaulting the Brotherhood's island stronghold would be suicide.

Besides, Zhao wasn't the only scientist in the world who could manufacture those kinds of drugs, so even if he were eliminated, Navuh would get someone else to take his place.

All that remained for Kian to do was beseech the Fates and hope for the best.

That wasn't a strategy, though.

When he and Toven joined Anandur and Brundar in the SUV, Kian's phone buzzed with a text message, and as he pulled it out of his pocket, he smiled when he saw it was from Syssi.

Allegra is asking when Daddy's coming home. She won't have dinner without you.

Such a simple message, but it grounded him. This was why they fought—for the chance to have everyday moments, family dinners, and children who could ask innocent questions without knowing how close they'd come to losing everything.

He texted back; *I'm on my way.*

2

FENELLA

The Hobbit was packed, and it buzzed with energy. Every table was occupied, with standing room only at the bar.

Fenella spun a Guardian's fountain pen between her fingers, letting the performance build as the crowd leaned in with anticipation. It seemed like every immortal in the village wanted one more reading before she left in less than a week.

"This pen," she announced, holding it up to catch the light, "has a secret."

"Don't they all?" someone called out, earning scattered laughter.

"Oh, but this one is special." Fenella closed her eyes, making a show of concentration, and suddenly she felt it—a genuine flash of emotion from the object. Loneliness. Distance. The image of a smiling, beautiful woman with loving eyes. Not a lover, though, that wasn't the energy she was sensing.

A mother.

Morrison, the Guardian who'd handed her the pen, shifted uncomfortably.

"To your mother," Fenella continued, the real impression blending seamlessly with her performance. "You write every week, telling her about your life here, but you leave out all the exciting parts because you don't want her to worry."

Morrison's jaw dropped. "That's exactly—how could you possibly—"

"But here's the thing." Fenella rode the wave of genuine psychometry while adding her theatrical flair. "The pen is getting frustrated. It wants to write the truth. It's tired of editing out all the exciting bits. 'Dear Mother,'" she affected a deep voice, supposedly the pen's, "'Today I fought three Doomers before breakfast. You should have seen me, Ma. I was magnificent.'"

The crowd roared with laughter, but Morrison's eyes had gone soft. "I do miss her," he said quietly, just loud enough for Fenella to hear over the noise.

"I bet your mother misses you, too," she said, dropping the performance for a moment. "Perhaps you should take some time off and go visit your mum." She handed the pen back.

"Thank you," he mouthed before melting back into the crowd.

"Who's next?" Fenella called out, shaking off the emotional residue. These authentic glimpses were becoming more frequent, and she wondered if her ability was growing naturally or if the brooch was amplifying it. "Come on, don't be shy. Only five more nights to discover what your belongings think of you!"

From his corner table, Din caught her eye and raised his glass in a salute. His laptop was open, and he was supposedly grading final exams from his students, but he couldn't possibly concentrate with all this noise. His attention never strayed from her for long, those intense eyes of his tracking her movements with a mixture of pride and possession that made her happy and irritated at the same time.

Being a woman was complicated.

On the one hand, Din's possessiveness excited her, heating her blood and making her want him, but on the other hand, she didn't want to be possessed, not even by a male who loved her and would fight dragons for her.

Fenella wasn't a damsel in distress, and she'd been taking care of herself for a long time without Din's help. Come to think of it, perhaps she'd been lucky rather than unlucky. If Din had stayed around and they had become a couple fifty years ago, she would have been spared all the misfortunes that she'd endured, but she would have also missed out on the adventures and all the good times she'd had. She wouldn't have discovered her strength and become so fiercely independent.

In a way, he'd done her a favor by acting like an ass and walking away, because otherwise she wouldn't be the woman she was now.

She blew him an air kiss and mouthed, "I love you."

Din pretended to catch the kiss in his fist, and the grin that spread over his face transformed him from handsome to irresistible. "I love you," he mouthed back.

They'd been saying it a lot, but each exchange still

sent a thrill through her. After her resistance had finally cracked and her fear of connection had been conquered, she couldn't imagine a day without telling Din how strongly she felt about him.

"My turn!" A guy pushed forward, holding out his wallet.

Fenella recognized him. Garrett was a Guardian, and he was a shameless flirt. He'd been hitting on her all evening long despite knowing that she was with Din.

"Let's see what secrets your wallet holds," she said, taking the leather billfold. She didn't feel much of anything. Some wallets were like that—too new, too impersonal. But she could work with that.

"Your wallet is having an identity crisis," she announced. "It's practically empty, which makes it question its purpose in life. 'Am I a wallet,' it asks itself, 'or am I just a flat leather decoration?'"

"Hey!" Garrett protested as the crowd laughed. "I have money!"

"Three dollars and an expired coupon for frozen yogurt don't count," Fenella continued. "Your wallet is considering running away to find a Guardian who doesn't spend it all on drinks."

"There is no better way to spend money than on a beautiful bartender..." Garrett leaned over the bar, his smile turning suggestive.

She wanted to tell him that he had been spending money on whiskey, not her, although his tips had been generous, when she saw Din looming behind the Guardian, looking pissed.

Fenella leaned her elbows on the bar and looked into Garrett's smiling eyes. "Your wallet isn't done talking. It just whispered to me that it's desperately in love with my boyfriend's money clip, and they're planning to elope to Vegas." She pursed her lips. "Sorry to disappoint."

The crowd laughed again, but Garrett wasn't done. "Din is a lucky guy, but if you ever want to trade up to a younger model..."

Din put his hand on Garrett's shoulder. "I believe you've had too much to drink. Fenella made her position clear. You should say goodnight and go home."

The entire speech had been delivered in a measured tone, but Fenella knew Din well enough to sense that he was angry. Immortals lived by different standards than humans, and this young Guardian had crossed the line.

Garrett turned, looked up to meet Din's eyes, and seemed to realize his mistake. Din might be a scholar now, but he had been a warrior in the past, and he'd probably seen more battles in person than Garrett had on the screen. The promise of violence lurked in his stance, controlled but unmistakable.

"I was just—"

"Leaving," Din suggested pleasantly. "To work on your manners."

Garrett backed away, hands raised. "I was just teasing. No harm meant."

"None taken," Fenella said brightly. "But your wallet is still disappointed in you!"

As Garrett retreated, Fenella reached for Din's

hand. "My hero. Defending my honor from aggressive wallets and their owners."

"Brat," he murmured, but his eyes were warm. "You were handling it just fine. I did it more to teach Garrett a lesson than anything else."

"I enjoyed watching you go all Highlander warrior." She tugged him closer. "Very sexy, Professor."

He leaned down to kiss her, quick but thorough, and the bar erupted in whistles and catcalls.

"Get a room!" someone shouted.

"We have one," Din shot back. "We just haven't made it back there yet."

More laughter.

Fenella pushed him back toward his table. "Go pretend to grade papers. I have thirsty immortals to serve and embarrass."

He squeezed her hand once more before returning to his corner, and Fenella dove back into the performance.

The night flew by in a blur of readings, drinks, and laughter. She told a wine opener that it was developing a drinking problem, convinced a set of car keys they were suffering from commitment issues because they were always jingling around with other keys, and helped a bookmark confess its secret desire to write a novel.

The brooch seemed to whisper truths to her, and she learned to ride the line between truth and theater, giving people what they came for while honoring what she sensed.

"Last call!" Atzil announced from behind the bar, and groans echoed through the room.

"One more reading!" someone pleaded.

Fenella shook her head. "Not tonight. You'll have to wait until tomorrow. Absence makes the psychometry grow fonder!"

The crowd gradually dispersed, people finishing their drinks and heading for the door. Soon, only a few remained, and then just Din, nursing his whiskey while she helped Atzil clean up.

"Fenella," Atzil called, looking a little nervous, which wasn't like him. "Can I speak with you for a moment?"

"Of course."

Atzil glanced at Din, who was pretending to be absorbed in his grading project, then back at her. He rubbed a hand over the back of his cropped hair.

"I just wanted to say that you've transformed this place," he said. "I love watching you work."

Fenella felt her throat tighten. "I just tell silly stories."

"You do it so naturally, you don't realize the impact you have on people." He reached under the bar, pulling out a small, wrapped package. "I have something for you. For the trip."

"I'm not leaving until Tuesday, and even that's not a sure thing. We might leave later than that."

"I want you to take it." Atzil handed the package to her. "I don't want it lying around the bar."

Taking the package, Fenella had a moment of panic thinking that it was a parting gift, but then Atzil had given her so many compliments that it didn't make sense for him to fire her.

She unwrapped it carefully, finding inside a beautiful silver flask engraved with Celtic knotwork.

"For emergencies in the desert," Atzil said. "It's insulated to keep liquids either hot or cold."

"Atzil, this is beautiful. Thank you."

"I'm glad you like it." His voice roughened. "I also wanted to tell you that your job will be here when you return, even if you take a month, a year, or a decade. The Hobbit isn't the same without you."

It was a relief to hear him say that. She needed confirmation that her job would be waiting for her when she came back.

"Fates, I hope it won't be that long." She set down the flask and pulled him into a hug.

Atzil stiffened for a moment—he wasn't a demonstrative male—then returned the embrace.

"I'll miss this place," she said against his shoulder. "I'll miss you."

"Then you'd better come back quickly." He pulled away, clearing his throat. "Now go. Your professor is waiting."

She tucked the flask into her bag, gave the bar one last look, and headed for the back where Din was still pretending to grade papers.

"Everything alright?" he asked.

"Atzil gave me a beautiful present, and for a moment, I was afraid that it was a parting gift, but he told me to come back quickly."

Din frowned. "We don't know how long it's going to

take, so Atzil should not count on you returning to the Hobbit anytime soon."

"He knows that." Fenella took off her apron and tucked it into her bag. "But knowing and hoping are two different things." She slung the strap of her satchel over her shoulder. "Ready to go?"

"Have been ready for a while." Din closed his laptop and slipped it into his messenger bag.

As they started the walk home, he gave her hand a light squeeze. "You were magnificent tonight."

"I'm magnificent every night."

"Yes, you are."

The moon was nearly full, casting everything in silver light as they walked through the village pathways, and except for the distant sounds of night birds and other nocturnal creatures, the night was quiet.

"Are you excited about Egypt?" Din asked.

"I'm a little nervous," she admitted. "I've never been there, and Jacki said that it wasn't safe. I'm not really worried because you will be with me, and hopefully, Max will come along, and Ell-rom will be there as well. I just don't want any unnecessary excitement, you know what I mean?"

He nodded. "The market incident has shaken you."

"It did, but more than that was hearing what was prevented by that chance encounter. Life is so fragile, Din, even for immortals, and there are a lot of bad people out there."

"I can't argue with that."

"And you know what's worse?" She turned to look at him.

"What?"

"That it's impossible to tell the bad actors from the good. That guy in the market looked so mundane. Just a pudgy human who looked no different than the other people standing in line. Nothing was menacing about him, nothing to indicate that he was evil, a monster plotting to murder tens of thousands of people."

Din lifted her hand and kissed her knuckles. "The Fates intervened and saved all those lives. I am grateful."

"So am I." She leaned against his arm. "But the Fates will not always be there to prevent disasters, and I have zero confidence in humanity. Now, every human I look at is a potential terrorist, a mass murderer. I don't know how to get past it."

He wrapped his arm around her. "I will not let anything happen to you. You can trust in that."

"I know." She reached up to touch his face. "That's what makes it bearable."

"I love you." He kissed her softly.

"I love you," she said when they came apart, the words feeling so natural now that she had gotten accustomed to saying them. "Think anyone's taking bets on whether we'll make it home or just scandalize the neighborhood?"

"We are fortunate that the shutters are down for the night. No nosy neighbors can watch us from behind their curtains."

She pulled him down for another kiss, longer this time, deeper.

"Home," Din said roughly when they parted. "Now.

Before I forget that I'm no longer a Highland barbarian."

Her hand flew to her chest in mock horror. "A Highland barbarian?" She let her expression turn teasing. "I would love to meet him, but all I get are empty promises."

"Oh, really?" Din's eyes began glowing. "I wouldn't want to be known as the Highlander who doesn't keep his promises." Moving faster than she could track, he scooped her into his arms and broke into a jog.

Fenella laughed. "What are you doing?"

"Isn't it obvious? I'm taking you to my lair so I can ravish you in private."

3

LOKAN

The Beijing skyline glittered beyond the floor-to-ceiling windows of Lokan's office, a forest of glass and steel reaching toward the smoggy afternoon sky. He stood with his back to his desk, listening to his assistant rattle off the day's remaining appointments while his mind processed the emoji that had appeared on Carol's phone mere minutes ago.

A sailboat. Such a simple image to upend nearly two years of carefully constructed cover. The sad part was that he and Carol had grown to love the business they were building, and somewhere along the way, it had stopped being just a cover.

It would be difficult to leave everything behind and run. Carol would be heartbroken.

"—and the textile consortium meeting at four," his assistant continued. "Will you need the conference room prepared, sir?"

"Cancel it," Lokan said, turning toward the guy, his voice and expression conveying the same measured calm he'd perfected over centuries. "In fact, cancel everything for the rest of the week."

"Sir?" The guy's eyes turned round.

"I just received word that Moda Devula, our largest buyer in Milan, is canceling their order for next year's spring collection. I have to go there and try to save the situation. Carol and I need to fly out immediately."

Everyone in the office knew that his power of persuasion was unmatched, but it was only effective in person. They assumed it was his charm, and Lokan wanted to believe that it played a part, but mostly it was his compulsion power that did the heavy lifting.

His thralling and compulsion abilities had been growing stronger since he'd mated Carol, and unlike before, he could now manipulate the minds of some immortals in addition to those of humans.

It was just one more benefit of having the most amazing, courageous female in the world as his mate, and given who his aunt was, that was saying something.

Right now, his legendary persuasion powers were an excellent pretext for picking up and leaving on a moment's notice. Later, they might save him and Carol from getting caught by his father's goons.

His assistant wrung his hands. "I understand, sir, but the consortium meeting has been planned for months. Mr. Zhang will be furious."

Lokan put his hand on the guy's slim shoulder. "Apologize profusely and offer to reschedule. I trust you to explain the emergency."

Even though Hai was a spy for the CCP, he was a

good guy, and Lokan felt guilty about him finding himself without a job once he realized that his boss was not coming back, and also having to explain to his superiors how he hadn't known his boss was leaving for good.

"Please book two first-class tickets to Milan on the next available flight for me and Carol. And two economy tickets for Samir and Gandel."

He couldn't leave his bodyguards behind without it looking suspicious, but he planned on getting rid of them the same way he'd done many times before when he'd needed to slip away.

"Yes, sir." Hai dipped his head. "Should I arrange the usual hotel?"

"The Principe di Savoia. The penthouse, if it's available." Details mattered. A panicked flight looked like running. A business trip to a familiar hotel seemed more routine. "Also, call the garage. Have them prepare the Mercedes."

As his assistant hurried to comply, Lokan used the landline to call Carol, knowing it was monitored.

"Darling," her voice carried the perfect blend of professional courtesy and intimate suggestion that marked their public relationship. "I was just about to call you."

She'd left the office right after receiving the emoji from Kian, with the excuse of having to prepare for the gala, when in fact she had gone to pack.

"I'm afraid I have bad news about the Moda Devula order," he said, knowing she'd respond appropriately. "They are throwing a tantrum and threatening to cancel the order. We need to fly out tonight to save the situation."

"Tonight? But we have the charity gala to attend—" She broke off with a perfectly timed sigh. "I guess business has to come before pleasure, although the gala is also business."

He chuckled. "In the high fashion world, they often come together. Can you clear the rest of your schedule?"

"Of course, darling. For how many days do I need to pack?"

"A week should do it, but just in case Francesca plays hardball, pack for two."

Hopefully, Carol could fit everything she couldn't part with inside one suitcase and a carry-on.

They wouldn't be returning to Beijing.

"How long do I have?"

"Be ready in about an hour." Lokan set down the phone and walked over to his private bathroom, locking the door behind him.

His go-bag was hidden in the ceiling tiles—cash in multiple currencies, his crypto keys, and several passports for him and Carol with different identities. Everything fit inside a single leather satchel.

In his private quarters, which were adjacent to the office, he changed clothes, trading his business suit for a pair of dark jeans and a cashmere sweater. Comfortable for travel, but still expensive enough to fit his image. The suit went back into the closet.

Back in his office, he made a show of gathering files, his laptop, and various business documents.

His assistant knocked and entered, holding printed airline tickets. "The 7:45 flight to Milan via Munich," he said. "First class was fully booked, but I managed to secure two business class seats together. The layover is long, though, six hours."

That was perfect.

"Excellent work." Lokan made a mental note to have money transferred to Hai's account once they were safe. The guy had been a good assistant, efficient and discreet. "I'll need you to handle things here while I'm gone."

Hai dipped his head. "Of course, sir."

Lokan found his bodyguards in their usual spots, one by the elevator and one by the stairwell. Professional, alert, and completely unaware they were guarding someone who'd been feeding intelligence to their greatest enemy for years.

"We are leaving in an hour," Lokan announced. "Urgent business in Milan."

Gandel, the senior of the two, frowned. "This is sudden."

"I have to save this deal or we go under. We invested heavily in new equipment to take on this order. I need to charm Francesca in person."

"Is Carol going with you?" Samir asked.

"Naturally. Now stop asking questions and go pack your things. We don't have much time."

The guards exchanged glances. They were good soldiers, trained to follow protocol, but Lokan was their boss, and even though they reported to Navuh, technically they were supposed to answer to him.

"The car will be here in forty-five minutes." He checked his watch with apparent impatience.

Lokan returned to his private apartment and began packing. Most of his belongings were at Carol's, and she knew what to pack for him, but he needed to maintain appearances and get to the car with at least a carry-on.

His bodyguards were down in the garage already, waiting by the car, and as he rode down in the elevator, he thought about the plan he'd memorized for months.

Milan was a feint, of course. They'd never make it past Munich. But the guards would continue to Milan without them, controlled by his thrall and compulsion. They would stay in the hotel and pretend that Lokan and Carol were there, maintaining the ruse for as long as possible.

His guards were standing by his gleaming black Mercedes. He'd miss it, oddly enough. Two years of driving Beijing's chaotic streets, Carol beside him, laughing at his cursing in languages no one else understood.

When he pulled up into the garage of her building she was already waiting, a vision in designer clothes and carefully applied makeup, every inch the successful businesswoman. Two Louis Vuitton suitcases and a matching carry-on stood to attention beside her.

"Darling," Carol purred as he stepped out of the car and opened the door for her. "This is terribly inconvenient. I hope Milan is worth missing the gala."

"I'll make it up to you," he promised, playing his part.

When they were seated in the car, he turned around and looked at his bodyguards, and after implanting a thought in both of their minds to go to sleep, he watched them slump in their seats.

Thankfully, the two weren't particularly strong-minded, so his thralling and compulsion worked on them to some extent. It wouldn't be as strong or last as long as it would on humans, but it would still do the job.

Leaning over, he planted a kiss on Carol's mouth. "It finally happened. We are going home."

A brilliant smile spread over her face. "It was time to go. I don't know what prompted the emergency evacuation, but I'm glad."

He put the car in gear and drove out. "Kian is convinced that my father is hiding things from me, which means he suspects me of being disloyal."

Carol frowned. "He's been suspecting that for a long time. What has changed?"

"Kian has just prevented four major terror attacks that the Brotherhood was planning in cooperation with the Revolutionary Guard. The captured Doomers shared a worrying story about chemical enhancements that have been ongoing for over a year, which I was previously unaware of. No one has mentioned to me the laboratory that has been built on the island or the scientist who was experimenting on our people. That means that my father instructed everyone to keep it from me."

Carol reached over and took his hand. "I'm glad that we made it out in time."

He winced. "I hope. Let's not celebrate before we are safe in the village."

She glanced at the bodyguards sleeping in the backseat. "According to the plan, we will give them the slip in Munich, and they will continue to Milan. Are you sure you can pull it off?"

He nodded. "They will stay in our hotel suite and keep up appearances for as long as possible."

Carol leaned back in her seat and let out a breath. "We are so fortunate that you can thrall and compel immortals. None of this would have been possible otherwise."

He smiled. "Don't forget that I can also dreamwalk. I can control these two from afar and reinforce the thrall while they are sleeping."

"You are incredible, darling." She reached for his hand. "You should wake them up now, or they will get suspicious."

Reluctantly, he did as she instructed.

The ride to the airport was tense beneath the casual chatter. Carol kept up a steady stream of complaints about Milan Fashion Week, and the difficulties of dealing with prima donnas like Francesca Sobiouti, who was in fact one of Turner's operatives and would back up their claims if asked.

Lokan responded with appropriate sounds while his mind churned with details of their escape plan.

Beijing Capital International Airport sprawled before them like a small city, all gleaming terminals and endless humanity. Perfect for getting lost in the crowds, but that wasn't the plan.

"Your guards look nervous," Carol murmured as they headed for security.

"They are always anxious in crowds," he said. "They are concerned about being able to protect me."

They cleared security without incident, the guards flashing credentials that got them waved through with their weapons. The terminal stretched before them, duty-free shops and restaurants, and gates leading to everywhere and nowhere.

"Lounge?" Carol suggested. "We have time."

The appearance of calm mattered. They checked into the business class lounge, where Lokan ordered drinks for the four of them.

Sipping her drink, Carol observed the bodyguards who were sitting at another table to give them privacy. "Are they on their phones scrolling through TikTok, or are they getting calls?"

Lokan followed her gaze. "Probably TikTok. I'm sure they've already reported the impromptu trip."

Carol pulled out her phone, snapping a selfie with the drink. "For my vlog."

When the boarding announcement came forty minutes later, they gathered their things casually; Carol touched up her lipstick, and Lokan ensured that they didn't forget anything.

"Sir." Gandel's voice was tight with barely controlled tension.

Fuck! They were busted.

It was time for plan B.

They turned, Carol's expression one of mild annoyance at the interruption.

"Yes?"

"I've been ordered to inform you that Lord Navuh wishes you to stay in Beijing. You need to cancel your trip."

Lokan pretended to let surprise and irritation war on his face. "I will call him. We have to go to Milan or the company goes under." He pulled out his phone, the one issued by the Brotherhood.

"I must insist." Gandel's hand moved to stop him, not quite touching him but making the threat clear.

They needed to get rid of the bodyguards, but it had to be done somewhere where no one would notice two grown men sleeping in the middle of the airport. After the guards were dealt with, he and Carol would continue to their alternative route.

"Fine," Lokan sighed with frustration that wasn't at all feigned. "Carol, darling, call Francesca and try to mollify her."

Carol's expression was perfect—annoyance mixed with resignation. "She's going to be furious."

"Can't be helped." He turned back to Gandel. "I assume we're returning to the office?"

"Yes, sir."

They gathered their luggage, Lokan grumbling about wasted tickets and failing business. Around them, passengers streamed toward the gate, oblivious to the drama playing out in their midst.

The walk back through the terminal felt endless. Security personnel were again retrieving their luggage, which took over an hour. They wheeled their luggage toward the exit, and the automatic doors whooshed open, Beijing's polluted air hitting them like a wall.

Lokan decided that the best place to leave his sleeping bodyguards would be in the car.

"You can wait here. I'll get the car," Samir offered.

"We'll just walk over there." For his plan to work, Lokan needed the car to stay in the parking lot.

The moment they were all inside the vehicle, this time with the bodyguards insisting on sitting up front and Lokan and Carol in the back, Lokan entered their minds, sending them into deep sleep.

"Do we destroy their phones?" Carol asked.

He shook his head. "It doesn't matter. The moment they get a call and don't respond, my father will assume I killed them. We can just leave them here. The thrall will eventually dissipate, and if not, their brethren will find them here once they arrive."

He took his own Brotherhood phone and dropped it onto the back seat.

Surprisingly, it was difficult to say goodbye to this last thing that connected him to his home.

"Let's get the luggage."

After retrieving their things, they locked the car, and Lokan threw the key under it.

Getting back on the street, they hailed a taxi, and Lokan, along with the driver, loaded their luggage into the trunk.

"Where to?" the driver asked.

"The train station," Lokan said loudly so the people standing on the sidewalk would hear them. "Quickly. We're late."

As the taxi pulled away, Carol leaned against Lokan, every line of her body radiating tension as well as excitement.

His mate loved these kinds of games.

"The train station wasn't part of the plan," she said. "Are you improvising?"

"Not at all. That's not where we are going." He leaned forward, pulling out a thick stack of bills. "Uncle, how would you like to earn a month's salary for one fare?"

The driver's eyes widened in the rearview mirror. "Where do you want me to take you?"

"The night market in Dongcheng. Then forget you ever saw us."

"I've already forgotten," the man said, snatching the bills.

"They'll have watchers at every major airport within five hundred miles," Carol whispered in his ear. "We can't go to Munich."

Lokan cast a silence bubble around the two of them. "We go to Mongolia, and from there to Russia."

She patted her curls. "It has been a long time since I've spoken Russian."

The night market materialized around them, a cacophony of sights, smells, and humanity. Perfect for disappearing.

They paid the driver extra to wait, then melted into the crowd.

New clothing from one vendor, boots from another, backpacks and hair dye from yet two others. The dye was for later, once they found lodging for the night. When they returned, the elegant businessman and his designer-clad companion had vanished, replaced by backpackers in worn jeans and practical boots.

Carol shed a few tears over having to leave the designer wardrobe and the luxury matching luggage that would have to stay behind, but Lokan kissed away her tears and promised to replace every item.

"Ready for an adventure?" he asked, shouldering the hiking pack.

"Always." She shouldered hers. "I've always wanted to see the Mongolian steppes."

They walked back to the taxi hand in hand, two young-looking travelers in a city of millions. Behind them, their old life burned like bridges that they'd never cross again. Ahead lay adventure, and eventually home.

The driver looked surprised at their transformation but said nothing. Money bought silence as effectively as compulsion, but Lokan was going to use thralling and compulsion as well once the driver's services were no longer needed.

4

AREZOO

The lunch rush hit the café like a tidal wave, and Arezoo barely had time to breathe between taking orders, preparing drinks, and delivering trays to tables. The line at the counter stretched almost the entire length of the café area, filled with impatient immortals seeking their midday caffeine fix and a bite to eat.

"One cappuccino, extra foam," Arezoo called out, sliding the cup across the counter to a waiting guy. "Your turkey avocado wrap will be out in just a moment."

She wiped her hands on her apron and turned to the next customer, remembering to smile despite her aching feet.

It sucked being the only human working with an immortal and a hybrid Kra-ell who both looked as fresh as they had in the morning and could keep going until closing without needing a break.

A small voice in the back of her head whispered

that she could be an immortal too if she chose one of the guys who'd signaled their interest. The problem was that even thinking about being intimate with a male made her nauseous, or worse, sweaty.

Would this ever go away? Would she one day feel attraction to someone again?

Arezoo hadn't been this way before the abduction. She'd been a typical teenager who had crushes on movie stars and gossiped with her friends about their boyfriends and who had dared to do what. She'd even gotten excited hearing some of those tales.

Not anymore, though.

Perhaps she should schedule a call with the clan's psychologist and get herself sorted out.

"Arezoo!" A familiar voice cut through her unpleasant thoughts.

She turned to see Drova weaving through the tables, her tall, slim frame making it easy for her to navigate between them. The Guardian uniform looked good on her, even without the insignia she coveted but wouldn't receive until she graduated from the training program.

"Can I get you a juice box?" Arezoo asked while pumping syrup into a latte.

The box only appeared to contain juice but was actually filled with synthetic blood for the Kra-ell, who couldn't consume anything else. Well, except for black coffee and alcohol, which Drova had no problem with.

Her friend leaned against the counter. "No, thank you. I'm not hungry." She looked at the packed tables.

"The whole village must have decided to have lunch here today."

"It surely looks like it." Arezoo finished the latte and started on the next order. "Don't you have Guardian training?"

"Lunch break." Drova shrugged. "Not that I need it. I had a nice drink of fresh blood yesterday, so I'm good for the next two days. But the other Guardians in training need food, so we are on a break, and I thought I'd stop by and see how you were doing."

Arezoo loaded a tray with three drinks and two sandwiches. "I'm swamped, as you can see, and my feet are killing me."

"I'll take it." Drova snatched the tray from Arezoo's hands before she could protest. "Where does it go?"

"Table seven, the one under the willow tree." Arezoo pointed. "But you shouldn't be doing this. You don't work here."

"I can help a friend if I want to." Drova was already moving toward the table, balancing the tray with ease. "Besides, we can talk while we are delivering the orders."

Arezoo was too tired to argue, so she nodded and followed Drova with a coffee carafe to refill cups on the way.

When she returned behind the counter, Aliya took over the deliveries so Arezoo could stay in one place. "One iced Americano, one blueberry muffin," Arezoo announced, setting them on the pickup counter.

"Your mother and aunts must be proud," Drova said. "The grocery store is really happening."

"They're excited." Arezoo started on another espresso. "They cleared out the house Ingrid arranged for them. Every piece of furniture is gone, and they're scrubbing every surface in preparation for the refrigerators and shelving units that are supposed to arrive tomorrow or the day after." She felt a twinge of guilt in her stomach for not being there to help. "I should be there scrubbing with them, but I need this job. My mother offered to pay me, but I can't take money from her. My sisters will help her."

"I get it." Drova crossed her arms over her flat chest. "Working for family is complicated. That's why I'm happy to be in the Guardian program instead of training with my mother."

Their eyes met, and Arezoo felt a kinship with the Kra-ell girl. They weren't even the same species, and yet they had a lot in common. They were both refugees from oppression and had controlling mothers. Both of them were carving out their own paths, separate from their mothers' expectations.

The difference was that Drova was her mother's only child, and that she was a warrior born and bred and seemed to fear nothing, while Arezoo was afraid of her own shadow.

Drova's lips quirked in what might have been a smile on a more expressive face. "I'm a better fighter than my mother, and she's even acknowledged that, but that was it. I've never heard a compliment from her."

Was she really better than Jade?

If so, what was she doing in training?

"My mother is not as bad. I think she said once or

twice that I was a good daughter. She tells me she loves me often enough, though, so I'm not complaining."

Wonder emerged from the back with a fresh tray of sandwiches. "Arezoo, these need to go to—oh, hello, Drova."

"Hi." Drova saluted Wonder. "How are you doing?" she added with a smile that looked so fake it was comical.

Drova had admitted to Arezoo that polite conversation was still a struggle for her and the other Kra-ell. It wasn't part of their culture, and it felt uncomfortable, but they were trying to integrate.

"Very well, thank you," Wonder answered with a straight face.

"Where do these need to go?" Arezoo asked.

As Wonder directed her to the table, Drova pulled out her phone and checked the time. "Damn. I need to get back." When she lifted her head, a smirk spread across her face. "Look who's just shown up."

Arezoo followed her gaze and felt her stomach flip. Ruvon had just walked into the café, looking a little nervous. He always looked like that, even when he wasn't trying to flirt with her, hunching his shoulders as if trying to make himself smaller.

It was a shame, really.

He was a tall man, and if he straightened his back, he would appear even taller. Perhaps even handsome.

When he spotted her behind the counter, his face lit up with a smile that transformed his usually plain features, making him look almost attractive.

"Good luck," Drova said, clapping Arezoo on the

back as gently as she could, which was forceful enough to make her stumble forward. "There is nowhere to hide this time," she whispered in Arezoo's ear. "Nowhere to run."

"Drova!" Arezoo hissed, but her friend was already heading out.

Ruvon joined the line, patiently waiting his turn. Arezoo found herself stealing glances at him between orders, noting how he kept checking something on his phone, then looking up at her, then back at his phone. He also carried a wrapped package under one arm.

By the time he reached the counter, her palms were sweating. She wiped them discreetly on her apron.

"Hello, Arezoo," he said, his voice soft enough that she had to lean forward to hear him over the noise of the café.

"Hi." She forced herself to meet his eyes. "What can I get you?"

"Two cappuccinos and two blueberry muffins, please."

Two? Arezoo's heart sank a little. Of course, he was meeting someone. Why else would he order two of everything?

She rang up his order while Wonder prepared it, and as he walked away, searching for a table, she tracked his movements, waiting to see who he was meeting.

The café was still packed, but just as he was starting to look discouraged, a couple stood to leave, and he quickly claimed their spot, setting down his order, his laptop, and the wrapped package while they were still clearing away their used dishes.

Arezoo tried to focus on her work, but her eyes kept drifting to his table. He'd opened his laptop and started working on something, occasionally glancing toward the counter. The second coffee and muffin sat untouched across from him.

When she passed by his table carrying a carafe, he turned to her. "Arezoo?"

She paused, the tray heavy in her hands. "Do you need a refill on your coffee?"

He hadn't touched his coffee yet, so she knew that wasn't why he'd called.

Ruvon shook his head. "Could you join me for a few minutes?" He gestured to the empty chair across from him. "The coffee and muffin are for you."

"Oh." The word came out as barely more than a breath. "I can't. I'm working, and we're so busy—"

"You can take a break," Wonder said from behind her, materializing there like some matchmaking apparition. "Fifteen minutes."

Arezoo opened her mouth to protest, but Wonder was already taking the carafe from her hands. "Go on. Your feet must be killing you."

They were. Arezoo had been at it for four hours straight, and her arches ached with every step. The prospect of sitting down for a little bit was too tempting to resist.

"Thank you," she said to Wonder, then turned to Ruvon. "I have fifteen minutes."

His smile could have powered the entire village. "Please, sit."

Arezoo sank into the chair with a grateful sigh and reached for the coffee. The first sip was heavenly. "This is exactly what I needed. Thank you."

Ruvon watched her with an expression that could only be described as adoration, and it made her shift uncomfortably in her seat. She wasn't used to being looked at like that—like she was something precious and fascinating.

She'd been looked at by men before, but those looks had been covetous, and they'd always made her uncomfortable. Even her father's friends had sometimes looked at her like that, and it had disgusted her. They were married, and they had soft bellies and soft chins from overeating.

Ruvon didn't look at her as if she were a piece of meat. He looked at her as if she were special.

"I have something for you," he said, pushing the wrapped package across the table.

Arezoo's hand froze halfway to the muffin. "For me? Why? It's not my birthday."

He shrugged, but she could see the tension in his shoulders. "I saw this in a used bookstore and thought you might like it. It's nothing. Just a book."

"You shouldn't buy me gifts."

What did he expect in return?

"It's nothing. It just looked like something that you would enjoy."

A used book probably didn't cost much, and she loved books, so he was right about that, but she should still refuse it. Accepting gifts from a man she barely knew and who clearly had feelings for her that she couldn't return, wasn't wise.

But in the end, curiosity won, and she pulled the package closer, starting to unwrap it carefully.

"A book of Persian poetry." Arezoo's breath caught.

The leather binding was soft with age, and the pages were edged in gold. She opened it carefully, revealing pages of beautiful calligraphy with delicate illustrations in the margins. This wasn't some mass-produced volume—it was old, probably valuable, definitely special.

"Ruvon." She ran her fingers over a page. "This is beautiful."

"You like it?" The hope in his voice made her chest tight.

"It's the nicest gift anyone has ever given me." The words were out before she could stop them.

"That's music to my ears." Joy replaced his uncertainty.

She turned the pages slowly, drinking in the beautiful words. Her grandmother had owned a book similar to this, though not nearly as fine. She'd read from it in the evenings, her voice soft and melodious, bringing the words to life.

"Do you like poetry?" she asked, looking up at him.

Ruvon shifted in his seat. "I don't know if I like it or not. I've never really read any. I mean, in the Brotherhood, we didn't exactly have poetry readings. And after we escaped, I focused on learning useful things. Poetry might be beautiful, but it is not useful."

Arezoo felt a pang of sympathy.

She couldn't imagine growing up without the beauty of words, without stories and verses to soften the harsh edges of life.

"Would you like to hear one?" she asked on an impulse.

His eyes widened. "Please."

She flipped through the pages, looking for something appropriate. Not a love poem—definitely not that. Something else, something safer.

She found one about dreams and hope, about the resilience of the human spirit. Her teardrop translator would mangle it, turning the music of the Persian language into functional but artless English. Still, she wanted to share this piece of her culture with him, and that was the only option available to her.

Her English wasn't good enough to translate the words by herself and try to imbue them with music.

As she began to read, the words flowed like water, even though she could hear the translator's echo turning them into something else. The rhythm was lost, the rhyme scheme destroyed, but the meaning—hopefully—remained.

"In the garden of dreams, where hope takes root, the soul finds strength to bear its heavy load. Though storms may rage and darkness may dispute, the heart remembers light along the road."

She continued through three more stanzas, aware of Ruvon's complete attention. Leaning forward, his coffee forgotten, he looked into her eyes, his dark gaze never leaving her face.

When she finished, the silence between them felt charged.

"That was beautiful," he said. "Thank you."

Arezoo closed the book carefully, running her hand over the cover. She should give it back. It was too much, too valuable, too meaningful. But her fingers wouldn't let go.

"I shouldn't accept this," she said, not looking at him.

"Why not?"

"Because..." She struggled for words. "Because this is not just a used book. It's an expensive gift that I don't deserve."

"You deserve it," Ruvon said quietly. "You deserve beautiful things. You deserve to have someone think of you when they see something lovely. That's all this is—I saw it and thought of you."

Arezoo felt tears prick at her eyes and blinked them away.

"Now I owe you a gift," she said, trying to lighten the moment.

Ruvon shook his head. "You don't owe me anything. The look on your face when you opened that book, the joy in your eyes, that's the greatest gift I could ask for."

The words should have come across as cheesy, but his sincerity made them sound authentic, meaningful, and she believed him when he said her happiness was enough for him.

"My break is almost over." She took a sip of her coffee. "I wish I could stay longer, but I can't."

Another beautiful smile brightened his face. "Thank you for sitting with me and for reading to me."

Arezoo stood, cradling the book against her chest. "Thank you for this. I'll treasure it."

"I'm glad." He gathered his things but left her coffee and muffin on the table. "Those are yours. You barely touched them."

"I'll finish them behind the counter," she promised.

He nodded, shouldering his laptop bag. "Maybe... maybe sometime when you're not working, you could read me another poem?"

It wasn't quite asking for a date, but it was close, and Arezoo considered it. "Maybe," she said, which was more than she'd thought she'd offer. "If you have time to stop by the café tomorrow, I'll ask Wonder for a longer break." She forced a smile. "Hopefully, the place won't be as busy as it was today."

He nodded, looking satisfied as if he'd won a bet with someone, or just with himself. "I'll be here."

5

DIN

Din pushed the remnants of scrambled eggs around his plate, watching Fenella demolish her third piece of toast with an enthusiasm that made him smile. She ate like someone who'd learned never to take food for granted, or maybe she just had a ravenous appetite.

"I want to go help Kyra and her sisters today," she said between bites, gesturing with a piece of bacon. "They're getting the refrigerators and shelving units delivered, and they could use some immortal muscle."

Din set down his coffee cup. "Today?"

She nodded. "They probably started hours ago." Fenella pulled out her phone and checked the time. "Fates, it's after ten already. You should have woken me up earlier."

It hadn't escaped his notice that she'd started invoking the Fates. It was a small thing, but to him it was another brick in the foundation of the life Fenella was building in the village. She was accepting the clan's beliefs and customs.

"You needed the rest." Usually, she was too exhausted after her nightly performances at the Hobbit to do anything other than shower and fall asleep, but last night she'd summoned energy for some fun times in bed.

She grinned. "Whose fault was that, Professor? You're the one who carried me in your arms all the way to my room with plans to ravish me."

He leaned forward. "But then you decided to first practice your psychometric abilities on various items of my clothing."

"I was trying to see if I could read the history of your shirts," she managed to say without laughing. "I thought it would be an academic exercise. How was I supposed to know that they were all imbued with lustful thoughts about me?"

He chuckled. "It should have been obvious. Do you have any idea how sexy you are when you do your readings? Every night, I sit in that corner and watch you perform, dreaming of the moment I can snatch you away and hoard you all for myself."

"Oh, shucks." Shira waved a hand. "Aren't the two of you cute?"

He'd forgotten she was even there. "Aren't you late for your shift?"

"I am." She shuffled the rest of her eggs into her mouth and pushed to her feet. "I'm out of here. Be good, children. If the cat in the hat comes knocking, don't let him in."

Fenella laughed. "Echoes of story-time corner at the library?"

Shira nodded. "I love that book." She bent to kiss Fenella's cheek and waved at Din. A moment later, the front door closed with a bang, and they were alone.

Fenella pushed back from the table, her expression growing serious. "They need help. Max is on duty, stuck in the dungeon and dealing with Doomers and ugly humans, so that leaves only Ell-rom to help the sisters move heavy equipment. He's strong, but he could use some help."

Din thought of the finals waiting on his laptop, each one a hundred pages of undergraduate attempts at archaeological analysis. He'd promised himself he'd finish grading them before they left for Egypt, which was only three days away, but this was important to Fenella, and he could finish the grading on the plane or in the hotel.

"The delivery probably hasn't arrived yet," he said.

"Maybe not, but we should go. They might need help with other things."

Din stood and started gathering the breakfast dishes.

"Leave those," Fenella said. "I'll deal with them later."

"Or we could take two minutes and do them now."

She rolled her eyes. "You're such a professor. Everything has to be in its proper order."

"And you're such a bartender. Everything can wait until later."

"Exactly."

They compromised by quickly rinsing the dishes

and leaving them in the sink, then headed out into the bright morning sun.

"It's strange," Fenella said as they passed an immortal jogging along the path. "Everyone is going about their day like the world didn't almost end."

"Maybe that's the point," Din suggested. "We keep living because that's what defeats evil. Every normal day is a victory."

She slipped her hand into his. "That's very philosophical."

"Occupational hazard. Spend enough time studying dead civilizations, and you start thinking about what makes them fade into nothing but pages in history books."

She cast him a sidelong glance. "And your conclusion is?"

He shrugged. "There is no one answer. Natural disasters, famines, plagues, wars. Weak leadership or power-hungry leadership—both can be disastrous."

She chuckled. "It's like that song about a hundred ways to die. Have you heard it?"

"Can't say that I have."

For the next several minutes, she sang to him the verses she remembered, making him laugh, and then they walked in silence, comforted by the warmth of their conjoined hands.

It felt nice.

Instead of being two, they were now one—an island of strength and unity in a chaotic world.

As they approached the house that had been designated for the temporary store, Din could hear voices and the distinctive sound of heavy equipment being moved. Inside, two Guardians were maneuvering a commercial refrigerator cart while Ell-rom guided them through the narrow doorway.

"Careful with the door frame," Soraya said, her hands fluttering nervously. "We just had it painted."

"We've got it," one of the Guardians assured her.

Din quickened his pace. "Need another pair of hands?"

Ell-rom's face lit up with relief. "Perfect timing, Din. This is the third one, and there are two more plus all the shelving units."

"Where do you want me?" Din started rolling up his sleeves.

Soraya looked like she might cry with gratitude. "You are angels, both of you. The refrigerators need to go along the back wall, and the shelving..." She gestured vaguely at the empty space. "Everywhere else, I suppose. We have a plan. Somewhere." She looked around frantically. "Rana! Where's the floor plan?"

"I have it!" Rana emerged from another room, waving a piece of paper. "But I think we need to make adjustments to it. The refrigerators are bigger than what we planned for."

Din joined the Guardians and Ell-rom, taking a corner of the massive unit. It was awkward to maneuver, even with immortal strength.

"On three," one of the Guardians said. "One, two..."

They lifted in unison.

After days of grading papers and sitting at his laptop, using his muscles felt good, necessary even.

"Through the door," Ell-rom directed. "Watch the—"

A scraping sound made Soraya gasp.

"It's fine," the Guardian quickly assured her. "It just brushed the frame. No damage."

They got the refrigerator inside and positioned it against the back wall, then returned for the next one.

Fenella joined her cousins in unpacking the shelving units and organizing the parts by function.

"I can't believe this is happening," Parisa said. "Our own store."

The morning fell into a rhythm of lifting, carrying, and arranging. Din enjoyed the physical exertion and the camaraderie of shared labor.

The Guardians were surprisingly good-natured about the constant adjustments Soraya demanded; "—move this refrigerator two inches left, no wait, maybe three inches right—no, to the left. Sorry. My mistake."

After the last unit was in place, the Guardians apologized for having to leave.

Din and Ell-rom were left alone to tackle the shelving units, which came with instructions that seemed to have been translated through several languages before reaching English.

"I think this diagram is upside down," Ell-rom said, turning the paper one way, then another.

Din studied it over his shoulder. "No, I think it's... actually, you might be right."

"Let me see." Fenella abandoned her unpacking to join them. "Oh, for Fates' sake. Look, ignore the diagram. It's obvious how these go together."

"Obvious to you, maybe," Din said. "Some of us like to follow instructions."

"Some of us overthink everything." She grabbed two pieces of the metal frame. "See? Tab A into Slot B. You don't need a doctorate to figure that out."

Jasmine joined their group. "I once tried to assemble a coffee table from IKEA and ended up with a modern art sculpture, but I'm willing to give it a try."

In the end, they somehow managed to figure out the shelving system.

The key, Fenella had said, was to have one person read the instructions aloud while everyone else ignored them and used common sense. Soon, they had a production line going—Din and Ell-rom assembling the frames, and the ladies attaching the shelves and adjusting the heights.

"Are you all packed for Egypt?" Jasmine asked as they worked.

"I haven't even thought about packing," Fenella admitted. "In fact, I don't own any luggage."

Din's hands stilled on the frame he was attaching. He'd been offering to take her shopping for weeks now, but she'd always found excuses—too busy at the bar, too tired, not in the mood. He'd begun to suspect it was less about time and more about her reluctance to venture outside the village again.

"You need luggage," Kyra said. "And clothes for the desert. It's hot during the day but can get cold at night."

"And comfortable shoes," Jasmine added. "Lots of walking on uneven ground if we're visiting archaeological sites."

Fenella sighed. "I guess I need to go shopping."

"I'll take you," Din offered. "Tomorrow? We could make a day of it."

He expected her to deflect again, to find another excuse. Instead, she nodded. "Yeah, okay. Tomorrow."

She didn't sound enthusiastic, but at least she'd said yes.

"It'll be fine," he said quietly. "We'll go to an upscale mall where there is zero chance of encountering Doomers or Revolutionary Guard terrorists."

She winced. "That's not a guarantee of safety. One of their targets was a large shopping mall. Remember?"

She was right about that.

"What about a Walmart or a Target?" Jasmine suggested. "It's not glamorous, and the merchandise is basic, but maybe that's better for a place like Egypt. The last thing we need is to look like rich tourists."

Fenella snorted. "Most of us can blend in, but Jacki, with her blond hair and translucent skin, is going to stick out like a sore thumb."

Jasmine shrugged. "She has bodyguards, and Kalugal can shroud her appearance to make her look like an ugly shrew. So, how about Walmart? Do you want to go?"

"Sure. I don't need anything fancy. Shoes, though, I'd rather buy something good."

"REI," Jasmine said with conviction. "Perhaps we should go there first. They have everything we need. Pricy, but then with the clan covering the expenses, we don't need to worry about that, right?"

"If you say so." Fenella sighed. "I don't care where

we shop as long as it's out of the way." She shook her head. "I still can't wrap my head around how close this city came to a horrific bloodbath. That scumbag recognizing Soraya and Rana was like divine intervention."

"The Fates work in mysterious ways," Ell-rom said. "What seemed like misfortune became the key to saving many thousands of lives."

"Right." Fenella attached another shelf with more force than necessary, bending the metal. "Sorry about that." She straightened it back. "But I'd prefer if the Fates could work their mysteries to prevent crap like that from happening in the first place."

Din reached over and put his hand over hers. "We don't have to go if you're not ready. We can order from a catalog and pay for express delivery."

She seemed to consider that for a moment, but then shook her head. "I want to try on what I'm buying." She attempted a smile. "Besides, what are the odds of running into another terrorist? Lightning doesn't strike twice in the same place, right?"

"Right," Din agreed, though privately he wondered if the odds held any significance when it came to Fenella. She seemed to attract trouble like a magnet.

As they continued working, the shelving units began to take shape around them, and the empty house was transforming into something that actually resembled a small store.

"What kind of luggage should I get?" Fenella asked. "I always just threw things in a backpack or duffel bag."

"Something with wheels," Jasmine said. "Trust me, your back will thank you."

"These are the last two units," Ell-rom announced, dragging over another flat-pack box.

"Good." Rana flexed her hands. "My fingers are starting to cramp from all these tiny screws."

"Almost done," Soraya said, though she looked ready to collapse.

It was easy to forget that the women were still human and didn't have the same strength and stamina as the immortals.

"You should take a break," Din suggested. "Walk over to the café, get something to drink, and rest. We can finish here."

Soraya shook her head. "We are almost done for today. I'd rather finish here and go to the café to celebrate when it's done."

Her tone brooked no argument, and Din figured that it was better just to let it go.

He and Ell-rom made quick work of the final units while the women began discussing product placement. Where should the spices go? Would the tea selection be better near the front or the back? Should they organize by cuisine type or product category?

"I'm still amazed that you're doing this," Fenella said to Soraya. "Opening a store in a new country, in a language you're still learning. You're so brave."

Soraya shook her head. "We're not brave. We're desperate. There's a difference."

"You are brave," Kyra said. "Desperation might have been the catalyst, but what you're doing now, building something this community needs, that takes courage."

"Besides," Parisa added with a smile, "we're not

doing it alone. Look at all of you, giving up your morning to help us."

"That's what family does," Fenella said.

Din saw the emotion that flashed across the sisters' faces at that statement.

Family.

Such a loaded word for women who'd been betrayed by those who should have protected them.

"Well," he said, setting down his tools, "I for one think that we've earned a lunch break."

"I'll stay here." Soraya put her hands on her hips. "I should start cleaning the shelves."

"I'll stay too." Yasmin walked up to her.

"Nonsense," Fenella said. "We'll bring lunch back for everyone. Din's buying."

"I am?"

"Yes, love. You are."

6

KIAN

K ian's office felt smaller with six people crammed around his conference table, which was covered with reports, tablets, and a laptop containing information that could shift the balance of power in their ongoing war with the Brotherhood.

"Let's start with what we know about our chemist." Kian touched his tablet, and Dr. Marcus Zhao's face appeared on the wall-mounted screen. The son of a Chinese immigrant father and a seventh-generation American Irish mother, he was handsome, in his mid-thirties, and wore elegant wire-rimmed glasses. His slight smile bordered on a smirk, making his expression look almost mocking.

"Dr. Marcus Zhao," Kian began, reading from the file Roni had compiled. "MIT graduate, summa cum laude. PhD in neurochemistry from Stanford. Professor at Berkeley for the past eight years, specializing in cognitive enhancement and neurotransmitter manipulation."

"Impressive," Turner murmured, studying the professor's list of publications. "Over sixty peer-reviewed papers. Multiple patents."

"He's brilliant but unorthodox," William added, pulling up another screen. "Gives off a vibe of the mad scientist. Three ethics violations at Berkeley, all related to pushing boundaries in human trials. Nothing serious enough to lose his position, but enough to establish a pattern."

Kaia leaned forward, her fingers dancing across her tablet. "His research focus is fascinating from a purely scientific standpoint. He was working on compounds that could enhance neural plasticity, improve reaction times, and reduce the need for sleep. His research hadn't reached the stage where he could experiment on humans, so it was still entirely theoretical. Frankly, I don't think he had any chance of getting approval for human trials."

"Limitations he no longer has to worry about," Onegus said. "Immortals can survive what would kill humans."

Kian studied Zhao's photo again. That slight smile bothered him. "I wonder whether he needed to be coerced or if he jumped at the chance to experiment without restrictions."

"According to the interrogations, they threatened to harm his sister," Julian said. "Classic leverage."

"Yes, but..." Kaia pulled up another file. "Look at his publication history. The last two years before his kidnapping, he was increasingly frustrated with institutional review boards. Multiple papers include barely veiled complaints about 'arbitrary limitations' and 'bureaucratic interference with scientific progress.'"

"You think he went willingly?" Turner's expression was skeptical. "Not that it matters. We can't do anything about it anyway. The only thing we need to figure out is the level of enhancement these drugs can provide and if they cause long-term damage. I would be thrilled if those Doomers burn out and we don't have to worry about them."

"I think it's possible he didn't resist as hard as we might expect," Kaia said. "For someone with his mindset, the opportunity to test his theories on subjects that can survive extreme enhancement might be irresistible. But then Turner is right about it being irrelevant."

"He's been working on this for over eighteen months already," Kian said. "If his initial test subjects survive and prove worthy of the investment, he'll keep perfecting his formulas until he's able to create an unstoppable army for Navuh. William, show us the timeline."

William replaced Zhao's photo on his screen with a chart. "Based on multiple interrogations, we've established a rough timeline. Zhao was taken about eighteen months ago. The first three months seem to have been spent setting up the laboratory and establishing baseline tests. In month four, the first enhancement trials began. Twenty test subjects, fifteen casualties."

Julian huffed out a breath. "Casualties is a washed

term. The Doomers didn't die, but the neural damage was severe enough that they had to be retired."

A euphemism for elimination. Even the Brotherhood wouldn't keep violently insane immortals around.

William continued. "The next stage was a refinement period. Smaller test groups and adjusted formulas. Success rate improved from twenty-five percent to nearly fifty percent."

"Still unacceptable losses by any reasonable standard," Turner murmured while jotting notes on his yellow pad.

"The Brotherhood doesn't operate by reasonable standards," Onegus said.

"The next stage was the establishment of the three-tier system. Level One becomes stable and reproducible. Level Two begins trials. Level Three..." William paused. "Level Three remains problematic. It pushes immortal physiology beyond sustainable limits. The subjects become incredibly strong and fast, but the mental degradation is severe. Paranoia, hallucinations, uncontrollable rage."

"The brain can't handle the overstimulation," Julian explained. "Even immortal neural tissue has limits. Push too hard, and you get cascading failures throughout the nervous system."

"Yet they keep trying," Kian mused. "Which means that either Zhao thinks he can solve it or Navuh doesn't care about the casualties."

"Both," Turner said flatly. "Zhao gets to push the

boundaries of his science, and Navuh gets enhanced warriors. The failures are just the cost of progress."

Kian turned to Julian. "You've analyzed the blood samples. What's your opinion?"

Julian pulled up a diagram. "It's genius-level work, to be honest. Zhao created compounds that enhance our already-superior muscle fibers and hyper-stimulate our neural pathways."

"Could you replicate it?" Kian asked.

"Given enough time and test subjects willing to risk their sanity? Possibly. But why would we want that?"

The suspicion in Julian's eyes was insulting. Did he think Kian would ever want to subject any of the Guardians to such horrors?

"Understanding how it works might help us counter it," he said. "Maybe find weaknesses."

"There are the obvious ones," Julian said. "The enhancements require constant maintenance. Several daily doses for optimal performance, and a minimum of one a day to avoid withdrawal symptoms. The compounds are metabolized quickly by immortals."

"The question is whether Zhao can stabilize Level Three," Kaia said. "If he can maintain those physical enhancements without the mental degradation..."

"We'd be facing warriors we simply can't match physically," Kian finished. "We need to push the Odu project and create mechanical warriors."

Onegus lifted a hand. "Let's slow down for a moment and think it through. We don't often engage with Doomers, and when we do, it's usually against a small cell. Even if we build an army of Odus, we still won't be able to storm the island with them or take them to clean Doomer infestations wherever we find them. What we need to focus on is protecting the village, and for that, an army of indestructible Odus would be invaluable. But perhaps our castle in Scotland needs them more than we do. Its main line of defense is the constant shrouding they use to mask their location, but it's not effective against immortals."

"They have explosives along the roads and the bridges." Kian shifted in his seat. "But you are right about them being more exposed than we are. I would prefer them to move here so we can combine our forces and enhance our defenses, but I can't force them to do so."

Theoretically his mother could command them to move for their own safety, but that wasn't how Annani worked. She would never force them to do anything that they didn't want to. She could be persuasive, though.

Kaia let out a breath. "I'm glad that we have other options because we are still very far from designing anything as complicated as the Odus."

"I don't need a perfect replica," Kian said. "Can you build something functional, even if it's not as advanced as the original Odus?"

Kaia looked uncomfortable. "What you are talking about is completely autonomous combat units. That's something that will require years of machine learning and then testing before it can be mass-produced."

He was well aware that what he was asking of her was not achievable in the time frame he needed, but if he didn't push, they wouldn't have a solution even ten years from now.

"We need options, Kaia. And I don't like the position we are in."

"I'll redouble our efforts," she promised.

"Do what you can," Kian said before turning to Julian. "Can you prepare medical protocols for treating enhancement drug withdrawal? If we capture more enhanced Doomers, we need something to keep them alive for interrogation."

"You are right that the withdrawal might kill them," Julian warned.

"Then figure out how to manage it. We need intelligence, not corpses."

7

LOKAN

The modest family home in the Mongolian countryside was a far cry from the luxury living Lokan had grown accustomed to during his time in Beijing. The single-story structure, with its weathered wood siding and tin roof, sat surrounded by endless grassland that stretched to the horizon. But it was safe, and that was all that mattered.

"Thank you again for having us," Lokan said in his limited Mongolian.

Their host was a man named Batbayar, who was part of Turner's extensive worldwide network of contacts. He nodded. "Let me take you to your room."

His wife and five children, ranging from perhaps six to sixteen, peered with curiosity at the guests.

After they settled in their room, Carol pulled the box of hair dye from her bag. "I suppose it's time to say goodbye to my beautiful golden locks."

Lokan pulled her into his arms. "You are beautiful to me no matter what color your hair is."

"You have to say that because you are my mate." She kissed him. "I wonder if Oyunaa knows what to do with this. Despite my extensive espionage experience, I've never attempted to disguise my appearance and therefore never colored my hair before."

"Can I help?" He looked at the box. "I'm sure instructions are included."

Carol smiled. "This home has one bathroom to serve everyone. I don't think they would be okay with us hogging it for the time needed to apply the color, and they would be too shy to interrupt. With Oyunaa there with me, they will be less timid."

"You are so wise." He leaned to kiss her forehead.

After Lokan explained what Carol needed, the women ducked into the bathroom, and he was left alone with Batbayar and the children. He attempted a conversation with his broken Mongolian, and the children giggled at his pronunciation.

"You... businessman?" Batbayar asked.

"Yes," Lokan said. "Traveling north. I have business in Russia."

Batbayar nodded, seeming satisfied with the vague explanation. In this part of the world, people knew not to ask too many questions of travelers who paid in cash and came recommended by trusted contacts.

An hour later, Carol emerged transformed. Her distinctive blonde hair had now turned a rich brown, making her blue eyes seem even more striking. She touched it self-consciously, turning to show him the back.

"Well, Ricky?" she said, using the fake name they'd agreed upon. "What do you think?"

Lokan grinned. They'd been amusing themselves during the journey by quoting old episodes of *I Love Lucy*.

"You got some splainin' to do, Lucy," he replied in an exaggerated accent, earning a laugh from Carol.

Their hosts looked confused by the exchange but smiled politely. The language barrier was both a blessing and a curse—it prevented real communication but also meant fewer questions.

Dinner was a simple affair of mutton stew and milk tea, shared around a low table with the entire family. The children gradually warmed up to them, two of the boys even attempting to teach Lokan a card game using enthusiastic gestures.

"Tomorrow, train?" Batbayar asked as they cleaned up.

"Yes," Lokan confirmed. "North train. Early morning."

The man nodded. "I drive you. Station far."

Later that night, lying on a thin mattress in the guest room, Lokan held Carol close. "I'm sorry about your hair, but you really look beautiful as a brunette, which is not good because you are still too noticeable."

She lifted her face to him. "So, what are you saying? I did it for nothing? I should have just wrapped a scarf around my head."

"You can do that in addition to the color."

She sighed. "At least we're together. Lucy and Ricky, international spies."

"They would have been the worst spies ever." Lokan chuckled. "Lucy would have blown their cover in the first five minutes."

With the thin walls and the family sleeping in the next room, even that little laugh felt like a stolen intimacy. Carol's curvy body was nearly impossible to resist, but Lokan had to limit himself to soft caresses, and once she fell asleep, so did he.

Morning came too soon.

Oyunaa prepared a hearty breakfast and packed food for their journey, refusing Carol's attempts to pay extra for the provisions.

The ride to the train station in Batbayar's ancient truck was bumpy and cold, the morning air sharp. When Batbayar pulled their bags from the back, Lokan left an envelope with extra cash on the driver's seat. It was more than they'd agreed on, but the family's hospitality deserved a reward.

After they said their thanks and goodbyes and walked away, Lokan turned to watch the guy pick up the envelope and take out the cash. He looked up and waved, mouthing a thank you.

"How much did you give him?" Carol asked.

"Twice what we agreed on." Lokan wrapped his arm around her middle, scanning the busy train station for any sign of an immortal presence. So far, he had found nothing, but he had a feeling that their luck would run out at some point.

They boarded the northbound train, finding their compartment in the second-class sleeper car. It was clean but basic—two narrow bunks and a small table between them.

"At least it doesn't smell like mutton." Carol sat on the lower bunk.

"Give it time." He put their packs under the bunks. "Once everyone starts unpacking their lunches…"

She glared at him. "Don't jinx it."

The train lurched into motion, beginning its long journey north toward the Russian border. The Mongolian steppes rolled by, endless grassland broken only by occasional clusters of gers and wandering livestock.

They'd been traveling for no more than two hours when Lokan felt it—that distinctive prickle of awareness that meant other immortals were near. He kept his expression neutral, not wanting to alarm Carol, but his muscles tensed.

"What is it?" she asked quietly, always attuned to the slightest change in him.

"Company," he murmured. "Stay here. Lock the door after me."

"Ricky—"

"Please, Lucy. Trust me."

She nodded, and as he stepped into the narrow corridor, he heard the click of the lock behind him.

Two immortals were making their way through the train car, checking each compartment as they went.

Lokan reached out with his mind, an ability his father didn't know the true extent of. Navuh believed his son could only thrall and compel humans. He still had no idea that Lokan's ability had grown and that he could now also thrall and compel some immortals, particularly those whose minds hadn't been strong to start with and later had been weakened by Navuh's ongoing compulsion.

One of the warriors paused with his hand on a compartment door five down from theirs. Lokan slipped into his mind with relative ease, finding the weakness he expected. Years of being compelled by Navuh had left fractures, gaps in mental defenses that Lokan could exploit.

Turn around, he suggested. *You've checked this car already. Move to the next one.*

The male frowned, confusion flickering across his features. His partner looked at him questioningly.

"We've already checked this car," the first one said, sounding uncertain.

"No, we didn't," the second protested. "We just got here."

You did, Lokan pressed, expanding his influence to include the second immortal. *You're being thorough. The next car hasn't been checked yet. That's where they are probably hiding.*

"Right," the second tracker agreed slowly. "The next car. Come on."

As they turned and headed back the way they'd come, Lokan maintained his mental pressure until they were out of his range. Only then did he allow himself to breathe, leaning against the corridor wall.

A soft knock came from behind. "Ricky?"

"It's clear," he said.

When Carol unlocked the door, he slipped back inside.

"Are they gone?" She put the dagger she'd held in her hand back into its scabbard.

"For now." He sat beside her, pulling her close. "We need to get off at the next station. Once they don't find us in any of the other compartments, they will be back, and I will have to repeat the thrall." He kissed her forehead. "I bought us a little time, nothing more."

They spent the twenty minutes or so until the next station in tense silence, Lokan extending his senses for signs of his father's minions returning.

The train slowed as they approached a small town, which was little more than a cluster of buildings around the rail line.

"Let's go." He gathered both their bags.

They disembarked with a crowd of locals, Lokan steering them immediately away from the platform. The town was small enough that strangers would be noticed, but hopefully, they could find transportation before the fighters realized their targets were no longer on the train.

A battered van sat outside the town's only store, its owner loading supplies into the back. Lokan approached him, pulling out a stack of bills.

"Excuse me," he said. "Is your van for sale?"

The man, grizzled and weather-beaten, looked at him like he'd grown a second head. "No."

Lokan showed the man the wad of bills, which represented more money than the van had been worth new. "I need it now, and you can buy a better one with this."

He could thrall the man to agree to sell them the van, but whenever money could do the talking, he preferred to let it do so.

The man's eyes widened. He looked at the money, then at Lokan, then at Carol standing with their bags. He must have realized that they were in trouble and were desperate for a vehicle because his expression softened,

"It runs," he said. "Mostly. The heater doesn't work, and it pulls to the left."

"Perfect," Lokan said, pressing the money into his hands. "Keys?"

Still stunned, the man handed them over. Lokan helped him unload his supplies, then turned back to place a mental suggestion.

You sold the van to a local family, he implanted. *A couple with three children, moving to Ulaanbaatar. They paid a fair price, and you were happy to help them.*

The man nodded slowly, the false memory taking root. "Good luck in the city," he said, addressing the fictional family his mind tricked him into seeing.

Lokan and Carol climbed into the van, which smelled strongly of motor oil and rotting vegetables. Carol wrinkled her nose but said nothing as Lokan started the engine. It coughed, sputtered, then caught with a roar.

"Well," she said as they pulled away from the town, "this is certainly a step down from your Mercedes."

"Beggars and choosers and all that. Besides, it's

perfect for this area. No one is going to pay attention to it." Lokan wrestled with the steering wheel as the van pulled strongly to the left, just like its previous owner had warned.

"Are we going to sleep in this thing?" Carol asked, eyeing the filthy interior.

"Hopefully not. I'll call Turner's contact once we're clear of the town. I hope he will be able to arrange lodging for us."

"Preferably with a shower," Carol said. "And clean sheets."

He laughed. "In this area, that's like asking for a five-star hotel, but maybe we'll get lucky." He pulled out his clan phone with one hand while fighting the van's steering with the other.

"Are you calling Turner's contact?" Carol asked.

He shook his head. "I want to give Kalugal an update. He asked me to keep him posted."

His brother answered right away. "Are you okay?"

"Yes. We're on the move. Father sent warriors after us, and two were searching the train we were on. I redirected them, we got off and bought a van from a random guy."

"Be careful," Kalugal said. "Navuh has chemically enhanced warriors, and the ones the clan captured were somewhat resistant to compulsion. Toven had to push to break through, at least with one of them."

"Great." Lokan let out a breath. "Just what I need."

"Navuh is probably worried about what you know and what you can reveal. That's why he sent men after you the moment your bodyguards reported your sudden travel plans. He's not stupid, and he has good instincts."

"I know." Lokan grimaced. "I spent a thousand years with him, and I know him much better than you do. Still, I had no idea about the chemist and the program to enhance warriors that he was running for over a year. I was completely in the dark about that, so it would seem that I don't know much after all."

"Take your time, Lokan. Let him think you're rushing for the nearest exit while you actually go to ground."

"Easy for you to say," Carol muttered. "You're not riding in a van that smells like something died in it."

Kalugal laughed. "You'll get used to the smell. In an hour, you won't even notice it."

"Right," she grumbled. "I think I'm going to empty my bottle of perfume on this thing."

"The glamorous life of international fugitives." Kalugal chuckled. "Look, take the long way around. Maybe even double back south for a bit before heading north again. The last thing Father will expect is for you to move away from your destination instead of toward it."

Lokan saw the strategic sense in that, but one look at Carol's expression told him she wasn't on board with extending their time on the road, especially in this van.

"We'll consider it," he said. "Right now, we need to find somewhere safe for the night. I can call the same contact Turner gave me before, or perhaps he has another one in case the first one sold us out. Not that I think he did that, but to be safe."

"I'll call Turner," Kalugal said. "They'll reach out to you."

"Thank you."

After ending the call, Lokan glanced at Carol. "You heard him."

"No," she said flatly. "I want to get to the village as quickly as possible. The sooner we are there, the sooner we will be safe." She gestured at the van's interior. "I can't stand this. Whatever this is."

"Fermented vegetables," Lokan offered. "With notes of diesel fuel and wet dog."

Despite herself, Carol laughed. "You forgot the undertones of despair and broken dreams."

"Ah, yes, how could I miss those?" He reached over to take her hand. "We'll find somewhere clean to stay tonight. I promise."

"With a shower," she emphasized. "A hot shower. That's non-negotiable."

"With a shower," he agreed. "Though in rural Mongolia, 'hot' might be optimistic."

She sighed, settling back in the cracked vinyl seat. "How did we go from a Beijing penthouse to this in less than forty-eight hours?"

"Careful planning and excellent life choices," Lokan said dryly.

"Clearly. Though I suppose it could be worse." She squeezed his hand. "At least Lucy has her Ricky."

He chuckled. "And they are riding into the sunset in what smells like a compost heap."

"That's why Ricky better find that shower soon, or Lucy's going to make him sleep in the stinky van."

It was getting dark when Lokan's phone chimed with a message. He read it and smiled. "Turner's network came through. They found us a place forty miles to the north of here."

"With a hot shower?" Carol asked hopefully.

Lokan reread the details. "Private bathroom. That's all it says."

"I'll take it."

8

SYSSI

The family was growing, and the dining room was a little crowded with the addition of several highchairs, but no one minded rubbing elbows while cutting Okidu's delicious roast or spearing fingerling potatoes with their forks.

Okidu hovered around them, refilling wine glasses and picking up empty platters while murmuring apologies for having to reach over. He'd outdone himself tonight, which was an achievement since he cooked elaborate dinners for the family every Friday.

Perhaps he'd made a special effort because everyone was in attendance for a change. Usually, some of the family members had other plans. Alena and Orion often dined with Toven and Mia and their extended families, while Jacki and Kalugal were either traveling or attending various fundraisers in the city.

"More wine, mistress?" Okidu asked Syssi.

"Just water for now, thank you." She placed her hand over her glass.

That earned her a curious look from Amanda. "Do you have news you would like to share with the rest of us?"

Syssi's cheeks heated at the implication. "I wish, but no. I'm just not a big fan of wine."

Amanda pouted. "That's disappointing. And how can you not like wine?"

It was disappointing but expected. Merlin's fertility potions had helped them conceive Allegra, and Syssi was grateful. To hope that they would work a miracle again so soon was overly optimistic.

"I just don't like the taste. If I'm drinking alcohol, I prefer a sweet and tangy cocktail."

"Like a margarita." Amanda leaned back in her chair with her wine glass in hand. "Which reminds me that we haven't had a margarita party in forever. We should have one." She turned to Alena. "Are you game?"

Alena shrugged. "Sure. As long as it doesn't involve any of your other crazy schemes."

"What crazy schemes?"

Syssi chuckled. "The witchy dancing in the woods, for one."

A smile spread over Amanda's beautiful face. "Ah, those were the days. How I miss them. But I was thinking of something less adventurous, like a karaoke party."

"I would love that," Alena said. "Just tell me when and where, and I'll be there."

Alena was a gifted singer with a powerful voice, so naturally the idea excited her, but Syssi still remembered the last time she and Amanda sang while drinking margaritas. Her sister-in-law had many talents, but singing wasn't one of them. She sang loudly and off-key.

Amanda turned to Jacki. "How about you, darling? Do you like to sing while drunk?"

Jacki smiled. "As much as the next girl, but if you want me to come to your party, it will have to wait until I'm back from Egypt."

"Right." Amanda's face fell.

At the far end of the table, Annani sat with Allegra on her lap, engaged in an animated conversation with her granddaughter.

"Nana pretty," Allegra declared, patting Annani's cheek. "Like Princess Sparkle."

Annani's melodic laugh never failed to raise goosebumps on Syssi's arms.

"Where is your doll, sweetheart?" Annani asked.

"In her bed." Allegra shifted on her grandmother's lap. "Sleeping."

"I see." Annani kissed the top of her head. "Does she have a pretty bed?"

"Very pretty." Allegra launched into a detailed description of the miniature bed Syssi had ordered for her from an artisan on Etsy.

Evie gurgled something incoherent between spoonfuls of mashed potatoes. She was seated on Annani's other side, mostly content to listen to her older cousin talking.

Syssi had never encountered a child who liked mashed potatoes as much as Evie did, especially when the ratio between potatoes and butter was equal parts.

"They grow so fast." Alena cradled little E.T. against her shoulder. "I try to savor every moment."

Orion leaned over and kissed her cheek. "We can have more, you know. Seventeen sounds like a good number to me."

Instead of laughing him off, Alena smiled. "Fates willing. I thought I was done at thirteen, and then this little miracle arrived. I wouldn't mind three more."

As all eyes turned to Jacki for some reason, she lifted her hands in the air. "It's up to the Fates. By the way, do you know that the grand opening of the village's first grocery store is this Monday?"

Syssi shook her head. "This morning they were still assembling shelves, and they are planning to open on Monday? What's the rush?"

"I don't know, but I'm happy that it's happening before we leave for Egypt." Jacki reached for a piece of baguette. "I'm curious to see what they've done with the place."

"They want it to be a gathering place, not just a store," Syssi said. "Somewhere people can get a taste of different foods. I like the idea of having more dining options in the village. When the permanent store is up and running, it will have a seating area where people can eat the prepared food they bought at the store."

As Annani and Alena discussed the kinds of ready-made foods they would appreciate in the store, and later Amanda and Alena assembled a playlist for the karaoke party, the mood around the table appeared to be relaxed, but Syssi sensed an undercurrent of tension

—the more bothersome topics dancing at the edge of discussion but not quite breaking the surface.

The recent terror threat, Lokan's escape and current fugitive status—these heavier matters waited like storm clouds on the horizon.

"I spoke with Lokan right before coming over here." Kalugal set down his fork, apparently deciding to end the pleasant veneer they had all been maintaining. "He and Carol are in Mongolia, doing their best to evade our father's minions."

Kian frowned. "I wasn't aware they were followed into Mongolia. I thought they ditched the bodyguards at the airport and escaped."

"They did, and Turner found them a safe house across the border for the night, but when they boarded the train the next morning, they encountered Doomers. Lokan thralled them to get rid of them, and he and Carol got off at the first stop after that. He bought an old van so they wouldn't have to rely on public transportation, where they are easier to find. I told him to take it slow and continue in a roundabout way."

Kian didn't look happy, his fingers drumming a staccato beat on the table. "I should send Guardians to help them. The Doomers Lokan encountered must have been the normal rank-and-file. If your father sends enhanced Doomers after them, Lokan might not be able to enter their minds and redirect them as easily."

Kalugal nodded. "I warned him, and I contacted Turner about finding them another safe house, but I agree that they might need help. It will take time for Guardians to get to them, though, and in the meantime, they should just lie low. Perhaps stay in the safe house."

Kian leaned back in his chair. "I still don't understand why Navuh suspected Lokan. We didn't act on any of the information he provided in a way that could have exposed him."

"Navuh could have sensed that something was off," Jacki said. "He knows his son."

"I regret not being able to be here when Lokan and Carol arrive at the village," Kalugal said, returning to his meal. "Jacki and I could have thrown a big welcome party for them."

"Do you want to postpone your trip to Egypt?" Kian asked. "The search for Khiann has waited this long—"

"No," Annani interrupted. "We cannot delay. Every day matters. I feel it..." She trailed off, but Syssi understood. The goddess had her own form of knowing, not visions exactly, but a deep intuition honed over millennia.

"I wasn't planning on postponing." Kalugal gave her a small smile. "My people found another figurine that might have been made by the same artisan who made yours, Clan Mother, or it could be a copy of a copy."

"Another one of me?" Annani asked.

"No, it's a different one. There is also a possible additional figurine in a private collection of someone I know by reputation, and I plan to make him an offer he can't refuse to purchase it."

"Antiques dealers are worse than arms dealers sometimes," Orion said.

Kalugal cast him a smile. "That's not an issue for compellers, right?"

Orion shrugged. "Snakes are stubborn, and many of them are immune to mind manipulation. Don't assume that your tricks will always work."

Kalugal sighed. "You are right. Let's hope this guy has a malleable mind."

Syssi tuned out the artifact acquisition discussion, her mind circling back to Lokan and Carol, stranded somewhere in Mongolia, hunted by Doomers sent by his own father.

"If Navuh catches them, would he... eliminate Lokan?" Syssi phrased her questions in a way the young children wouldn't understand, but they seemed to sense the increased tension in the adults around them.

E.T. whimpered softly, and Alena adjusted him against her shoulder.

Kalugal took a long sip of wine before answering. "I've thought about little else since they ran. Betrayal is not something our father can forgive. He would try to extract information from Lokan using any means available to him but would probably imprison him somewhere secure instead of doing something that our mother would never forgive him for."

"You don't sound certain," Annani observed.

"Because I'm not." Kalugal met her gaze. "Navuh crossed a line I never thought he would when he authorized those massive terror attacks, especially the one at the concert. I don't think I know him anymore. Something has changed, and I would like to find out what it is. When I talk with my mother, I'll ask her if she's noticed anything."

Annani shook her head. "Areana will not answer any questions about your father. Do not even try."

Kalugal closed his eyes briefly. "The truth is that I fear for her. What if Navuh knows about our communications with her? The device we gave her is undetectable, but my mother might not be as circumspect as she believes. Someone could have noticed something."

That was a constant danger, but the weekly conversation with Areana was a lifeline for both Annani and her. If she ever decided that it was time to leave her deranged mate, that was the only way she could request help.

"Perhaps I should summon a vision," Syssi murmured.

"And ask what?" Kian gripped her hand under the table. "Whether Navuh knows about Areana's little betrayal? Or about an escape route for Lokan and Carol?"

When put like that, he was right that requesting a vision would be futile. Those were not the type of questions that the universe answered.

Kian squeezed her hand gently. "Lokan and Carol are both capable people, and I will send a team to protect them. That's much more helpful than asking the universe for answers. You know that you shouldn't squander your gift."

He was right, of course.

Her reservoir wasn't limitless.

She'd realized months ago that, unlike the Supreme Oracle of Anumati who could summon visions at will and en masse, Syssi's gift was more like a battery that needed to be conserved and saved for moments of necessity.

Finding Khiann was a necessity. Lokan, Carol, and even Areana could take care of themselves.

9

AREZOO

T he Pearl's opening day dawned bright and clear, and Arezoo arrived with her mother at five in the morning to help with the final preparations.

The transformed house barely resembled the empty shell they'd worked so hard to clean and organize just days before. Now the shelves were stocked, the refrigerators were filled, and the air was perfumed with the scent of freshly made bread that had been baking since three in the morning.

"Arezoo, sweetheart, can you arrange these pastries in the display case?" Parisa called from the kitchen-turned-bakery, her face flushed from the heat of the ovens. "Mind the glazed ones—they're still warm."

"Of course, Aunt Parisa." Arezoo carefully transferred the delicate pastries, each one a small work of art.

The cream-filled profiteroles glistened with

caramel, while the walnut cookies bore intricate patterns pressed into their golden surfaces.

Her mother emerged from the room that they'd converted from a bedroom into a cold storage room, carrying a crate of cucumbers. "The vegetables are just beautiful. Look at how green these are. I'm tempted to bite into one just to see how juicy it is."

"Then do it," Arezoo said. "They belong to you."

Soraya shook her head. "Just take the crate."

"Where do you want them?" Arezoo took it from her mother's hands.

"The produce section near the front. People like to see fresh vegetables first thing, especially the green ones. They set the tone."

Soraya's eyes sparkled with an excitement Arezoo hadn't seen since… well, ever. This store represented so much more than just a way to earn a living. It was their declaration of independence, their stake in this new life.

By seven-thirty they were ready to open the doors, and Arezoo took her position behind the register, running through the system one more time.

William had installed a modern point-of-sale setup that seemed almost too sophisticated for their small operation. Still, Arezoo had mastered it quickly thanks to her experience working the café register.

"I'm nervous," Yasmin admitted, adjusting a pyramid of pomegranates. "What if no one comes?"

"They'll come," Rana said with characteristic confidence. "The village residents have been waiting for this."

The bell above the door chimed at precisely eight o'clock. Their first customer was Wonder, Arezoo's boss from the café, carrying a woven basket.

Arezoo wanted to ask who was handling the morning traffic in the café, but Wonder just walked in with a bright smile and her imposing height, making the converted living room feel smaller. "Congratulations on your opening," she said. "I've come mainly for the fresh bread, which I could smell from the café, and whatever else catches my eye."

"Welcome to The Pearl," Soraya said. "Please, look around. The fresh bread is in the back room, still warm from the oven."

As Wonder browsed, more customers arrived—first a trickle, then a steady stream. Arezoo's fingers flew over the register, ringing up purchases while listening to the delighted exclamations over her aunts' baking.

With the variety of items for sale, it was much more complicated than working the register at the café. Thankfully, they had decided to sell fruit and vegetables in packages, so weighing things was not necessary. If she had to do that as well, she would have probably needed help.

"The almond cookies are incredible," one immortal said after tasting a sample from Yasmin's tray. "I'll take three packs."

They had only prepared ten, which in retrospect was too few.

The morning rush exceeded their wildest expectations, and Arezoo barely had time to think between customers, but she thrived on the energy. This was different from the café—this was theirs, their success, their contribution to the community that sheltered them.

Not that she was quitting the café. For now, she would work mornings in the store and afternoons in the café. Hopefully, it was all going to work out.

"We need more flatbread," Parisa called out around ten o'clock. "I'm starting another batch. We're nearly sold out."

"The sourdough too," Yasmin added. "Who knew immortals loved bread so much?"

"Everyone loves fresh bread," a customer in line said. "And the smell alone is enough to lure everyone in the village to your store."

"Good to know," Rana said. "I thought to post daily specials on the clan's bulletin board, but maybe the smell is enough of an advertisement."

"It certainly is," said a Guardian whom Arezoo recognized as one of the regulars from the café.

His basket was full of vegetables, bread, frozen steaks, and a container of Soraya's special herb blend.

"That'll be eighty-seven dollars and thirty cents," she told him.

"That's very reasonable and worth every penny just for the convenience and the wonderful service." He handed over his card. "I'll be back for more tomorrow," he promised.

The compliments warmed Arezoo's heart. The clan members weren't shopping at their store out of pity or to show their support. They truly appreciated what The Pearl had to offer.

As she fell into a rhythm of ringing up purchases and putting them in paper bags, Arezoo let her thoughts drift to the poetry book she'd left hidden under her pillow in her room. She'd spent a couple of hours with it last night, carefully turning each page, marveling at the craftsmanship as much as the written words.

She'd never owned anything so beautiful, so aesthetic. Everything in her life had been practical, functional. Even the few books she'd managed to keep had been cheap paperbacks, easily replaced. But this was a work of art in every sense of the word, pleasing to the eye, to the touch, and to the soul.

Rana's excited chatter pulled Arezoo out of her musings, and she smiled at her aunt, who was engaging customers in conversation, asking if there was anything they would like that they couldn't find in the store, and writing the items in her notepad.

As the bell chimed again, something in Arezoo's gut tightened even before the door opened and Ruvon walked in. Her customer-friendly smile faltered for just a moment before blooming into something more genuine for him.

He had a nice dark green shirt on instead of his usual blues and grays, and he'd had his hair styled. The changes were subtle but noticeable, at least to her, and she had to admit that he looked good.

"Welcome to The Pearl," she said. "How are you today?"

His face lit up at her warm greeting. "I'm well. Congratulations on the opening. The store looks great."

"Thank you. We're a bit overwhelmed by the response, but in the best way. My aunts' baked goods are nearly sold out already."

"Then I should grab some before they're all gone."

"You should. They are in the other room."

When he returned a moment later with several items stuffed in his basket, she smiled at him once more. "Thank you again for the poetry book. I spent a couple of hours reading through it last night. It's the most beautiful thing I've ever owned. The binding, the gold leaf, the calligraphy—every page is a work of art."

Ruvon seemed to grow in height with each compliment. He straightened, his shoulders squaring, and his entire posture shifted from uncertainty to satisfaction and even pride. His smile transformed his whole face, softening the sharp angles and bringing warmth to his eyes, which usually seemed shadowed.

The transformation was remarkable.

"I'm so glad," he said, and his voice was different too —richer, more confident. "When I saw it, I could picture you reading it, running your fingers over the pages. The store owner said it was from the early nineteenth century, from Isfahan. The paper was handmade, and a master illustrator did the decorations."

It must have cost him a small fortune, but it wasn't polite to ask how much he'd spent on the gift.

"I can tell," Arezoo said. "Each margin is unique. I found myself studying the artwork as much as reading the poetry." She hesitated, chewing on her lower lip. "The truth is that I never would have thought about something like that, let alone wanted it. Somehow, you knew what would please me better than I knew myself."

Color rose in his cheeks, which was both adorable and surprising.

She was well aware that Ruvon's youthful looks were misleading and that he was old enough to be her great-grandfather. He shouldn't be this shy around a girl like her.

"I've always liked books, even though I don't get to read much. But what caught my attention was how beautiful this little volume was. I thought that something so unique and pretty should belong to you because you are unique and pretty."

Arezoo felt a flutter of something—not fear, not exactly discomfort, but an awareness of being seen.

The color on his face deepened, and he raked his fingers through his hair. "I'm so bad at this."

"No, you're not." She paused, searching for the right word. "It was an incredibly thoughtful gift, and I appreciate it greatly. Really."

When he smiled and stood taller again, she suddenly understood something profound. She had power here—the power to build him up or tear him down with a word, a look, a smile.

Was this why some men feared women so deeply? This power to affect them with such small gestures? She thought of the systems designed to strip women of their agency, voice, and presence in public life. If a smile could transform a man's entire bearing, if disappointment could crush his spirit, then those who built cages for women did so out of weakness rather than strength.

It was a disturbing thought, but also an enlightening one. She'd grown up seeing male power as absolute, overwhelming. She'd always hated that, rebelled quietly against it, and couldn't understand it. Now she suddenly did. Women had power that men feared.

The disturbing thoughts must have shown on her face because Ruvon's shoulders began to slump again, uncertainty creeping back into his posture. He was so attuned to her moods that it was almost frightening. They weren't even a couple, and she'd done nothing to encourage his affections beyond basic politeness, yet her emotional state affected him profoundly.

She quickly offered another smile. "The book is perfect. I feel transported every time I open it, like I'm entering a magical world where everything is beautiful and nothing harsh can intrude."

The transformation happened again—spine straightening, chin lifting, that warm light returning to his eyes. Such a small thing, her approval, yet it changed everything about how he carried himself.

"Your gift means so much to me, but I can't keep chatting with you. There is a line of waiting customers behind you."

"Of course." He stepped aside. "I'll just browse for a bit."

As Arezoo rang up the next customer's purchases and the next, she watched Ruvon selecting more items and putting them in his basket. A loaf of sourdough, some of Yasmin's sugar cookies, a container of her mother's spice blend, and fresh vegetables that he examined with amusing seriousness.

"These tomatoes are perfect," the woman at the register was saying. "But these were the last ones. When will you get more?"

"We'll restock daily," Arezoo said, but she wasn't sure of that.

"Wonderful. I'll be back tomorrow, then."

Fenella emerged from the cold storage room. "You are completely out of grapes!" she announced with a mixture of triumph and dismay. "I can't believe how fast they went."

"At this rate, we'll be sold out of everything by noon," Soraya called back, but her tone was joyful rather than worried.

"That's a good problem to have," Parisa said. "Better than sitting on inventory."

When Ruvon approached the register with his selections, Arezoo was ready with professional friendliness that held just a touch more warmth than she offered other customers.

"Did you find everything you needed?" she asked, beginning to scan his items.

"Yes, and several things I didn't know I needed," he replied with a small smile. "Your aunts' baking is dangerous. I may have to increase my training to compensate."

She laughed. "You have nothing to worry about. I hear that immortal metabolism is amazing, and that it's really difficult to gain weight."

"It is," he admitted, then seemed to gather his

courage. "Arezoo, I was wondering—that is, if you have time—would you perhaps read another poem for me some time? When you're not busy, of course."

She glanced around. The initial rush had calmed somewhat, and Rana had returned to help with customer questions, freeing Soraya to restock the shelves.

"I'm working the afternoon shift in the café. If you stop by near closing time, we can read some poetry over coffee."

His entire face brightened. "Really? That would be wonderful. Thank you."

She finished ringing up his purchases, their fingers momentarily brushing as she handed him the bag. Neither of them pulled away immediately, though the contact was brief and could have been dismissed as accidental.

"Fifty-three fifty," she said.

He handed her his card and carefully gathered his purchases. "I'll be at the café."

"See you later," she promised.

After he left, Arezoo found herself touching the spot where their fingers had met, wondering at her own boldness. When had his presence shifted from threatening to... whatever this was?

Another wave of customers arrived, and she lost herself once more in the rhythm of ringing up orders, taking payments, and putting groceries in bags. Still, throughout it all, she kept thinking about power and fear, about the delicate dance between men and women, and about the way a smile could transform someone's entire being.

The poetry book waited under her pillow in her room, patient as only ancient things could be. And somewhere in the village, a male walked taller because she'd acknowledged his gift with genuine pleasure.

Perhaps this was what healing looked like—not a dramatic revelation, but small moments of connection that slowly rebuilt trust in the possibility of kindness.

FENELLA

I t was Fenella's last night in the Hobbit before the trip to Egypt, and the thought was discomforting and exciting at the same time.

It was strange how the nightly performance had become her routine, her life. Every day, she found herself looking forward to the start of her shift, and she knew she was going to miss it. Still, at least Din was accompanying her on the trip, so she wasn't leaving behind every aspect of her new life that had brought her stability and satisfaction after half a century of uncertainty and constant vigilance to just survive.

"You are quiet," Din said, his hand tightening over hers.

"I'm thinking about tomorrow." She glanced up at him. "Hard to believe that after all the delays, it's finally happening."

He nodded. "Still scared about going?"

"A little, but I want to go. I want to help find Esag and maybe Khiann, if Esag can help with that. It would be nice to find out whether my ability can contribute something meaningful instead of just entertaining drunk immortals."

The truth was that Fenella wouldn't have minded if her ability were only good for entertainment. In fact, she might have preferred it because it placed much less responsibility on her shoulders, but she felt indebted to the clan and the Clan Mother.

"I like watching you entertain people. Anyone who's bringing smiles to people's faces is doing a better service to humanity than most."

"That's so sweet of you to say." She stretched up on her toes and kissed his cheek. "But are you planning to sit in your corner every night I work? Even after we get back?"

"Where else would I sit?" He arched a brow. "Would you prefer if I sat at the bar?"

Had he misunderstood her questions, or was he pretending?

"What I meant was that you must have better things to do than watch over me every night for hours. Won't you get bored? There must be something else you'd rather do than watch me pour drinks and make up stories."

"Like what? Sit at home and watch television?" He shook his head. "I'd rather be where you are."

It was touching, really, but it was a bit obsessive. "If the roles were reversed, would you want me sitting in that corner every single night, just watching you work?"

He considered this as they passed under a large oak tree. "I would, but what would you rather do?"

Fenella thought about it for a moment and realized that she would have most likely done the same thing. "Most nights, I'd want to be where you were. I'd want to be near you. But some nights..." She smiled at the image forming in her mind. "Some nights I'd probably stay home, run a bubble bath, pour myself a glass of wine, and watch terrible movies or reruns of shows I've seen a dozen times."

"That sounds lovely. Maybe I should try that. Though I'd probably read instead of watching television."

"Of course, you would, Professor."

"We complement each other. You introduce me to the joys of mindless entertainment, while I bore you with archaeological journals."

She bumped his shoulder. "You don't bore me. Much."

"Such enthusiasm." But he was smiling. "We should put in a request for our own place when we get back. Somewhere we can both have terrible movie nights or reading nights as the mood descends."

"I've already done that," she admitted. "Not officially, but when I visited Ingrid's design center, I implied that we would like our own place when we return from Egypt."

"Good." He lifted their conjoined hands and kissed her knuckles. "It's time we let Shira and Thomas have some peace and quiet."

"Did either of them complain?"

He shook his head. "No, but I don't want to overstay my welcome. By the way, we could visit Scotland if you want. I can show you the castle, introduce you to my mother…"

She definitely wasn't ready for that. "Let's not plan too far ahead. I prefer to take things one day at a time."

"Of course." He smiled tightly. "No pressure."

As they got closer to the Hobbit, Din suddenly slowed considerably as if they had all the time in the world.

"Come on, we need to hurry, or I'll be late." She tugged on his hand.

"Atzil can manage by himself for a few minutes." Din gestured at the sky. "It's such a beautiful night. The moon is almost full. We should take a moment to appreciate it."

"We can appreciate it after my shift." She pulled on his hand again, but he seemed determined to dawdle. "Din, seriously. What's gotten into you?"

"Nothing. I just think we rush too much. Always hurrying from one thing to the next without stopping to—"

"You're stalling." The realization hit suddenly.

Was he reluctant to share her with her audience, wanting to have her all to himself for a little longer?

"I'm not stalling. I'm being philosophical about the passage of time and—"

"Din."

"I'm serious."

"Right." She stopped pulling and stepped closer,

reaching up to touch his face. "Are you jealous? Do you want to keep me all to yourself?"

"You caught me." He leaned into her touch. "Am I being ridiculous?"

"A little bit." She rose on her toes to kiss him quickly. "But it's sweet. Now come on. I don't want to be late on my last day."

When they reached the Hobbit, Fenella noticed something odd. The windows were dark, as usual, the shutters preventing the light from leaking through to the outside, but it was also quiet. The Hobbit wasn't soundproofed like the residences in the village, and usually she could hear chatter and music as soon as she turned into the pathway leading to its front door.

"That's weird," Fenella said as Din reached for the door handle. "Is anyone even there?"

"Let's see." He opened the door, and as they stepped into the dim interior, she waited for her eyes to adjust to the darkness. But then, the lights suddenly blazed on, and the bar erupted in whistles and applause.

"Surprise!"

Fenella gaped, processing the scene.

The bar was packed—fuller than she'd ever seen it before. Banners reading 'Good Luck in Egypt' and 'Don't bring back any Cursed Mummies' hung from the ceiling. Every regular was there, plus faces she didn't expect to see.

"Oh my God," she breathed. "You knew about this?"

"I may have been informed that my stalling services were required."

"I'm going to kill you later. Slowly."

"I look forward to it."

Atzil walked over, his chiseled jaw squared in an almost comical grin. "The guest of honor has arrived." He pulled her into a brief embrace before letting her go.

Still reeling, Fenella let herself be pulled into the crowd. Hands patted her back, voices called out greetings and jokes. Someone pressed a drink into her hand —whiskey, neat, just how she liked it.

"Speech!" someone called out, and others took up the chant. "Speech! Speech!"

"Oh no," Fenella said. "I don't do speeches. I do psychometric readings."

"Then read something!" Morrison suggested, producing a bar spoon. "Tell us what this spoon thinks about your trip!"

Laughter rippled through the crowd, and Fenella felt herself relaxing. These were her people, her community. The panic receded, giving way to warmth.

"Fine." She took the spoon with exaggerated ceremony. "Let's see what wisdom this spoon has to share."

She closed her eyes, making a show of concentration. The now-familiar tingle of the brooch seemed to pulse against her chest, and for a moment, she felt something from the spoon—countless hands, endless stirring, the satisfaction of creating something that brought pleasure.

"This spoon is having an existential crisis," she announced. "It's thrilled that I'm going to Egypt because it's always dreamed of stirring ancient cocktails. It wants me to find a recipe for Cleopatra's favorite drink and bring it back. It has aspirations, people. Don't let its humble appearance fool you."

The crowd laughed and applauded. More objects appeared—a bottle opener that apparently yearned to free ancient wine from archaeological sites, a cocktail shaker that claimed past lives as various vessels throughout history.

"Your turn!" Fenella called out. "Who wants to try reading me?"

What followed was a hilarious reversal. Her regulars took turns 'reading' various bar tools, each interpretation more ridiculous than the last. Graham insisted a corkscrew was writing her memoirs. Someone else claimed a jigger had commitment issues because it could never hold on to liquid for long.

They were terrible at it, but that was the point. Their attempts were filled with inside jokes and references to past nights, a greatest hits compilation of her time at the Hobbit.

"Alright, alright!" Atzil called out eventually. "Enough amateur hour. Let's have a proper toast. Whiskey for everyone, on the house!"

The front door opened right as a cheer went up, and Fenella's jaw dropped as Kyra entered, followed by her sisters. All of them. Even Soraya, who looked extremely uncomfortable but determined.

"I can't believe you came to my bar."

"We had to come," Soraya said, chin lifted. "We couldn't miss your send-off."

Rana leaned to whisper loudly in her ear, "We were curious about this den of iniquity you work in."

"It's cozy," Yasmin offered diplomatically.

"I can see why you love it," Parisa said.

Behind them, Arezoo slipped in, looking radiant in a way Fenella hadn't seen before. She'd done something with her hair, and was that lip gloss?

"You look amazing," Fenella told her.

Arezoo blushed. "It's Laleh's doing. She said I couldn't come to a party looking like I was going to clean houses."

"Everyone!" Atzil called out, raising his glass. "A toast to Fenella, who has brought magic to the Hobbit. May your journey be safe, may your discoveries be plentiful, and may you come back soon because I can't handle these drunken idiots alone!"

"Hey!" several people protested, but they were laughing.

"To Fenella!" the crowd chorused, and drinks were raised and downed.

"I believe this calls for entertainment of a different kind," someone said—MacGregor, one of the Guardians. "We can't send our lass off without a few songs."

What happened next would be burned into Fenella's memory forever.

Three Guardians began singing in harmony, their voices filling the bar with Scottish ballads. She vaguely recognized the songs from her youth.

The crowd swayed along, and Fenella was swept up in the sounds of those deep voices that reminded her of home.

"Clear the floor!" Tavish called out suddenly. "We need space!"

People pushed tables and chairs back, creating a clear space in the center of the bar. Fenella's eyes widened as two Guardians produced swords and laid them crossed on the floor.

"Seriously? You are going to do the Highland sword dance for me?"

The guys grinned and assumed their places.

The three who had sung before started singing again, and the dancers began their performance, their feet moving in intricate patterns between and over the blades. The crowd clapped in rhythm, and Fenella noticed Kyra's sisters joining in, their faces smiling and alight with joy.

This was what she'd always wanted without realizing it. Not just safety, not just a place she could hide in, but a community, belonging, the freedom to celebrate and make as much noise as she pleased without fear.

When her eyes misted with tears, Din wrapped his arm around her middle. "You okay?"

"Perfect," she said, and meant it.

The acceptance of these people melted the last sheet of ice protecting her heart, this community that embraced her with open arms.

Another dancer took the floor, and this time, people began joining in around the edges, attempting Highland steps with varying degrees of success. Jasmine pulled Ell-rom into the mix, laughing as he tried to follow her movements. Even some of Kyra's sisters were drawn in.

"Dance with me," Fenella said to Din.

"I don't really know how—"

"You're a Scot. It's genetic."

"That's not how genetics work."

"Din." She took his hand. "Just move your feet and make your woman happy."

His resistance crumbled at that. "How can I refuse when you put it like that?"

They joined the dancing, and Din's movements were not at all awkward or amateurish. Instead of her guiding him, he guided her through the steps, patient when she stumbled, delighted when she got it right.

When they took a break from the dancing, she leaned in and kissed him on the lips. "Thank you."

"For dancing? You forced me."

"For this." She gestured at the people around them. "I know you had something to do with organizing it."

"I may have mentioned to Atzil that you deserved a send-off. The rest was all him and your admirers."

"My admirers?"

"Love, half of this village adores you, and the other half just hasn't met you yet."

11

DIN

The clan's airstrip stretched ahead in the early morning light, the tarmac still radiating yesterday's heat despite the cool dawn air. Din followed Fenella down from the bus to where Okidu was pulling out everyone's luggage and arranging it in a neat row.

"Look at that." She stared at the sleek private jet waiting on the runway. "We're traveling in style."

Din studied the aircraft with a more critical eye. It was a Gulfstream GIVDP, if he wasn't mistaken, which was top of the line, but after the landing gear malfunction on his flight from Edinburgh to New York, he couldn't help but view it with suspicion. Private jets, in particular, were prone to accidents because they typically had less rigorous maintenance schedules than commercial airliners.

"You look like you're calculating crash statistics," Max said from behind him.

"Not at all," Din lied smoothly.

Kyra elbowed her mate. "Don't tease him. After what happened to him in New York, it's natural that he's nervous about flying."

"That was a commercial flight with hundreds of passengers," Max pointed out. "This is Kalugal's private plane. He's not going to skimp on maintenance when his own family is on board."

It was a fair point, but Din's unease persisted nonetheless. Kalugal's crew was performing final checks, and through the cockpit window, he could see two pilots running through their pre-flight checklist.

He didn't know that private jets required a co-pilot, but this was going to be a long flight, so perhaps they were going to take turns.

In addition to Shamash, whom Din regarded more as a babysitter than a guard, Kalugal had brought only two men, and Din wondered if that was enough protection for their group. According to Jacki, Egypt was hostile and dangerous to foreigners.

"Is that sufficient protection?" He gestured at the men.

Kalugal handed the baby carrier where Darius slept peacefully to Shamash. "You forget that with my compulsion ability, I can freeze everyone within earshot with one command. In addition, I maintain a substantial security force in Egypt to guard my dig sites and also cover my private residence in Cairo, where we will be staying."

"How substantial?" Din pressed.

"Twenty-three men, all former special forces who are familiar with the area and speak the language."

Kalugal's lips twisted in a smirk. "Trust me, Professor. I've been managing Egyptian operations for decades. We'll be well protected."

Jacki wrapped an arm around her husband's waist. "You need to show Din your Professor Gunter disguise."

"Oh, *ja*," Kalugal affected a German accent. "When I flew commercial and had to go through airports, I wore the disguise of an older gentleman." He smiled. "Regrettably, my shrouding doesn't work on security cameras, and if the operators are located beyond my sphere of influence, they see the real me and not my shroud."

The guy was scarily powerful, which was not immediately apparent because he was easygoing, exuding charm, and exhibiting a sense of humor. Nevertheless, Kalugal was a force to be reckoned with, and Din was glad to have him on their side.

Jasmine and Ell-rom joined them, the former looking eager while the latter appeared his usual stoic self.

"This is exciting," Jasmine said. "My first time visiting Egypt. I've always wanted to see the pyramids." She turned to Ell-rom. "Remember I showed you that documentary about them?"

Ell-rom nodded. "The one that claimed they were power plants and not burial sites."

Kalugal chuckled. "Let's get on board, and I'll tell you my version of what the pyramids were used for and how old they really are."

Din was familiar with all the conspiracy theories

surrounding the pyramids, and he was curious to hear which one Kalugal favored. Most of them were nonsense, but not all.

The interior of the jet was even more opulent than he'd expected—cream leather seats that looked more like armchairs, polished wood panels, crystal decanters secured in a bar that would have done credit to a luxury hotel.

"Which seats would you like?" he asked Fenella.

"By the window, definitely." She was already moving toward a pair of seats midway down the cabin. "I want to see everything."

As they settled in, Fenella carefully placed her carry-on bag in the overhead compartment. The figurine Kalugal had gifted to the Clan Mother was inside, entrusted to Fenella's care, wrapped in silk and nestled in a specially designed case. The Clan Mother had insisted that Fenella take it, hoping it might trigger additional visions.

"Nervous?" he asked, watching her fidget with the seatbelt.

"A little, but not about flying. You?"

He smiled. "I'm crossing my fingers for no trouble, mechanical or otherwise."

Their host stood near the bar. "Ladies and gentlemen, welcome aboard. Once we're airborne, I'll be happy to serve drinks. We have a fully stocked bar, and I've made sure to include some exceptional whiskies for those with sophisticated palates."

"Now you're talking," Max said, claiming seats for himself and Kyra across from Din and Fenella.

The pilot's voice crackled over the intercom, instructing everyone to buckle up and announcing their departure.

When the engines revved up and the vibration traveled through the airframe, Din gripped the armrests.

"Hey," Fenella said. "It's going to be fine. Lightning doesn't strike twice in the same place, right?"

He forced his hands to relax. "I'm not sure about that."

She leaned closer. "Tell me something fascinating about Egypt."

"What would you like to know?"

"Anything. You're the professor. Profess."

As the jet began to taxi, Din fell into lecture mode. "Most people think of Egypt as just pyramids and mummies, but the civilization spanned over three thousand years. To put that in perspective, Cleopatra lived closer in time to us than to the builders of the Great Pyramid."

"Seriously?" Fenella's eyes widened.

"The official history dates the building of the Great Pyramid at around 2560 BCE. Cleopatra died in 30 BCE. That's over two thousand five hundred years later, and she's been dead for just over two thousand years."

"Oh, wow."

"The Great Pyramid is much older than that," Kalugal said. "It was already ancient when the Clan Mother was born."

The acceleration of takeoff pressed them back into their seats, and Din closed his eyes, forcing himself to relax. He'd never been afraid of flying, and even during the emergency landing on the river, he hadn't been overly concerned. Not for himself anyway. It was only after the fact, when he'd learned what could have happened, that the fear had set in.

"See?" Fenella said. "We survived the takeoff."

"I'm more concerned about the landing," he pointed out.

"Pessimist." But she said it with affection.

Kalugal unbuckled and stood, steady despite the slight turbulence. "Now then, who wants a drink? We have approximately fifteen hours to Cairo, with one refueling stop. Might as well enjoy ourselves."

"I'll have whatever single malt you're proudest of," Max called out.

"A man after my own heart." Kalugal walked over to the bar. "Din? What's your pleasure?"

"The same," he said.

"I could make cocktails," Fenella offered, starting to rise. "Jacki, what would you like?"

Jacki shook her head. "Thank you, but I prefer not to drink during flights. Too dehydrating, and I have this little one to think of." She adjusted Darius's carrier. "Perhaps some sparkling water with lime?"

"Coming right up," Kalugal said. "Fenella, what can I get you?"

"Whiskey, neat," she said, settling back into her seat. "When in Rome and all that."

"Excellent choice." Kalugal began pouring with the skill of a professional bartender. "You know, this particular bottle comes from a distillery near Inverness. Twenty-five years old, finished in sherry casks. I'd be curious to hear the opinions of my Scottish guests."

Din accepted the crystal tumbler, inhaling the complex aroma. "Speyside?"

"Highland, actually, though you're close. The distillery sits right on the border between the two regions."

The whiskey was exceptional, all smoke and honey with a finish that seemed to last forever.

"So, Kalugal," Max said, leaning back with his drink. "You promised us a story about the pyramids."

"What they teach in universities about the Great Pyramid is absolute nonsense. Four thousand five hundred years old? Built by Khufu with copper tools and slave labor?" He laughed. "The real story will blow your minds."

The guy should have been an actor.

Kalugal leaned forward conspiratorially. "The pyramid is at least 12,000 years old, and some say that it's much older than that. Personally, I think it's more like 36,000 years old. It was built by the gods, of course, with the gods' technology. The limestone casing? Those weren't just decorative stones. They were precision-cut insulators!"

Max cast Din a knowing smile. "What say you, Professor? Is that right?"

Din nodded. "Kalugal's right about the casing stones. Each one weighed 15 tons and was polished to a mirror finish with tolerances of one hundredth of an inch. But here's what's fascinating—the pyramid's latitude coordinate is the exact same number as the speed of light in meters per second. Coincidence? Obviously." He laughed. "The longitude coordinate matches nothing, so there's that."

"The longitude matches nothing yet!" Kalugal slapped his armrest. "The Great Pyramid wasn't a tomb. It was a massive piezoelectric power generator. The granite in the King's Chamber contains high concentrations of quartz. When the Earth's seismic activity compressed these crystals, it generated electricity. The whole structure was essentially a giant battery."

Din nodded. "The Queen's Chamber had those mysterious shafts that contained salt deposits and zinc and copper residue. Those are chemical components of batteries. And get this—when they analyzed the mortar between the blocks, they couldn't replicate it with modern chemistry. It's stronger than the stone itself."

Kalugal settled back into his armchair-like seat at the front and swiveled it electronically so that he was facing the rest of the group. "But power generation was just the beginning. The pyramid's shape creates a natural resonance chamber. Those granite beams above the King's Chamber? They're tuned to specific frequencies. The harmonic vibrations could have been used to achieve altered states of consciousness and communicate with others on faraway planets."

"The mathematical encodings are everywhere," Din added. "The pyramid's base perimeter divided by its height equals 2π. The King's Chamber dimensions encode the Pythagorean theorem, centuries before Pythagoras was born, even according to the official dating of the place, and the descending passage points directly to where the star Thuban would have been in 10,500 BC."

Kalugal, who was still hanging on to the bottle, poured himself another shot. "Tesla understood this. He wanted to recreate the pyramid's wireless power transmission system at Wardenclyffe. The pyramid sent energy through the ionosphere to receiving stations, smaller pyramids, around the world. That's why you find pyramids on every continent."

"The erosion patterns on the Sphinx prove it matches the alternative dating," Din said. "Dr. Robert Schoch's analysis showed water erosion from torrential rains that haven't occurred in Egypt for at least 10,000 years. The establishment archaeologists went crazy trying to discredit him."

Kalugal raised his glass. "If we have time to visit the Great Pyramid, you'll feel the energy yourself. That structure is still active, still transmitting on frequencies that humans can't feel. The pharaohs didn't build it. They found it, long after the original builders vanished in the great cataclysm."

He smiled at his captivated audience. "And I haven't even told you about the underground city beneath it yet, or the crystal capstone that could focus energy beams into space. But we'll save that for when we're there, standing in the shadow of that great mystery."

Fenella gaped at them both. "You can't be serious. That sounds like science fiction."

Kalugal shrugged. "Even all those millennia ago, the gods possessed incredible technology, but it all fell into disrepair when contact with Anumati was severed and eventually eroded to such an extent that almost nothing is left. That's what I'm looking for—traces of that technology. Before Aru and his team arrived, we knew very little about the gods' history and who they were, so my interest in archaeology was mainly to find proof of what I suspected all along. Technically, my assumptions were confirmed by these new arrivals from Anumati, but after years of digging, I can't just abandon my favorite hobby, so I keep digging."

"What are you hoping to find?" Fenella asked.

"Information. I love discovering and deciphering ancient writings. In my latest excavation, we've uncovered a cache of cuneiform tablets that appear to be trade records, but with some fascinating anomalies."

"What kind of anomalies?" Din asked.

"References to goods that don't match any known Egyptian or Mesopotamian terms. Descriptions of materials with properties that seem impossible for the period." Kalugal took a sip of his whiskey. "One tablet mentions a cloth that 'captures the sun's light and holds it through the night.'"

"Phosphorescent fabric?" Din suggested. "That would be anachronistic by several millennia."

"Exactly." Kalugal nodded. "Another describes containers that 'preserve food as fresh as the day of harvest for a full turning of the seasons.'"

"Some kind of preservation technology," Ell-rom mused. "Perhaps chemical?"

"The implications are staggering," Din said. "If these tablets are authentic—"

"Oh, they're authentic," Kalugal assured him. "I've had them tested six ways from Sunday. The clay composition, the writing style, even trace elements in the stylus marks all date to the Third Dynasty."

"The gods had access to things we're only now rediscovering," Fenella said.

"That's what I think." Kalugal took a sip from his whiskey. "But that's not something any respectable archeologist can suggest."

"What else?" Din asked.

"Architectural plans that don't match any known structures. Mathematical proofs that shouldn't have been discovered for another thousand years. And my personal favorite—medical texts describing surgical procedures that we only perfected in the last century."

"The gods wouldn't have shared everything," Max said. "But some information must have leaked out."

Kalugal refilled their glasses. "Perhaps we'll find more clues on this trip. The figurines are our priority, though. We need to locate Esag, and with his help, hopefully we will find Khiann."

Max raised his glass. "To successful hunting, then. May we find what we seek in Egypt."

They toasted, crystal chiming against crystal.

"You know," Fenella said, "I've been wondering about something. If Esag survived the destruction, why didn't he try to find other survivors? Why didn't he come looking for Annani?"

"Perhaps he tried," Jacki suggested. "But the world is a big place, and immortals went into hiding. It would have been nearly impossible for him to find any of the others."

"Maybe he thought that they were all dead," Kyra said. "He was far enough away to survive, but he might have assumed no one else did."

"Well, that got dark quickly," Max said. "How about we talk about something more cheerful? Like, how many ways the Egyptian authorities might try to kill us?"

"Max!" Kyra smacked his arm.

"What? I'm being practical. We're heading into a country where the Brotherhood has a significant presence and influence. I'd like to know what we're walking into."

"The situation is tense but manageable," Kalugal assured them. "We have security, and we'll be staying in my house and not a hotel. I've been doing this for years, Max. I know how to keep my people safe."

Din appreciated the reassurance, but he noticed Fenella had gone quiet beside him. When he glanced over, she was staring out the window at the clouds below, her expression distant.

"What are you thinking?" he asked.

She turned to him with a rueful smile. "Just processing the fact that we're flying into danger. Again. I thought I was done with that when I reached the village. I just wish the world wasn't so full of people trying to kill each other."

"Amen to that," Jasmine said from across the aisle. "Though if it wasn't, we'd be out of a job."

"Speak for yourself," Din said. "I'd be perfectly

happy studying ancient civilizations without people trying to blow themselves up, along with as many innocent bystanders as possible."

"Where's the fun in that?" Ever one to trip over himself as he tried to lighten the mood, Max grinned. "Nothing like a little danger to spice up academic research, true?"

"Your definition of 'little' needs work," Kyra told him.

As the banter continued, lifting the collective mood, Din relaxed into it, enjoying the camaraderie.

"More whiskey?" Kalugal offered, bottle in hand.

"Why not?" Din said. "It's a long flight."

12

ANNANI

A nnani's stomach fluttered with a sensation she had not felt for a long time.

She was nervous.

She had dragged her feet telling Wonder about the possibility of finding Esag, but now that the expedition to Egypt had left, she could no longer delay. The problem was that what she had to share was a mix of hope and uncertainty.

Perhaps she should have told Wonder sooner. Right after Fenella had touched the figurine and seen those visions, Annani should have called Wonder and told her the good news. But something had held her back, the same instinct that made her cup her hands around a candle flame a moment before the advent of a gust of wind that would have extinguished it.

It was a gut feeling that had warned her it was too early, but then guilt interfered, whispering that her friend would not forgive her for keeping this a secret from her.

When the doorbell chimed, she rose to her feet and waited for Ogidu to escort Wonder inside.

Her butler entered her receiving room and bowed. "Mistress Wonder is here, Clan Mother."

"Thank you, Ogidu. Please show her in."

Her butler bowed and stepped aside, and then Wonder was there, filling the room with her impressive height and the positive energy she carried these days.

It was good to see her so confident and contented. She had not been that way as Gulan.

"Annani!" Wonder smiled.

Annani opened her arms, and Wonder crossed the room in three long strides, enveloping her in an embrace that lifted her slightly off her feet. They both laughed at the awkwardness of it—Wonder having to bend nearly double and Annani having to stretch up on her toes.

"Some things never change," Wonder said, setting her down gently. "We are still a mismatched pair."

"And yet we were perfect together." Annani took Wonder's hand and led her to the sofa.

"How was your day at the café?" she asked to start the conversation.

"Less busy than usual. The Pearl is the new attraction now, stealing some of my customers. Not that I mind. The village needed another casual dining place."

Annani tilted her head. "Do the sisters serve food in their grocery store? I was not aware that they have dine-in arrangements."

"They don't, but people buy their ready-made items

and take them home. Once the new place is built, though, there will be outdoor seating on the roof of their store, which will serve as a back terrace for the office building. I expect many more of the café customers will opt for that."

Kian had mentioned that over dinner at his house and had even shown her the plans.

"It is going to be a very nice addition to the village center," Annani said. "I am looking forward to the day it opens."

Wonder nodded. "So, what's the occasion? You didn't invite me to talk about the new grocery store."

Annani laughed. "I remember that expression on your face. It is the same one you always had when you suspected me of coming up with another scheme that would get us in trouble."

"That's because you have the same guilty look on your face you always had when you were about to drag me into one of your shenanigans. I often wondered where the fountainhead of all those crazy ideas was."

"They were not crazy. They were fun."

Wonder's laugh was rich and full. "You always made it sound like such wonderful adventures. 'Come on, Gulan, it will be fun,' you'd say. And then we'd end up hiding in the storage chambers and secret passages while half the palace guards searched for us."

"Poor Gulan." Annani squeezed her hand. "But maybe forcing you to go against your careful and calculated nature helped shape you into the strong female you are today."

"Strong?" Wonder shook her head. "I was terrified

half the time. But I could never say no to you, and not just because you were the princess and I had to obey your wishes. You'd look at me with such excitement, such certainty that whatever mad plan you'd concocted would work out perfectly, that I just got swept away."

"My plans usually worked."

"After significant modifications to account for reality," Wonder corrected. "You always forgot about little details like guards, or walls, or the laws of physics."

They smiled at each other, the weight of shared history like a familiar cloak wrapping around them both. But Annani could see the question in Wonder's eyes, the awareness that she had not been invited here to reminisce.

"There is something I need to tell you." Annani tightened her fingers around Wonder's hand. "I should have told you about it sooner, but I did not want to get your hopes up for nothing."

Wonder frowned. "Don't keep me in suspense. Just tell me what it is."

Annani contemplated the best approach to tell Wonder about Esag and decided to start at the beginning.

"Kalugal and Jacki found another figurine in Egypt that resembles in style the one Kalugal found of you. Only this time, the figurine was of me."

Wonder gasped. "Do you think the same person carved them both?"

Her friend had always been sharp. "Yes and no. Mine was a copy of an original that was carved by the same person who carved yours. When Fenella held it, she saw visions of the carver copying an older original, which was signed at the bottom." She took a deep breath. "The name of the artist was Esag son of Agnon."

Wonder went very still, her hand trembling in Annani's grasp. "Esag?" The name came out as barely more than a whisper. "But that would mean that he—"

"Survived." Annani squeezed her friend's hand. "The inscription read, 'Blessed be the memory of the most radiant princess who was taken from us too soon.' He thought we had all died, Gulan. He carved figurines of us to keep our memory alive."

Tears gathered in Wonder's eyes but did not fall. She had not always been good at controlling her emotions, but she had gotten better at it after her resurrection.

"Fenella's talent works best when Kyra and Jasmine join forces with her. That is why they all boarded Kalugal's jet this morning and left for Egypt. They are going to follow the trail of figurines that will hopefully lead them to Esag, and if we find Esag..."

"We might find Khiann," Wonder finished. She pulled her hand free and stood abruptly, pacing to the window. "Anandur had to know about this and didn't tell me." She turned back to Annani. "Did you or Kian order him to keep this from me?"

Shaking her head, Annani rose to her feet and walked over to her friend's side. "We did not, but he might not have known the details. And even if he did, he probably wanted to spare you disappointment the same way I did. Finding Esag is not assured. In fact, the chances of finding him are very slim."

"He should have told me anyway. We're fated mates and we don't keep secrets from one another." Wonder closed her eyes briefly. "Did he think that I was still pining after Esag?"

"Oh, my dear Wonder." Annani patted her friend's arm. "Men are foolish creatures, but your Anandur knows how much you love him. In his mind, he was protecting you from disappointment if the search proved fruitless."

Wonder's broad shoulders sagged. "That sounds like him."

"Hope can be cruel when it is snatched away. I also wanted to spare you that if possible, but I knew you would be angry at me if I kept it from you."

Wonder moved back to the sofa, sinking into the cushions. "Can I at least see the figurine?"

"I gave it to Fenella to take with her, hoping she might glean more memories from it. But I took photographs." She sat next to Wonder. "Do you want to see them?"

"Yes, please."

Annani reached into the hidden pocket of her gown and withdrew her phone. She had taken multiple photos of the figurine from every angle, just in case it got lost and this was all that remained of it.

She handed the phone to Wonder, watching her friend's face as she studied the images.

"It's so beautiful," Wonder breathed. "The detail is extraordinary. I never knew Esag had such artistic talent."

"And this is not even his work. According to

Fenella, the artist who made this copy was never satisfied with his attempts to match the original. He felt he could never capture the perfection that Esag had achieved."

Wonder enlarged the image, studying the face carved in miniature. "It does look like you. Not just the features, but something about the expression. That little tilt to your chin when you're planning something devious."

"I do not tilt my chin when planning," Annani protested.

"You absolutely do. It's your tell." Wonder handed the phone back, but her expression had grown distant. "If Esag made these, mine and yours, he must have cared for me more than I thought he did."

Wonder had been in love with Esag, and he had let her down. Annani could see how knowing that he had carved her likeness, thereby preserving her memory, must have stirred up old feelings and old questions.

"Of course, he did. His marriage was arranged, and he was doing what was expected of him."

Wonder nodded. "What I don't get is how he knew about the fate that befell me. He wasn't there when I fell into the chasm, and yet Jacki saw the whole story when she touched my figurine."

"I have a theory about that," Annani said. "What if Esag developed foresight abilities over the centuries? What if he had visions, and he imbued his work with them?"

Wonder shook her head. "If he saw me falling into the chasm, he knew that I wasn't dead and that I was in

stasis, buried somewhere in the desert. Why didn't he look for me?"

"Maybe he did," Annani said softly. "Maybe he also saw what happened to Khiann and looked for him too. That is what I am hoping for. Perhaps he doesn't have the resources to find Khiann, but he could point us in the right direction."

They sat in silence for a moment, the weight of desperate hope pressing down on Annani instead of uplifting her.

Wonder straightened, shaking off the melancholy. "The threads of fate are weaving the tapestry of our lives, and the pattern is starting to emerge. It's all coming together."

13

FENELLA

The cabin lights had dimmed hours ago, transforming the luxurious interior into a cocoon of shadows and soft breathing. Fenella shifted in her fully reclined seat and adjusted the blanket over her legs.

Her body thrummed with an energy, excitement about their destination, restlessness from being confined in a metal tube hurtling through the night sky, and the scent of Din's cologne that was driving her nuts. She wasn't used to having him near and not being able to play.

He appeared to be dozing, a little cramped on the narrow bed created by flattening the seat, one hand resting on his thigh beneath the cashmere blanket. His chest rose and fell in a steady rhythm that should have been soothing, but instead made her hyperaware of his proximity.

She glanced around the cabin. Across the aisle, Max had his arm around Kyra, both of them sound asleep.

Further back, Jasmine was curled on Ell-rom's chest while he was watching something on his tablet with earphones on and the screen dimmed. Even Kalugal seemed to be asleep along with his wife and son.

The gentle hum of the engines created a white noise that masked most small sounds, which was perfect.

A wicked idea began to form in Fenella's mind, one that would shock her stuffy professor, but that made her want to push boundaries even more just to see his reaction.

She shifted closer to him, letting her thigh press against his. His eyes opened immediately.

"Can't sleep?" he whispered, his Scottish accent more pronounced in his drowsy state.

"No," she breathed, turning her head so her lips were near his ear. "I'm feeling antsy."

His body tensed, responding to the seductive quality in her tone or maybe just to the pheromones she must be emitting. "Fenella..."

"Shh," she murmured, her hand snaking beneath his blanket. "Everyone's asleep."

"Not really," he said, but his voice had gone rough. "Immortal hearing, remember?"

"Then they'll politely pretend they can't hear anything," she countered, interlacing their fingers before slowly guiding his hand to rest on her thigh. "Just like we pretend that we can't hear what they are doing."

"No one is doing anything they are not supposed to," Din protested, but didn't pull his hand away. "This is—"

"Exciting?" she supplied. "Thrilling? Daring? Unlike anything my proper professor has done before?"

She felt more than heard his sharp intake of breath as she guided his hand to where she needed it.

"You're going to be the death of me," he muttered, but she could hear the capitulation in his voice. His properness was crumbling under her touch.

"What a way to go," she teased, moving her hand to his belly.

"Fenella." Her name came out as half-warning, half-plea.

She turned more fully toward him, using the movement to drape her blanket over both of them. In the dim cabin light, his eyes began to glow, and she had the absurd idea of telling him to put on his sunglasses.

"Close your eyes," she murmured. "They are a dead giveaway." When he obeyed her command, she caught his ear between her teeth, and as he shivered, she kissed the spot. "I want to play," she whispered into his ear, letting her breath ghost over the sensitive skin.

His fingers brushed against the gusset of her panties, providing the friction she so desperately needed. Fenella bit back a moan.

She had him.

Her straightlaced, proper professor was doing something wonderfully improper.

"You are insane," he said, but his fingers were moving.

"Insane with need," she breathed, sliding her hand into his pants and cupping him over his cotton shorts.

She felt him tense, every muscle going rigid. "Oh my. Someone's very interested in playing."

"Witch," he accused, but the word held no heat—or rather, it held nothing but heat.

"Yes," she said, beginning a slow, torturous rhythm with her hand.

As his fingers slid beneath her underwear, Fenella had to bite her lip to suppress a gasp.

"Shh, we need to be quiet," he reminded her, the smugness in his whisper making her want to do something that would wipe that satisfaction right off his face.

Two could play at that game. She adjusted her grip, changing the pressure in a way that made him inhale sharply through his nose.

Fenella delighted in the way Din's control frayed at the edges.

They found a rhythm, hands moving in concert beneath the blankets, the danger of discovery adding an edge that made every touch electric.

Fenella had never done anything like this—had never even imagined the possibility of doing something so daring. The girl she'd been back in Scotland would have been scandalized, and the immortal she'd become during her years of running would have seen it as an unnecessary risk.

But the person she was now, safe and loved by this magnificent man—this version of Fenella wanted to grab every moment of joy, every chance to feel alive.

"You're thinking too much," Din whispered, his

fingers finding a spot that made her thoughts scatter like startled birds.

"Pot, kettle," she managed, increasing her ministrations in retaliation.

His head dropped back against the small pillow, and she watched his throat work as he swallowed hard. The sight sent a bolt of satisfaction through her. This controlled, careful male was coming undone because of her touch, in a cabin full of immortals with exceptional hearing.

The power of it was intoxicating.

"I can't believe we're doing this," he breathed, the words barely audible even to her.

"I can't believe it took us this long to try," she countered, shifting slightly to give him better access while maintaining a slow, lazy rhythm with her hand. "All those nights at the bar, we could have been having so much fun."

"The bar?"

"Why not? That storage room is very private. It has a lock..."

"You're incorrigible," he said, but his fingers were doing something that made coherent thought increasingly difficult.

"You love it," she gasped, then bit her lip hard to keep from making more noise.

"I love you," he corrected, the words fierce despite being whispered. "Even when you're trying to corrupt me thirty thousand feet in the air."

"Especially then," she insisted, her movements

becoming more urgent as pressure built low in her belly. "You like being corrupted by me."

His only response was to demonstrate just how skilled his hands could be when properly motivated. Fenella had to turn her face into his shoulder to muffle the sounds trying to escape her throat.

"That's it," he encouraged, his voice strained as her hand continued its work. "Let go. I've got you."

And he did. Even in this mad moment of public intimacy, she felt safe with him, protected. He would never let anything bad happen to her, would never judge her for her desires, would never make her feel ashamed for wanting what she wanted.

The realization, combined with her trust and his expert touch, pushed her over the edge. She bit down on his shoulder through his shirt, her body shuddering with release as waves of pleasure washed over her. Through the haze of sensation, she felt him tense beside her, his climax following hers.

They lay frozen for long moments afterward, breathing carefully controlled, hands still beneath the blanket but no longer moving. Fenella lifted her head from his shoulder, wondering if she'd left teeth marks through the fabric.

"Well," she whispered, a giggle trying to escape. "That was..."

"Insane," he finished, but he was fighting a smile. "What am I going to do about the mess?"

"Take off your underwear and go commando."

He groaned. "We're never doing this again."

"Liar. Do you need me to help you?"

"No. I've got it."

"I need to visit the lavatory," he said after performing the complicated maneuver under the blanket.

"I wonder why," she teased, earning herself a look that promised retribution later.

He slipped out of his seat with admirable grace, considering the circumstances, and Fenella watched him make his way to the back of the plane. No one stirred, the cabin maintaining its illusion of slumber, but she wasn't fooled. Immortal hearing meant that someone must have been aware of their clandestine activities.

The thought should have mortified her. Instead, it sent another little thrill through her system. Perhaps there was a little bit of an exhibitionist in her.

Who knew?

Love was liberating. Evidently, having a partner she felt safe with was all the encouragement she needed to start experimenting with what brought her pleasure.

When Din returned, he slid back into his reclined seat with a carefully blank expression. "You look entirely too pleased with yourself," he whispered.

"I have good reason to be." She snuggled against his side with the smugness of a cat who'd gotten the cream. "I've just inducted my proper Scottish professor into the mile-high club. That's worth a little satisfaction."

"Inducted, corrupted, led astray," he muttered, but his arm came around her, pulling her closer. "What's next? Public indecency in the Cairo Museum?"

"Now there's a thought," she mused, feeling him tense. "All those dark corners, hidden alcoves, the mummy exhibit..."

"Absolutely not," he said with mock firmness. "I'm an archaeologist, not a tomb raider of virtue."

She laughed softly against his chest. "Tomb raider of virtue? Did you really just say that?"

"My brain's not fully functional yet," he defended. "Someone scrambled my circuits at high altitude."

"Poor baby," she cooed with false sympathy. "Maybe you should get some sleep. We still have long hours in the air."

"As if I could sleep now," he said. "I'll be spending the rest of the flight wondering who knows."

"If anyone does, they're probably impressed. I doubt anyone suspected you had it in you."

He pressed a kiss to the top of her head. "You're a terrible influence."

"The best kind of terrible." She yawned, feeling drowsy now that the adrenaline was receding. "Wake me when we get to Cairo?"

"Of course." His hand stroked through her hair, gentle and soothing. "Sleep, my wicked witch."

She smiled against his chest, feeling accomplished and content. It had been risky, potentially embarrassing, and definitely outside both their comfort zones. Still, it had also been a moment of connection that belonged to no one but them, even if others had been peripherally aware of it.

"Din?" she murmured, already half-asleep.

"Hmm?"

"We're definitely doing that again."

His chest rumbled with quiet laughter. "We'll see about that."

LOKAN

The afternoon sun beat down on Lokan's head as mercilessly as it scorched the dusty outskirts of Choibalsan, turning the air into shimmering waves of heat that made the distant mountains dance like mirages. The small town represented a significant detour from their route toward the border with Russia, but Kian had insisted that they needed protection and shouldn't attempt the crossing alone.

So here he was, standing beside the van, one hand shading his eyes as he scanned the road.

"Are you sure this is the right place?" Carol asked.

"These are the coordinates Turner sent, and it matches his description—a desolate stretch of road two kilometers outside of Choibalsan. It's far enough from curious eyes but close enough to the airport to make sense as a rendezvous point."

"They're late," Carol said from her perch on the van's bumper.

"They didn't provide the exact time. Just to be there between two and three in the afternoon."

"They are costing us a day. We could've reached the border today."

He sighed. "That was Kian's entire point. He doesn't want us crossing the border without protection. Chances are that my father's minions are guarding each crossing."

A distant thrum caught his attention, but it wasn't the sound of a vehicle approaching, and Lokan's muscles tensed as he identified that it was made by helicopter rotors.

"Get in the van," he ordered, already moving toward the driver's door.

Carol stood up, but instead of following his instructions, she lifted her hand. "It's probably the Guardians."

"Carol—"

"How on earth would the Brotherhood know to look for us here?"

She had a point, but he still preferred for them not to be sitting ducks in case she was wrong.

"You're probably right but get in the van anyway." He strode toward her, ready to throw her over his shoulder and shove her inside the vehicle.

He was too late.

The aircraft appeared over a low rise, painted white with commercial insignia on the tail, and as it circled their position, looking for a place to land, Carol began bouncing on her toes.

"It's them! I can see Grant through the window. That enormous bald head of his is unmistakable."

Relief flooded through Lokan, but then what she'd said registered. "Why is he bald?"

Immortals didn't lose their hair like humans did.

"He shaves his head. Don't ask me why. Something about wanting to look like Kojak."

"Who's Kojak?"

Carol huffed. "Where have you been living? Under a rock? He was the most famous television detective of the seventies and was named one of the greatest TV characters of all time."

He grimaced. "Actually, I was living under the proverbial rock. I didn't get to watch much television on the island."

Her expression turned remorseful. "My poor baby. We are going to watch it together as soon as we are in the village."

The helicopter landed on a relatively flat patch of ground, less than a hundred meters away, kicking up a cloud of dust that had them both shielding their faces with their arms and turning away. When the rotors powered down, three figures stepped out, carrying enough weaponry to assault a fortress.

"Carol!" The bald Guardian opened his arms wide as she ran toward him.

Lokan watched with amusement as his mate was engulfed in the Guardian's embrace, her feet leaving the ground as he spun her around. The other Guardians waited their turn, grinning broadly.

"Put me down, you giant oaf," Carol laughed, smacking Grant's shoulder. "You're going to break my ribs."

"As if." Grant set her down. "You're much tougher than you look." He kept his hands on her shoulders. "Fates, it's good to see you safe, even if your hair is a mousy shade of brown. Why did you color it?"

"Always with the compliments, Grant. Do you make all the girls swoon with those one-liners?" She let the other two embrace her as well.

Lokan observed the group from a few feet away, marveling at the camaraderie between his small mate and the three hulking Guardians. She'd trained with them only for a short period of time, but it seemed that she'd earned a place in their hearts.

"Hello, Lokan." Grant extended his hand. "I'm Grant. This is Camden and Dougal. We're your escort to the border."

"Thank you," Lokan said. "Though I wasn't expecting an aerial arrival. I was about to throw Carol in the van and speed away."

"Smart instincts," Camden said. "Turner's contact suggested this after our flight was delayed, and we gladly accepted his offer."

"Speaking of which." Dougal opened one of the large duffel bags they'd brought. "Compliments of Onegus." He pulled a compact submachine gun along with extra magazines out of the bag. "I hope you still remember how to use this."

"An MP5?" Carol's eyes lit up. "Oh, you beautiful man. Give it here."

"Thought you'd approve." Dougal handed the equipment to her. "Grant has your tactical vest and sidearm.

Lokan, we brought you an AK-47. Figured you knew how to handle it."

Lokan accepted the familiar weight of the rifle. He'd carried one through half the world's conflict zones over the decades. "It's like riding a bicycle," he murmured.

"A deadly bicycle," Grant agreed. "Right, let's get this gear loaded and get moving." He looked at the van and winced. "Is that thing operable?"

"It runs better than it looks," Lokan said. "You can tell the pilot that he can leave."

Grant turned around and signaled to the pilot.

The guy gave him a two-fingered salute, and a couple of moments later, took off, kicking up another cloud of dust.

"I wish we could just take a ride in that helicopter," Carol said. "Regrettably, even if we can thrall the pilot to take us over the border, the Russians will shoot it down."

"Or force us to turn back," Lokan added.

"One more thing." Grant reached into his pocket and pulled out two small cases. "Earpieces compliments of William."

"Thank you." Lokan reached for the cases and handed one to Carol. "Are these the ones that filter compulsion?"

"No, just regular Guardian communications," Grant said.

"Good enough." Carol put the case in her pocket.

They piled into the van, the Guardians somehow

managing to fit themselves and their equipment into the back.

"Fates," Camden muttered. "This is cozy."

"It was all we could get on short notice," Carol said. "And I'll have you know that I spent an hour this morning cleaning it. You should have smelled it before."

"What was it hauling? Dead yaks?" Grant snorted at his own lame joke.

As Lokan pulled onto the rutted road, Carol twisted in her seat to face the Guardians. "So, what's the deal with the enhanced Doomers Kian warned us about? The two Lokan encountered on the train were nothing special. He thralled them to turn around with ease."

"You were lucky." Grant leaned forward, his jovial demeanor nowhere in sight. "The three we encountered during the raids were nothing like what we've been used to."

"I watched one take three shots to center mass and keep fighting," Camden added. "Their pain tolerance is through the roof."

"Supposedly, some of them can go weeks without sleep," Dougal continued. "Just imagine what that means. They can keep hunting without stopping for rest."

"That's impossible." Carol waved a dismissive hand. "Not even immortals can do that."

Grant shrugged. "That's what Toven got out of the Doomer he interrogated, and he used compulsion, so the bastard couldn't lie."

"Toven barely managed to break through." Camden

met Lokan's eyes in the rearview mirror. "No offense, but you couldn't have done that."

"None taken," Lokan said. "I'm only a three-quarter god, and until I met Carol, I could only thrall and compel humans." He cast her a fond smile. "You make me a better male."

"Of course, Ricky."

"Ricky?" Grant asked.

Carol laughed. "Meet Lucy and Ricky. Those are our fake identities."

"I see," Grant said. "Well, we are here in case you encounter enhanced Doomers. Your mind tricks might not work on them."

"Speaking of Doomers," Lokan glanced at the three Guardians in the mirror. "Did you encounter any at the airport?"

Dougal nodded. "We spotted at least two outside the terminal, but they were focused on people going in, not those coming out. We managed to slip past them easily enough."

"Why didn't you just take them out?" Carol asked. "It would have been nice to just drive to the airport and fly out of here."

"Because there might have been more of them," Lokan said.

"Correct," Grant agreed. "Turner's contact was waiting for us with a taxi outside, and he took us to the helicopter rental place. You'd be amazed at what tourists will pay for tours of the Gobi. We learned that Westerners use them to conduct aerial photography expeditions, and wealthy hunters use them to look for argali sheep. It's a thriving business."

Lokan chuckled. "It's fascinating what people come up with to make money. Entrepreneurship drives innovation even here."

"How far to the safe house?" Camden asked.

Dougal checked his phone. "Three hours, give or take. It's a farm outside Sükhbaatar. The owners are visiting relatives in Ulaanbaatar tonight, so we will have the place to ourselves."

"Convenient," Lokan muttered. "Turner's global network of operatives is impressive. He has contacts everywhere."

Grant's stomach chose that moment to rumble loudly. "Please tell me there's someplace to stop for food. I haven't eaten since yesterday's airline meal, and that barely qualified as food."

"There are no dining options on this route." Carol reached for her bag. "But I bought supplies this morning. I've got dried meat, bread, some fruit that's probably bruised by now, and these fried pastry things that the vendor assured me were a local delicacy."

"You're a lifesaver." Grant took what she offered. "Literally. I was about to start eyeing Dougal like a piece of meat."

"I'm all gristle," Dougal protested. "Camden would be much more tender."

"I hate you both," Camden said, but he was grinning as he bit into one of the pastries. "These are actually good. What are they?"

"Khuushuur," Carol pronounced carefully. "Fried meat pockets."

When they were done eating, Grant looked at Lokan through the rearview mirror. "I wonder how long your father has suspected you of double-crossing him."

The blunt statement was like a kick to the gut, even though it shouldn't have been. His father didn't deserve his loyalty.

"I didn't double-cross him. I only supplied information that was important to protect the clan."

"It doesn't matter," Carol said. "We're out now. That's what counts."

She was right, of course. But some part of him was still wrestling with the betrayal—not his betrayal of Navuh, because he didn't feel like he'd actually betrayed his father, but his father's betrayal of him.

Some foolish part of him had hoped that Navuh loved him in his own twisted way and that he wouldn't hurt him.

Maybe he had?

After all, if he'd suspected Lokan of betrayal, he could have detained him a long time ago during his mandatory monthly visits to the island. And yet he hadn't.

What had changed, though?

Why had he decided to make his move now?

Was it because Lokan had attempted to run?

Probably. Maybe his father had waited for definitive proof before moving against him. Not only that, he'd sent the regular rank and file after him when he could have sent his new enhanced warriors.

Perhaps he actually wanted Lokan to get away?

15

FENELLA

Fenella pressed her face to the SUV's window, watching the chaotic Cairo traffic. The city blurred past in a kaleidoscope of colors, honking horns, and more people on the streets than she had seen anywhere else. After the serenity of the village and then the long flight, the sensory assault was overwhelming.

Watching a motorcycle weave between cars with three people balanced precariously on its seat, she asked, "Is it always like this?"

"This is actually light traffic," Kalugal said from the front passenger seat. "Wait until you see rush hour. It's like watching a choreographed disaster that somehow never quite happens."

His driver, a stern-faced man named Ahmed, navigated the chaos with the calm of someone who'd long ago made peace with Cairo's anarchic traffic laws. They were in a convoy of three black SUVs, Kalugal's security detail split between the vehicles.

"How large is this city?" Fenella asked. "I mean people-wise?"

"The Greater Cairo metropolitan area has a population of approximately twenty-two million." Jacki lifted a stuffed toy Darius had dropped and offered it back to him. "But the city proper is home to about eight million."

That was a lot of people, and it seemed like they were all out on the streets.

"How far to your estate?" Din asked.

"Another twenty minutes, assuming no accidents block the roads." Kalugal turned to face them. "You'll love the house. It's an old Ottoman-era mansion I've spent a lot of money restoring."

The city gradually gave way to more affluent neighborhoods, the buildings growing larger and more ornate.

When they finally turned through a set of massive iron gates, Fenella felt like she'd entered another world. The estate was surrounded by high walls topped with decorative ironwork that concealed some very non-decorative security measures.

The house itself took her breath away.

Three stories of honey-colored stone and graceful arches, with intricate wooden balconies and windows screened by latticework. Gardens surrounded it, an oasis of green and serenity in the dusty, noisy city.

As their convoy pulled up to the main entrance, staff emerged from the house like a well-orchestrated welcoming committee. At their head stood a young man in his late twenties, slim and neat in pressed khakis and a white shirt, his smile bright and full of straight white teeth against olive skin.

"Professor Gunter!" He bounded down the steps. "Everything is prepared as you requested. The rooms are aired, and the meal is almost ready to be served, and I have gathered the items you asked us to locate."

It took Fenella a moment to recall that Kalugal used the pseudonym Professor Gunter when traveling, and she wondered if he was also shrouding his appearance to resemble his chosen avatar.

"Excellent work as always, Joseph." Kalugal clapped the young man on the shoulder. "Everyone, this is Joseph, who keeps this place running. Joseph, our guests."

Joseph dipped his head. "Welcome to Cairo. If you need anything during your visit, I am at your service. No request is too small or too strange. The professor has trained me well in anticipating the unexpected."

His English was accented but clear, and his grammar was correct.

When they were ushered inside, Fenella tried not to gape like a tourist. The entrance hall soared three stories high, with a fountain in the center and staircases curving up on either side. The walls were covered in geometric tile patterns that seemed to shift and dance in the light filtering through stained glass windows.

"The bedrooms are on the second floor," Joseph said as other staff took their luggage. "The entire east wing has been prepared for your exclusive use."

Kalugal grinned. "What he means is that he's quarantined you away from my archaeological specimens and reference library. He lives in fear that guests will accidentally break something priceless."

"It happened once," Joseph said. "And the vase was already cracked."

"It was also three thousand years old," Kalugal countered.

Joseph shrugged as if to say it hadn't been his fault that Professor Gunter's guests were clumsy. It made Fenella like him immediately.

As they were shown to their room—a spacious suite with high ceilings and doors opening onto a shared balcony overlooking the gardens, Fenella set her bag on the bed. Annani's figurine was inside, and she was acutely aware of how precious it was and how carefully she needed to handle it.

"Dinner will be served in one hour," Joseph said from the doorway. "I hope it will give you enough time to freshen up." He dipped his head again and closed the door behind him.

Fenella sank onto the bed, suddenly feeling exhausted. The flight, the time difference, and the sensory overload of Cairo hit her all at once.

"You alright?" Din sat beside her, pulling her against his side.

"I'm tired and a little overwhelmed. It will pass."

"We can skip dinner if you want to. We'll just shower and get in bed."

She shook her head. "I'm hungry. The prepackaged meals on Kalugal's jet were not that great. I'm surprised that he didn't assign one of his guys flight attendant duties to serve us proper meals."

Din chuckled. "Or brought Atzil along."

An hour later, refreshed after a shower and a change of clothes, they gathered in what Kalugal called the small dining room, though it could have comfortably seated twenty. The table groaned under the weight of dishes, and Fenella's mouth watered. There was roast lamb, stuffed vegetables, multiple types of rice, flatbreads, salads, and other dishes that Fenella couldn't identify but smelled amazing.

"Yusuf, or Joseph as he likes to be called these days, grew up poor and hungry," Kalugal said as they took their seats. "That's why he's convinced that running out of food is the worst possible hospitality failure, and he always makes the chef prepare twice as much as needed."

"It all looks and smells amazing," Kyra said.

Jacki waved a hand over the offerings. "Let's eat."

"Don't mind if I do." Fenella reached for one of the platters and scooped a generous portion of rice with roast lamb onto her plate.

After they were finished and the staff had cleared the main courses, Kalugal led everyone to a spacious salon. "I'm curious to see what my team has found while we were gone."

"Shall I bring the items now, sir?" Yusuf, aka Joseph, asked.

"Please," Kalugal said. "But first, my guests are in dire need of strong coffee." He smiled at Kyra, who had started to doze off. "We are not done for today, my dear."

She shook herself. "We are not?"

"I want us to examine the figurines before we retire for the night."

"Of course." She straightened her back. "Coffee will be helpful, though."

A few minutes later, a server arrived with a tray of small cups that emitted a strong aroma of coffee.

It was sweetened with too much sugar, but whatever was in that stuff was like a booster shot of energy, and after finishing her cup, Fenella felt like she could dance the night away. Either that or have her way with Din on that beautiful bed in their room.

What they had done on the jet had been just the appetizer.

With coffee and dessert consumed, she half expected Kalugal to invite everyone to a smoking room, or maybe to the garden she'd seen from the window of her room, but he didn't. Instead, he opened the large wooden box that Joseph had put on the side table beside him and peered inside.

"Shall I take the items out?" Joseph asked.

"No need, thank you," Kalugal said. "We would appreciate some privacy, though."

"Of course, sir." Joseph dipped his head and ushered the rest of the staff out of the room, closing the double doors behind him.

Kalugal leaned forward conspiratorially. "Yusuf used to be one of my diggers. He showed up at the site one day, skinny as a rake, claiming he had experience.

He didn't, of course, but he was so eager to learn, so quick to pick up English and adapt to whatever was needed. I promoted him to site assistant, then house manager when I realized his real talents lay in organization rather than excavation."

"He seems very capable," Jasmine observed. "An intelligent fellow."

"He is, and what's more, he might be a Dormant."

That got everyone's attention, and Fenella regarded their host with a frown. "What makes you think so?"

"It's just a hunch." Kalugal smiled. "Sometimes I get them." He turned to Din. "That's how I knew that David, Sari's mate, was a Dormant, and I brought him over to her as a gift with a ribbon on top." He pretended to tie an imaginary ribbon in the air.

Din snorted, and Fenella wanted to ask him what the heck Kalugal was talking about, but maybe she should wait until they were alone to hear that story.

"If you suspect him, why haven't you tested him?" Kyra asked. "With males, it's easy. All he has to do is fight an immortal for a minute or so to activate the immortal's venom glands and get bitten."

"Selfish reasons, I'm afraid." Kalugal lifted his coffee cup and took a sip. "If he turns out to be a Dormant and transitions, he'd need to come to the village. And I like having him here, running my house."

"That's not fair to him," Jasmine said.

"I know." Kalugal had the grace to look a little sheepish. "The truth is that at first, I thought he had a wife and children because he told me he did when I hired him. If he transitioned, he would have to leave his family, and that seemed cruel. But it turned out he'd lied about that to get the job. He thought I'd be more likely to hire a family man out of pity."

"So now that you know he's single, why not test him?" Fenella asked.

"I keep putting it off, but Jasmine is right that it's not fair to him."

"If testing a potential male Dormant is so uncomplicated," Fenella said. "Get one of your men to wrestle with him until things get aggressive enough for venom production, then a bite, and see what happens. Why make it more complex than it needs to be?"

"Because change is complex," Din said. "Even good change."

Kalugal saluted him with the coffee cup. "You are not wrong, Professor." He put the cup on the table next to the wooden box and put the box in his lap. "Let's see what treasures my team has found."

He pulled out several cloth-covered figurines and started unwrapping them one at a time. Most were simple and not particularly artistic. But one made Fenella's breath catch.

It was a figurine of a girl on the cusp of womanhood, eleven or twelve years old, and she was carved with exquisite detail and painted with care. The face was serene, beautiful, with elaborately styled dark hair and a gown that seemed to flow despite being made of stone. Even in miniature, the sculpture radiated a sense of life.

"This one is unlike the others." Max leaned forward for a better look.

Kalugal lifted the figurine, turning it to examine the base. "There's a mark here, but I don't recognize it." He pulled out his phone and snapped a photo. "I'll send this to the Clan Mother. It might be ancient Sumerian or a simple artist's mark."

"What did the dealers say about it?" Ell-rom asked.

"Let's see." Kalugal unfolded a note that had been wrapped together with the figurine.

"The expert Joseph took it to said it was contemporary—beautifully handmade but probably created within the last decade. But looking at it..." Kalugal shook his head. "There's something about it that feels older. Perhaps it's another copy of an original that had been carved much earlier."

"Should I give it a try?" Fenella asked, "Maybe I can see something useful."

Kalugal handed it over, and Fenella cradled it carefully in her palms. The stone was cool, smooth, and seemed to pulse with energy.

When she felt Kyra's hand on her shoulder and Jasmine's on her other side, she took a deep breath to center herself and prepare for their combined abilities to create the amplification she needed.

"Ready?" she asked them.

They nodded, and Fenella closed her eyes, opening herself to whatever impressions the figurine might hold.

The vision came gradually, like fog clearing from a window. She saw hands—young hands, steady and sure, working with tools on stone. The hands belonged to a man, though she could only see him from chest to fingers as if she was seeing what he had been seeing as he'd worked. There was an electric lamp next to him, confirming what the expert had said about the contemporary origins of the figurine, but it was an old and rusted lamp, and the workshop was cramped and dusty.

There was something infinitely sad about the way he carved, though, deliberate but with melancholy. When he paused to examine his work, she got the sense that he was satisfied with his creation, but that profound sadness permeated everything around him, including the beautiful figurine.

Through the workshop's single window, she could see a narrow alley, lined with crumbling stone buildings that looked ancient and decayed. Laundry hung between windows, and somewhere a child cried. It was clearly a poor neighborhood, the kind of place where people scraped by day to day.

The vision faded, leaving Fenella blinking in the bright light of the sitting room. Beside her, Kyra and Jasmine were also coming back to themselves.

"Well?" Kalugal demanded. "What did you see?"

"A young man," Fenella said. "Working in what looked like a very poor area. Old buildings that were falling apart. He was carving with such sadness, like each stroke hurt him."

"I saw the same," Kyra confirmed. "His hands were not only young but also unmarred. That's peculiar for someone in his line of work, which makes me think that he was immortal. And if I'm right, we might have just witnessed Esag working."

"But why would he be living in poverty?" Fenella asked. "With all the natural abilities of an immortal, he could have done better for himself."

"Maybe he's hiding from something," Max suggested. "Or someone."

"Or maybe it's not Esag at all," Din said. "Maybe it's his descendant, someone who inherited the talent and maybe even apprenticed with him. A child born to an immortal male would have been human. Not even a Dormant."

"Why the sadness, though?" Fenella touched the figurine again, feeling an echo of that profound melancholy. "This feels personal, like a loss the carver experienced directly, like the girl was a relative. Maybe a sister of his."

"What about the mark on the base?" Kyra asked. "The Clan Mother might recognize it."

"I've already sent it." Kalugal wrapped the figurine in its cloth, but instead of putting it back in the box, he put it aside. "The Clan Mother should be awake by now, but perhaps she is busy and didn't see my message yet."

16

AREZOO

The morning rush hit the café like a tsunami, and Arezoo was regretting switching shifts with Aliya. It was only seven-thirty, and she was already overwhelmed. She dodged between tables, balancing a tray loaded with cappuccinos and pastries, while trying to remember which orders belonged to which customers.

Working the register at her mother's grocery store was child's play compared to this. There, she could stand in one spot, smile, ring up purchases, and place the groceries in bags. Here, she was moving constantly.

Not that Wonder's job was any easier. She was making the coffees, ringing up the orders, and handing out the sandwiches and pastries.

"One almond croissant, one double espresso," Arezoo announced, setting the items before an immortal she recognized but couldn't name. They all started to blur together after a while. Like mannequins in a store window, they were all so perfect that it was difficult to tell them apart, and they even dressed the same, or almost the same.

"Thanks, Arezoo." He smiled at her. "Busy morning, eh?"

"Very," she confirmed, already moving to the next table. "Enjoy your breakfast."

She paused at the corner table where Parker and Lisa sat, their heads bent together over a shared muffin. The young couple came early in the mornings before heading out to the school they both attended. They were looking at each other as if the other person were their entire world.

"Can I get you anything else?" Arezoo asked.

Lisa looked up. "Oh! Um, maybe another orange juice?"

"Just one?" Arezoo glanced between them.

"We're sharing," Parker said as a grin lit his handsome face.

How old was he? Maybe Laleh's age? Lisa seemed to be a little older, but she was still the perfect age to be Laleh's friend.

Maybe she should say something?

Perhaps some other time. Arezoo still didn't feel confident enough to just start a conversation. Better yet, she could ask Drova to say something. On second thought, weren't these teenagers the very ones she'd compelled to steal things for her?

Yeah, Drova probably wasn't the best choice for that.

"I'll be right back with your order." Arezoo moved to the next table, but her mind remained on the young couple.

Parker was already immortal, Drova had told her that, and Lisa was a Dormant, waiting to transition when she was old enough to have sex with an immortal.

What were they waiting for?

Lisa was at least sixteen. Girls much younger than her were getting married in Iran, and even though Parker was younger, he was for sure up to the task.

The thought surprised Arezoo with its boldness. Since when did she have opinions about other people's sex lives?

They were clearly in love, though. They looked fully committed to each other, and Parker could give Lisa immortality right now and make her safe instead of waiting. Why delay?

She knew the answer, of course. The clan had rules about age and maturity. But in the world Arezoo had left behind, girls younger than Lisa were routinely married off to older men. Her own father had started receiving offers for her when she turned fourteen. Luckily, her mother was a strong woman who fought for her daughters. She had found fault in each of the potential matches and convinced her husband that his daughters were worth much more than what was being offered, and that he should wait for the right match.

His greed had saved her from an early marriage, though it hadn't saved her from being kidnapped and—

No. She wouldn't think about that. Not here, not now, not while she had customers to serve and had to pretend to be a normal girl living her normal life.

After delivering the juice to Parker and Lisa and noting their easy mutual affection, she wondered what it would feel like to have that.

The thought of Ruvon flickered through her mind, and she quickly pushed it away. He would be disappointed today when he came for his usual visit and didn't find her there.

They'd fallen into a routine over the past few days, of him arriving near closing time, ordering coffees and pastries for both of them, and her reading to him from the poetry book.

Somewhere along the way, her wariness of him had faded into something close to friendship. He listened with such intensity, asked thoughtful questions about the meanings behind the verses, and shared his interpretations, which often surprised her with their profound insight. But she knew he wanted more. It was in every look, every careful gesture, and every cup of coffee and pastry he bought for her.

He had feelings for her, romantic feelings, while she felt... what? Companionship? A growing fondness that was definitely not love?

"Order up!" Wonder called from behind the counter.

Arezoo hurried over to collect the plates, her mind still churning.

Was she being unfair to Ruvon? Leading him on by spending time with him when she knew she couldn't return his feelings? Or was friendship its own valid thing, separate from romance?

The morning rush eventually slowed to a manageable pace, and Arezoo finally got a chance to catch her breath. She grabbed a sandwich from the display, turkey and avocado on sourdough, and sat at the counter to eat.

"Are you okay?" Wonder asked.

"I forgot how intense it gets here in the mornings."

Wonder's expression softened with sympathy. "I appreciate you switching with Aliya."

"She and Vrog are working on something important." Arezoo took a bite of her sandwich.

Wonder chuckled. "Maybe they are working on a baby."

Arezoo blushed. "Do they want a child?"

Wonder shrugged. "I don't know. The Kra-ell revere children as much as immortals do, but they take their procreation duties even more seriously than we do, so it's possible."

Arezoo didn't even know if Vrog and Aliya were married. Not that it mattered in the village. Everyone knew who was with whom, and that was enough. Nothing official was required. Her Aunt Kyra and Max were not talking about getting married, but they were talking about having a baby so Jasmine would have a sister or a brother.

Wonder sighed. "Did you hear from your aunt since she went to Egypt?"

Arezoo shook her head. "No, why?"

"Do you know why she went there?"

"Something about looking for artifacts that will help find the Clan Mother's lost husband."

"Yes, well." Wonder pushed a strand of hair behind

her ear. "Eventually. But before that, they need to find Khiann's best friend, Esag, and they hope he will be able to help them find Khiann."

"I heard my aunt talking about it with my mother, but I didn't pay attention to the details."

Why was she telling her all that?

Wonder let out a breath. "When I was a girl in Sumer—and yes, I'm that old—I fell desperately in love with Esag, Khiann's squire. Annani was in love with Khiann, so, of course, I had to be in love with his best friend. Besides, he was tall and handsome, with the most beautiful red hair, like flames in sunlight. I was convinced he was my destiny."

Wonder was mated to a Guardian named Anandur, who fit that description perfectly. It was confusing.

"What happened?" Arezoo asked instead of trying to figure it out.

"As it turned out, he wasn't my destiny." Wonder's smile turned rueful. "Though it took me an embarrassingly long time to realize that. A soothsayer told me that my future was with a giant of a man with red hair. Esag fit that description, so I assumed he was the one."

"But he wasn't?"

"He wasn't. He cared for me, but not enough to leave his awful but rich fiancée. And for my part, what I thought was love was attraction mixed with wishful thinking. I wanted so badly for him to be my destiny that I ignored all the signs that he wasn't."

Arezoo set down her sandwich. "How did you know that he wasn't the right one?"

"I met Anandur." Wonder smiled. "After Esag broke

my heart, I escaped the palace and joined a caravan bound for Egypt. An earthquake happened, and I tried to save as many people as I could, but eventually I fell into the chasm as well. If I were human, I would have died, but I was immortal, so I entered a state of stasis and remained buried for five thousand years. When I woke up, I didn't remember who I was, let alone Esag, the guy I was supposedly in love with. I won't bore you with all the details of how I met Anandur, how we fell in love, how I finally remembered Esag but realized that I loved Anandur with everything I had, and that Esag wasn't the real deal for me."

"Fate must have worked very hard to make you and Anandur happen. He wasn't even born yet when that soothsayer told you about him. Maybe that's why you had to fall in love with Esag and have your heart broken. So you would escape and go to sleep for five thousand years."

Wonder laughed. "You make me sound like Sleeping Beauty."

"You are beautiful, and you slept for five thousand years, so yeah. That fits."

Wonder shook her head. "You know what's funny? When I was young, I didn't think anyone would ever want me. I was so tall for a woman in those days, and strong, stronger than even the immortal males. I could lift things that warriors struggled with. Annani was like this perfect doll, deceptively delicate and stunning, while I was..." She gestured at herself with a self-depre-cating laugh. "This."

Arezoo couldn't hide her shock. "But you're

gorgeous! How could you think no one would want you?"

"Different times, different standards," Wonder said. "Back then, most people were much smaller. I was too big, too strong, too awkward. Boys didn't find me attractive."

"What about Esag?"

Wonder smiled. "He didn't seem intimidated by my strength, and he was nice to me. He found me attractive, just not enough to leave his awful fiancée for."

"It's strange how we see ourselves," Arezoo said. "And how others see us."

"Indeed." Wonder straightened, preparing to return to work. "The saddest thing is when people settle for less than they deserve because they don't believe they deserve more. Both parties suffer in that equation—one from not being truly loved and appreciated, the other from knowing deep down that they're someone's compromise."

She walked away, leaving Arezoo alone with her sandwich and her suddenly complicated thoughts. Was that what she was doing with Ruvon? Letting him hope for more because she felt sorry for him?

The comparison with Wonder's story was uncomfortable.

Like Wonder had been different from the females of her time, Ruvon was different from other immortal males in the village. Not as classically handsome, not as confident, and probably convinced that no immortal female would choose him. He might have even been spurned by some.

Arezoo liked Ruvon, enjoyed his company, and appreciated his kindness. She loved how his whole demeanor changed when she read poetry to him. But there was no spark, no flutter in her stomach when he smiled, no desire to close the distance between them.

Was she being cruel by being kind to him? Or was there value in friendship itself?

Perhaps she could help build Ruvon's confidence without misleading him. Show him that he was interesting and valuable, help him see his own worth, so he could eventually pursue someone who would love him the way he deserved.

It didn't have to be romantic to be meaningful.

17

ANNANI

The Pearl hummed with activity as Annani stepped through the doorway with two of her Odus flanking her like sentinels. The scents of fresh bread, cardamom, and cilantro enveloped her, triggering memories of markets from the past.

"Clan Mother!" Soraya stepped from behind the register and bowed low. "What an honor to have you visit our store."

Annani glided forward, her silk gown whispering against the floor. "I have heard so many good things about it that I had to come not only to see but also to shop."

She motioned for Ogidu and Oridu to take baskets and go about their task of collecting ingredients for the evening meal.

"You must try our new tea blend." Rana was practically vibrating with excitement. "Yasmin has quite the gift for combining flavors."

"Then I shall have some." Annani followed her deeper into the store.

The transformation of the space amazed her. What had been a regular house just days ago now bloomed with new life and purpose. Shelves lined the walls, stocked with a variety of items. The refrigerated section hummed quietly, keeping produce crisp and dairy fresh. Everywhere were careful touches that spoke of pride, like the hand-lettered signs written in chalk on small blackboards, the artfully arranged displays, and the small potted plants at the register.

A flash of movement caught her eye, and Annani spotted a small figure attempting to hide behind Yasmin's skirts. Little Cyra peered out at her shyly, her dark eyes wide.

"Hello, sweet one," Annani said gently, bending down to the child's level, which, given her diminutive stature, required little effort. "Have you been helping your mother in the store?"

Cyra nodded solemnly but did not leave her hiding spot.

"She's been very helpful," Yasmin said, running a loving hand over her daughter's hair. "Haven't you, sweetie? She helped arrange some of the lower shelves this morning."

"This is wonderful." Annani smiled at the child. "You are such a big girl."

The child nodded in agreement, which was adorable.

"Tell me, Cyra. Have you had any more dreams about the doll man?" Annani asked bluntly.

Normally, she would not have pressed, but she felt in her gut that they were getting close to finding Khiann, and the little girl with her strange dreams, which could be prophetic, might provide a crucial piece of information.

The child's eyes widened further, and she shook her head vigorously, pressing closer to her mother's leg.

Interesting. The denial was too quick, too emphatic. Either she had dreamt of him again and was frightened, or she was picking up once again on Annani's own thoughts about Khiann trapped in stasis somewhere in the desert.

If the child was indeed an empath, as Annani suspected, being around so many immortals with their heightened emotions must be overwhelming—no wonder she hid behind her mother's skirt.

"It is alright, my dear girl," Annani soothed. "Dreams cannot hurt us. They are just stories our sleeping minds tell us."

But were they?

In Cyra's case, Annani wasn't so sure. Empaths often receive information through dreams, processing during sleep what they absorbed during waking hours. She could have peeked into the child's mind to see what she was hiding, but Cyra was so young that an intrusion like that could potentially harm her.

Annani straightened, offering the child a reassuring smile before turning to Soraya. "Everything looks wonderful. The entire village is talking about The Pearl."

"Really?" Rana's face flushed with pleasure.

"My dear, everyone loves the store. I have heard nothing but praise."

The sisters exchanged delighted glances. It was such a change from when they had first arrived—haunted, broken, and jumping at shadows. Now they stood proud, met eyes directly, and smiled without reservation. They had found their purpose, and with it, their dignity.

"Business has been even better than we hoped," Soraya said. "We've had to triple our bread production, and we still sell out by mid-morning."

Yasmin chuckled. "That's because Parisa is a magician with dough. People are placing special orders for all kinds of occasions or just for everyday consumption."

"As they should." Annani smiled. "Talent should be recognized and rewarded."

She walked through the store with the sisters trailing behind her, pointing out special items and sharing their plans for the future establishment, when they would have more space and could offer a wider selection of items.

Their enthusiasm was infectious.

They spoke of adding a small café area to their proposed site, where people could enjoy tea and pastries, and of expanding their ready-for-the-table section. Yasmin was even thinking about hosting cooking classes.

"You have thought of everything," Annani complimented them.

A steady stream of clients moved through the store

as they talked. Each was greeted warmly, like a friend or a neighbor, and not just a customer.

The sisters were not just running a store; they were also managing a family business. They were building relationships, weaving themselves into the community's fabric.

"Mistress." Ogidu dipped his head as he approached her. "We have gotten all the items on our list. Shall I proceed to pay?"

Annani glanced at the laden baskets both Odus carried. "Did you leave anything for the other customers?"

"The selection remains ample," Oridu assured her, missing the joke.

Despite their emerging sentience, the Odus still did not understand most humor and took everything literally.

As they walked up to the register, Soraya shook her head. "It's on the house, Clan Mother. Your money is no good here."

"Nonsense. I will pay like any other customer."

"But you're not any other customer," Soraya protested. "You're... you're..."

"A resident of this village who wants to support your business," Annani said. "If you refuse my money, how can I shop here with a clear conscience?"

"Please," Rana added her voice to her sister's. "Let us do this one small thing. After everything you've done for us—"

Annani shook her head. "If you insist on this course, I am afraid I will have to take my business elsewhere.

My Odus will continue shopping at the supermarket in town where they do not object to accepting my money."

Soraya's stubborn streak had met its match in Annani's determination, and as she looked to her sisters for support, they both shrugged helplessly.

When the Clan Mother decided something, arguing was futile—a lesson most clan members had learned a long time ago.

"Very well," Soraya said with a sigh that suggested great suffering. "But at least allow me to give you the family discount."

"You will charge me the same price as you do everyone else," Annani countered. "Or shall we continue this delightful debate? I have all day."

Soraya's shoulders slumped in defeat. "Before today, I had never met anyone more stubborn than I am." She completed the transaction and accepted the credit card Oridu handed her.

Once the receipt was printed, Annani stepped forward and pulled the startled woman into an embrace.

"Your success brings me such joy. Keep up the good work and never doubt your worth, my dear one."

Soraya stood frozen for a moment, then slowly, tentatively, returned the embrace. When they parted, her eyes were suspiciously bright.

"Thank you, Clan Mother." She bowed.

A slight tug on Annani's gown drew her attention downward. Cyra had emerged from behind her mother's skirts, her little arms raised in the universal child gesture for 'pick me up.'

"I want a hug, too."

Annani's heart melted. "Of course, sweetness. Come here."

She lifted the child easily, settling her on her hip. Cyra immediately wrapped her arms around Annani's neck, burying her face against the goddess's shoulder.

"You have a very special little girl," Annani told Yasmin, who was watching with a mixture of pride and concern. "You should bring her to visit me. Perhaps we could have tea parties with Phoenix. She is about Cyra's age. Would you like that?"

The child nodded against her shoulder, not lifting her face.

"Little girls transition just from spending time around me," Annani told Yasmin, keeping her tone light. It was a lie. The little girls transitioned with the help of a small transfusion of her blood, but that was a secret known only to Alena, Kian, and Toven.

"I thought she was already too old for that," Yasmin said uncertainly. "I thought she needed to be under two years old."

"We can give it a try." Annani smiled reassuringly. "If it works, great, and if not, she will have to wait until she is old enough for the venom bite."

She set Cyra down gently, the child immediately retreating to her mother's side but watching Annani with those too-knowing eyes of hers.

"We should go," Annani said, glancing at her Odus, who stood patiently with their purchases. "Thank you for the lovely visit. Your store is a true asset to our community."

As more customers entered, the lunch rush began in earnest. Annani made her farewells, accepting hugs from all the sisters and even managing to coax a shy wave from Cyra.

She put her protective sunglasses on before stepping outside into the midday sun, and as Ogidu helped her into the golf cart, Oridu secured their purchases in the back.

"Home, Clan Mother?" Ogidu asked as he started the electric motor.

"Yes, please." Annani reached into the pocket of her gown for her phone.

She found a message from Kalugal that had been received a couple of hours ago, probably when she was preoccupied at the store. As she read it, she excitedly pressed on the two images he had sent her.

The first showed the bottom of a figurine with strange markings she didn't recognize, and the second...

Annani's heart seemed to stop.

The figurine depicted a young girl with delicate features and elaborately braided hair, captured in stone with loving detail.

It was Tula, Wonder's little sister. She would have recognized that face anywhere, and the artist had perfectly captured her mischievous streak and the stubborn tilt of her chin.

Memories flooded back. Tula playing along with Annani's shenanigans, much more comfortable participating than her older, more careful sister. Laughing at one of Annani's more outrageous schemes.

Tula was all grown up now, trapped with Areana in Navuh's harem on the Doomers' island, and according to Carol, she was quite a beauty. She was not Navuh's concubine, who, surprisingly, was loyal to Areana, but she was a prisoner, nonetheless, trapped in that gilded cage he had built for his mate and her ladies-in-waiting with no hope of escape.

It must have been Esag who had carved Tula so lovingly.

He had preserved her image in stone with the same loving attention he had given to Annani's likeness. Was he creating a memorial to everyone he had lost? Trying to ensure they would not be forgotten even if he believed them all dead?

The thought was so achingly touching that Annani felt tears prick at her eyes.

She quickly typed a response to Kalugal.

The figurine depicts Tula, Wonder's younger sister. This is definitely Esag's work, even though the mark at the bottom holds no meaning I can decipher.

After sending the message, she looked up to find they were nearly home. "I have changed my mind. Please take me to the café."

"Of course, mistress." Ogidu changed direction at the next path intersection.

Annani clutched her phone, staring at Tula's stone face.

How would Wonder react to seeing her sister's image captured in stone? It would be painful, certainly, but also proof that Esag had cared enough to preserve her memory. Every figurine they found was another piece of the puzzle, another step closer to finding the artist.

And if they found Esag, perhaps they would also find Khiann.

The café came into view, its outdoor seating area bustling with the lunch crowd.

When Ogidu parked the cart, the three of them stepped out and entered the enclosure. Several customers looked up, stunned to see her walking in, but Annani merely smiled and nodded, her attention focused on Wonder.

"Annani?" Wonder's hand flew to her chest. "Did they find Esag?"

"Not yet." Annani gestured for Wonder to follow her as she walked behind the structure to where the vending machines stood under the shade of trees. "I have other news."

"What news?"

Annani held out her phone, the image of Tula's figurine filling the screen. She watched as Wonder took it with steady hands.

For a long moment, Wonder said nothing, her eyes tracing every detail of her sister's carved features. "She looks exactly as I remember her. Every detail... her hair, the way she held her head, that little smile she'd get when she was thinking of mischief." A tear slipped down Wonder's cheek. "He captured her so perfectly."

"It had to be Esag," Annani said.

"He's honoring us," Wonder said, still staring at the

image. "He thinks we are dead and he's trying to make sure we're not forgotten."

"But we are not dead," Annani said. "We are here, and Tula is with Areana."

"Trapped on that island with no hope of escape," Wonder said bitterly. "With no chance at a real life."

Annani touched her friend's arm. "She could have escaped when we saved Carol. She chose to stay with Areana. Tula is no longer the young girl you remember, and she makes her own decisions."

Wonder nodded. "Maybe that's what irks me the most. She chose Areana over me."

18

DIN

Din draped his arm over his face as the harsh Cairo sunlight shone right into his eyes through the latticework screens.

He'd been awake for over an hour or maybe even more, content to lie still and watch Fenella sleep. Her dark hair was spread across the pillow, looking like spilled ink, and her expression was peaceful and relaxed, a rare occurrence during sleep. She still had nightmares, probably about her captivity in the hands of that monster that they still kept alive in the dungeon for whatever reason.

They'd already pumped him for the information he could give, and Max was being super-secretive about the reason they were keeping the demon alive.

Din had his suspicions, though.

Now that it had become known that the Brotherhood was employing a chemist to enhance a select group of fighters with drugs, the fake doctor's action seemed to make more sense. They had wondered where he'd gotten the special drugs he'd used on Fenella and Kyra, and now the mystery was solved.

The question was how he'd kept that information from Toven, and if he had kept that back, chances were he had hidden other things as well.

In a way, it was good news because if compulsion didn't work to loosen his tongue, Din could think of other methods that would be much more satisfying to him and Max.

They could take turns beating the crap out of the devil's spawn.

Fenella stirred, burrowing deeper into the pillow, and just like that, all of the negative thoughts that had been swirling in his head were banished.

Din smiled.

His sexy bartender was decidedly not a morning person, but it was time to get up. They had plans today, and as much as he'd like to let her sleep until noon, that wasn't an option.

Shifting closer, he breathed in the scent of her hair, different than her usual floral shampoo.

Kalugal had outfitted the house with top luxury brands of everything, and Fenella had cooed with pleasure when she discovered the display in the bathroom.

In some things, she was very easy to please. In others, well, she required patience and finesse.

He pressed a gentle kiss to her temple. "Time to wake up, *mo ghràdh*," he murmured against her skin.

She made a sound that might have been a protest and pulled the covers up over her head.

"Come now," he coaxed, tugging the blanket down

enough to expose her face. "We have ancient mysteries to solve, remember? Lost immortals to find?"

"Ancient mysteries can wait," she mumbled, eyes still firmly closed. "Sleep now. Mystery later."

He chuckled, trailing kisses along her jaw. "What happened to my adventurous Fenella? The one who couldn't wait to explore Cairo?"

"She's sleeping. Leave a message."

"I have a better idea." He captured her lips in a proper kiss, soft and sweet, the kind that usually made her melt against him.

Her eyes fluttered open, hazy and unfocused. "That's cheating," she accused, but her lips curved in a smile.

"All is fair in love and mystery," he said, helping himself to another kiss.

"Pretty sure that's not how the saying goes." She kissed him back, her arms coming up to wrap around his neck.

For several long moments, they traded sweet, lazy kisses until a knock at the door rudely interrupted them.

"Breakfast in thirty minutes," Joseph's voice sounded through the door.

"Go away," Fenella said.

Din gasped. "You can't talk to him like that," he whispered.

She rolled her eyes. "Why not?"

There was a long moment of silence on the other side of the door, and Din imagined Joseph opening and closing his mouth, trying to come up with a proper reply to the rude guest.

"Professor Gunter asks that everyone be seated around the table at nine sharp."

"We'll be there," Din called back before Fenella had a chance to insult the poor guy again.

She groaned, flopping back against the pillows. "Do we have to? Can't we just stay here and let everyone else chase down the figurines? They can bring them here, and I'll do the reading after I'm properly rested."

"And miss all the sightseeing? Besides, you'd never forgive yourself if they found something important without you." He climbed out of bed, padding toward the bathroom.

"Ugh, you are right," she muttered, but he heard the rustle of sheets that meant she was getting up. "I want to see Cairo. Do you think we'll get to tour the pyramids today?"

"Not likely." He paused with the toothpaste in hand. "I'm sure Kalugal has the whole day planned out."

Precisely at nine o'clock, he and Fenella entered the dining room to find most of the group already assembled. Kalugal sat at the head of the table, looking every inch the distinguished professor in his crisp white shirt, a kerchief tied around his neck, and khaki pants. Little Darius sat in his highchair, chewing enthusiastically on a piece of pita.

"Good morning," Kalugal said cheerfully. "Please join us. I trust you slept well?"

"I did." Fenella sat on the chair that Din pulled out for her. "The mattress is heavenly. Can we get the brand for the village homes?" She scrunched her nose. "On second thought, maybe that's not a good idea. No one will want to get out of bed."

"I slept like the dead." Max loaded his plate with eggs and beans. "Which is appropriate, given where we're going today."

Kyra elbowed him. "Don't be morbid at breakfast."

"How is stating facts morbid? We are literally going to search for someone who's been presumed dead for five thousand years."

"But he is not dead," Fenella said. "I thought you were referring to the pyramids." She turned to Kalugal. "Will we have time to visit them today?"

"Not today," Kalugal said, "First, we find Esag, and if there is any time left, we can go sightseeing. And on the topic of Esag, I have good news. The Clan Mother responded to my message about the figurine."

Everyone's attention sharpened, and even Darius stopped chewing and looked expectantly at his father.

"What did she say?" Jasmine prompted when Kalugal took too long to respond, overdoing the dramatic effect.

"The figurine is of Tula, Wonder's younger sister, as she appeared five thousand years ago." His expression grew somber. "We know that she's alive because she's my mother's lady-in-waiting, stuck with her in my father's harem on the Doomers' island."

A heavy silence fell over the table. Din had heard about Areana, Annani's sister, Kalugal and Lokan's mother, and Navuh's mate, who chose to remain trapped in that fortress of an island with her abhorrent truelove mate. Her friend Tula declined freedom as well, opting to stay by Areana's side.

For a long time it had been a secret, but eventually, most clan members had learned about Areana's whereabouts and how she'd been found thanks to Carol's incredible bravery.

"Does Wonder know about the figurine?" Max asked.

"The Clan Mother didn't share that information with me." Kalugal picked up his coffee cup. "But I'm sure she has told Wonder about Esag and Tula. She did not recognize the mark, but that does not negate Esag being the creator of Tula's figurine. It's obvious that the same artist created the figurines of Wonder, Annani, and Tula, and based on the impossible memories embedded in one of them, the artist has the gift of foresight."

"Esag," Fenella said. "It can't be anyone else."

"I agree," Kalugal said. "Which brings me to today's plans. The dealer who sold the Tula figurine has a shop in Khan el-Khalili, the old bazaar in historic Cairo. It's a tourist area, which I'm sure you will all enjoy. Surprisingly, it's also where authentic pieces can be found at bargain prices." He chuckled. "It occurred to me that the vendors conspire to place a valuable artifact in one of the stores occasionally, so when the story spreads, it lures hordes of tourists to buy counterfeits at outrageous prices."

Din nodded. "It's easy to swindle people who don't know what to look for."

Kalugal nodded. "Fortunately, I know exactly what

to look for. My people heard about a figurine in a private collection that seemed promising, but when they requested a picture and forwarded it to me, I realized right away that the piece was not only done in a completely different style but also wasn't worth even a fraction of the price the dealer was asking for."

"Good for you," Max said. "When do you want to leave?"

"As soon as we are done with breakfast and the security briefing." Kalugal turned to his wife. "What are your plans, darling? Do you want to join us on the scavenger hunt?"

She shook her head. "I'll sit this one out. The markets are dangerous, and our sweet little Darius is still human, still vulnerable."

Kalugal cast her an adoring look. "You are so wise, my mate. I'll leave my two men with you."

"I prefer that you have them protecting you and your group. The regular security people are enough to keep me and Darius safe in the house."

He leaned over and took her hand. "When I'm not around to protect you, I worry. Having my men watch over you and our son eases my mind."

"I know. But what about you?" She waved a hand over everyone gathered. "I'm safe in the house, but you are going out there. You need the protection more than I do."

Kalugal grinned. "We will be perfectly safe. With me, Max, Din, Ell-rom, and a human security detail, no one will get close enough to breathe the wrong way at us."

She nodded, casting him a loving smile. "I didn't know that you were taking some of the security team with you. Now I'm not worried."

Pouting, he put a hand over his chest. "You wound me, my love. Am I not enough to protect everyone?"

With his compulsion ability, he probably was.

Max cleared his throat. "At this rate, we will never leave."

"Right." Kalugal turned back to the group, lifting his hand. "I'll have Ahmed brief you on security protocols for the market."

As if summoned, the stern-faced security chief entered the room. He was obviously human, probably in his fifties, with the kind of weatherbeaten face that spoke of years in the harsh Egyptian climate.

"Good morning," he said in accented but clear English. "Allow me to explain safety procedures for touring the bazaar."

Din settled back in his chair, prepared for what would likely be unnecessary but well-meaning advice. Beside him, Max had adopted a similar posture of polite attention.

"You need to stay together at all times," the chief said. "The market is a maze, and it's easy to get lost, even easier to get separated. Pickpockets work in teams. One distracts while others grab valuables."

Standard tourist warnings. Din nodded along, noticing Fenella hiding a smile behind her coffee cup.

"Second, do not accept tea from vendors unless you intend to buy. It creates an obligation. They will pressure you, follow you, make scenes."

"Good to know," Kyra murmured.

"Third," Ahmed's expression grew more serious, "and this is most important—the ladies must always remain in the center of the group, with the men surrounding them."

The amusement faded from Din's face, and he noticed Max responding in the same way.

"Excuse me?" Fenella set down her cup with a sharp click.

Ahmed seemed oblivious to the shift in atmosphere. "The local young men make sport of harassing foreign women. Following, making suggestive and offensive comments, touching, grabbing, and worse. They are very aggressive, and sometimes things can get ugly before the police arrive. It's safer if the ladies are protected by their male escorts at all times."

Kalugal set down his coffee cup. "Ahmed's warnings aren't exaggerated, I'm afraid. You might remember the CBS correspondent who was assaulted in Tahrir Square during the 2011 celebrations? She was there with her crew, surrounded by security, covering what should have been a joyful event." He paused, meeting each woman's eyes in turn. "A mob of men surrounded her, separated her from her team, and subjected her to a brutal sexual assault that lasted nearly thirty minutes. Her own security couldn't reach her through the crowd. It took a group of Egyptian women and soldiers to finally pull her to safety." His jaw tightened. "This wasn't in some dark alley or lawless area—this was in the city's main square, during a public celebration, to a prominent journalist with professional security. That's the reality we're dealing with in Cairo."

A stunned silence followed.

Din hadn't been aware of that, and given the others' responses, neither had they.

"It is an unfortunate reality," Ahmed said with a shrug that suggested he found it distasteful but inevitable. "Western women, especially, are targets. They see movies, think all foreign women are... available."

Fenella tensed beside him, and Din's heart ached for her. She'd told him about her years on the run, how she'd had to constantly calculate her safety, modify her behavior, and shrink to avoid unwanted attention.

"How is it allowed to happen?" Fenella asked. "Who raises men who do such things?"

Ahmed shook his head. "These men are like pack animals when they sense vulnerability. Terrible things happen to women who walk alone or even in small groups."

Max's jaw had gone tight. "What do the police do about this?"

Ahmed's laugh was bitter. "Police are men too. Often worse. They see Western women as rich targets for bribes or..." He trailed off, but his meaning was clear.

"Fantastic," Fenella muttered. "Just fantastic. Now I just want to go home where women are treated as people."

Din reached for her hand under the table, giving it a

reassuring squeeze. "We will keep you safe. You know we will."

She glared at him. "I'm not worried about that with Kalugal and you guarding us. I'm just disgusted and disappointed that this barbaric misogyny exists anywhere in the world."

"Are there any other concerns we should know about?" Ell-rom asked, probably trying to change the subject.

"Watch for vendors who get too close," Ahmed continued. "Some use children who are also very aggressive, pulling on clothes and crying, all to distract you while their accomplices rob you. Also, some areas of the market are known for..." he paused, seeming to search for appropriate words, "unsavory activities. Drug deals, other illegal business. I will guide you away from these."

"We appreciate your expertise," Kalugal said diplomatically. "Your concerns are noted."

Din felt nauseous. The casual way Ahmed discussed women being harassed, as if it were just another hazard like pickpockets or aggressive vendors, sat poorly with him, and the others seemed similarly affected.

Jasmine shifted in her chair. "Perhaps we could modify the formation, and instead of hiding the women in the center, we could pair up? Each woman with a male escort?"

Ahmed looked skeptical. "Too risky. The men here do not respect such arrangements. They see an attractive woman with a foreign man and think she is a prostitute. It makes the harassment even worse sometimes."

"Of course, it does," Fenella said under her breath.

"We'll take appropriate precautions," Kalugal said. "Thank you, Ahmed. Please ready the vehicles for us. We will be right out."

As soon as the door closed behind the guy, Fenella exploded. "Pack animals? Sport? What the hell?"

"It's disgusting," Kyra agreed. "Though not surprising. Too many places in the world are like this."

"The question is how do we handle it," Max said. "Because I guarantee if someone lays a hand on either of you, I'm going to tear them apart with my fangs."

"That's the least of my concerns," Ell-rom muttered under his breath.

Din studied him with a frown. What did he mean by that? What could be worse than that? And when he glanced at Jasmine, she looked on the verge of panic.

"Perhaps the two of you should stay behind," he suggested gently.

Ell-rom shook his head. "It's going to be fine."

Jasmine patted his hand. "Of course, it is. Kalugal can freeze a crowd with one command." She looked at their host with desperation in her eyes. "Right? You can do that?"

"Of course." Kalugal regarded Ell-rom with curiosity. "Don't worry, Prince. I'm like an entire army. When we rescued Jasmine and Margo from the cartel, I froze the entire staff. No one could move a finger. Even the gods couldn't do what I did."

"I like the sound of that," Fenella said, some of her tension easing. "Go, Kalugal." She pumped her hand in the air.

Din felt slightly offended that Fenella valued Kalu-gal's protection more than his, but it was tough to compete with a powerful compeller.

Kalugal swept his gaze over his guests. "Despite the heat, I suggest full coverage. The less skin showing, the less unwanted attention."

"Wonderful," Fenella sighed. "Death by modesty in the Cairo heat."

As they filed out to prepare, Din took Fenella's hand. "Are you alright?"

She tilted her head, considering. "I'm angry. Not scared, just... angry that this is how the world works in too many places."

"I know," he said softly. "And I'm sorry."

"Not your fault." She squeezed his hand. "Though I appreciate you not going all Highland warrior and vowing to protect my honor."

"I didn't have to. It's a given."

19

LOKAN

The safe house creaked with age as Lokan walked across the floorboards to finish packing their belongings.

Through the grimy window, he could see the rising sun over the Mongolian steppes, and somewhere in the distance, a dog barked, welcoming the new day.

The family who owned this place had been gone all night, just as Turner's contact had promised, but they were supposed to return by midday, and it was time to move.

"Check weapons, documents, and supplies," Grant said from the main room. "Make sure nothing gets left behind."

"Don't leave a mess," Carol added. "These people don't have a maid to tidy up after us."

Lokan zipped the backpack closed and glanced at her. Even after a night of rest, shadows lingered under her eyes. The tension was taking its toll on her.

"Ready?" she asked after making the bed.

He nodded. "You?"

She shrugged. "As ready as one can be for sneaking across international borders while being hunted by enhanced killing machines."

"When you put it like that, it sounds almost exciting."

She smiled. "Darling, your idea of exciting needs work."

When they walked into the main room, Grant looked up from the topographical map that was spread across the kitchen table. "Good timing. We need to discuss the route."

Lokan joined them at the table, noting the various markings on the map. The official border crossings were circled in red, with X marks through each one.

"Turner's contact supplied intel," Dougal said. "Suspected mercenaries have been spotted at every major crossing point between here and Kyakhta. They're not even trying to be subtle about it. It's like they want you to know they're there."

"They are herding us." Lokan studied the map. "Trying to force us into a specific route where they can ambush us."

"That's what we were thinking," Grant said.

Carol leaned over Lokan's shoulder. "What's the alternative?"

Dougal traced a finger along the map, following a winding route through what seemed to be empty terrain, but then most of Mongolia was like that.

Mountain passes. "This region here is too tricky for vehicle passage, so it's likely to be ignored."

"Ignored by whom?" Lokan asked. "The Mongolian border patrol?"

Camden nodded. "Yes, and I bet your father's minions will not bother for the simple reason that there are too many of those mountain passes, and they don't have enough enhanced fighters to cover each one of them in addition to the regular border crossings, even if they pair them with normies. Smugglers have been using these routes for decades. Drugs going north, weapons coming south. It's rough terrain, but passable if you know what you're doing."

"And do we know what we're doing?" Carol asked.

Grant's grin was sharp. "I've been through worse. At least here we don't have to worry about IEDs."

"Just enhanced immortals who can go weeks without sleep and are resistant to mental manipulation," Carol said dryly. "That's so much better than improvised explosive devices."

Grant shrugged. "At least you can see the enhanced Doomers coming."

"True," Carol conceded.

"Since the van can't make it through the passes," Lokan said. "We'll be on foot for parts of it. We'll have to leave some of our things behind."

Dougal looked up from the map with a triumphant smile on his face. "Not necessarily. We can use motorcycles—dirt bikes that are built for rough terrain." He tapped a spot on the map. "Starting here, we can make the border in about four hours if we push hard."

"Motorcycles," Carol repeated. "Because nothing says 'stealthy border crossing' like the roar of engines in mountain passes."

"Would you prefer walking?" Grant asked. "Because that's about a three-day trek through rough terrain. Once the Brotherhood realizes that we are not showing up at any of the official crossings, they will figure out we had to go through the mountains, and they'll find us before we make it halfway."

She held up her hands in surrender. "Motorcycles it is, though I've never driven one. I've sat behind a biker plenty of times, but that doesn't count as experience, right?"

Lokan quashed the flare of jealousy Carol's reminiscing had brought about. His mate had a rich history of lovers, and it was best if he didn't think of that. It wasn't as if he had been a monk while waiting for her to enter his life.

"You can ride with me," he said. "I've had plenty of experience with bikes."

"When?" She turned to him in surprise. "You never mentioned being a motorcycle enthusiast."

He shrugged. "I've lived for a very long time, sweetheart. You pick up skills if only to alleviate the boredom."

"My mate, the biker spy." Carol patted his arm. "You continue to surprise me. But I still want my own bike. I'm a fast learner."

"Where can we get bikes?" Lokan asked.

"Already arranged," Grant said.

Lokan arched a brow. "Another of Turner's contacts?"

"Who else?" Dougal said.

"Right." Grant rubbed his hands together. "But we are getting only three bikes, so we will have to pair up. We should move out. Our window is narrow, and every minute we delay gives the Brotherhood more time to tighten the net."

As they loaded into the van one last time, the vehicle groaned under the weight of five immortals and their gear. Lokan took the wheel, with Carol sitting in the passenger seat beside him and the three Guardians arranging themselves among the supplies.

He opened the window, enjoying the crisp morning air, which was a stark contrast to Beijing's perpetual smog. Under different circumstances, Lokan might have taken pleasure in admiring the stark beauty of the landscape and the way the grasslands seemed to stretch forever beneath an endless sky, but his attention was focused on the road, on the mirrors, on signs of pursuit.

They rode in tense silence, the only sounds the van's laboring engine and the rattle of equipment in the back.

The meeting point was an abandoned petrol station, its pumps long dry and its building half-collapsed from neglect. But as they got closer, Lokan saw three motorcycles waiting in the shadow of the ruins, next to a flatbed truck and a lone figure.

"That's our contact," Dougal said.

Lokan pulled up beside the bikes, studying the man

who stepped forward to meet them. Middle-aged, Mongolian features, with the hard look of someone who'd spent most of his life exposed to the elements.

"You're late," the man said in accented English.

"Traffic was murder," Grant replied, clearly delivering a code phrase since there had been absolutely no traffic the entire way.

The man nodded, satisfied. "Follow the tracks north for five kilometers, then bear east at the split rock. The pass begins there."

"Did your people notice any suspicious activity on the routes?" Camden asked.

"Government patrols increased yesterday, but they focus on the valleys, not the high passes. Still, be careful. The mountains have eyes."

The guy didn't wait for a response. He simply climbed into the truck and drove away.

"Subtle fellow." Carol walked over to the bikes.

"In this business, chattiness is not a virtue." Grant followed her to inspect the bikes. "Not pretty, but functional."

Carol chuckled. "You should post a meme with that line, under the heading of 'things you can say to your bike but not to your girlfriend.'"

"Right." He frowned, clearly confused.

"Just forget it." She waved a hand.

They redistributed their supplies into backpacks that could be worn while riding. Everything else would have to be abandoned with the van. Lokan felt a pang watching Carol sort through their belongings, deciding what little they could keep from their Beijing life.

Grant took the lead bike, Lokan swung onto the second and Carol climbed on behind him, her arms wrapping tightly around his waist. Camden and Dougal took the third.

The engine rumbled to life beneath him.

"If you drop me off this thing, I'm filing for divorce," she said against his ear.

"We're not married," he pointed out, revving the engine.

"Then I'll marry you just so I can divorce you."

He laughed. "We are getting married when we get to the village. That's a promise. Now, hold tight. This is going to be rough."

She pressed her soft body to his back. "You have to ask me first, lover boy, and tempt me with a huge diamond ring."

"Done."

They set off across the steppes, following tracks that were barely visible in the sparse grass. The bikes handled the terrain better than expected, though Lokan could feel Carol's grip tighten with every bump and dip.

The split rock appeared exactly where their contact had said it would, a massive boulder cracked down the middle as if struck by a giant's axe. They turned east, and the terrain began to change almost immediately. The grasslands gave way to scrub, then to bare rock as they climbed.

"How are you doing?" Lokan asked.

"Peachy," she said, though her death grip suggested otherwise. "Contemplating the life choices that led to this moment."

The path, such as it was, wound between increasingly large rocks and steep drop-offs, but Grant led them well, choosing routes that the bikes could handle while maintaining decent speed. They'd been climbing for perhaps an hour when Camden, who along with Dougal was bringing up the rear, suddenly accelerated past them.

"Company!" he said into the comm. "Two bikes, coming up fast!"

Lokan risked a glance back and saw them—two motorcycles kicking up dust clouds as they pursued.

"How did they find us so quickly?" Carol asked. "Do those drugs induce precognition?"

Lokan wondered the same thing. There was no way his father's goons could have found them so fast out here without inside information. He hadn't even seen any drones hovering above that could have been collecting and transmitting information.

"Questions later," Grant said. "Camden, you and Dougal are with me. We'll try to lead them away. Lokan, maintain course. The pass levels out in about three kilometers. We'll regroup there."

Before Lokan could protest, the Guardians peeled off, heading down a side trail that led back toward the lower elevations. The pursuing bikes split up, one following the Guardians, one continuing after Lokan and Carol.

"We can handle one," Carol said.

Lokan reached out with his mind, trying to connect with the pursuer's, a move he'd done countless times before, but this time, he hit a wall of chaotic energy that nearly made him lose control of the bike.

"I can't get into his head," Lokan said through gritted teeth. "It's like trying to grasp smoke filled with broken glass."

The pursuer was gaining on them, close enough now that Lokan could see some details of who the biker was, and what he saw wasn't good. The guy was big, dressed all in black, and when their eyes met in the mirror, the Doomer smiled, and it was not a sane expression.

"I bet it's one of the enhanced ones." Lokan revved the engine, going maximum speed.

Carol's hold on him tightened. The distance between them and the pursuer grew longer.

The trail ahead forked, with one path continuing up toward the pass and the other disappearing between two massive rock formations. Lokan made a split-second decision, yanking the bike toward the rocks. It was a risk since the path might dead-end, but they needed to break the line of sight and give themselves options.

The passage between the rocks was barely wide enough for the bike. Stone scraped against their thighs as they squeezed through, the engine's roar echoing off the walls.

They burst out into a small canyon, perhaps fifty meters across, with walls too steep to climb, but there were boulders scattered throughout, and the remains of what might have been an old shepherd's shelter.

Lokan killed the engine behind the largest boulder, and they dismounted quickly.

"Options?" Carol already had her weapon out.

"In an enclosed space, he has all the advantages. Enhanced strength, enhanced speed, and apparently enhanced resistance to mental manipulation."

"Then we don't fight fair," she said. "We fight smart."

The sound of the pursuing motorcycle echoed into the canyon, then cut off abruptly. Silence fell, broken only by the whisper of the wind through the rocks.

"I know you're here," a voice called out. "Lord Navuh wants you alive, but he didn't specify in what condition. Your female, however, is expendable."

Carol's expression hardened. "Expendable?" she whispered. "I'll show him expendable."

"Wait," Lokan cautioned, but she was already moving, using the boulders as cover to circle toward the canyon entrance.

The enhanced Doomer appeared between the rocks. Up close, Lokan could see the signs of what the chemicals were doing to him—the micro-tremors in his hands, the dilated pupils, the way his head cocked at odd angles as if listening to voices only he could hear.

This thing was eventually going to fry his brain, but regrettably, not soon enough.

"Come out, brother," the Doomer sing-songed. "I promise to make it quick for your worthless human. A mercy, really. Better than what awaits her in the island's whorehouse."

Rage, cold and precise, flooded through Lokan.

He stepped out from behind the boulder, hands in the air, his rifle left behind. "Let's discuss terms."

The Doomer wasn't going to kill him because Navuh wanted his wayward son alive, but he might shoot him to disable him.

The Doomer's grin widened. "Terms? You have no leverage for terms."

"You can't kill me," Lokan said calmly. "My father will execute you on the spot if you do. And you can't capture me either. I have a lot of money that could be yours if you just let us go."

He knew the guy wasn't going to do that. He was just buying time for Carol to creep into position.

"You think I care about money?" The Doomer laughed. "I'm the future of the Brotherhood. Enhanced. Evolved. I haven't slept in six days, and I feel invincible."

"You feel insane," Lokan corrected. "The drugs are destroying your mind. I can sense it from here—the chaos, the fractures. How long before you snap and lose your mind completely?"

The Doomer's expression darkened. "Long enough to complete my mission."

He moved faster than any immortal should. But Lokan had been expecting it, diving to the side as the Doomer's fist shattered the rock where he'd been standing. Stone shrapnel peppered his back, tearing through his jacket.

Carol's shots rang out from across the canyon, precise three-round bursts aimed at the Doomer's center mass.

He staggered but didn't go down, the bullets barely seeming to register through whatever chemical cocktail was flooding his system.

"Pathetic," he snarled, turning toward her.

That was his mistake. Focused on Carol, he didn't see Lokan retrieve the blade from his boot.

Lokan moved with all the speed his three-quarter-god heritage granted him, driving the blade between the Doomer's ribs and up into his heart, but even that wasn't enough to drop him.

Hopefully, Carol would know what to do.

The enhanced immortal spun, backhanding Lokan with enough force to send him flying into the canyon wall.

Stars exploded across Lokan's vision, and he tasted blood. But he'd done enough. The Doomer stood swaying, looking down at the blade protruding from his chest with something like surprise.

It wasn't enough to kill him, but the three rounds Carol emptied into his back, right where the blade was, should do the trick.

"I'm... invincible..."

"You're dead." Carol stepped out from behind cover. "You just haven't figured it out yet."

The Doomer took one step toward her, then another. But his legs gave out on the third, and he collapsed to his knees. He tried to speak, but only blood came out of his mouth, and he pitched forward.

Lokan wasn't taking any chances. He confirmed the kill with a close-range burst into the Doomer's head. There was no regenerating from that.

"I don't think he has any plans of waking up," Carol noted dryly as she rushed to Lokan's side, her hands gentle, checking his injuries. "What's broken?"

"A couple of ribs, but I'll heal." He clasped her fingers. "We need to move, my love. His partner might have dealt with our friends."

As if summoned by his words, motorcycle engines roared in the distance, growing closer. Lokan tensed, ready for another fight.

"It's them," Carol said. "It's our guys."

The two motorcycles carrying Grant, Camden, and Dougal roared toward them, coming to a stop a few feet away.

Camden whistled low at the sight of the dead Doomer.

"Enhanced?" Grant asked.

"Very," Lokan confirmed. "Resistant to mental manipulation and with enhanced strength and speed."

"Ours wasn't," Camden said. "Standard Doomer, went down with conventional tactics. Seems they're mixing teams."

"We need to move," Grant said. "That gunfire will have attracted attention, and where there are two, there might be more."

Lokan retrieved his blade, wiping it clean on the Doomer's clothes before returning it to his boot.

As they prepared to leave, Lokan took one last look at the corpse. The face, even in death, showed signs of madness—the price of Navuh's enhancement program.

"What is he thinking, creating these abominations?" he murmured.

Dougal snorted. "As if the unenhanced ones are not freaks. They are all monsters."

Not all of them, but Lokan was in no state to argue with the Guardian. He was about to ride for hours with broken ribs.

As they mounted up and continued toward the pass, leaving the canyon and its grim contents behind, Lokan couldn't shake the image of those mad eyes.

20

FENELLA

The Khan el-Khalili bazaar assaulted Fenella's senses the moment she stepped out of the air-conditioned vehicle. The heat hit her first, a wall of dry air that seemed to suck the moisture from her lungs. Then came the smells—spices and incense, leather and metal, sweat and garbage, all mixing into a stinky potpourri that made her eyes water.

Then there was the noise, with vendors shouting about their wares and waving potential shoppers over, tourists haggling in a menagerie of languages, Arabic music spilling from shops, and the constant hum of too many people crammed into the narrow medieval streets.

"Stay close," Ahmed barked, already looking harassed even though they'd been there less than a minute. "Do not walk away from the group! Do not stop for vendors!"

Easier said than done. They hadn't made it more

than ten feet before sellers descended on them like hawks on prey.

"Beautiful lady! Come see! Best prices!"

"Papyrus! Real papyrus! Not fake!"

"Perfume oils! Cleopatra's secret!"

Fenella was squeezed between Din and Max, with Kyra on Max's other side and Jasmine behind with Ellrom. Kalugal led the way with Ahmed, while two more security guards brought up the rear. Their formation might have been meant for protection, but it made navigating the narrow alleys nearly impossible. It was like trying to drive a tank through the market.

"Scarf for lady?" A vendor somehow managed to shove a piece of silk in Fenella's face. "Beautiful scarf for beautiful lady!"

"*La, shukran,*" Din said firmly, shoving the guy and his scarf away from her.

"You speak Arabic?" she asked, impressed.

"Just the useful phrases. No, thank you. How much? Where's the bathroom? Those sorts of things."

"Husband buy!" The vendor with the scarf wasn't giving up. "Good husband buy beautiful things for beautiful wife!"

Din rolled his eyes and pulled out his wallet. "How much?"

She put a hand on his arm. "Din, no—"

"Tourists buy things," he said quietly. "It's for our cover."

They were undercover?

Nobody had told her that. She would have put on her oversized sunglasses instead of the small ones.

Oh, well. Next time.

And so it began. The scarf was just the appetizer that had whetted Din's appetite. Once Din had been given permission to spend money on her, there was no stopping him. At the next stall, he bought her a silver bracelet. Then, leather sandals with long straps meant to wrap around her calves. A small inlaid box that the vendor insisted was made from real ivory, which made Fenella want to gag and throw it at the vendor's head until Din convinced her that it was fake ivory and no elephants had been harmed to produce it. The last one, for now, was a bottle of perfume oil that supposedly contained jasmine from Aswan.

"You're being ridiculous," she hissed as he examined a display of painted plates. "We're supposed to be looking for figurines, not redecorating our non-existent Cairo apartment."

"The dealer said his cousin sells figurines," Din said quietly, gesturing for the seller to wrap three plates. "Information comes with a price tag, and these plates are it. Jacki can give them to someone on their staff."

Fenella wasn't buying it. "That's the fifth cousin with figurines we've heard about." She watched the pile of packages in Din's arms grow. "They are playing you."

"I can help carry," one of Kalugal's guards offered, taking a couple of packages from Din.

"Thank you, Ibrahim," Din said.

None of the stores had air-conditioning, and after over an hour of touching all kinds of figurines and other artifacts that could loosely be classified as such, Fenella felt sweaty and dirty, and none the wiser.

She'd opened herself to impressions several times, with Kyra and Jasmine maintaining light contact by touching her arm or her shoulder and theoretically amplifying her abilities, but most of the items were completely flat, with no memories embedded in them whatsoever. The few fragmented visions she'd gotten had been frustratingly mundane.

"This is useless," she muttered, setting down yet another figurine of Anubis that had only emitted a trace of irritation. "We are not going to find Esag by browsing tourist shops."

"Patience," Kalugal said. "This is where we found the other figurines."

They reached another shop, which was larger than the others they had visited so far, and the proprietor spoke excellent English and seemed to know his merchandise.

Din walked over to an ornate brass lamp that Fenella had to agree had some charm to it despite being ugly, but it wasn't worth carrying with them through the market, let alone taking back to the village.

"We don't even have a house, Din," she protested.

"We will." He motioned for the shopkeeper to wrap it up.

Shaking her head, Fenella moved over to the figurine collection, with Kyra falling in step with her.

"Anything?" Kyra asked quietly.

"The usual tourist junk made in China and pretending to be authentic." Fenella picked up a small statue of Isis. "Nothing."

"My dear ladies!" The proprietor appeared at her

side, all obsequious smiles. "You have excellent taste! That statuette of Isis is very special. Very old!"

Yeah. Perhaps it was two months old, the time it took to ship it over from China.

"How old?" Jasmine asked.

"Oh, perhaps one hundred years! Maybe two hundred! From my grandfather's collection!"

Fenella set it down carefully. She didn't see the point in crushing his sales pitch. "It's lovely, but not what we're looking for."

His expression shifted, becoming calculating. "Ah, you are collectors. What are you interested in?"

"Unusual pieces." Kalugal joined them. "Unique. Pieces made by real artisans and not mass-produced overseas." He pulled out his phone and showed the guy a picture of the figurine modeled after Wonder's sister.

The man's eyes shone with the excitement of a shark identifying prey. "Unique is difficult to come by. Expensive."

"Money isn't an issue," Kalugal assured him. "For the right kind of item."

Another furtive glance. Then the proprietor leaned closer. "I know of such an artist. Very talented and very strange. He comes by occasionally and sells one or two pieces. Very unusual work. I pay him top pound because his pieces sell for much more and never stay on display for more than one day. I don't have anything of his at the moment, but if you leave me your contact information, I will let you know as soon as he delivers another piece."

Fenella's pulse quickened. "Do you know where he lives?"

"The City of the Dead." The man shuddered slightly. "Al-Qarafa. It is not a safe place for tourists. You shouldn't go there. Wait until he comes here."

Obviously, the guy didn't want to be cut out of the deal, and he wasn't going to tell them where to find the artist. He might even be lying about his living in the City of the Dead just to discourage them from attempting to find the craftsman.

Fenella turned to look at Din, signaling with her eyes that he should just reach into the human's mind and pluck the information out of there.

"Does he have a name?" Din asked.

Fenella hoped he'd understood her eye signals.

"He calls himself Isa. He doesn't talk much. Just brings pieces, takes money, and disappears again."

"When was he last here?" Kalugal asked.

"Maybe two weeks? Three? He's not regular." The man studied them with shrewd eyes. "So, you are not just interested in his work but in him in person?"

Kalugal nodded. "I have a project I would like to discuss with him."

"I could maybe arrange an introduction," the shop-keeper said. "For a fee."

"That won't be—" Kalugal began, but stopped mid-sentence. His posture had shifted subtly, and then he flashed the proprietor a charming smile. "Actually, yes. Let's discuss terms. Inside your office, perhaps?"

The guy looked puzzled but pleased. "Of course! This way!"

Kalugal followed him, but instead of going into his cramped office, he herded their entire group toward the back door. "Everyone out. Now. Act natural."

"What's wrong?" Fenella whispered.

"Suspicious company about to enter." He pulled the shop door shut behind them and turned to the confused proprietor who'd followed them out. "You're closing early today and going home. Lock the door."

"Yes... Yes, of course." The proprietor fumbled for his keys, moving like a sleepwalker.

"This way," Kalugal directed, leading them not back into the main bazaar but down a narrow side alley. "Quickly, but don't run."

They followed, packages rustling, trying to look like a group of lost tourists, except for Ahmed and his two companions, whose eyes darted in all directions.

"Are they following?" Max asked, his hand drifting toward where Fenella knew he had a weapon concealed.

"Not yet, but they might once they realize—there." Kalugal grabbed a door handle seemingly at random, only to find it locked. A quick twist of immortal strength broke the mechanism, and he ushered them all inside what appeared to be a carpet shop's storage room.

They emerged into a different section of the market, and Kalugal kept them moving, taking seemingly random turns until Fenella had no idea where they were.

"Why didn't you just shroud us?" Din asked quietly as they paused in the shade of an archway. "You can make us look like different people to whoever was following us."

Kalugal gestured with his chin at Ahmed and the guards. "Because my security team would not understand what's going on and might run off screaming about dark magic or djinn. As I said earlier, it's hard to find reliable security in Cairo."

"Fair point," Din conceded.

"Who was watching us?" Fenella asked. "Brotherhood goons?"

"I'm not sure," Kalugal admitted. "They were watching us through the display window, so I couldn't sense if they were immortals. They could have been just common thieves who zeroed in on tourists who are buying everything in sight." He gave Din a pointed look.

"Hey, I was maintaining our cover," Din protested, shifting his armload of packages. "And nothing in here is particularly valuable."

"You bought the lamp," Fenella said flatly.

"It's a nice lamp, and it was well priced."

"We don't have a house!"

"We will, and I want us to decorate it. I could see this lamp over a reading chair."

He was so cute that she felt like kissing him right then and there, but it really wasn't the time or the place. "You're impossible."

"I prefer adorable."

"If you two are done," Max interrupted their banter, "maybe we should focus on the fact that we just got actual intelligence? This Isa character in the City of the Dead sounds promising."

"That's true," Kalugal said. "I peeked inside the shop-keeper's mind and, surprisingly, he was telling the truth about that. But we can't go there today. We need to lose the tail, go home, and explore the place tomorrow."

"The City of the Dead," Jasmine mused. "That's the cemetery district where people live among the tombs, correct?"

"Indeed," Kalugal confirmed. "Many thousands of people make their homes there, some families for generations. It's a maze of mausoleums, crypts, and improvised housing. Easy to get lost in, easier yet to disappear in."

"Sounds perfect for someone who wants to stay hidden," Ell-rom observed.

"Right then," Ahmed said, finally finding his voice. "Professor, please, we should return to the cars. This is becoming dangerous."

Kalugal turned his most charming smile on the man. "Ahmed, my friend, I apologize for the excitement. Academic passion sometimes overrides common sense. You're right, of course. Let's return to the house."

The security chief looked mollified. "The vehicles are parked near the Khan. We'll need to backtrack carefully."

"Lead the way," Kalugal said.

They began the journey back through the market, taking a circuitous route to avoid retracing their steps and traversing their earlier path. Fenella kept checking over her shoulder, searching for faces that appeared too often or eyes that lingered too long.

"Stop that," Din murmured. "You're attracting attention."

"Says the man carrying half a bazaar's worth of merchandise."

"Touché."

They were nearly back to the main thoroughfare when it happened.

A man stepped out of a shop directly in front of them—tall, European features, eyes that tracked their group with predatory interest. Not a local. Not a tourist either.

"Keep walking," Kalugal said quietly. "Don't react."

They passed the man, who made no move to follow or intercept. But Fenella could feel his gaze burning into her back.

"Doomer?" she breathed.

"No. But he might be working for them."

"Reporting," Max said. "Or he could be just a random dude with a resting bulldog face."

When they reached the vehicles without further incident, got inside, and pulled away from the Khan, Fenella let out a sigh of relief.

"Well," she said, settling back in her seat. "That was educational."

"We learned about Isa," Kyra pointed out. "That's progress."

Fenella touched the scarf Din had bought for her, the silk cool and soft beneath her fingers.

Din's ridiculous shopping spree was kind of sweet.

He'd bought her things simply because he wanted to, prompted by a street vendor who had suggested that a good husband should buy his wife nice things.

"Thank you." She leaned against his shoulder.

"For what?"

"For the lamp. It's hideous, but I love it."

KIAN

K ian reviewed the latest reports on his tablet while in the background, Onegus and Turner brought Jade up to date.

Two situations, both critical, both demanding resources he didn't have. His jaw tightened as he read Grant's update about the enhanced Doomer attack in Mongolia. Thankfully, Lokan and Carol had managed to kill him, but the fact that Lokan alone hadn't been enough was concerning.

The guy was a one-thousand-year-old immortal, a three-quarters god, and a compeller.

"My Russian contacts are ready to retrieve them once they cross the mountain pass," Turner said. "They are impersonating Russian soldiers, which should be enough to keep the Doomers away. They don't want to get into an altercation with the Russian army. It should be smooth sailing from there."

Kian wasn't sure about that. Navuh was getting bolder.

"We have good news from Egypt," he said. "They've identified a potential lead—someone called Isa living in Cairo's cemetery district. They are going to try to track him down tomorrow."

Turner tilted his head. "The City of the Dead. Now that should be interesting. Why would an immortal live in a place like that?"

"Anonymity?" Onegus suggested. "Besides, they don't know if it's Esag. It might be just some random human who's good with his hands."

Jade leaned back in her chair. "I know that you are all concerned with finding the Clan Mother's mate, but the enhanced Doomer situation is more urgent, and I have a solution. You should mix up the teams so there are at least two Kra-ell warriors in each one. You should have also sent Kra-ell with the Guardians to Mongolia. We can match the enhanced strength of the Doomers. Your Guardians cannot unless they are wearing exoskeleton suits, which is impractical in most situations."

She was right, and there were plenty of capable Kra-ell available, but not all of them wanted to serve on the force.

"There aren't enough of you to put two with each team," Kian stated the obvious.

She regarded him for a long moment with those big eyes of hers. "Right now there aren't, but I can convince more to join the force. When they hear about the enhanced Doomers, they won't be able to resist the challenge to prove that they are the superior warriors. Also, as those who already joined the force have proven, we don't require a lot of training to be ready for action."

She was right about that as well. The Kra-ell were natural killers, and the hardest part of training them was keeping them in line and having them follow orders. The easiest thing was just to unleash them on Doomers and watch them tear them apart, enhanced or not.

Onegus grinned as if Jade had delivered him the best news of the day, and in a way, she had. "If you can get more of your people to join, I will include at least one Kra-ell warrior with every strike team."

"Good." Jade offered him a rare smile. "I'm glad that you accepted my offer so eagerly."

"We don't have the luxury of refusing help," Kian said. "I've instructed William to accelerate the Odu development program, but regrettably, they won't be ready anytime soon. We need soldiers, disposable ones. I don't want to lose Guardians or Kra-ell to those enhanced monsters."

The temperature in the room seemed to drop. Onegus's expression darkened, and even Turner looked uncomfortable.

"What if they become sentient?" Onegus asked. "I'm not comfortable with regarding them as disposable, even if they start as machines. If they end up as people, they need to be treated accordingly."

"They will not be sentient," Kian said. "I'm not talking about the original Odus who have become part of our family. The new models William and Kaia are developing will be stripped down. They will need to be capable of learning and making tactical decisions, but they won't have the capacity for emotions or self-awareness."

Turner still looked skeptical. "Things rarely go according to plan when you're dealing with artificial intelligence. The ability to learn and make decisions can lead to all kinds of unintended consequences."

"Do you have a better idea?" Kian challenged. "We're facing an enemy that's stronger and faster and outnumbers us at least a hundred to one. If we continue on the same trajectory as we are now, we will be wiped out."

Turner was quiet for a long moment. "I don't have a better idea, and I'm not opposed to developing an army of Odus. What I'm cautioning against is treating them as disposable machines. We should treat them as soldiers."

Kian snorted. "Am I the only realist here? Navuh is treating his fighters as disposable. Most politicians treat their soldiers in a similar manner. It's rare to see any politician who genuinely cares about the human lives lost to wars."

Turner nodded. "We are different, but I get what you are saying. So, how is William going to ensure that our cyborg army doesn't become sentient?"

"Simple," Kian said. "No curiosity subroutines, no self-reflection protocols, no emotional simulation. They'll be tools, nothing more."

"The Kra-ell have a saying," Jade said. "'The sword that thinks is the sword that chooses.' Be careful what you wish for, else your tools might decide they have better uses for themselves."

"I'm not an expert, so I leave this to those who are." Kian turned to Onegus. "Anything else on the agenda for today?"

"Just a reminder that you wanted to bring in the paranormals from Safe Haven and potentially use them in our new spy division. Eleanor is waiting for instructions."

"Call Eleanor and ask her to propose solutions. She's intelligent and cunning. She can take the time to consider the options and possible challenges and come up with better ideas than I would, especially given the little time I'll have available to dedicate to this."

Onegus flashed his famous megawatt smile. "They say that necessity is the mother of invention, but it's also a catalyst for change."

Kian frowned. "What are you talking about?"

"You're actually trusting someone else to make decisions. That's growth."

"I am asking Eleanor for options and suggestions. I will still make the decisions, so maybe there is less growth than you think," Kian muttered.

Onegus lifted his hands in mock surrender. "One step at a time. Maybe one day you'll be able to cross that bridge."

22

LOKAN

The motorcycle's engine whined in protest as Lokan downshifted, struggling up the steep grade. Loose rocks scattered beneath the tires, tumbling into the darkness below. The mountain pass had narrowed to little more than a goat track, barely wide enough for the bikes, with a sheer drop on one side that disappeared into shadows.

As the bike lurched over another outcropping, Carol's arms tightened around his waist, and his healing ribs protested, but he didn't say a thing. Having her body pressed to his was soothing to his soul.

The terrain had deteriorated so much over the past hour that he regretted having bikes and not yaks. The animals were well adapted to the cold, high altitude, and rugged, steep terrain.

They would have also made little to no noise and not attracted unwanted attention.

The yaks' smell was another issue, which would

have bothered Carol, but given all their advantages, Lokan was sure she wouldn't have objected.

Not that what was coming off the bikes was pleasant. They were overheating, and the acrid smell of burning oil filled the air, mixing with the sickly-sweet scent of engine components that were starting to melt.

If the bikes lasted all the way through, he would count it as a miracle.

Ahead of them, Grant's bike suddenly lurched, and the Guardian raised a fist as he dismounted. "Hold up," he said.

Lokan brought his bike to a halt, and he and Carol got off.

"What's wrong?" He walked up to where Grant was standing at the edge of the path.

The Guardian pointed ahead to where the track seemed to disappear entirely, replaced by a series of rocky ledges that would require climbing rather than riding. "We need to ditch the bikes. We can't get them through that."

"Bloody hell," Camden muttered. "The contact said this was passable."

Dougal joined them. "For smugglers on foot, maybe, or mountain goats."

Lokan studied the terrain with a sinking feeling. "I was just thinking that we would have been better off riding yaks, and that Turner's contact should have thought to warn us that even mountain bikes were not the best choice for this terrain. Now we are stuck making the rest of the way on foot, and that's going to take much longer than we accounted for."

They would run out of supplies, but as immortals, they would survive. The bigger problem was that the longer they were exposed, the more vulnerable they were.

"Maybe we should backtrack and find another route," he suggested. They'd already deviated significantly from the planned path to avoid potential ambush points, and he wasn't at all sure that there was a more accessible route.

"Lokan," Carol said quietly, and something in her tone made him follow her gaze.

She pointed at the sky. "Can you hear that?"

He focused, trying to ignore all the nocturnal noises and isolate a sound that didn't belong. He heard it then, the distant whine of a small engine. Once he knew what he was looking for, it was easy to spot the small dark shape in the clear night sky.

"A drone," he said. "Two o'clock, about three hundred meters up. We wouldn't have heard it over the engine noise if we hadn't stopped."

"How long has it been tracking us?"

"Damn." Carol pulled her weapon. "We need to shoot it down. It's transmitting our location."

"Don't." Lokan put a hand on her arm, lowering it. "They already know where we are. It's better to let them think we're unaware of it while we plan."

Carol snorted. "Too late for that. They saw us looking up. This thing is transmitting in real time."

"It's dark," Camden said. "They might not see details."

Lokan's mind raced through their options. The

drone changed everything. Even if they found a way to continue with the motorcycles, they'd be tracked. The enhanced Doomers could be closing in already, guided by real-time surveillance.

"We don't have much choice," he said. "We need to leave the bikes, continue on foot, and pretend that we didn't notice the drone. If they think we don't know that we are being followed, they won't send people after us in the mountains. They will just wait for us to come to them. We let Turner's people know what's going on and ask for help. Perhaps they can mobilize the Russian army and send it this way. I'd rather we get caught and brought in for interrogation than fall into the hands of Doomers."

His father's minions would kill Carol and the three Guardians on sight. The Russians, on the other hand, would take them into custody. That wasn't ideal, but manageable.

"We have a lot of gear to carry," Dougal pointed out, gesturing at their supplies. "We are already down to the minimum. We can't leave anything behind."

The Guardian was right, but there wasn't much they could do about it.

"We need help." Lokan told him his idea and then sent a text to Turner.

With that done, he shouldered his pack, wincing as it pressed against his still-tender ribs. "Let's move. The drone is small and built for surveillance. It can't keep tracking us for long on one battery charge. Eventually, it will have to return for recharging. So, stay alert and listen for it. When we can no longer hear it, we could potentially find cover."

These mountains were mostly bare, so he didn't hold out much hope of finding a place to hide. His original idea was still the best, provided that Turner could pull that off.

As they began the arduous climb over the rocky ledges, the irony wasn't lost on Lokan. They were reduced to climbing through mountains like he had done hundreds of years ago.

"This reminds me of Afghanistan," Grant muttered, hauling himself over a particularly challenging section. "Except with immortal drug-enhanced hunters instead of Taliban."

"And no air support," Camden added.

"What were you doing in Afghanistan?" Lokan asked.

Grant cast him an apologetic smile. "That's classified information. Sorry, Lokan."

Well, at least it gave him something to think about. What could the clan possibly want with Afghanistan? Had their people been there and needed to be evacuated? Or maybe they had gone to save someone important or a friend?

"The drone is gone," Carol said.

To his great shame, he hadn't been paying attention. Not that it mattered. There hadn't been any places to hide before, and there weren't any ahead.

"I need to rest," Carol said quietly. "Can we take a break?"

"We can't stop here," Lokan said. "We need to find better cover first."

"Where?" She took a sip from her canteen. "There isn't even a tree in sight."

"There should be caves," Dougal said. "I'm on the lookout for those."

"When we get to the village," Carol murmured, "I'm sleeping for a week."

"Only a week?" He pressed a kiss to her temple. "I'm not getting out of bed for a month. We will watch reruns of *I Love Lucy* and all of your other favorite shows, stuff our faces with ice cream and popcorn, and do other fun stuff without having to worry about being discovered."

They'd lived with the fear of discovery for far too long, and they both needed a real vacation to recharge.

"I wish," she said. "We'll have to go through debriefing, then find a house we like, your brother will want us to come for dinner at his place, my friends will want me to come over to theirs..." She sighed. "Maybe we should stay in Mongolia and become yak herders."

"Right." He laughed. "My cosmopolitan mate a yak herder. I can just picture you doing that with a designer clip over your nose."

"True." She straightened, squaring her shoulders. "Let's keep moving, people. We don't have all night...oh wait, we do."

They resumed their trek, following what might generously be called a path through the rocks, and as they got lower down the mountain, the landscape became less severe. The drone didn't return, which

Lokan didn't know what to make of, but the good news was that they were now trekking through scattered pine forests that provided some cover from aerial surveillance. On the other hand, the trees also limited visibility, making it easier to ambush them.

Lokan constantly scanned their surroundings, every shadow potentially hiding an enemy. The enhanced Doomer from the canyon had moved faster than anything he'd encountered before. If more were coming, they needed to be ready.

"Movement ahead," Grant whispered.

Everyone froze, weapons coming up smoothly. Lokan extended his senses, feeling for the telltale presence of immortal minds. Instead, he found something else entirely.

"Humans," he said quietly. "Six of them. Military, by their mental patterns."

"Border patrol or Turner's people?" Carol asked.

"Wrong location for border patrol," Camden said. "We are still many kilometers from the border."

Through the trees, Lokan could make out lights—flashlights moving in a search pattern. Occasionally, he caught the sound of Russian voices, though distance made the words indistinguishable.

"It's more likely the welcoming committee Turner arranged," Dougal said hopefully. "I just didn't expect them to cross so far into Mongolia to get us."

Neither had Lokan.

He closed his eyes, extending his mental reach toward the approaching soldiers. Human minds were usually easy to read and influence, but he needed to be closer to do so. From this far, he could potentially get glimpses of their thoughts.

Hopefully.

The moment he touched the first mind, he immediately felt that something was off. These weren't the disciplined thoughts of a professional soldier. There was an eagerness there, an anticipation that spoke of a man expecting action, expecting a payday.

"Mercenaries," he whispered. "Or rogue soldiers doing some freelance work."

"You think they are paid by the Brotherhood?" Carol moved her hand to her sidearm.

"Possibly. I can't get deep into their mind from this far away. They seem to be looking for someone." He gave it another try, straining to collect more fragments of thoughts. "They're looking for us. Four men and a woman."

The patrol was getting closer, their search pattern methodical. In a few minutes, they'd be within visual range even in the darkness.

"I can handle this," Lokan said. "Human minds are easy to—"

"You," one of the Russians called out in accented English. "We know you're there. Come out. We mean no harm."

Everyone tensed. Carol was already aiming her weapon in the direction of the voice.

"We are sent by a mutual friend," the voice continued. "To escort you to safety. Please, no shooting. We are all friends here."

"Could be legitimate," Camden whispered. "Turner's people would know our group composition."

"The Brotherhood knows it as well," Grant countered. "This feels like a trap."

Lokan had to make a decision. They could fight, but gunfire so close to the border would bring every patrol in the area. They could run, but the Russians knew their position now. Or he could trust in his abilities and handle this his way.

"Stay here," he told the others. "I'll verify their intentions."

Before anyone could protest, he stood and stepped into view, hands visible but ready to move if needed. "I'm here," he called in Russian. "Approach slowly."

Six men emerged from the trees, weapons lowered but not put away. They wore Russian military uniforms, but Lokan's enhanced vision caught details that didn't fit—non-regulation boots, personalized equipment, the too-casual way they held their weapons.

The leader, a grizzled man with sergeant's stripes, smiled broadly. "Ah, excellent. You match description perfectly. You are expected, yes? Transportation is waiting."

Lokan reached into the man's mind, expecting the usual ease of reading human thoughts. Instead, he found focus, discipline, and underneath it all, a core of absolute certainty about their mission.

These men had been paid, but not by the Brotherhood. The mental signature was different—cleaner, more professional. Turner's network, most likely. But something still felt off.

"Where is this transportation?" Lokan asked, maintaining his mental probe.

"Less than two kilometers down the mountain. Your friends can come out now. We all want to go home, yes?"

The sergeant's thoughts remained consistent: escort the targets to the vehicles and deliver them to the extraction point. Simple. Professional. But there was something else, a slight note of discord that made Lokan hesitate.

"Carol," he said without taking his eyes off the Russians. "Bring the others. It's safe."

She emerged first, weapon still ready, followed by the three Guardians. The Russians showed no surprise at their appearance, which meant they'd known exactly where everyone was hidden.

"Ah, the famous Carol," the sergeant said with another broad smile. "Such beauty! No wonder you risk so much to protect her, yes?"

Carol's expression could have frozen fire. "Let's skip the charm offensive. How do we know you're really Turner's people?"

The sergeant reached slowly into his pocket, producing a sealed envelope. "Message for you. Authentication, I am told."

Grant took the envelope, examining it carefully before opening it. His expression shifted from suspicion to relief. "They are legit. These are our escorts."

Lokan still couldn't shake the feeling that something was wrong. He pushed deeper into the sergeant's mind, past the surface thoughts to the darker corners where secrets hid.

And there it was. A secondary payment, already received. A promise of more to come, from someone who wanted to know the route they'd take, the safe houses they'd use, the extent of Turner's network in the region. It wasn't necessarily someone in the Brotherhood, but who else would want that information?

"Sergeant," Lokan said calmly in Russian. "Tell me about your other employer."

He could have compelled the man to tell him what he wanted to know, but Russians were notoriously difficult to compel and thrall. Lokan was surprised he managed to get the few flashes of memories that he got.

The man's smile faltered for just a moment before returning full force. "We work for your friend, help you reach safety."

"The ten thousand euros in your account say otherwise," Lokan continued, plucking the figure from the man's startled thoughts. "Who's paying for information about our route?"

The other Russians shifted nervously, fingers moving closer to triggers. The Guardians responded instantly, weapons coming up in smooth precision.

"Now, now," the sergeant said, but sweat had begun beading on his forehead. "No need for unpleasantness. Yes, okay, someone pays for information. But harmless information only! Route, timing, nothing more. We still take you to safety, everyone wins."

"Who?" Carol's voice was ice.

"I don't know," the sergeant admitted. "Electronic transfer, encrypted communications. They want to know about the network, about how people move through the region. Information only, no interference with mission."

Unless the sergeant was an exceptional actor, which he wasn't, he really didn't know who his secondary employer was. The Brotherhood didn't operate that way.

They might use humans, but it was usually done by thralling and not by anonymous money transfers. Then again, things were changing, and Navuh's army of goons was becoming more sophisticated. On the other hand, what were the chances that the Brotherhood had infiltrated Turner's network?

That wasn't likely.

"Here's what's going to happen," Lokan said, using his compulsion and hoping it would work. "You're going to report to that other client that we never showed up, that you waited at the rendezvous, but we must have taken a different route. You're going to forget everything about this encounter."

His head ached from how strongly he had pushed with his compulsion. These men had strong wills, and their suspiciousness made their minds almost impenetrable.

"Yes... We waited," the sergeant said slowly, his eyes glazing. "But no one came. Different route, probably."

"Exactly," Lokan confirmed. "Now, you're going to return to your vehicles and drive back to your base."

When the Russians turned and began walking back the way they'd come, Lokan still wasn't ready to celebrate. There was a good chance that the compulsion wouldn't last, and they would turn around.

When they didn't, he let out a relieved breath. "I didn't think it would work."

Carol clapped him on his back. "You are a three-quarter god, my love. Of course, it worked."

"Impressive," Grant said. "But what about our extraction?"

"We have to continue on foot," Lokan said. "Someone's compromised Turner's network, at least partially, and we don't know who it is."

"You think that it's the Brotherhood?" Camden asked.

Lokan shook his head. "They don't operate like that. Besides, their infiltrating Turner's operation is unlikely."

"Could it be Gorchenco?" Carol suggested. "The last we've heard of him, he was in a vegetative state after a stroke, but the guy could have made a deal with the devil and recovered, or it was all a ruse to throw off his enemies while he regrouped. He knows you, and if he figured out your connections to the submarine fiasco, he wants you dead. He also has extensive connections in Russia."

Lokan winced. If that was true and Gorchenco recovered, it was bad news. The Russian mafia boss had a good reason to suspect Lokan of sabotaging his deal to sell a Russian nuclear submarine to the Chinese. Gorchenco also knew Turner, and he worked with

Navuh, supplying the Brotherhood with weapons. The guy was smart, and he could've figured it out, especially if he had access to an information leak from Turner's network or the Brotherhood.

Perhaps he was the reason Navuh suddenly suspected Lokan.

Could that be the missing piece of the puzzle?

"That actually makes perfect sense. We should have taken Gorchenco out when we had the chance. We won't be safe in Russia." He pulled out his phone and typed a long text to Turner, explaining what happened.

23

DIN

The City of the Dead was like something out of a fever dream. What had begun a long time ago as Cairo's historic cemetery had evolved into a sprawling necropolis where the living made their homes among the dead. Mausoleums served as houses, tomb courtyards became living rooms, and ancient crypts had been converted into shops and workshops.

The juxtaposition was surreal.

Laundry lines were strung between centuries-old headstones, satellite dishes were mounted on Ottoman-era tombs, and children were playing football, the proper one, in what had once been sacred burial grounds.

Ahmed looked like he was about to pop a vein. "This place is not good for outsiders."

Din couldn't fault the guy for his succinct assessment. The narrow alleys between the tombs created a maze that seemed purposely designed to disorient visitors. The morning sun barely penetrated here, blocked by improvised roofs and awnings that had been constructed over the centuries. The air was thick with dust, cooking smoke, rotting garbage, and the underlying mustiness of ancient stone.

"It's like a city within a city." Fenella's eyes darted around. "How many people live here?"

"Half a million, give or take." Kalugal consulted a hand-drawn map. "Some families have been living here for generations. They're born here, live here, die here, and are buried here. The cycle continues."

A group of children appeared from behind a crumbling wall, hands outstretched, voices raised in a chorus of pleas for money. Ahmed shooed them away with sharp words in Arabic, but they simply retreated to a safe distance and continued following their group.

"Should we give them something?" Jasmine glanced at their escort of ragamuffin children.

"No," Ahmed said firmly. "Give to one, and hundreds will come."

The security team, which Kalugal had beefed up for today's excursions, formed a protective box around them as they pressed on.

Locals watched them pass, some with curiosity, others with suspicion, a few with barely concealed hostility. Foreigners weren't welcome here, especially those who didn't give money to the begging children.

Still, Din trusted Ahmed's experience that giving them money would only make things worse.

"This way," Kalugal directed, studying his map. "The

workshop should be in the older section, near the Mamluk tombs."

The architecture, if one could call it that, changed as they moved deeper into the cemetery. The newer additions gave way to ancient structures, some dating back to the medieval period. These tombs were more elaborate, with carved stone façades and ornate Islamic calligraphy that had survived centuries of weather and neglect.

"How does anyone find anything here?" Max grumbled, sidestepping a pile of garbage that had been dumped in front of a fifteenth-century tomb. "It's worse than the bazaar."

"That's probably why the carver likes this place," Din said. "If you wanted to hide, this would be perfect. You don't have an official address, so there is no government oversight. You're a ghost."

An elderly woman sat in the doorway of a converted mausoleum, watching them with sharp eyes as she sorted through a pile of electronic components. The incongruity of ancient stone and modern circuit boards perfectly captured the strange reality of this place.

"We need to turn left at the tomb with the blue door." Kalugal held the map up, comparing what had been hand-drawn to what was in front of their eyes.

Eventually, they found the door, but it was more by chance than by what was on the crude map.

It was a Fatimid-era tomb whose entrance had been fitted with a bright blue metal door that appeared to have been salvaged from elsewhere. Beyond it, the alley narrowed even further, forcing them to walk in single file.

"I don't like this," Max muttered. "Too confined. No escape routes."

Din silently agreed. The walls pressed in on either side, and the only way out was forward or back the way they'd come. They could easily get boxed in and robbed.

Well, not easily. They had a formidable compeller who could redirect any would-be attacker.

Ell-rom didn't seem worried, though, and Din wondered whether he was just a stoic male or if he was hiding unparalleled fighting abilities. After all, he was no ordinary hybrid. He was half god, half Kra-ell, royal on both sides.

Powerful blood circulated in his veins.

Kyra stopped, her hand going to the amber pendant at her throat. "I feel something." She closed her eyes. "We are getting closer." She opened them. "That's all I got." She turned to Jasmine. "Maybe you can find out more."

"We need to get to an intersection," Kalugal said. "It will be pointless to do it here."

As they began to move, Din was glad to see the alley widening ahead and branching off in several directions.

Jasmine declared the spot perfect for scrying, and when they stopped and gathered around her, she reached into her bag and pulled out a stick that was about a foot long. It was just a simple twig, which she must have stripped and sanded down herself.

That was what she used as a scrying rod?

Din had never seen one used outside of academic discussions about ancient divination practices, and the ones he'd seen were much more intricate, carved with symbols and other decorations.

Jasmine held the stick loosely in her hand, closed her eyes, and took a deep breath. At first, nothing happened. Then, slowly, the tip of the rod began to dip, pulling downward and to the left.

"Until not too long ago, I would have called it mumbo jumbo," Max muttered. "But she found Ell-rom and Morelle using this stick."

"The proof is in the pudding," Fenella said.

They chose the alley that Jasmine's stick indicated, winding deeper into the cemetery. The tombs here were even older, some partially collapsed, while others had been reinforced with modern materials in haphazard attempts at preservation. The residents were fewer, and the alleys quieter.

"We're being watched from all over," Ahmed said quietly. "I don't know if they are curious or hostile."

Din had noticed it too. Faces in windows that disappeared when he looked at them, shadows that moved just at the edge of vision. The locals were tracking their progress, probably wondering what had brought such an unusual group to this corner of their domain.

"Just keep moving," Kalugal advised.

They turned another corner and found themselves in a small courtyard surrounded by ancient tombs. Unlike the rest of the cemetery, this area had been kept relatively clean. The stones had been swept, and the worst of the decay had been repaired. It felt almost cared for.

Jasmine's rod pointed firmly toward a tomb entrance sealed with a steel door. Unlike the improvised barriers they'd seen elsewhere, this one looked professionally installed, complete with multiple locks and a security camera mounted above it.

"This is it," Kyra said with certainty. "The one we're looking for is in there."

"The good news is that we are in the right place," Max said. "The bad news is that we need to figure out how to get in without starting an international incident."

"In front of a crowd of onlookers," Din added, noting movement in his peripheral vision.

They'd attracted quite an audience along the way, but everyone was maintaining a careful distance and doing a good job of staying hidden.

Kalugal studied the door. "How about I just knock?"

"Wait," Fenella interrupted. "Look."

She pointed to a small brass plaque beside the door, so tarnished it was barely visible against the ancient stone. Arabic script had been etched into the metal, along with a symbol that looked familiar.

"That's the same mark that was on Tula's figurine," Jasmine said. "The one the Clan Mother couldn't identify."

Excitement thrummed through Din. They'd actually located Esag's workshop.

"Can I knock now?" Kalugal asked.

"With five locks and security cameras, the owner is well aware of us standing out here," Max said. "There is no need to knock."

"We could just wait," Ell-rom suggested.

"In this neighborhood?" Ahmed shook his head. "We shouldn't stay here. Word has already spread about a group of tourists with private guards, which indicates that they are wealthy. The hoodlums are assembling while we stand here, exposed."

He was right. They were attracting too much attention. But they'd come too far to leave empty-handed.

"I'm going to knock," Kalugal said. "And if no one responds, I can get us in quickly and quietly. Ahmed, have your men secure the perimeter. The rest of you, stay with me and get ready for anything."

Din did not agree with Kalugal's plan. What right did they have to break into someone's home or workplace?

"We shouldn't," he said as Kalugal knocked. "I mean, we shouldn't enter if he doesn't open the door."

Kalugal turned to him. "I will compensate him for any repairs or damages and more." He lifted his face to the security camera above the door. "You hear that? We need to come in because we are not safe out here. I'll pay for a new door and its installation."

The first lock yielded to Kalugal's strength with barely a whisper of protest. Then the second, then the third. Each one had been quality hardware, but nothing that could stop an immortal determined to enter.

The fourth lock gave way, then the fifth. Kalugal

grasped the handle and looked back at them. "Move to the side. He might be in there and shoot first."

They nodded as one, weapons appearing in the hands of those who carried them. Din moved closer to Fenella, shielding her with his body.

The door swung open on well-oiled hinges, revealing darkness beyond. No alarms sounded, no traps sprang. Just silence and the musty smell of enclosed space mixed with something else—stone dust and oil, the scent of a workshop.

Kalugal entered first, followed by the rest in a practiced formation. The entrance led to a narrow corridor that sloped downward, carved directly into the bedrock. Modern LED strips had been mounted along the walls, providing dim but adequate lighting.

"This passage isn't part of the original tomb." Din ran his hand along the wall. "This tunnel was carved much later. See the tool marks? Modern equipment."

They descended perhaps twenty feet before the corridor opened into a larger space. Kalugal found a light switch, and suddenly the room blazed with illumination.

Din's breath caught.

It was indeed a workshop, but unlike any he'd expected. Traditional tools mixed with modern equipment—ancient chisels alongside electric grinders, weathered wooden benches next to a new ventilation system. Shelves lined the walls, holding blocks of various stones, bottles of pigments, and reference books in multiple languages.

But it was the works in progress that drew the eye.

Figurines in various stages of completion covered every available surface. Some were roughly carved, barely more than shaped stone. Others were nearly finished, awaiting only final details or touches of paint. The style was unmistakable—the same flowing lines, the same attention to proportion, the same indefinable quality that made them seem almost alive.

"Look at this," Jasmine called from across the room. She stood before a wall covered in photographs and sketches. Not ancient drawings, but modern photos printed on regular paper. They showed figurines from multiple angles, some of which Din recognized from museums, while others he'd never seen before.

"He's documenting his work," Kyra said wonderingly. "Keeping track of where they end up."

Fenella moved among the sculptures like someone in a trance, her hands hovering over them but not quite touching. "The energy in here is incredible."

FENELLA

The workshop exceeded Fenella's expectations, although the truth was that she hadn't known what she expected to find. It wasn't just the huge number of figurines, although there were hundreds of them lining shelves, covering work-benches, and tucked into every available space. It was the sheer energy that pulsed from them. Her psycho-metric ability, even without touching anything and without Kyra and Jasmine augmenting it, thrummed with awareness, compelling her to touch everything.

She felt like a vampire who smelled blood.

Bad analogy, but whatever. "Holy mother of pearl," she breathed, turning in a slow circle. "Look at all of that."

Each figurine was unique, capturing not just phys-ical features but the essence of the person portrayed. That was the hallmark of true artistry. Very few could achieve that ineffable quality.

One was of a warrior woman with fierce eyes and a

proud chin. Another of a child caught mid-laugh, joy radiating from the stone. An elderly man whose carved face held mirth and wisdom, his expression conveying his amusement at the folly of youth.

"Don't touch anything," Max warned.

"I wasn't going to," Fenella said, but her fingers were itching to make contact, to dive into the memories these pieces must hold. "This is his life's work."

Din moved closer to examine a section of shelving. "I think they are organized according to a timeline. The style evolves subtly over time."

He was right. She was no expert on antiques or even on styles, but the pieces on the higher shelves looked older and displayed a different technique than those on the lower shelves, which were newer and showed refinements in method and experiments with different stones and pigments. It was like watching Esag's artistic abilities grow over the centuries.

"But where's the artist?" Max asked the question that was on everyone's mind. "This place is obviously in active use. Some of these pieces are still damp."

"Someone's coming," Kalugal said sharply, and everyone tensed.

Footsteps sounded in the corridor above, belonging to more than one person. There were three of them.

"Defensive positions," Max ordered quietly. "But don't look aggressive. We are the trespassers here, and we didn't come to fight."

Din pulled Fenella back and tucked her behind his solid frame. She wanted to protest and say that she wasn't some damsel who needed protecting, but common sense prevailed as the tactical part of her brain recognized the wisdom. She wasn't a warrior. Her value was in her ability, not her fighting skills.

The footsteps stopped just outside the entrance. Then three figures appeared in the doorway.

The one in the center had to be Esag. Tall and lean, with flame-red hair and freckles. His face was young. Like all immortals, there had been no weathering over the thousands of years of his existence, but his eyes held the weight of that long life. He wore simple clothes, dust-covered from work, but his hands bore no signs of wear. Immortal healing made them look like the hands of a scholar, not a craftsman.

The two flanking him were dark-haired, one slightly taller than the other, both carrying themselves with the easy confidence of warriors despite their civilian clothing. They weren't threatening, not really, but they exuded confidence that implied they didn't consider the immortals and humans in front of them particularly dangerous, and that was a little scary.

Kalugal, Ell-rom, Max, and Din were not weaklings, and Esag and his friends' assessment of them must have revealed that.

For a long moment, the groups simply stared at each other. The tension in the room ratcheted up another notch.

"Well," Esag finally said in proper English, sounding like he had grown up in London. "This is unexpected, and I don't know if I should say that I'm glad to discover that not all immortals are dead, as my companions and I believed, or not."

"We come in peace." Kalugal lifted his hands. "And before we commence with introductions, I want to apologize for breaking into your workshop and reiterate that I will pay for the new locks and their installation."

Esag smiled. "I saw your message on the security camera. Couldn't you have waited until our arrival?"

"I apologize again, but our group attracted a lot of attention, and I wanted to get everyone inside for their safety. Especially the ladies."

Esag nodded. "Your apology is accepted. Now, please tell us who you are, how you found us, and why you searched for us."

"My name is Kalugal, and these are my companions. We came looking for you, Esag. We didn't know whether your two companions survived as well."

Confusion creased Esag's brow. "How do you know my name? And how is it possible that you are here? We thought all the immortals perished with the gods. You are the first ones we've encountered in five thousand years. How did you know to look for me?"

"Your figurines." Fenella stepped out from behind Din despite his attempt to keep her back. "The ones you made of the people you thought lost. Kalugal is a collector, and he discovered three of them. They led us to you."

His name had been carved on the bottom of the figurine she'd seen in her vision, so for now, that explanation should suffice. Too much information all at once would shock the poor guy.

Esag's face went white. His companions moved closer, protective, but he waved them back.

"Which figurines?" he asked.

"The one that started our search was of Gulan, nowadays going by the name of Wonder."

"Gulan." The name came out as barely a whisper. "You found my carving of Gulan, and you speak of her as if you know her, just using a different name."

"We do," Max said. "Gulan was buried and in stasis until not too long ago. Construction started where she was, and a water pipe burst. That's how she was revived. Poor thing didn't remember who she was and what had happened to her, but eventually, her memories returned, and the merciful Fates led her to our clan."

"Clan?" One of Esag's companions tilted his head in confusion.

"Perhaps we should all sit down for this," Kalugal suggested.

"Of course." Esag waved a hand toward his large worktable. "Roven and Davuh will get another bench."

So, those were their names. The Clan Mother had told them about the two Guardians who had accompanied Esag on his search for Gulan, but Fenella had forgotten them.

Once both benches had been dusted and the table cleared, they all somehow squeezed into the available space.

Kalugal cleared his throat and assumed the mantle of authority that came so naturally to him. "We search on behalf of someone who never gave up hope of finding other survivors. Someone who is very dear to you and who survived the bombing of the assembly because she escaped beforehand."

Fenella had to hand it to Kalugal. The guy knew how to build up suspense.

Esag regarded him with suspicious eyes. "None of the gods escaped. If they did, we would have felt their presence, their influence on these wretched humans."

"Maybe some did," Kalugal said.

One of Esag's companions shook his head. "We went back, years later, when the poison had faded. There was no one left. The assembly hall was a crater, the palace turned into rubble, and everyone and everything were dead for many kilometers in all directions."

"As I said, the goddess escaped before the bombing."

"Who?" the taller companion asked.

"Before I answer that," Kalugal said, "I need to know who I'm talking to. Are you Davuh or Roven?"

"I'm Davuh, and this perpetual optimist on Esag's other side is Roven. We were tasked with retrieving Gulan, who escaped with a caravan heading for Egypt, but regrettably, we didn't reach her in time. We thought that she perished in the earthquake that preceded the bombing." He cast a glance at Esag. "You said you saw it in your dream."

Esag nodded. "Sometimes I get prophetic dreams. I know they are special because I feel like I'm right there when they are happening. They don't have the same quality as regular dreams." He shook his head. "I see the events unfolding through the eyes of someone who was there, but I can't do anything to change the event or the outcome. I'm trapped in the past as a helpless observer. I hate those dreams. I hate seeing people I care about dying or being buried alive." He leveled his gaze at Kalugal. "Who was the one who survived? Tell me."

Kalugal smiled. "The princess. The most radiant one."

Fenella had a feeling that Kalugal wasn't going to tell Esag about Areana and Toven yet. He wanted to make sure that Esag and his companions were trustworthy first.

For a long moment, Esag and his two friends just gaped, and then Esag whispered, "Annani is alive?"

Kalugal nodded. "She is alive, and she is the Mother of the Clan. The matriarch of many immortals. Your princess singlehandedly preserved the traditions and knowledge of the gods and helped humanity, or at least part of it, to make strides toward enlightenment as the gods had intended."

Davuh swayed on the bench, Roven made a sound that might have been a sob, but it was Esag's reaction that broke Fenella's heart. He seemed to crumple, his head falling into his hands.

"I can't believe she's alive," Esag murmured. "It makes sense, though. Who else would have fought for women while Mortdh's patriarchal sacrilege ruled supreme?"

"She sent us to find you," Fenella said.

"It was the figurines," Kalugal explained. "I found the one you made of Wonder, I mean Gulan, many years ago. My mate, Jacki, who can read memories and emotions embedded in objects, held it in her hand and saw what happened to Gulan. You must have embedded your dream into the figurine you carved of her."

Esag nodded. "I carved it right after I had that dream. It was still painfully fresh, and I transferred the pain into my work."

"It's a beautiful piece," Kalugal said. "The next one we found was even more exquisite. It was one of Annani. This time, Fenella read it. She has a similar talent to my Jacki, but she needs Kyra and Jasmine's boost." The two lifted their hands when Kalugal said their names. "Anyway, the figurine wasn't your original. Someone was copying your work, and she saw in the memories he had embedded in his work the original he was copying. When he lifted the figurine to examine it, she saw the engraving on the bottom with your name and your dedication to the princess."

"And then Kalugal's people found Tula's figurine," Fenella said. "The breadcrumbs, or rather the figurines, led us here."

Tears misted Esag's blue eyes. "I thought they were all dead."

"Most are," Kalugal said. "But some survived."

Esag looked up at Kalugal with eyes that held millennia of pain. "Where is Annani? Can we see her?"

Kalugal nodded. "She is in America. But first, I need you to know that Navuh survived as well, and he's not a friend of hers. He has an army of immortals at his command, and he wants to do away with Annani and her clan."

"That son of a traitor." Esag spat on the floor. "The murderer. I wish he were dead."

Kalugal shifted uncomfortably on the bench, causing everyone else sitting on it to move a few inches over. "Well, I can't really blame you for that sentiment, but without him, I wouldn't be here."

Esag looked like Kalugal had just dumped a bucket of ice on his head. "Did he send you?"

Kalugal threw his hands in the air. "Oh, no. I'm here on behalf of Annani, and this handsome, tall guy sitting on Roven's other side is Annani's half-brother, Ell-rom, and he is the son of Ahn and a lady you've never heard of. Max and Din are Annani's great-great-great-grand-sons." He pointed at each of them when he said their names. "Fenella, Kyra, and Jasmine are all the descen-dants of a mystery Dormant who lived eight hundred years ago."

Davuh frowned. "So, what did you mean by saying that without Navuh, you wouldn't be here?"

Kalugal sighed dramatically. "Do you remember that Princess Areana left the palace to join Mortdh in his northern estate?" When Esag nodded, he continued. "Navuh escorted her part of the way, and they fell in love. When Mortdh bombed the assembly and died along with the other gods, Navuh took over his father's harem and married Areana. I am their son, but I escaped my father's tyranny, and the merciful Fates led me to the clan. I'm now the beloved nephew of Annani and a dear cousin to her children." He flashed the three immortals a charming smile. "Any questions?"

Esag's expression was unreadable. "A million of

them. But first and foremost is, what do you want with us?"

The smile slid off Kalugal's face, and Fenella expected him to say that the Clan Mother needed Esag to help her find Khiann, but something in Kalugal's eyes shifted, and the smile returned. "I'm here to welcome you to the clan. All three of you. There is no reason for you to live alone in this hellhole. We have a beautiful place in America, with many single immortal females that would be delighted to meet three strapping immortal males."

At that, Roven straightened, and his eyes started glowing. "Count me in."

"How do the three of you speak such good English?" Fenella blurted.

Esag smiled. "You might be too young to know this, but Britain occupied Egypt for about forty years, and it maintained its presence even after declaring Egypt independent. The last British troops left in 1956. That's a very long time for an immortal to learn a language." He looked at Kalugal. "How old are you if you don't mind me asking?"

"I'm a little older than Fenella, but not by much. I escaped my father's tyranny during World War II." Kalugal continued with his story of how he and a group of select soldiers had found their way to America, and then one day, the Fates had decided that it was time for them to find a home with Annani and her clan.

Fenella listened with interest, Kalugal's story filling some of the gaps in what she knew about his history and how he'd come to be part of the clan.

"Did you carve the figurines to make a living?" Jasmine asked. "Or did you carve them to commemorate everyone you thought you lost?"

Esag's hand went to a pendant at his throat—a small carved stone Fenella hadn't noticed before. "I had some talent when I started, and it was a good way to make a living in relative anonymity, but when I got better, I started creating figurines of people I cared about." He sighed. "Forgive me for getting emotional, but this is difficult for me. For us." He looked at his friends. "After all these years of mourning them, we find out that the princesses are alive. But one is married to Navuh, and the other is the mother of an entire clan."

"Annani is waiting to meet you," Fenella said. "And I'm sure that you want to meet her and Wonder, I mean Gulan. From what I was told, you won't recognize her. She's not the shy girl she used to be."

Esag looked down at his hands. "I wronged Gulan. I hope she forgave me."

"She did," Jasmine said. "She is happily mated to a redheaded Guardian who looks a little like you."

A smile bloomed over Esag's face. "I'm happy for her."

"We haven't had family in so long," Roven said.

"You can have it now." Jasmine reached for his hand over the table. "The clan is more than just a safe haven. It's a community. A place where you can be yourself and not hide anymore. I'm also a newcomer to the clan, and I was welcomed with open arms. You will be too."

Esag looked around his workshop. "I don't mind

leaving this place behind, but I want to take my work with me. At least some of it."

"Don't worry about that," Kalugal said. "I can have a crew pack everything up and ship it to the States, and as for your travel arrangements, I have enough seats on my private jet to offer you a ride. The three of you will be traveling in style."

KALUGAL

Kalugal watched with satisfaction as Esag, Davuh, and Roven took in the splendor of his Cairo estate. After the dusty, cramped confines of the City of the Dead, the mansion's soaring ceilings and marble floors must have seemed like a step into another world.

"Welcome to my home away from home," Kalugal said, spreading his arms wide. "The one I have in America is very different than this one. You'll see when you get there. In the meantime, you're safe here."

Roven let out a low whistle as his gaze traveled up the curved staircase to the stained-glass skylight three stories above. "Are you that rich? Or is Annani paying for all of this?"

That was a direct question that might have been considered rude by some, but Kalugal had no problem answering it. "I'm not financially reliant on the clan. I'm a self-made billionaire." He liked how it sounded, and even more how round the three immortals' eyes had gotten after hearing him say that.

"What do you do?" Davuh asked.

"I'm an investor. I identify new emerging technologies, purchase them, develop them, and then sell them."

"Sounds complicated," Esag said. "I thought you were into antiques."

"My hobby is archaeology, but as in everything else I do, I go all in. No half-measures for me."

The upstairs door opened, and a moment later, Jacki descended the stairs with Darius in her arms. Their son's face lit up at the sight of his daddy, or maybe the new people, and he immediately began babbling in his unique mixture of baby talk and actual words.

"Hello," Jacki said, her smile warm and welcoming. "I'm Jacki, Kalugal's wife, and this little charmer is our son Darius."

Kalugal watched with amusement as the three ancients seemed to melt at the sight of the little boy.

Darius, who was usually shy around strangers, seemed fascinated with Esag's flaming red hair, and he reached out his chubby arms toward him.

Jacki and Kalugal exchanged glances. "He wants you to hold him," she said. "Which is surprising since he is usually reserved around strangers."

Esag grinned. "Babies love me." He reached for the boy with the assurance of someone who had been holding babies his entire life.

As Darius settled happily into Esag's arms, he immediately reached for his flame-red locks.

"Don't pull, Darius," Jacki warned.

"That's okay," Esag was still grinning. "I don't mind."

Joseph chose that moment to appear. "Professor Gunter, the room is ready." He smiled at their new guests. "I have to apologize, but with so many guests staying at the mansion right now, I have you all staying in one suite. It's spacious, and I had two additional beds delivered, but ideally, I would have you each staying in your own room."

"That's okay," Davuh said. "We are used to sharing, and we've never stayed in an affluent house like this, so this is an upgrade."

"Thank you, Joseph," Kalugal said.

"If you'll follow me," his house manager motioned toward the stairs, "I'll show you to your room so you can freshen up." He gave their dusty old clothing a once-over. "I will bring your luggage up."

"We don't have any," Esag said. "We will go back to pack our things later."

"Would you allow me to offer you a change of clothing?" Kalugal suggested as tactfully as he could. "I have plenty of new things I can part with, and we are all about the same size."

The males looked uncomfortable, but given the look Joseph was giving them, they must have realized that staying in this house came with certain standards, which they were not meeting.

"Thank you," Esag said.

After Joseph left them to scavenge for clothing in Kalugal's closet, Kalugal led them up the stairs to their bedroom.

"When I renovated the house, I turned all the rooms into suites, so you will have plenty of space despite having to share." He opened the double doors and motioned for them to go in.

The large double bed was in its usual place, and the two portable single beds occupied the space that had previously been the seating area. Joseph had pushed the couch against the foot of the double bed, and somehow it all worked well.

"Good man," Kalugal murmured. "I'm lucky to have him, and I would hate to lose him."

"Why would you lose him?" Roven asked. "People here would kill for his job."

Kalugal sighed. "I've long suspected that Joseph might be a Dormant, but I've been dragging my feet about telling him that and testing him. It's not fair to him, though."

"We haven't encountered any Dormants in five thousand years," Esag said. "But then it's not like they have their genetic makeup tattooed on their foreheads. How can you identify Dormants when you don't know who their parents are?"

Kalugal tapped his nose. "I have a sense for it. Or at least I believe I have. Testing my hypothesis should be easy enough with a male Dormant, though."

"Do you intend to induce him yourself?" Esag asked.

"I'd rather not. Perhaps I'll ask one of my men to do it; however, I need to tell Joseph first." He chuckled. "I can just imagine his reaction. He already thinks I'm strange."

Esag frowned. "He called you Professor Gunter. Is this the last name you are going by?"

Kalugal nodded. "When I travel. In the village, I'm just Kalugal."

"I could induce him for you," Davuh offered. "It has been over five thousand years since I induced a Dormant."

Kalugal smiled. "Do you think you still know how to do it? I mean, biting is instinctive, but the trick is to stop before killing the guy."

Davuh looked offended. "This is not something an immortal ever forgets."

"I'll take your offer under consideration," Kalugal said, right as Joseph entered with a pile of clothing.

"Thank you, Joseph." Kalugal took it from him and placed it on one of the beds, waiting for the guy to leave. "After you have freshened up, I will arrange a video call with the Clan Mother. She will be overjoyed to talk to you."

Esag swallowed. "Did you tell her that you found us?"

"Not yet. I will deliver the good news while you are showering and give her time to prepare emotionally for the conversation with you. She will be overjoyed."

"We need time to prepare to speak to our princess as well," Esag said. "I still think that I'm dreaming."

Kalugal nodded. "I understand, and I know how to help you relax. When you come downstairs, I'll treat you to some excellent whiskey and cigars."

Roven grinned. "You are officially my favorite guy."

"Hey, I thought I was your favorite." Davuh pretended offense.

"You've been moved down to second place." Roven clapped him on his back. "Kalugal wins."

"What about me?" Esag asked. "I'm the one who fed and clothed you for five thousand years, you ungrateful mongrels."

Kalugal observed their banter with a smile. "I'll leave you gentlemen to shower and change, and I will do the same." He brushed a hand over his khaki pants. "I'm dusty and sweaty, and Joseph will have an aneurysm if I show up like this to dinner."

He walked out of the room and closed the door behind him.

Joseph was waiting for him on the second-floor landing. "Is there anything else you need from me before dinner, sir?"

"Yes. I'd like you to contact our usual shipping crew. We have a workshop full of artifacts that need to be carefully packed and sent to America."

They had a dedicated and trustworthy team that they used for smuggling all the archaeological finds out of Egypt. He wouldn't entrust a task like that to anyone else.

"Consider it done, sir. I'll make the arrangements immediately. Anything else?"

Kalugal leaned against the balustrades. "How would you like to work for me in my other home in America?"

The transformation in Joseph was instant and dramatic. His usual composed demeanor cracked like an egg, revealing pure, undiluted excitement beneath. "America, sir? Of course. When do I leave?"

Chuckling, Kalugal lifted his hand. "Not so fast. I'd need someone to take over here first. This house doesn't run itself."

"I'll find the perfect replacement!" Joseph said immediately, practically vibrating with energy. "Ahmed's son Hamid is smart and a hard-working young man. Naturally, he's very trustworthy given who his father is. I could train him. How long would I have? When would we leave? What would my duties be?"

Kalugal held up a hand. "Slow down, Joseph. Nothing's decided yet. First, I would like to interview the young man."

"Of course, sir. I'll go check on the preparations for dinner and call the shipping team."

"Please do."

If Kalugal's hunch about Joseph being a Dormant proved wrong, he could find him a job in his office building in Los Angeles. The guy was intelligent and eager to please, so finding something for him to do wouldn't be a problem.

Kalugal found Jacki in their master suite, relaxing on the couch with a book.

"Where is Darius?" he asked.

"Shamash has him. How are our guests doing?"

"Nervous about talking to Annani." He wanted to sit next to her, but he was dusty and didn't want to dirty the fine fabric covering the couch. "I should hit the shower and would love for you to join me. I need someone to reach that spot on my back that I always miss, and I promise to return the favor."

She laughed. "Is that so?"

"Yes. It is." He offered her a hand up.

26

ANNANI

As Annani selected Wonder's contact on her phone, her heart raced with a mixture of joy and excited anticipation. She was about to tell her that they had found Esag. After five millennia, another piece of their shattered past had been recovered.

"Wonder," she said the moment her friend answered. "Drop whatever you are doing and come to my house immediately."

"What's wrong?" Wonder sounded alarmed.

"Nothing is wrong. Everything is wonderfully, gloriously right. They have found Esag, Roven, and Davuh. They are all alive."

Wonder, or rather Gulan, had not known the other two, but she had heard their names and knew that they had been sent with Esag to search for her.

The silence on the other end stretched for several heartbeats. "Where did they find them? And how? Was it the figurines?"

"In Cairo, and yes, they followed the trail of figurines."

"I can't believe it," Wonder breathed.

"Believe it and come over as fast as you can. Kalugal is arranging a video call."

"Yes. I'm leaving right now."

"Hurry," Annani urged. "Kalugal said he would call after they had had time to shower and change, but I do not know how long that will take."

"I'll be there in five minutes," Wonder promised and ended the call.

Annani set down her phone on the coffee table and leaned back. Over five thousand years had passed since she had seen Esag's face, heard his voice, and watched his easy smile. He had been Khiann's closest friend, his squire, his confidant. In her memories, he was forever young, and she wondered if he still looked the same: that flame-red hair, that goofy smile, that irreverence.

She rose from the couch and began pacing, unable to contain the nervous energy coursing through her.

Ogidu appeared in the doorway. "Is everything alright, Clan Mother? Can I get you anything?"

"Everything is perfect," she told him. "Wonder is coming over, so please have tea and refreshments ready, though I doubt either of us will be able to eat anything."

"Of course, Clan Mother." He bowed.

Annani moved to the window, looking out at the pathway outside her home. She could just imagine Wonder running like the wind to make it there in five minutes.

True to her word, Wonder arrived on time, barely pausing to knock before Ogidu opened the door. She swept into Annani's living room like a force of nature, her face alight with emotion and her eyes sparkling with excitement.

Annani crossed to her friend and took her hands. "Come, let us sit together and wait like we used to."

They settled onto the sofa, side by side, hands clasped between them like young girls sharing secrets, and for a moment, Annani was transported back to those days in the palace when they would sit just like this, planning adventures or discussing the latest court rumors.

"Where was Esag living in Cairo?"

"The City of the Dead, of all places," Annani said. "When they found his workshop, it was filled with shelves upon shelves of carvings."

"I never knew he had such talent," Wonder said.

"Neither did I, but he has been honing his craft for millennia. They found him returning to the workshop with Davuh and Roven." Annani squeezed Wonder's hands. "All three of them thought they were the only immortals left in the world. Can you imagine how lonely they were?"

Wonder's eyes glistened with unshed tears. "We've all thought we were alone at some point. At least they had each other."

"True." Annani glanced at her phone, willing it to ring.

"If I had awakened from stasis in Cairo instead of Alexandria, perhaps our paths would have crossed."

Wonder sighed. "Imagine how different my life would have been if I had run into Esag after waking up."

"The Fates work in mysterious ways," Annani said. "If you had found Esag back then, you might not have found Anandur, who was always your destiny."

Wonder's expression shifted, a shadow of old pain crossing her features. "I wonder if Esag carved my image because he felt guilty. He did break my heart."

"I guess that he cared more than he could show at the time," Annani suggested. "He could not get out of his engagement to Ashegan without bringing ruin to his family. He did what every dutiful son would have done."

Wonder sighed. "You're right, of course. And it no longer matters. I have Anandur, and I wouldn't trade him for anyone. I'm eager to introduce them. I think they'll like each other."

As Annani's phone chimed, they both tensed.

She accepted the video call and cast it to the large wall screen in front of them. The image that appeared stole her breath.

Three faces filled the screen, but Annani's attention locked on to Esag. He looked exactly as she remembered—that distinctive red hair curling at the ends, those smiling blue eyes, and the freckles that were scattered across his nose and cheeks.

"Princess Annani," Esag breathed, and his voice broke on the word, and then he and his companions were kneeling on the floor in Kalugal's office with their heads bowed.

"Please rise," she said. "There is no need to bow. It is

not done these days, and I do not expect it from anyone, especially not from old friends."

They rose, sitting back on the couch in Kalugal's office.

"You have no idea how good it is to see you alive and well," Esag said.

Tears prickled Annani's eyes. "I feel the same. I always hoped that you, Roven, and Davuh survived. It is wonderful to see your faces."

Esag's gaze shifted to Wonder, and his expression became even more stunned. "Gulan? You look so different. So beautiful."

Wonder smiled. "Thank you. I am different, and I no longer go by the name Gulan. That name belonged to the servant girl you knew five thousand years ago. I'm called Wonder now."

Esag seemed incapable of taking his eyes off her. "Kalugal told us that you go by that name now, but he said you would explain the choice. Why Wonder?"

She smiled. "When I woke from stasis, I had no memory of who I was. Some children on the street called me Wonder Woman because, apparently, I resembled the actress who portrayed her. I liked the sound of it and decided to adopt it."

"It suits you," Esag said. "In more ways than one. You are beautiful, strong, and brave."

"Flatterer," Wonder accused, but she was smiling through misty eyes.

Esag leaned closer to the camera. "Kalugal mentioned that you woke up from stasis in Egypt."

"I did, but I didn't stay there long. There was an

incident, and I had to escape. I boarded a cargo ship heading to America and somehow found my way to Annani's clan. The Fates must have guided me."

Esag nodded. "Even if we had ended up in the same city, it's unlikely that our paths would have crossed, given that twenty-two million people live here."

"How have you been?" Wonder asked, and there was weight to the question that spoke of their history.

Esag's expression softened. "Lonely. Grateful for Davuh and Roven, but lonely." His gaze flickered between Annani and Wonder. "And you? I'm told that you are married now."

"I am. Anandur is my truelove mate," Wonder said, but there was no cruelty in the emphasis, just stated fact. "You'll find this amusing, but he looks a lot like you. He's tall, red-headed, has freckles, and fancies himself a comedian. Apparently, I have a type."

Esag's laugh was genuine and warm. "I cannot wait to meet him. He must be truly extraordinary if he is like me."

This time, both Wonder and Annani laughed.

"I see that you are still as modest as you were back then," Wonder said.

His expression sobered. "Time beat some humility into me. I'm not as full of myself as I used to be."

"I'm surprised," Wonder said. "You developed an artistic talent and also a prophetic ability. Those two should have made you even more full of yourself than you were before."

He shook his head. "Both were expressions of my

grief. I think that is all the three of us have been doing throughout the millennia."

"I'm sorry," Wonder said. "You must have been so sad…"

Annani felt like an observer to their reunion, which was appropriate, she supposed. They needed this moment to acknowledge their past and establish their present. But after several more exchanges, she could no longer contain the question burning in her chest.

"Esag," she said, drawing his attention back to her. "I must ask you something important. How did you know what happened to Gulan? You were not there when the earth swallowed her, and yet you imbued her figurine with that memory."

"I have prophetic dreams sometimes," he said. "I dreamt about her trying to save people and falling into the chasm."

Annani's heart thundered in her chest as she gathered the nerve to ask the next question. "Have you had any prophetic dreams about Khiann?"

Pain, old and deep, flashed across Esag's features. "I dreamt of Khiann. Many times. But those dreams reflected the wishes of my heart. My mind refused to accept his death. They were not prophetic."

"Tell me about your dreams."

"I see him sleeping," Esag said slowly. "In stasis, like Gulan was. But that is impossible. Khiann died with the other gods in the bombing."

"No," Annani said. "He did not."

All three males leaned forward, their attention laser-focused on her words.

"Princess?" Davuh prompted when she paused to gather her thoughts.

"After you three left to search for Gulan, Khiann left with a caravan, and he was caught in the same earthquake as her, but we were led to believe that Mortdh assassinated him. There were witnesses, and I believed their testimony that they had seen Mortdh take Khiann's head. Only recently has it occurred to me that my father might have compelled their testimony as a way of getting rid of Mortdh. Mortdh intended to kill Khiann; there is no doubt in my mind about that. However, he and his men might have arrived too late and never found Khiann, as he was lost in the earthquake. That was what the witnesses came to tell my father, but he changed their memories to suit his needs."

The implications hung heavy in the air. Esag's face had gone pale beneath his freckles.

"If Khiann is in stasis..." Esag's voice was hoarse. "If my dreams were true visions..."

"Then he has been sleeping in the desert for five thousand years, just as Gulan had," Annani finished. "And we need to find him."

Wonder's grip on her hands tightened. "The dreams you've had, Esag—were they detailed? Did you see landmarks, anything that might help locate him?"

Esag closed his eyes. "It was just an endless desert." He opened them. "I could never bring myself to carve a figurine of Khiann. It was too painful. Maybe if I carve one now, the dreams will give me more guidance."

"You will do that right here in the village," Annani

275

said. "We need to celebrate this reunion properly. You will never be alone again. You will have a community, a family."

"Family," Roven repeated. "I'd almost forgotten what it felt like to have family beyond us three."

"You'll be reminded soon," Wonder assured him. "And then you might yearn for solitude. This place is a hive of gossip."

"I can live with that," Davuh said.

"How soon can you get here?" Annani asked.

"Kalugal is making arrangements for my workshop contents to be shipped over to the village," Esag said. "I want to supervise the packing of the more precious items, all the figurines of those we lost, but I can leave the tools, materials, and commercial pieces for his team to take care of."

"Very well," Annani said. "I want to extend my warm welcome to the three of you. I want you to know that you are loved, you are wanted, and you are coming home."

27

LOKAN

awn's colors across the Russian sky were magnificent, but Lokan barely noticed the beauty. His body ached from the night-long trek through increasingly rugged terrain, his ribs were still healing because he hadn't had proper rest, and his head hurt from maintaining constant vigilance and casting his mental net around. Carol was also exhausted and operating on pure determination, which he knew was the case, not because she'd complained but because she hadn't cracked a single joke or even talked in hours.

"River crossing ahead," Grant said from a few paces ahead of them. "About half a klick."

The extraction point lay just beyond that river, and Lokan was grateful to see the end of this journey. They'd been walking for over twelve hours since abandoning the motorcycles, pushing through rocky terrain that was meant for mountain goats and not people.

"Finally," Carol muttered. "I'm about ready to swim back to America at this point."

Lokan was so glad to hear her joke again. "Almost there, my love," he assured her.

When they reached the tree line above the river, Grant held up a fist, signaling them to stop. The water below ran fast, swollen with mountain runoff. A narrow wooden bridge spanned the rapids, looking about as sturdy as one would expect in these parts.

"I don't like it," Camden said, studying the crossing through binoculars. "It's too exposed. Perfect for an ambush."

"Everything has been perfect for an ambush in these damn mountains," Dougal grumbled. "It's a strategic nightmare, but we can't second-guess every meter of terrain or we'll never make it to the extraction point."

Lokan reached out with his senses, searching for the telltale presence of immortal or human minds and found nothing, but he didn't trust himself, especially given the pounding headache he'd developed. Immortal thoughts were harder to detect from a distance, and that held even truer for enhanced immortals, whose minds were harder to penetrate.

"I'm not sensing any thoughts," he reported. "But that doesn't mean it's clear. My headache might be interfering with my extrasensory perception, and it's also possible that the ambushers are so empty-headed that they are difficult to detect."

That hadn't gotten him the chuckle he'd hoped for from Carol.

"We have no choice," Grant said. "We have to cross.

We go fast, one at a time. I'll take point, then Carol, then you. Camden and Dougal, you provide cover until we are across, then follow."

Grant made it halfway across the bridge when the world exploded into chaos.

Gunfire erupted from concealed positions on both banks, the sharp crack of AK-47s mixing with the deeper boom of shotguns. Grant dove forward, rolling across the remaining planks as wood splintered around him.

"Contact left and right!" Camden said into the comm while returning fire.

Lokan grabbed Carol and pulled her behind a fallen log as bullets whizzed overhead. He reached with his mind, suddenly focused by the adrenaline rush, and this time he got something. The mental signatures that met him were human, tinged with greed and desperation rather than the focused malevolence of Doomers or human assassins.

Low-level mercenaries or bandits, who shouldn't be challenging to take out.

"Not Brotherhood," he said into the comm, squeezing off a burst toward muzzle flashes on the far bank. "Humans."

A voice called out in accented English from across the river. "You surrender now! We only want the woman and the pretty boy. Others can go!"

"Charming," Carol muttered. "They know how to make a girl feel special."

"I'm offended," Camden said through the comm. "Am I not a pretty boy?"

"Gorchenco must be behind this," Lokan growled. "My father wouldn't have wanted Carol."

She cast him an incredulous look. "Yes, he would, Lokan. He would use me to interrogate you."

That hadn't occurred to him, but she was right. His father would absolutely torture her to get him to talk.

More gunfire, but it was undisciplined, spray-and-pray tactics rather than aimed shots. These weren't soldiers or even professional criminals. These were opportunists hoping for an easy payday.

There was obviously a bounty on his and Carol's heads, but the question was who had put it up, Gorchenco or Navuh?

Did it matter?

Lokan wasn't about to let himself get caught alive, regardless of who wanted his head.

"Camden, Dougal, flank left," Grant's voice crackled over their earpieces. "I'll draw their fire. Lokan, can you get into their heads and redirect?"

"Working on it," Lokan replied, though the distance and chaos made it difficult for him to do so. He needed to be closer.

"I have an idea," Carol said. "Cover me."

Before he could protest, she was moving, not away from danger but toward it. She sprinted along the riverbank, using trees for cover, drawing fire away from their position. The attackers, focused on what they saw as the prize, shifted their attention to track her.

Which was precisely what she'd planned.

With their focus redirected, Camden and Dougal

moved like shadows through the trees, their immortal speed and strength turning them into blurs of motion. The first scream came seconds later as Dougal reached the nearest gunman.

Lokan used the distraction to push forward, closing the distance to the main group of attackers. As he moved, he reached out with his mind, finding the chaotic thoughts of greedy men.

Five million rubles... American dollars better... the Pakhan wants them alive... especially the woman...

He found what seemed to be their leader, a rough-looking veteran whose thoughts were more organized than the rest. Lokan slipped into his mind like a knife between ribs.

Drop your weapon, he commanded. *Tell your men to stand down.*

The man's hands began to loosen on his rifle, his face going slack.

"Hold your position, soldier," a voice called out in Russian, and a figure emerged from the trees on the far bank—tall, well-dressed despite the wilderness setting, and with the demeanor of a man used to being obeyed.

"Let me guess," Lokan called out, buying time as he tried to penetrate the newcomer's mental shields. "You work for Dimitri Gorchenco."

The man smiled. "Colonel Volkov, formerly of the GRU. Now a freelance contractor with a very lucrative offer on the table. You've caused the Pakhan considerable losses, Mr. Lokan. He wants to discuss that with you. Personally."

"I'm sure he does," Lokan replied, noting that Grant

had made it to cover on the far bank and was working his way toward Volkov's position. "But I'm afraid I have prior commitments."

"A shame." Volkov raised his hand, and more fighters emerged from concealment. Twenty, maybe twenty-five total. "We'll have to do this the hard way then."

What followed was a massacre, though not the one Volkov had planned.

Grant hit the first group like a hurricane. Bodies flew, bones cracked, and weapons were turned on their owners and their comrades.

Lokan was impressed. Even he had a hard time thralling under pressure, while the three Guardians were doing that in addition to physically fighting.

Camden and Dougal carved through the left flank with the same brutal efficiency. These might have been hard men, veterans of Russia's criminal underworld, but they were still only human. They stood no chance against immortals.

Meanwhile, Carol had circled back and was picking off stragglers with precise shots, cutting off their retreat routes.

Lokan focused on Volkov, battering against his mental shields with increasing force. The man had a strong mind and was well trained, but he was still human. Still breakable.

"You don't know who you're dealing with," Volkov gasped, blood running from his nose as Lokan's mental assault intensified. "Every criminal from here to Moscow is looking for you. Every corrupt cop, every soldier who needs extra money. You'll never make it out of Russia."

"I beg to differ." Lokan pushed harder.

Volkov's shields shattered like glass. His eyes rolled back, and he collapsed, his mind overwhelmed by the forced intrusion. Lokan rifled through his memories with no regard for the damage he caused.

There. The bounty notice was distributed through Gorchenco's network. Five million American dollars for Carol and Lokan, delivered alive to the Pakhan. Every criminal organization in the region had been alerted.

But there was more. Someone in Turner's network was feeding information to Gorchenco. Not a name, just a stupid code that would have made Lokan laugh under different circumstances.

Foxhound.

Someone was watching too many old action movies.

Lokan withdrew from Volkov's mind, leaving the man drooling and twitching on the ground. Around them, the ambush had turned into a rout. Bodies littered both riverbanks, and the few survivors were fleeing into the forest, their greed overwhelmed by terror.

Grant materialized beside Lokan with barely a spatter of blood on his tactical vest. "You okay?"

Lokan nodded. "Gorchenco has put a bounty on Carol and me," Lokan said. "Every criminal in western Russia is looking for us. And someone in Turner's network is feeding him information."

Grant's expression darkened. "The extraction point might be compromised."

"My thoughts exactly." Lokan pulled out his phone. "I need to warn Turner."

He typed quickly, explaining the situation and the code name Foxhound. Turner's response came within minutes.

No idea who that is, but I will find out. Wait for the new extraction point coordinates.

"We'll have a new location shortly," Lokan told the others.

Carol dropped to the ground and sat amidst the carnage. "I'll rest in the meantime."

The text from Turner with the new coordinates arrived only a few minutes later.

Lokan showed them to the others. "Fifteen kilometers northeast."

"On foot?" Carol asked. "That's another three hours minimum."

Camden gestured toward the trees. "The mercenaries didn't get here on foot, and I heard engines revving up, probably used by those who escaped. I bet there are vehicles left behind we can use." His gaze swept over all the dead bodies around them.

"They'll be looking for those vehicles," Dougal pointed out.

"They'll be looking for us regardless," Grant said. "Speed trumps stealth at this point. We take the vehicles."

They found two battered SUVs and a military-style truck that had seen better days. They loaded into the two SUVs, not because they needed both for the five of them, but because they might need to split up. Grant took the wheel of the lead SUV with Camden riding shotgun. Lokan drove the second vehicle with Carol beside him and Dougal in the back.

The vehicles roared to life, and they tore off down the rough forest road.

Lokan's phone buzzed with another message from Turner. *Aircraft inbound. ETA to new extraction point: 43 minutes. Suggest you hurry. Local military responding to gunfire reports.*

"Perfect," Lokan muttered. "Because we need more complications."

"What now?" Carol asked.

"Military's mobilizing. We have forty-three minutes to make the new extraction point."

"Then drive faster," Dougal suggested from the back seat.

In the lead vehicle, Grant was setting a punishing pace, and behind him, Lokan pressed harder on the accelerator to keep up, the SUV's engine protesting as they flew over the uneven terrain.

They'd gone five kilometers when Lokan's phone rang. Turner's number.

"Change of plans," Turner said. "Original extraction point is compromised. We're rerouting again."

"Turner—"

"Listen carefully. There's an abandoned airfield twenty kilometers due east of your current position. The pilot will put down there in..." A pause. "Thirty-seven minutes. That's the best we can do."

"Understood." Lokan was already recalculating the route. "What about—"

The line went dead.

"East," he called to Grant over the comm. "Twenty kilometers to an abandoned airfield. We have thirty-seven minutes."

"Copy that," Grant responded. "Hold on to something."

The next half hour blurred in a chaos of speed, desperation, and barely controlled vehicles. They left the forest behind, tearing across open steppes that offered no cover but allowed for greater speed. Twice, they spotted helicopters in the distance, but whether military or criminal, the aircraft didn't pursue.

With five minutes to spare, the airfield came into view. Crumbling concrete buildings, a tower that tilted at an alarming angle, and a runway that looked like a collection of potholes held together by wishful thinking.

And descending toward it, engines roaring, was the most beautiful sight Lokan had seen in days—a cargo aircraft, sturdy and battered but airworthy.

They skidded to a stop near the runway as the plane touched down, bouncing alarmingly on the deterio-rated surface but maintaining control. The cargo ramp was already lowering before the aircraft fully stopped.

"Move!" Grant shouted.

They abandoned the vehicles and ran, Carol's hand in Lokan's as they sprinted up the ramp. The pilot was an older woman with grey-streaked hair, wearing a jumpsuit that bore no insignia. "Welcome aboard," she called back in accented English. "Next stop, somewhere that isn't Russia."

As the engines roared to full power and the abandoned airfield fell away beneath them, Lokan finally allowed himself to relax. They'd made it. Bloodied, exhausted, hunted by half the criminal underworld, but alive.

Carol collapsed against him, her head finding that familiar spot on his shoulder. "Next time we need to escape somewhere," she said, "let's pick a nice tropical island. With beaches. And drinks with umbrellas."

He laughed. "That description matches my father's island. You've already done that and ended up in his harem."

"Right." She scrunched her nose. "A different tropical island, then, somewhere in the Bahamas."

"Deal," he said, pressing a kiss to her hair. "Though knowing our luck, the island would probably turn out to be run by pirates."

"At this point," she murmured, "I'd take pirates over Russian mafia any day."

As the aircraft climbed toward cruising altitude, leaving Russia and its dangers behind, Lokan closed his eyes and let exhaustion claim him. They'd won this round, but Gorchenco needed to be dealt with.

That was tomorrow's problem, though. Today, they were still alive, and they were going home.

28

AREZOO

At five-forty in the afternoon only a handful of customers remained in the café, nursing their cappuccinos while Arezoo wiped clean the vacant tables and, together with Aliya, lifted all the chairs on top of them so they could hose down the floor.

The stragglers still had time, though. The café didn't close until Wonder closed the shutters on the serve-out window, so Arezoo couldn't tell them to get up and leave.

Ruvon should have gotten there already, though, and she wondered what was keeping him. Maybe he wasn't coming today?

For some reason, the prospect of him missing one of their poetry reading sessions upset her.

It shouldn't bother her since she wasn't really interested in him.

Well, she wasn't interested in him romantically, but

she considered him a friend, and she liked spending time with him. She didn't want to lose him.

She enjoyed their routine of coffee, pastries, and poetry. Nothing more. Nothing that should make her check her reflection in the espresso machine's chrome surface or wonder if she should have worn the blue blouse instead of the green. She didn't do that because of him. She just wanted to look well put together and professional.

She was done lifting the chairs on table five when Drova strode in, still wearing her Guardian-in-training uniform. Unlike other times, though, it wasn't in immaculate condition. Sweat darkened the fabric at her collar, and her usually severe expression held a hint of satisfaction that suggested a particularly grueling training session, at which she'd excelled and put the other trainees to shame.

She waved at Arezoo and continued to the counter. "Got some of those juice boxes in the fridge? I could use something cold and full of protein."

"Coming right up." Wonder reached for the special refrigerator they kept stocked for their Kra-ell customers. "Good training session?"

"The best." Drova's rare smile transformed her face. "We did hand-to-hand combat drills all afternoon. I dominated the session."

"Of course you did." Wonder handed her a box.

"Thank you." She took the box and turned around, leaning against the counter. "Guess who showed up at the gym today asking about private coaching?"

Something in Drova's tone made Arezoo pause. "Who?"

"Your poet."

"Really?"

"Mmm-hmm." Drova's eyes glinted with amusement. "I overheard him talking to Morrison about private strength training. Morrison passed him off to Gareth, who's apparently taking him on as a project."

Arezoo couldn't quite picture it. Ruvon seemed fragile and breakable next to the burly Guardian.

"Ruvon made him an offer he couldn't refuse. Come to think of it, I'm jealous. For that kind of money, I would have gladly trained him. Anyway, starting tomorrow, they will be meeting for an hour three times a week." Drova took another sip of her synthetic blood. "That's not nearly enough time to get seriously in shape, but I guess he needs to start somewhere. If your boy is serious about getting buff, though, he should train every day for a couple of hours."

"He's not my anything," Arezoo said automatically. "And he's definitely not a boy."

"Sure he's not." Drova's smirk was positively wicked. "That's why you're clutching that cleaning cloth like you are about to strangle it."

Arezoo looked down at her white-knuckled grip on the cloth and forced her fingers to relax. "I'm just surprised. Ruvon never mentioned wanting to train."

"Maybe it was a spontaneous decision," Wonder suggested from behind them, joining the conversation. "Perhaps one of his friends put him up to it." She smiled. "Girls put on makeup and nice outfits to attract guys, and guys work on their muscles to attract girls."

Arezoo had never been attracted to muscular men. She liked that Ruvon was smart and enjoyed reading. Still, his wish to do something different, to step out of his comfort zone, resonated with her.

It took courage to do so, and she was glad that Ruvon had found it in himself to embrace something new.

"Earth to Arezoo," Drova said, waving a hand in front of her face. "You went somewhere else for a minute there."

"Sorry. I was just thinking how much courage it takes to pivot and do something uncharacteristic. Ruvon choosing to start training at the gym is equivalent to you choosing to study math."

Drova winced. "Don't remind me. I'm so glad that I don't have to do that anymore." She slurped the last of her blood box and tossed it into the disposal receptacle. "I should go." She lifted her arm and sniffed her armpit. "Yeah, that's ripe. I need a shower."

Arezoo shook her head. "You are worse than the men."

"I'm better, you meant to say." Drova pushed away from the bar. "So much better." She waved goodbye to Wonder. "See you tomorrow, ladies."

After she was done wiping down all the vacant tables and lifting the rest of the chairs, Arezoo headed to the employee bathroom. She washed her hands, smoothed her hair, and even applied the lip gloss Laleh had given her.

Some inner sense told her that Ruvon was out there even before she opened the bathroom door, and when she saw him, her breath caught.

Ruvon looked different. No, that wasn't quite right —he looked like himself, but more. His posture was straighter, with his shoulders back and chin up. The usual button-down shirt had been replaced by a well-fitted Henley that emphasized broader shoulders than she'd noticed before, and his hair, usually somewhat unruly, had been styled with deliberate care.

But it was his smile that stopped her in her tracks. Gone was the uncertain, hopeful expression she'd grown accustomed to. This smile was confident, warm, and directed entirely at her.

What was responsible for the transformation? Had Ruvon spoken with the clan's psychologist and gotten advice on how to project confidence?

"Hello, Arezoo," he said, and even his voice sounded different. Deeper. More assured.

"Hi," she managed, acutely aware that she was staring.

Behind her, she heard the shutters closing and turned around. "Don't worry." Wonder smiled at her. "Your coffees and pastries are on the counter." She pointed to where she'd left them.

"Thank you," Ruvon said. "But don't close yet. I need to pay you."

"It's on the house." Wonder winked at him. "Have a lovely evening, you two." She pulled down the shutters.

"You look different," Arezoo said. "I mean good."

"Thank you." He took the plates to their usual table,

292

put them down, and pulled out a chair for her. "You look beautiful. But then, you always do."

The compliment, delivered without his usual stammering uncertainty, sent warmth spreading through her chest. She put their coffees down and sat, hyperaware of his presence as he took his seat across from her.

"Drova mentioned she saw you at the gym," she said, needing to fill the silence that suddenly felt charged.

"Ah." A slight flush colored his cheeks, the first crack in his newfound confidence. "I'm starting to train tomorrow. Kalugal has been complaining about many of us being out of shape, and he's right. We may not be soldiers anymore, but if the call comes, we are expected to mobilize to defend the village. I don't want to be the weak link."

She chuckled. "I doubt you would be defending the village with a rifle in your hands. Your job would be monitoring security screens and activating whatever booby traps are hidden around the perimeter."

He shrugged. "You are probably right, but in case I'm needed with a rifle in my hands or just my bare fangs, I want to be ready."

"Why now?" The question burst out of her before she could think it through.

His eyes met hers, direct and honest. "Because I want to be able to defend you. It's no longer hypothetical for me. Someone I care for needs my protection, and I would never forgive myself if I couldn't provide it."

That was sweet, but the village was far from

defenseless, and Arezoo doubted she would ever need Ruvon to fight for her.

"Ruvon—"

"I know what you're going to say," he interrupted gently. "You are going to tell me that you don't need my protection because the village is full of protectors, but I need to do this for me. I need to know that I'm capable of defending you. You were the catalyst."

She didn't know what to say to that, so she reached for the poetry book in her apron pocket and pulled it out. "Should we read?"

"If you'd like." But something in his tone suggested poetry was the last thing on his mind.

Nevertheless, she opened the book at random, finding a verse about transformation. How appropriate. As she began to read, her voice shook slightly.

"In the garden of becoming, where souls shed their winter skins..."

The words flowed between them, but for the first time, Arezoo found herself distracted by the man across from her. The way his dark eyes shone whenever he looked at her, glowing from the inside, and when he reached for his coffee and took a sip, she couldn't help but notice how perfectly shaped his lips were.

How come she'd never noticed that before?

"Arezoo?" He said her name softly, and she realized she was still staring at his mouth.

"I'm sorry. I got distracted for a moment." She looked down at the page, searching for the last stanza she'd read.

His smile turned teasing, another new facet to this evolving version of him. "It's the first time that Persian poetry can't hold your attention. If this poem is boring to you, you can switch to another."

"It's not the poem," she admitted, then immediately wanted to take the words back.

His expression shifted, hope blooming across his features. "It's not?"

She shook her head, unable to form words as he leaned slightly forward.

"Arezoo," he said, her name a caress. "What's bothering you?"

"Nothing." Her eyes shifted to his mouth again, and as hard as she tried to look away, she couldn't.

What was happening to her?

Had he put something in her coffee?

"Would you go on a real date with me?" The question came out of nowhere, finally enabling her to move her gaze from his lips to his eyes. "Not a poetry reading in a closed café, but a real date to a nice restaurant. I can make reservations at Callie's, and after dinner we could take a walk in the moonlight. Just the two of us."

The safe answer, the one she'd been prepared to give him for weeks, dissolved on her tongue. Sitting across from him now, seeing the vulnerability beneath his newfound confidence, and feeling the flutter of interest in her chest that she had lost hope of ever feeling again, Arezoo realized that she wanted to say yes.

"When?" she asked, and watched joy transform his face.

"Saturday? I could pick you up at seven."

"I'd like that," she said. "I don't think that you'll be able to get reservations at Callie's, though. I've heard that she's booked months in advance."

He reached over the table and took her hand, his larger one warm and surprisingly soft against hers. "Would you like me to take you out of the village? We could go to a restaurant in town."

That was too scary, and not because she would be alone with Ruvon. She just didn't feel safe leaving the village yet.

"I can't," Arezoo said softly. "The village is my sanctuary, and I'm still too afraid to leave its boundaries, even with a fierce protector at my side."

That got a laugh out of him. "Then I'll have to bribe someone to give up their reservations at Callie's or hire Atzil to cook us a private dinner."

Her eyes widened. "I don't want you to spend a lot of money just because I'm scared of going to the city. We can have a moonlight picnic at the lookout point instead."

His smile could have powered the entire village. "That's a wonderful idea. Is Saturday okay, or do you prefer a different day?"

She shook her head. "My evenings are free, so whenever you want is fine." She smiled. "I'll bring a small flashlight so I can read poetry to you under the moon. Unless you are sick of it and don't want to hear another stanza."

"Never." He gave her hand a gentle squeeze. "I could

listen to you reciting Persian poetry forever. The sound of your voice is music to my ears."

Arezoo smiled. "Then let me read to you some more."

She returned to the book, but the energy between them had shifted. Where before there had been careful distance, now there was possibility.

By the time she finished reading and it was time to go, Arezoo felt like she was floating. Maybe she didn't need to call Vanessa after all. Maybe her ability to feel attraction, to want connection, hadn't been destroyed. Maybe it had just gone into hiding and had been waiting for the right person at the right time.

"I'll walk you home." Ruvon offered her his arm.

She had forgotten to hose down the floor, but Wonder would forgive her for neglecting to do so one time. Besides, it wasn't dirty, and whatever crumbs there were now wouldn't be there in the morning once the night creatures picked it clean.

After a moment's hesitation, Arezoo took Ruvon's arm, surprised by how natural it felt to walk beside him this way. The evening air was cool and crisp, carrying an array of sweet scents from the flowerbeds.

Her family's home came into view too soon, and she regretted that their evening was drawing to a close.

"Thank you," she said as they stopped at the front door.

"Thank you for saying yes," he replied. "To the date, I mean. I promise to make it special."

"I'm sure you will."

He lifted her hand, hesitated, then pressed a gentle

kiss to her knuckles. The gesture sent tingling up her arm.

"Goodnight, Arezoo."

"Goodnight, Ruvon."

She watched him walk away, and when he turned at the corner to go, she waved back with a smile spreading across her face that she couldn't suppress and didn't want to.

The house was quiet when she entered, and she wondered where everyone was.

There was light in her mother's room, and she headed that way, finding her on the couch watching an Iranian channel on the television.

"Come," her mother patted the couch beside her. "A lot is happening back home."

"Good or bad?" Arezoo asked as she sat down.

"That depends on who you are asking."

"I'm asking you."

"It's good," her mother said. "I think."

29

FENELLA

Fenella kicked off her dusty sandals the moment she entered their bedroom suite, resisting the urge to collapse face-first onto the nice clean bed. After helping Esag, Davuh, and Roven wrap and pack hundreds of figurines for shipping carefully, and then spending the afternoon trekking through the pyramids and the surrounding desert, she felt like she'd been rolled in dust and sand and baked in an oven.

"I don't even want to sit down." She leaned down to pick up the dirty sandals and headed toward the bathroom. "I feel like I'm covered in five thousand years' worth of dust."

Din chuckled as he closed the door behind them, looking equally dusty and sweaty. His usually neatly combed hair stuck up at odd angles, and he had a tan that looked suspiciously dark, which made her think that it would probably wash off with some soap and water.

"The hazards of archaeological tourism." He followed her toward the bathroom. "Wait until you spend a day at a dig."

"Not planning to." She gingerly touched her hair and grimaced. "There's sand in places sand should never be. I need a shower. Actually, no—I need a shower and then a long soak in that glorious bathtub."

"That sounds like a plan," Din said. "Since we've all eaten out, we don't have to come down for dinner, and we can retire for the night."

There was a gleam in his eyes that hinted at his plans, and even though she was tired, she was entirely on board with them.

Fenella started on the buttons of her shirt. "Join me in the shower?"

His eyes darkened with interest. "I was hoping you'd say that. I need someone to scrub my back."

She rolled her eyes. "Is that the only reason you want to shower with me?"

"Among others," he murmured, reaching out to pluck a piece of straw from her hair. "How did that get in there?"

"From packing up Esag's workshop. Some of his older pieces were wrapped in straw." She pulled her shirt over her head. "Last one in the shower has to wash the other's back."

"Is that supposed to be punishment?" Din asked, but he was already stripping off his clothes with impressive speed.

They reached the bathroom door at the same time, both laughing as they squeezed through together.

"I guess we will be washing each other," Din said as he turned on the water in the shower, testing the temperature until he was satisfied that it was just right.

The bathroom was one of the bedroom suite's best features—marble everything, a shower large enough for four people, and a bathtub that could probably double as a small swimming pool. Steam was already beginning to fog the mirror as the shower reached the perfect temperature.

"Come here," Din said, his playful tone shifting to something warmer. "Let me help you with that hair tie."

She moved into his arms, sighing as his fingers worked through her tangled hair with gentle patience. There was something incredibly intimate about the care he took not to pull on her tangles. When he finally managed to free her hair from the elastic band, she released a breath.

"I didn't realize how much that bothered me until you took it off. I don't like pulling my hair into a ponytail."

"Then I'm glad I made it better." He pressed a kiss to her temple.

She turned in his arms, looking up at him. "I'm pretty sure my hair is now twenty percent sand."

"Thirty percent, at least," he agreed solemnly. "Possibly forty."

She swatted his chest. "Help me wash it."

"Yes, ma'am."

As she stepped into the shower, the first blast of hot water was heavenly. Fenella groaned in pure pleasure as it sluiced over her overheated, sweaty skin, watching the water turn beige as it swirled down the drain. "It's like we've just come back from the beach."

"It looks that way." He laughed.

"That's amazing." She tilted her head back. "I may never leave this shower."

"That would make flying home tomorrow rather difficult." Din reached for the shampoo. "I don't think Kalugal will be okay with me dismantling his shower and taking it with us on the plane."

"Details," she murmured, then made another pleased sound as his hands worked the shampoo through her hair. "Oh, you're so good at that."

"I have many talents," he said, his Scottish accent more pronounced as it always was when he was relaxed or aroused or both. "Hair washing is just one of them."

"What are the others?" she asked, eyes closed as he massaged her scalp.

"Well, there's my ability to spot ugly floor lamps and pay too much for them."

"That's a talent?"

"Absolutely. Not everyone can spot a truly hideous lamp at fifty paces. It takes a special eye."

"A special something, anyway," she agreed, then squeaked as he tickled her ribs in retaliation.

What started as playful soon shifted to something more as they took turns soaping each other's bodies. Din's hands were thorough, and Fenella returned the favor with equal attention to detail.

"You missed a spot," she said, running her soapy hand over her breast.

"Did I?" His voice had gone rough. "How careless of me."

"Very," she agreed, then gasped as he cupped her breast and thumbed her nipple.

"Can't miss such an important spot." He repeated on the other side.

He backed her against the shower wall and bent his head to twirl his tongue over her nipple. When he nipped it lightly, she jerked, and he laved the small hurt away and then flicked over it with the tip of his tongue.

She gasped when he rubbed two fingers over her entrance, and when he dropped to his knees in front of her, she threaded her fingers in his hair.

He picked up her leg and placed her foot on his shoulder, opening her to his gaze. She should have felt scandalized but didn't. There was nothing she felt like hiding from him, nothing she wanted to hold back. They were one.

He plunged his tongue into her, and when she rewarded him with a throaty moan, he switched to licking her clit.

Her knees buckled, and she would have collapsed if he hadn't been holding on to her, and then she was climaxing and barely aware of how she was still upright.

Suddenly, she found herself turned around, and her hands instinctively braced against the marble.

He wrapped an arm around her waist and entered her with one swift thrust, filling her so completely, so deliciously, that tears prickled her eyes.

What a strange time to get teary-eyed, but Fenella

didn't care. Din accepted her the way she was, and nothing she did could turn him off or bother him.

He started pounding into her fast and hard, the slapping sounds of their bodies against each other echoing in the enclosed shower.

Another orgasm rose within her, like a wave rushing to break against the shore, and when it crested and she yelled his name, he climaxed as well, filling her with his essence.

"Din..." she breathed.

"I love the way you say my name," he murmured against her neck.

She'd expected him to bite her as their passion crested like he usually did, but he didn't. Not this time.

It was a shame, really, and not just because she craved the venom trip. She could use the therapeutic effect that would have erased all the aches and pains from a long day of packing and trekking.

Fenella couldn't help but make a small sound of disappointment, but as her mind cleared, she remembered that Din had bitten her that morning, and usually he couldn't produce venom more than once a day. Besides, she would have blacked out, and they couldn't have enjoyed the bathtub together.

"I wish you could have bitten me," she said, running her hands through his wet hair. "I love your bites."

"I know you do." He kissed the spot he usually bit and withdrew his shaft. "You are a venom junkie."

"Your venom junkie," she corrected, then squealed as he turned her around and swept her up in his arms. "What are you doing?"

"Taking you to the bath, obviously. Can't have you walking on these wet floors."

"I'm immortal," she reminded him as he carried her to the tub.

"Better safe than sorry." He set her down carefully in the tub.

After fiddling a little with the water temperature, Din climbed in across from her, and they spent a few minutes just adjusting positions until they were comfortable, her back against his chest, his arms around her waist.

The bathtub was even better than the shower.

"This is perfect," she murmured, letting her head fall back against his shoulder.

"Mmm," he agreed, pressing a kiss to her damp hair. "Though I keep expecting Joseph to burst in with towels or tea or something."

"He wouldn't dare. Kalugal would have his head."

"Good man, Kalugal."

They floated in silence for a while, the hot water and lavender-scented bath oils working their magic. But as relaxed as her body was becoming, Fenella's mind kept circling back to tomorrow.

They were flying home, leaving this Egyptian adventure behind them and starting their lives together.

"I'm nervous," she said quietly.

Din's arms tightened around her. "About what?"

"About going home. About us."

She felt his body tense behind her. "What about us?"

"I've never lived with anyone before," she said in a

rush. "Not as a couple. What if the magic fades once we're back? What if you realize I'm terrible to live with? What if—"

"Fenella." He turned her in his arms so she was facing him, water sloshing dangerously close to the tub's rim. "Look at me."

She did, finding his eyes serious but warm.

"First of all, there's no magic to fade. What we have is real, built on love, friendship, and respect. That's not going anywhere. And secondly, we are truelove mates, as proven by all the obstacles we had to overcome to be together."

"But—"

"Thirdly." He placed a finger gently over her lips, "I already know that you're terrible to live with. You leave wet towels on the floor, you steal the blanket, and you have questionable taste in late-night television."

"Hey!" She tried to look offended but couldn't quite manage it.

"And I love all of it," he finished. "Even your silly reality show addiction."

"It's not an addiction," she protested. "It's a healthy interest in human drama."

"Of course, it is." He cupped her face, his thumbs stroking her cheekbones. "The point is, I know who you are, Fenella: the good, the bad, the occasionally criminally insane. And I want all of it. All of you. Wet towels and all."

She felt tears prick at her eyes. "You can't mean that."

"Have I ever lied to you?"

"Well, no..."

"There you have it." He leaned and kissed the tip of her nose. "I'm ready to tackle anything and everything with you. I would like to ask the Clan Mother to officiate at our wedding in a grand ceremony attended by the entire clan. I want it all."

He kissed her then, thoroughly.

This time, their lovemaking was slower and tender, rather than urgent. The warm water and oils made every touch silky smooth, every movement languid and deliberate.

When they finally emerged from the tub, the water had cooled and their fingers were thoroughly prune-like, but Fenella felt more relaxed than she had in a long time.

"I could sleep for a week," she announced, toweling off with one of Kalugal's luxurious Egyptian cotton towels.

"We have about ten hours before we need to leave for the airport," Din said, checking his watch.

He was so literal that sometimes it was funny.

Naked in bed, Fenella sighed contentedly as she curled into Din's side. "You know what I'm most excited about?"

"What's that?"

"Decorating our house. Making it ours." She propped herself up on an elbow to look at him. "I've never done that before."

He wrapped his arm around her. "We will go shopping together and find other hideous but unique items."

She laughed. "You have terrible decorating taste."

"My taste is not terrible," he protested. "It's eclectic."

"Din, you bought a lamp that looks like a brass octopus with tentacles."

"Octopus? It looks nothing like an octopus. That lamp has character," he insisted, then yelped as she poked his ribs. "Fine, if you hate it that much…"

"I love it," she admitted, settling back against him. "I love how excited you get about the weirdest things. Like that plate with the constipated camel."

"He's not constipated; he's contemplating."

"He's definitely constipated." She yawned. "But I love that you saw him and immediately thought, 'This needs to come home with us.'"

"You're mocking me," he said, but she could hear the smile in his voice.

"I'm not," she said seriously. "I do love it. No one else would get so enthusiastic about ugly lamps and constipated camel plates. It's very… you."

"I'm not sure if that's a compliment or not."

"It is." She pressed a kiss to his chest. "I love that you're already thinking about making our home special, even if your version of special is a bit strange." She yawned again. "I'm keeping you, you know. Terrible taste and all."

"Good," he murmured, pressing a kiss to her hair. "Because I'm keeping you, too. Messy bathrooms and reality-show addiction and all."

"Healthy interest," she mumbled, already half asleep.

"Of course. My mistake."

As sleep pulled her under, Fenella felt the last of her

anxiety fade away. "Love you," she whispered into the darkness.

"Love you too," came the reply, along with a gentle squeeze.

30

LOKAN

The cargo plane's landing gear hit the runway with a bone-jarring thump that woke Carol from her exhausted sleep. She jerked upright against Lokan's shoulder, blinking in confusion at the dim cargo hold around them.

"Where are we?" she mumbled, her voice thick with sleep.

"Finland," Lokan said, peering out the small porthole window at the grey dawn light illuminating the airport. Pine forests stretched beyond the runway, dark green against patches of lingering snow. "The pilot mentioned Rovaniemi."

Carol yawned. "Well, anywhere is better than Russia."

"It's also not the first time the clan has run an operation here," Grant said. "Finland is where the Kra-ell we saved from Igor's compound boarded our ship."

Camden started collecting their things. "No offense to the Russian people, but I'm very happy to be out of there. I thought that Putin was a strong leader, but it seems like that country is ruled by its criminal element."

Grant chuckled. "Aren't they all?"

Carol nodded, her curls bouncing enticingly even when tangled from sleep. "Most politicians are crooks who are in it for the money. It's a legal mafia."

"At least they are not trying to kill us," Dougal said.

"Yet," Lokan countered.

"Welcome to Finland, folks. Local time is 6:47 AM," the pilot's voice crackled over the intercom. "The temperature is a balmy two degrees Celsius. There's a van waiting for you on the tarmac—blue Ford Transit, the driver's name is Mikko. He's expecting you. Good luck to you all."

"Any chance this Mikko is going to try to collect a bounty on us?" Carol finger-combed her tangled hair with little success.

"I can vouch for him personally." The pilot walked into the cabin. "We are all old friends." She smiled. "You're safe here."

Once the cargo ramp had lowered with a hydraulic whine, letting in a blast of crisp Arctic air that made them all shiver despite their immortal constitutions, they rushed to put on their jackets.

"There's our ride," Dougal said, nodding toward a blue van parked some fifty meters away.

A tall, lean man stood beside it, wearing a green corduroy jacket and a gray scarf. His hands were in his pockets, and he was watching them with the relaxed alertness of someone with extensive military training.

311

Lokan could spot former Special Ops guys from a mile away, and this guy was entirely obvious.

They gathered all of their possessions, mainly weapons, plus what they had stored in their packs, and walked down the ramp. Lokan kept Carol close, his arm around her waist.

"Hello, Mikko," Grant said as they approached the guy.

He nodded, ice-blue eyes taking in their bedraggled state. "And you must be Turner's lost sheep. Rough journey?"

"You could say that," Lokan confirmed.

Mikko cracked a smile. "Come on, let's get you somewhere warm. We can swap war stories on the way. I'm sure you are eager for showers, coffee, and something to eat."

They piled into the van, Grant sitting next to Mikko, Lokan and Carol taking the middle row, and the two other Guardians in the back.

"The safe house is about forty minutes north," Mikko said as he pulled away from the airport. "Full amenities, hot water, proper beds, stocked kitchen. Turner said to take good care of you, so I got you the best."

"Thank you," Carol murmured. "A hot shower sounds like heaven."

"Any word on the situation with Turner's network?" Lokan asked.

Mikko shook his head. "It's under investigation. Turner is not the only one utilizing this wider network of operatives, and it is crucial that this Foxhound is found and eliminated; otherwise, the entire organization will collapse. Turner is now relying only on his close associates whom he knows personally. Like me."

"You served with him?" Grant asked.

"Delta Force, back in the day. Did a tour in Afghanistan together before he became a desk jockey." Mikko navigated the empty roads with the familiarity of someone who lived in the area. "I'm semi-retired, but when he called saying he needed a safe house and extraction for priority packages, no questions asked, I didn't hesitate."

"We appreciate it," Lokan said sincerely. "We've been running for days."

"So I gather. You all look like you've been dragged through several circles of hell."

"Only three or four," Carol said. "We skipped the really bad ones."

Mikko chuckled. "Turner's arranging a private jet for tomorrow morning. Again, because the larger network is compromised at the moment and he has to rely on personal contacts, it wasn't so easy to find someone immediately, and flying commercial is not advisable given your situation."

"It's all good," Lokan said. "We need to rest and resupply before the Atlantic crossing."

"Resupply." Carol perked up. "Does that include clothing that doesn't smell like motorcycle exhaust, fear, and sweat?"

"There's a shopping center about forty-five minutes from the house," Mikko said.

Carol made a small sound of longing that made

Lokan smile. His mate had left her entire designer wardrobe in Beijing, and while she'd been remarkably stoic about it, he knew how much she missed her nice things.

"Perhaps we should stop there before going to the safe house."

Carol turned to look at him. "I'm exhausted. I just want that hot shower and a bed. Shopping can wait."

He chuckled. "Those are words I never thought I would hear from you. What if I promise to make it quick?" he coaxed. "Just the essentials. Some proper clothing and luggage. Maybe some of that face cream you like that you had to leave behind."

"You don't even know what face cream I like," she protested, but he could see her resolve weakening.

"The one in the silver jar with French writing. Smells like roses and costs more than most people's mortgage."

Her eyes widened. "How do you know that?"

"Don't you know that I notice everything about you?"

From the back seat, Camden made a gagging sound. "Get a room, you two."

"That's literally where we're going," Carol shot back, but she was smiling now. "Fine. Shower first and then a quick shopping stop, and I mean quick."

"Thirty minutes, maximum," Lokan promised. "In and out."

"Famous last words," Grant muttered.

The drive continued through increasingly remote territory, the main roads giving way to smaller ones, then barely paved tracks through dense forest. Snow still clung to the gentle slopes despite the approaching summer, and Lokan was mesmerized by the stark beauty of the landscape.

"Pretty different from Beijing." Carol followed his gaze.

"Just a bit." He thought of their ultra-modern apartment, the constant noise and motion of the city, and the press of millions of people. Here, they might have been the only ones in the world.

"Which do you like better?" she asked.

He considered the question. "Honestly? Neither. Beijing was a useful cover, but it was never home. This is beautiful, but too isolated. I think..." He paused, searching for the right words. "I don't really care where I am as long as I am with you."

"Smooth talker," she accused, but there was a slight smile on her lips, and her eyes were soft.

The safe house appeared through the trees like something from a fairy tale—a traditional Finnish log cabin, but larger and more modern than the term suggested. Solar panels gleamed on the roof, and Lokan could see the subtle signs of security measures.

"Home sweet temporary home," Mikko announced, pulling up to the front door. "Fully stocked, alarm system's already disabled for your arrival. Code's 1847."

They climbed out, muscles stiff from too many hours in various uncomfortable positions. The air was even colder here, crisp and clean in a way that made Beijing's smog seem like a bad dream.

"This is perfect," Carol breathed, taking in the peaceful surroundings.

"Wait until nightfall," Mikko said, handing Grant a set of keys. "You can enjoy the Northern Lights out here. Quite a show if you're lucky."

"We could use some luck," Dougal said, hefting their gear from the van.

"Don't jinx it," Camden warned.

Mikko helped them unload, then leaned against the van. "The shopping center is located about fifteen kilometers down the road, then east at the crossroads. Can't miss it—the only commercial building for fifty kilometers. There is a car in the garage for your use, and the tank is full. I'll be back tomorrow morning at eight to take you to the airstrip."

"Thank you," Lokan said, shaking the man's hand. "We owe you."

"You owe Turner," Mikko corrected. "I'm just paying back old debts. Stay safe, stay inside, and try to avoid attracting attention if you do go shopping. I don't anticipate any Soviet spies out here, but you never know."

With that cheerful advice, he climbed back in the van and drove off, leaving them standing in front of their temporary sanctuary.

"First things first," Grant said. "We sweep the house and check security and supplies."

"First things first," Carol countered, "I shower. You can do whatever you want after I no longer smell like a yak."

"You don't smell like a yak," Lokan protested.

"You can't smell me because that's what you smell like, too. We've gone nose-blind to our own stench."

Grant sighed. "Fine. Camden, you take first watch. Dougal and I will do the sweep. Try not to use up all the hot water."

"No promises," Carol called over her shoulder as she headed inside.

The cabin's interior was as well-appointed as Mikko had promised—the main room combined living and dining areas, with a modern kitchen along one wall. A fireplace dominated another wall, stacked wood beside it. Hallways led off to bedrooms and bathrooms.

"Oh, thank God," Carol called from the bathroom. "There's actual soap. And towels. Clean towels, Lokan. Do you realize how wonderful that is?"

He was amused by her rapture over basic amenities. "You shower first. I'll check the supplies and see what we need to get."

"My hero." She started stripping off her clothes as she headed into the bathroom. "There are toiletries, first-aid supplies, and bathrobes in here," she called out.

"Good."

Lokan waited until he heard the shower start, then began exploring the cabin. The kitchen was indeed fully stocked—canned goods, dried foods, even fresh bread and milk in the refrigerator.

It was all basic and utilitarian, and it would do for now, but after years of living in luxury and playing the role of successful businesspeople, they had grown accustomed to better.

Fifteen minutes later, Carol emerged from the bathroom in a cloud of steam, her hair wrapped in a towel and wearing one of the bathrobes that was made for someone twice her size. "Your turn," she said. "It was a great sacrifice, but since I love you so much, I left you some hot water."

"Thank you." He kissed her as he passed. "I'll be quick."

The shower was indeed heaven. Lokan stood under the spray, letting the hot water wash away days of sweat and grime. By the time he emerged, he felt almost human again. Or immortal, rather.

He found Carol dressed in clothes that didn't quite fit—a pair of sweatpants that were too long and a sweatshirt that was too large.

"Where did you find those?" He waved a hand over her.

"In the closet. There is a matching outfit for you as well."

"Perfect." He opened the closet door. "Do you still want to go shopping, or will these do?"

She looked at herself and grimaced. "I can't arrive at the village looking like this."

"You look beautiful as you always do," he said. "It doesn't matter what you have on."

"You're so sweet." She smiled. "But I have no choice. I have to go shopping."

"Then let's make it quick. Clothes that fit, proper luggage, and maybe that face cream if they have it."

"They won't have it out here, and the clothing will be no better than what we had on the trek, but at least they will be the right size and clean."

Grant appeared in the doorway. "If you're going out, at least one of us needs to go with you."

"We'll be fine," Lokan said. "Unless you guys need to do some shopping as well?"

"We don't," Grant said. "But we are here to protect you. I should go with you."

Carol stretched on her toes to kiss Grant's cheek. "You forget that Lokan and I are not inexperienced civilians. We are both trained, and we know what we are doing."

Reluctantly, he nodded.

"Bring back food," Camden called from the living room.

"Pizza?" Dougal suggested hopefully. "Do they have pizza out here?"

"We'll see what we can find." Lokan ushered Carol toward the door before the shopping list could grow longer.

The car Mikko had mentioned was in the garage—an older model Volvo. The keys were on the hook by the door.

"Are you okay to drive?" Carol asked as she got in. "Did you sleep on the plane?"

"I dozed off for a little bit. That's enough for me."

It wasn't, and he was operating on fumes, but thankfully Carol didn't argue for a change, and soon they were driving through the Finnish forest.

"This feels so surreal," Carol said, adjusting the heater vents. "Three days ago, we were running for our lives through Mongolia, and now we're going shopping in Finland like a normal couple."

"We're not a normal couple." He smiled at her. "We're extraordinary people who happen to need new underwear."

She laughed. "When you put it that way, it sounds almost romantic."

"Everything is romantic with the right person," he said, reaching over to take her hand.

"Such a smooth talker."

"That's why you love me."

"Among other things." She waggled her brows.

The shopping center appeared exactly where Mikko had said, a modern building that looked almost alien, dropped into the wilderness as it was. The parking lot held a few dozen cars at most, all older models.

Carol squared her shoulders like a soldier preparing for battle. "Thirty minutes, starting now."

He chuckled. "You make it sound like a race."

They entered through sliding doors into fluorescent-lit normalcy. A department store anchored one end, a grocery store the other, with smaller shops in between. Music played softly over hidden speakers.

"Divide and conquer?" Carol suggested. "You get luggage and men's clothes, I'll handle women's wear?"

"Together," Lokan said firmly. "I'm not letting you out of my sight."

"Overprotective much?"

"Recently hunted by multiple armies," he countered.

"Fair point." She linked her arm through his. "Ladies' department first. I refuse to spend another minute in these sweats."

What followed was the most normal half hour they'd experienced in recent memory. Carol efficiently selected clothing appropriate for travel and in the correct size. She didn't bother trying anything on, claiming that she was old and experienced enough not to need that. She knew what looked good on her, and he couldn't argue with that.

"What about this?" She held up a soft blue sweater.

"Beautiful. It matches your eyes," he said without thinking. "But don't forget that the summer where we are going is not a Finnish summer. You won't need this in the village."

"True." She added it to the pile anyway.

He was wise enough not to ask why.

They found two rolling suitcases, and Carol discovered a face cream that wasn't French, but it made her happy nonetheless.

"Five minutes to spare," she announced, checking her watch. "Time to get food."

The grocery store was small but well-stocked. They loaded a cart with fresh produce, bread, cheese, and wine.

"Frozen pizza for Dougal." Carol added several boxes to the cart. "And beer. We've all earned it."

"We have." Lokan selected a bottle of whiskey that was basic but would do.

They were heading for check-out when Carol suddenly stopped, her hand tightening on his arm. "Lokan."

He followed her gaze to the newspaper rack. The headlines were in Finnish, but the photos were unmistakable—their faces, clearly taken from some identification database, stared back at them.

"International business couple missing," Carol translated with the help of her phone. "Feared kidnapped."

"Well," Lokan said, "that's not ideal."

"You think?" She pulled him away from the papers. "We need to go. Now."

They weren't famous or important enough to appear in a Finnish newspaper, so it was obviously Gorchenco's doing. He must have bribed the editor to run the story so that they would be easier to locate.

They checked out quickly, the teenage cashier barely glancing at them as she scanned their items. Still, Lokan felt exposed, watched, even though logic told him no one here would connect them to the newspaper photos of a cosmopolitan-looking couple.

Loading the car felt like it took forever, every passing stranger a potential threat. Only when they were back on the forest road did Carol relax.

"I'm so glad that I changed my hair color." She cast him a sidelong glance. "You shouldn't have shaved."

He lifted his hand to rub his jaw. "Yeah, I shouldn't have. Too late, though."

"We look nothing like the business executives in those photos." He gestured at their casual clothes. "Someone would need to pay close attention to recognize us from those."

They drove in tense silence for a few minutes before Carol spoke again. "You know what the funny thing is?"

"What's that?"

"Six months ago, seeing our faces in a newspaper would have been good for business. Now it's a disaster."

"Our definition of success has changed," he agreed.

"For the better, though." She squeezed his hand. "We are finally going home."

They pulled up to the safe house as the sun was setting. Grant met them at the door.

"Any problems?" he asked.

"Define problems." Carol handed him grocery bags.

Lokan showed him a photo of the newspaper on his phone, and Grant's expression darkened. "That's not good."

"Every intelligence service in the world will be looking for us," Lokan said.

"The good news is we brought pizza," Carol offered. "And beer."

Dougal appeared as if summoned by magic. "Did someone say pizza?"

"And beer," Camden added, joining them. "Blessed be the providers."

"I'll let Onegus and Turner know," Grant said, pulling out his phone.

Later, dressed in new clothes that fit, fed and warm, Lokan stepped out on the cabin's front porch with Carol. She'd wrapped herself in a blanket, steam rising from her teacup.

"Look," she whispered, pointing up.

The Northern Lights were dancing across the sky in ribbons of green and gold, nature's light show unfolding above the silent forest.

"It's beautiful." He pulled her closer.

"Think we can do normal after all we've been through?" Carol asked softly.

"Probably not," Lokan admitted. "We'll have to find ways to amuse ourselves, or we'll suffer from withdrawal symptoms. Those Perfect Match adventures might provide some much-needed adrenaline boosts from time to time."

Carol laughed. "I don't think they have anything as crazy as what we've been through lately."

"Probably not."

31

KALUGAL

The breakfast table groaned under the weight of excess food. Fresh pita bread, multiple varieties of cheese, olives, honey, jam, boiled eggs, ful medames, and enough other dishes to feed twice their number.

"Everything is so good." Jasmine helped herself to the fava beans. "Are we going to have fresh food on the flight or the same frozen meals as on the way here?"

Kalugal stifled the urge to roll his eyes. He was providing them with luxury transportation, and they were complaining about the service?

"Not the same, but still frozen. I have it delivered by a company that provides the same service to other small airlines. Perhaps I should bring Atzil with me the next time and have him prepare everything fresh on board."

Jasmine caught the sarcastic tone in his voice and lifted a placating hand. "I'm not complaining. The ready-made meals were fantastic. It's just that this is better, and I'm going to miss the variety."

"We can always replicate it back home." Kalugal poured coffee for Jacki. "I'll suggest it to Atzil. He's familiar with most of these dishes."

"Are you going to invite us?" Ell-rom asked.

Kalugal flashed him a smile. "Of course, my dear uncle."

There was no harm in reminding the prince of their familial connection. Everyone tended to forget that Annani and Areana were half-sisters, and that Kalugal's father was the grandson of Ekin, Ahn's half-brother. Essentially, they had the same blood running in their veins, mixed in with other enhancements.

He still didn't know what power Ell-rom was hiding under his stoic façade, but it had to be something major for Kian to keep it such a secret. Normally, Kalugal had no problem discovering everything Kian tried to keep from him, but this time, the security and secrecy around Ell-rom's abilities were tight.

When Joseph walked in from the kitchen carrying a fresh pot of coffee, Kalugal knew he wasn't there just to refill their cups, but he played along, lifting his empty one.

"Is Hamid here yet?" he asked.

"Yes, sir." Joseph poured the fragrant brew. "Should I show him into your study?"

Kalugal frowned at Joseph, who should have known better. "I don't allow anyone in my study while I'm not there. Keep him entertained until I'm done with breakfast."

Joseph swallowed. "Yes, sir. I will invite him to wait in my office."

"Excellent. I'll see him after breakfast."

The poor man looked like he had barely slept, and his brain was not operating on all cylinders. He'd probably been up late preparing detailed notes about the house's operations for his replacement. It seemed like Joseph was under the illusion that he was leaving with them later today.

Kalugal needed to have a talk with him and explain that he had to stay for a few weeks to train Hamid. Notes were great, but they couldn't replace in-person training.

"This is incredible," Kyra said, spreading soft white cheese on her bread. "What is it?"

"Domiati," Jacki said. "It's made from buffalo milk."

As the talk around the table continued about local delicacies, Kalugal rose to his feet. "If you'll excuse me, I have business to attend to."

"Hamid's interview?" Jacki asked.

"Among other things." He bent to kiss her cheek. "It shouldn't take long."

On his way to the study, Kalugal sent a text to Joseph to bring Hamid there.

Ahmed's son looked a lot like his father and carried himself with a similar, former military manner. "Thank you for seeing me, sir." He bowed.

"Sit, please." Kalugal motioned at the two chairs in front of his desk as he took his place behind it. "Your father has been working for me for many years, and Joseph speaks highly of you."

"He is too kind, sir."

Kalugal chuckled. "Joseph is many things, but overly kind isn't one of them. He says you are trustworthy, which is top priority for me, and that you have a good head for logistics."

Hamid shifted in the chair. "I'm looking forward to proving my worth."

Kalugal smiled. "The pay is generous, but the hours are demanding while I'm in residence. If you have a family, you won't be seeing much of them during those times. When I'm not here, though, there is very little to do, and you will need to be here only a couple of hours a day."

"I understand, sir. I was hoping to make my residence here."

Kalugal tilted his head. "What about your family?"

"I don't have one yet. I hope to save up before getting married."

"Smart man." He turned to Joseph. "Do we have any staff rooms available?"

Joseph seemed taken aback by the question. "I thought Hamid would be taking over my room."

"When his training is complete, sure, but you will still need your room until he is ready to take over." Kalugal shifted his gaze to Hamid, and after a quick peek into his mind, offered him his hand. "Welcome aboard, Hamid. You can start tomorrow."

The peek into the young man's head was just one more layer of precaution. Hamid was Ahmed's son, and Kalugal trusted Ahmed. The man had worked for him for many years, was well-paid, and had proven himself many times over. The son wouldn't risk his father's position.

"Thank you, sir." The guy shook Kalugal's hand.

Joseph waited until Hamid left with repeated thanks, before asking the question that was burning in his eyes. "I thought I was leaving today for America. I'm all packed."

Kalugal cast him an apologetic smile. "I'm sorry for not making myself clear. I need you to stay for at least a month to train Hamid. Your job might seem easy and simple to you now, but it is anything but. I can't entrust my household to an inexperienced man who's unfamiliar with its rhythm. He needs to shadow you for a few days until he gets the hang of it, and then you need to look over his shoulder while he tries to step into your shoes."

Joseph's face fell, the excitement dimming like a flame deprived of oxygen. "Are you sure that a month is needed, sir? I can probably teach Hamid everything in one week."

Kalugal leaned back in his chair. "Patience, my dear Joseph. Good things come to those who wait. Let's see first if Hamid is the right man for the job. When I return, I will evaluate his performance, and if I find it satisfactory, you'll fly back with me then."

"I... yes, sir. Of course." Joseph squared his shoulders. "That's a very sensible approach. I apologize for misunderstanding."

Kalugal felt like he'd kicked a puppy. "Don't view this as a negative reflection on my faith in you. The opposite is true. It's because I trust you that I want you to train your replacement so he can do just as good of a job."

"Thank you, sir. I understand completely, sir." Joseph managed a smile. "Shall I begin preparing a training schedule for Hamid?"

"That would be excellent, yes."

32

DIN

The private section of Cairo International Airport was a world away from the chaos of the main terminals. Din stood on the tarmac, watching as the ground crew prepared Kalugal's jet for departure. The morning sun was already fierce, promising another scorching day, but he barely noticed the heat. His attention was fixed on Esag and his companions as they carefully unloaded wooden crates that contained a treasure trove of figurines from the van.

"No, no," Esag said when one of the ground crew reached for a crate. "We'll handle these ourselves." Or something to that effect. Din understood more from the tone and hand gestures than from the language itself.

Davuh and Roven flanked their friend, each carrying a wooden crate with the reverence usually reserved for religious artifacts. Which, Din supposed, they were in a way. Five thousand years of memories were carved in stone, preserving the faces of a lost civilization of gods and immortals.

One of the two pilots walked over to the redhead. "We need to ensure proper weight distribution in the cargo hold. It's critical for flight safety. If cargo shifts during flight, it can affect the aircraft's center of gravity. In extreme cases, it could cause the aircraft to crash."

Din felt his stomach tighten at the implications. The more he learned about aviation, the less he trusted it. Statistics be damned—he'd experienced firsthand how easily things could go wrong.

"Show us where you want them and we'll help you secure them properly." Roven's tone brooked no argument.

The pilot nodded, recognizing a battle he had no chance of winning.

As the pilot and Esag's group got busy securing crates in the plane's cargo hold, Din remembered the packages he still had in the van. His lamp was too large and awkward for the cabin, so it would have to go in the cargo space as well, but the rest of his purchases could go into the overhead compartments.

As he retrieved it, he tried to fix the paper wrapping around the brass tentacles that was becoming undone. Well, they weren't really tentacles so much as artistically shaped arms, but that was what Fenella called them, and it had stuck.

"I can't believe you are taking this with you," Max said. "I'm sure you can find better stuff in L.A. It's not an antique, right?"

"It's not, but it has character," Din defended, though he was starting to question the purchase himself. Unlike all the mass-produced stuff from China, this was one of a kind.

"I'll take your word for it," Max said.

They joined the others at the cargo hold, where the pilots were demonstrating the proper securing technique to Esag's group. Specialized compartments with padding and adjustable straps would keep the crates immobile during flight.

Din handed over his lamp to one of the pilots. "I hope you have room for this."

"We'll find room," the guy said.

As he watched them secure it in one of the compartments, his mind churned with all the things that could go wrong. Shifted cargo affecting the plane's balance. Turbulence severe enough to break even these restraints. Mechanical failures, bird strikes, human error...

"Stop it." Fenella slipped her hand into his.

He glanced down at her. "Stop what?"

"Calculating all the ways we could die." She squeezed his fingers. "I know the face you make when you do that. Your jaw gets tight, and you get this little crease between your eyebrows."

"I'm not—" He stopped, realizing she was right. "Yeah, I do. I just can't help it. Ever since the water landing, I find it difficult to trust these flying death traps."

"I understand." Her eyes got clouded. "Once trust is lost, it is nearly impossible to recover."

Din felt shamed by her quiet admission. Compared to what she'd gone through, his brush with death was nothing.

With Fenella's exuberance and zest for life, it was easy to forget the nightmare she'd lived through. There were the occasional nightmares, but other than that, she never talked about it, and he didn't ask because he figured she'd tell him when she was ready.

He squeezed her hand. "You are much braver than I am."

Once everything was loaded and secured, the cargo hold was closed and locked, the ground crew moved on to final pre-flight preparations, and the passengers of Kalugal's luxury airline headed toward the stairs.

As Kalugal's men took everyone's carry-on luggage and packages to put in the cabin, Din contemplated never boarding another plane again, but given that his mother was in Scotland, and she still hadn't met Fenella, that wasn't an option. Besides, he had to take care of things at the university, and not everything could be done remotely.

"Are you still calculating?" Fenella asked as they paused at the foot of the stairs, letting Jacki navigate them first with Darius in her arms.

"Now I'm thinking about sea voyages. How do you feel about ships?"

"I've never been on a cruise, if that's what you're asking. Are you planning our honeymoon?"

Was that a hint? Should he be planning their honeymoon already?

"I hate flying," he admitted. "If I could, I'd never

leave the ground again. But I promised to take you to Scotland to meet my mother and visit all the places you grew up in." He gestured vaguely westward. "A ship is an option. Slower, but safer."

Fenella laughed. "A sea voyage from Los Angeles to Scotland? That would take weeks! Even months. They would have to go through the Panama Canal, or around South America, then across the Atlantic..." She shook her head. "That's assuming we could even find a passenger ship doing that route."

She was right, but the idea of weeks at sea seemed preferable to hours in the air. "Ships don't fall from the sky."

"No, they just sink," she pointed out. "Or catch fire. Or get hijacked by pirates."

"Modern piracy is actually quite rare—"

"Din." She stepped closer, placing both hands on his chest. "Life is scary. Bad things happen. But we can't avoid everything that's unsafe. That's not living—that's just existing, paralyzed by fear."

He covered her hands with his. "As I said, you are much braver than I am."

"I'm not," she said. "I'm a survivor. When shit happens and you manage to get out alive, it's a cause for celebration, for thanking Fate by embracing life instead of letting fear and despair bury you. That being said, I'm not looking for danger. I wouldn't have kept running for half a century and getting in trouble if I knew of a place like the village where I could be safe. I would have gladly stayed there."

"Not true. Until not too long ago, you were plotting

ways to escape the village. You felt trapped, and you wanted your freedom back."

A smirk lifted one side of her mouth. "Busted. I was just so used to roving that staying put in one place became difficult. It felt unsafe. Letting people in and planning a future terrified me."

"But it no longer does, right?"

She pouted. "It still does a little, but I know it's going to be okay because you are with me."

"I love you." He wrapped his arms around her and pulled her to him, pressing a kiss to her mouth.

"Move along, lovebirds!" Max called from the top of the stairs. "You're the last ones."

Fenella made a hand gesture toward Max that spoke louder than words, and kissed Din back. When she was done, she turned to Max with a triumphant smile on her face and only then led Din up the stairs.

The cabin was already filled with their companions.

It was a little more crowded on the way back than it had been on the way here, but there were enough seats for everyone.

"Ladies and gentlemen," the pilot's voice came over the intercom. "We're expecting a smooth flight to Los Angeles today, with a brief refueling stop in Paris. Flight time will be approximately eighteen hours. Please ensure your seatbelts are fastened for takeoff."

Eighteen hours, with two takeoffs and two landings. Din settled back in his seat and closed his eyes.

"Stop it." Fenella put her hand over his.

"I'm not doing anything."

"You're catastrophizing." She interlaced their fingers. "Tell me about your castle in Scotland."

It was a transparent distraction technique, but he let her get away with it. "There's a loch near the castle, surrounded by pines. In the early morning, mist rises from the water like something out of a legend. Sometimes red deer come to drink at the shore."

"That sounds lovely."

"I used to fish there, though my friends and I rarely caught anything. I think we were too loud, scaring everything away. Or maybe the fish just sensed us."

The engines roared to life, and Din's grip on Fenella's hand tightened involuntarily. She squeezed back, continuing to ask questions about the clan's home in Scotland as the plane began to taxi.

He continued, "In winter, the whole landscape transforms into something from a fairy tale. Though fairy tales in our homeland tend to involve more murders and fewer happy endings than the Disney versions."

She laughed. "Naturally. Can't have too much happiness in Scottish folklore."

The plane turned onto the runway, engines spinning up to full power.

He focused on Fenella's profile, the way the morning light caught the subtle highlights in her dark hair.

"Another adventure ending," she murmured as the plane began its acceleration. "And a new one beginning."

"Oh?"

She turned to face him, her eyes soft with emotion. "This one is more important than all the others. Our life together. Building a home, creating new memories, and figuring out how to be us without constant danger nipping at our heels."

Lately, the only danger that had nipped at Din's heels had been overeager students and overly competitive professors, but he chose not to point it out.

"I like the sound of that, though knowing you, you'll find trouble even in the clan's serene village."

"Probably," she agreed. "But at least I'll have your ugly lamp to defend myself with. One look at those brass tentacles and any unwanted guests will flee in horror."

He smiled at her attempt at humor. "It's not that bad."

"Din, it's an octopus. Made of brass. With eyes that seem to follow you around the room."

"It's not an actual octopus, and those are decorative gemstones, not eyes."

"Creepy gemstones," she corrected.

"Are they really arguing about that kitschy lamp again?" Max's voice carried clearly from somewhere behind them.

"It's not kitschy!" Din protested, twisting to look back. "It's—"

"Unique?" Kyra suggested sweetly. "Distinctive? A conversation piece?"

"An abomination," Jasmine added her opinion. "Though I'm sure it will look lovely in your home."

"It'll look perfect," Fenella said loyally, then spoiled it by adding in an undertone, "in the garage."

Din turned back to her with mock outrage. "The garage? The homes in the village don't have garages. Everyone parks in the underground structure."

"Oh, yeah. I forgot. A closet, then. Somewhere that guests won't accidentally see it and run away screaming."

Instead of answering, he responded with a kiss, ignoring the immediate chorus of whistles and catcalls from their companions.

"Children, please." Kalugal's voice rose above the silliness. "You are upsetting Darius."

"Sorry," Fenella called back, but she was still smiling.

The plane reached cruising altitude, and outside the windows, the desert gave way to the Mediterranean, a sheet of blue stretching to the horizon.

Fenella rested her head on his arm. "Maybe we should keep the lamp in the bedroom."

He raised an eyebrow. "Really? Suddenly it's no longer scary?"

"It is, which is why it could be an effective deterrent to intruders."

There were no intruders in the village, but he could understand Fenella's need to have something to defend herself with.

"So, it's a security measure?"

"Exactly."

"You're mocking my lamp again."

"I'm finding creative uses for it," she corrected. "There's a difference."

He couldn't argue with that logic, mainly because he was too busy being grateful. Grateful they'd found each other and gotten a chance at a future neither of them had dared hope for.

"I love you," he said quietly.

"I love you too," she replied, then added with a mischievous grin, "ugly lamp and all."

"It's not ugly, it's—"

"If you say 'artistic,' I'm moving to a different seat," she warned.

"I was going to say 'misunderstood and unap-preciated.'"

AREZOO

rezoo checked her reflection in the hallway mirror one more time, smoothing down the soft blue blouse she'd chosen after trying on almost every outfit in her wardrobe. She'd even let Laleh help with her makeup.

Now, waiting by the front door, she could hear her mother moving around in the kitchen, working on the feast she and her aunts were preparing for the celebration tomorrow. Kyra and Jasmine, along with Fenella, had found Esag and two other ancient immortals who had survived the destruction of their kind over five thousand years ago.

The entire village was going to welcome them, and Arezoo was planning to cheer loudly and give them the same warm welcome she and her family had received.

Speaking of welcomes, perhaps it would be better if Ruvon didn't come inside. Arezoo loved her mother dearly, but she wasn't an easy woman to get along with, and Ruvon was far too timid to withstand Soraya's intense scrutiny.

A small voice in the back of Arezoo's head whispered that he wasn't as timid as he appeared.

Ruvon only looked young and insecure, but he was much older than her mother and used to be a warrior in a brutal army. The problem was that Arezoo tried very hard to forget both facts. She much preferred the illusion of a shy, sensitive young man who hung on her every word and looked at her as if she were the morning and the evening star.

She was very good at compartmentalizing and allowing only safe topics in her conscious mind. Everything else, and there was a lot of it, had been shoved into inaccessible compartments that only existed in her subconscious and regrettably surfaced when she slept. It was rare that she managed a night without nightmares, without waking up gasping, her heart pounding, and covered in sweat.

Shaking her head, she dispelled the dark thoughts and decided to wait for Ruvon outside.

"I'm going out," she called to her mother.

"Enjoy your evening," her mother called back. "And don't stay out too late."

"I won't." Arezoo opened the front door and stepped out.

Her mother knew she was meeting Ruvon, and they were having a picnic at the lookout point, and surprisingly, she hadn't objected.

It was certainly unexpected progress. First the bar, and now this.

Maybe her mother was finally starting to see her as an adult.

A few moments later, Ruvon appeared from behind the bend, carrying a large woven basket in one hand and what looked like a folded blanket tucked under his other arm. He wore dark jeans and a soft gray Henley that fit him perfectly, both new. Arezoo had seen him enough times by now to recognize every item in his wardrobe, and it was clear that he'd gone shopping recently and gotten himself a few stylish outfits.

Was he trying to look nice for her?

The setting sun highlighted his newly styled hair, and when he looked up and saw her watching him, his whole face lit up with that smile that transformed him from plain to handsome.

"Hi," she said, suddenly feeling shy despite all the time they had spent together over the past weeks.

"Hi." His smile widened. "You look beautiful."

"Thank you." Her hand rose instinctively to her freshly styled hair. Laleh had curled it, and it was cascading in soft waves around her shoulders instead of being gathered in a braid as usual. "You look nice too."

"Thank you." He glanced down at his new clothing.

"Did you prepare all this?" She gestured at the basket.

"I wish I could say yes, but that would be a lie." He transferred the blanket to drape over the basket and offered her his arm.

After a moment's hesitation, Arezoo threaded hers

through it and was surprised to find the contact feeling natural, comfortable.

"Atzil prepared the food," Ruvon said. "My contribution was selecting the wine and the chocolate-covered strawberries for dessert."

"That sounds perfect," she said. "I love chocolate-covered anything."

He chuckled. "That's what Ingrid said."

"The designer?"

He nodded. "She's Atzil's partner, so she often stops by Kalugal's house when Atzil serves lunch or dinner for the men. When she heard about the picnic, she suggested the strawberries. And the wine."

Arezoo was starting to realize that the picnic had turned into a much bigger production than it was supposed to be.

"How many people know about our picnic?" she asked.

He looked embarrassed. "A few. At first, I was trying to get someone to give up his reservation at Callie's, so eventually all of my friends knew that I wanted to take you out on a date. No one had reservations for the coming days, and they kept asking if I had found anyone to trade with, so I had to tell them about the change of plans."

Arezoo let out a breath.

It wasn't a big deal, and most people had already seen them sitting together at the café, so their friendship wasn't a secret, and people had probably figured out that it would eventually turn into something more.

"Does it bother you?" he asked.

"No. We have nothing to hide."

"I'm glad."

They walked in silence for a few moments, following the path that wound through the village toward the lookout point. The evening was warm, with a gentle breeze carrying the scent of jasmine and other flowers from the gardens they passed.

"I hope no one else is there," Ruvon said as they navigated around a cluster of decorative boulders. "There aren't really any other private spots in the village suitable for a picnic."

"We could always have our picnic in the backyard of one of the unoccupied houses," Arezoo suggested, only half-joking. "No one would bother us there."

He glanced at her in surprise. "That's actually not a bad idea. Though it might be considered trespassing."

"In a village where everyone knows everyone? I doubt anyone would mind." She was warming to the idea. "But let's check the lookout first. I hope luck is on our side."

When they rounded the last bend in the path and found the lookout point empty, just as they'd hoped, Arezoo released a breath. The small lawn area with its single bench and sprawling oak tree commanded a spectacular view of the Malibu Mountains, with the ocean visible in the distance.

"Perfect," Ruvon murmured, and she wasn't sure if he meant the view or their privacy.

They spread the blanket under the oak tree, positioning it to take advantage of the view. Arezoo settled onto it, while Ruvon began unpacking the basket.

345

"Atzil has prepared enough food for an entire family," Arezoo said as container after container emerged. There was fresh bread, several types of cheese, olives, stuffed grape leaves, sliced fruit, miniature quiches, and all kinds of pickled vegetables.

"He said something about 'young love requiring proper fuel,'" Ruvon said, then immediately looked stricken. "I mean, not that he meant—"

"It's okay," Arezoo said. "Obviously, he would think that. It's a date after all, right?"

Ruvon nodded, looking relieved. "Yes. Our first official date." He pulled out a wine bottle and two glasses. "Which calls for a toast."

She smiled. "It does."

He fumbled with the corkscrew for a moment before managing to open the bottle. The wine was white, crisp, and cold, and Arezoo took a grateful sip as soon as he handed her the glass.

"To our first date." Ruvon raised his own. "May it be the first of many."

She clinked her glass against his. "To many more," she said with less enthusiasm than he had, not because she didn't want there to be more but because she was not an optimistic person.

Who knew what tomorrow held?

They began filling their plates, and as Ruvon piled olives on his, she couldn't contain her curiosity any longer.

"Can I ask you something?"

He looked up, wariness flashing across his features. "Of course."

"Your fashion transformation," she gestured at him, encompassing the clothes, the hair, the newfound confidence that seemed to radiate from him. "How did that happen and why?"

He glanced down at himself with a self-deprecating laugh. "It's Ingrid's doing."

"Ingrid? Why?" Arezoo asked.

He set down his plate and took a sip of wine before answering. "She said that I needed to elevate my appearance. I didn't even know that there was anything wrong with it, but she pointed out the ill-fitting clothing that had seen better days, the simple haircut that did nothing for my face, and my terrible posture. She offered to help me change all that, and I gratefully accepted her help."

"Good for you." Arezoo tucked a strand of hair behind her ear. "My sister Laleh did the same for me. She did my hair and makeup and helped me select the outfit."

He chuckled. "I'm glad that I wasn't the only one who needed help to prepare for courtship."

"Courtship?" Arezoo repeated.

"I'm sorry, that's such an old-fashioned word. I didn't mean to presume—"

"Ruvon." She waited until he looked at her. "It's okay. I'm fine with you courting me."

When his eyes widened with hope, she held up a hand.

"As long as you understand that I'm not like other girls you might have dated. I grew up very sheltered, and then..." She took a deep breath, forcing herself to

347

say the words she'd kept locked inside for so long. "I was also kidnapped and abused, and I'm still recovering from that trauma. I'm not ready for anything other than talking."

The confession hung between them in the evening air. It was the first time Arezoo had given voice to what had happened to her, acknowledging it outside of her own head. She didn't talk about the kidnapping, about what had been done to her and her sisters, and cousin. It was easier to forget, to move on, to pretend it was just a nightmare that had ended.

But that was hard to do when she still woke up gasping from dreams where she was back in that place, drugged and helpless. The memories were hazy, mercifully dulled by whatever they'd given her, but they were there, buried in her subconscious mind and emerging when her defenses were down.

"Arezoo," Ruvon said softly, and she realized that her hands were trembling. He reached out as if to take them, then stopped.

"I have no expectations," he said, his voice fierce with sincerity. "You're completely in charge here. You make the rules. I'm just grateful you're giving me a chance to spend time with you."

The statement stunned her. Where she came from, women had no power, no agency. Men made the decisions and set the rules. And Ruvon wasn't a product of the Western world, where women's rights were at least acknowledged, even if not always respected. He came from the same oppressive background she did, maybe worse.

Yet here he was, handing her all the power, and it was like a weight she didn't know she'd been carrying suddenly lifted from her shoulders.

"You really mean that," she said, and it wasn't a question.

"I do." He reached for her hand and squeezed it gently. "I know what it's like to have your choices taken away, to be trapped in a situation where you have no control. It has been a long time since I was in that situation, so I've had time to recover. You are still healing."

That was such a deep level of understanding, so unexpected, that it hit her like a kick to the gut.

When a tear slipped down her cheek before she could stop it, she pulled her hand free to wipe it away, embarrassed.

"I'm sorry, I didn't mean to—"

"Don't apologize," he said. "Not for this. Not to me."

She looked at him then and saw what had been in front of her the entire time but hadn't fully registered. Ruvon had escaped from the Brotherhood, from the same organization that had harbored her abuser, and it occurred to her that he had been abused as well. He'd risked everything to get away, to find freedom and a new life. He was like her—a survivor who'd clawed his way out of darkness.

She was still clawing.

That was why he understood, why he could offer her control without making it seem like a gift or a favor, but simply the natural order of things.

"We should eat," she said finally, taking a deep breath. "Atzil's feast shouldn't go to waste."

They returned to their plates, the atmosphere lighter somehow, as if her confession had cleared the air between them. The food was incredible—each bite perfectly seasoned and prepared with obvious care.

"This hummus is amazing." Arezoo spread more on a piece of bread. "I've tried to make it myself, but it never turns out this smooth."

"The secret is probably some impossible technique that takes years to master," Ruvon said. "Like removing each chickpea skin individually while chanting ancient culinary spells."

She laughed, nearly choking on her bread. "Ancient culinary spells?"

"Oh, yes. Atzil might hide a grimoire of secret recipes somewhere."

She hadn't known Ruvon had such a sense of humor. Perhaps their mutual confessions had liberated him as well.

"Protected by supernatural forces that strike down anyone who tries to steal them?"

"Exactly. Lightning bolts for anyone who dares attempt his special tahini blend."

They continued in this vein, creating increasingly absurd theories about Atzil's cooking secrets. The wine helped, loosening Arezoo's usual reserve and making everything seem funnier than it probably was. She felt light, almost floating, but in a good way—not the terrifying disconnection she'd experienced during her captivity, but a pleasant warmth that made her feel bold.

When they'd eaten their fill of the main courses, Arezoo pulled out the poetry book from her bag.

The leather cover was soft under her fingers, familiar and comforting.

"What shall I read tonight?" she asked, flipping through the pages.

"Whatever speaks to you." Ruvon leaned back on his hands.

She let the book fall open naturally, and her breath caught. It was a love poem, one she'd read alone in her room but had never dared to read aloud. The words seemed to pulse on the page, daring her.

"This one," she said, her voice barely above a whisper.

She began to read, the ancient words flowing like honey from her lips. The poem spoke of longing, of two souls reaching across impossible distances, of love that defied logic and circumstance. As she read, she became hyperaware of Ruvon's presence—the way he leaned slightly toward her, the way his breathing had deepened, the way his eyes never left her face.

When she reached the verse about a first kiss beneath the stars, her voice faltered. The air between them had become charged, electric with possibility. She looked up from the page to find Ruvon staring at her lips, his expression soft with wonder and want.

Something inside her shifted, a door opening that she'd thought was locked forever. Without letting herself think, without letting fear intrude, she leaned forward and pressed her lips gently to his.

It was barely a kiss, just the briefest contact, soft as

butterfly wings, and then she pulled back. But it was enough to send her heart racing, enough to make her feel like she'd stepped off a cliff into free fall.

Ruvon sat frozen, his eyes wide with shock. He didn't move, didn't breathe, just stared at her as if she'd cast a spell over him.

A giggle bubbled up from her chest, breaking the spell. "You look like you've been struck by lightning."

He blinked, coming back to himself. "I was. Did you just kiss me?"

"Yes." She was surprised by how steady her voice sounded, when inside she was anything but.

"Why?" The question came out as barely more than a breath.

She considered how to answer, then decided on simple honesty. "You have nice lips." She felt heat flood her cheeks. "I've never kissed anyone before. I wanted to know what it was like."

If possible, his eyes got even wider. "This was your first kiss?"

She nodded, suddenly shy again. "Was it... Okay?"

"Okay?" He laughed, but it was shaky, overwhelmed. "Arezoo, that was... I don't have words. A gift. Thank you."

"It was just a little kiss."

"You trusted me enough to choose me to be your first." He paused. "That's a precious gift," he added softly.

She noticed he made no move to kiss her back, to push for more, and her heart swelled with gratitude.

"I think it's time for those chocolate strawberries,"

she said, needing to lighten the moment before she did something really crazy like kiss him again.

"Right. Yes. Strawberries." He fumbled for the container, looking as shaken as she still felt.

The strawberries were perfect—ripe and sweet beneath a layer of dark chocolate. They drank more wine and read more poems, but the atmosphere had shifted. Every glance felt weighted, every accidental touch electric.

As the sun sank lower, painting the sky in shades of pink and purple, Arezoo realized something had fundamentally changed not just between them, but inside her.

Tonight, she had taken back a piece of herself she'd thought was lost forever. She'd chosen to kiss a man— this sweet, patient, understanding man who gave her all the power and asked for only her friendship in return.

KIAN

The early morning sun was strong enough in the summer to necessitate protective eyewear, and as Kian stepped out of the bus behind Syssi, he put on his sunglasses.

According to the latest updates, the planes would be arriving within minutes of each other—Kalugal's jet from Cairo along with his entourage and the clan's jet from Toronto carrying Lokan, Carol, and the three Guardians. Turner's associate had collected them from Finland and dropped them off in Canada, where Eric had collected them with the clan's jet and flown them home.

Syssi slipped her hand into his. "I'm so excited, but that's nothing compared to what Wonder must be feeling." He nodded, glancing to where the tall brunette stood with Anandur, their hands clasped, fingers interlaced.

Hopefully, Esag's appearance wouldn't cause a rift

between them. They were truelove mates, and there was no way Wonder had any feelings other than friendship left for Esag, but Kian didn't envy Anandur's position. If Syssi's former boyfriend suddenly appeared in her life, Kian wouldn't have been happy. But that was a small worry compared to the stress of the past few days. Lokan and Carol had been hunted across multiple countries, with enhanced Doomers on their trail, a snitch in Turner's network, and then fucking Gorchenco coming back from the dead and making things even more difficult for them.

He should have had the guy killed when he had the chance. He more than deserved it for what he had done to Ella.

Thankfully it all ended well, and Lokan and Carol, along with the three Guardians he'd sent to help them, were on their way home. The cherry on top, though, was the discovery of Esag and his companions.

It seemed like the Fates took pity on him sometimes and delivered occasional doses of good news to keep him going.

"It's a miracle that after five thousand years, we've found more survivors."

"The Fates work in mysterious ways," Syssi murmured.

"Indeed."

Kian watched Wonder smoothing her hands over her jeans, checking her hair, adjusting her collar. Anandur stood beside her, a mountain of barely contained tension.

"How are you holding up?" Anandur asked her.

Wonder's laugh was shaky. "I survived five thousand years in stasis and rebuilt my entire life. Yet the thought of seeing Esag again makes me nervous like that uncertain girl I used to be."

"You're not Gulan anymore," Anandur said. "You are Wonder now. Strong, confident, mated to a devastatingly handsome Guardian." He pretended to flip his hair back, which was ridiculous since his red curls were cropped short.

That earned him a small smile. "Devastatingly handsome?"

"I calls it like I sees it," he said and struck a pose, which made her laugh.

Brundar actually cracked what might have been a smile. His brother's antics had that effect occasionally, or rather rarely, and even then, only when Anandur couldn't see it.

"Aircraft on approach," Okidu announced cheerfully from his position by the bus door.

No one argued with his superior hearing.

They all turned to watch the sky, and soon Kian could make out the distinct shape of Kalugal's sleek jet approaching from the east and behind it, the clan's smaller plane.

"Both at once," Syssi said. "The Fates have a sense of drama."

The larger jet landed first and taxied to the hangar, where Kalugal's ground crew was waiting while the smaller one circled overhead.

When the runway was clear, the smaller jet aligned for approach and landed a few minutes later.

Kian waited patiently for the doors of both jets to open and for the passengers to spill out.

First to disembark were Lokan and Carol, and Kian started toward them when Kalugal's voice boomed across the tarmac. "Lokan!"

He practically sprinted toward his brother, the two meeting halfway in an embrace that brought a smile to Kian's face.

Carol hung back with the Guardians for a moment, letting the brothers have their reunion, before Kalugal pulled her into the hug as well.

"You finally made it," Kalugal said. "With enhanced Doomers and the Russian mafia on your heels."

"It was an adventure." Carol patted her curls, which were brown now instead of blond. "One I'd prefer never to repeat. And we couldn't have made it without these three." She motioned to the Guardians and then shifted her gaze to Kian. "Thank you for sending them to us."

As the reunion continued, Kian's attention was drawn to movement from Kalugal's plane. A figure emerged at the doorway, and even from a distance, there was no mistaking his flame-red hair.

Wonder made a sound—half gasp, half sob—and started forward. Anandur moved to follow, then stopped himself, fists clenched at his sides.

Esag froze at the top of the stairs, his eyes finding Wonder immediately despite the distance and the crowd and the five thousand years since they had last seen each other.

Wonder's long legs ate up the distance, and Esag met her halfway, the two colliding in an embrace that spoke of tremendous shared loss and the miracle of unexpected reunion.

"I thought you were dead," Esag's voice carried despite being muffled against Wonder's shoulder.

"We thought the same of you." Wonder pulled back to look at his face. "Esag, you haven't changed at all. Still the same red hair, the same freckles..."

"You've changed," he said wonderingly. "You look so strong, so confident. The Gulan I knew would never have run so fast in front of strangers."

"I'm Wonder Woman now, and I don't hide what I can do from my clan members." She turned, gesturing for Anandur to come over. "Esag, I want you to meet my husband, Anandur."

Esag grinned as he extended his hand. "Aren't you a handsome fellow. It's like looking in the mirror."

"Great," Brundar murmured. "Another clown."

Kian had a feeling that Brundar was right, and that Esag and Anandur were similar, not just in appearance.

Anandur shook the offered hand. "Wonder says that a lot. The same red hair, the same questionable sense of humor."

Esag laughed. "You're clearly a male of excellent qualities."

"Modest, too," Wonder added dryly. "You are practically like twins, born four thousand years apart."

Kian stepped forward. "Welcome to the clan. I'm Kian, Annani's son, and this is my wife, Syssi."

"The princess's son." Esag's eyes shone as he took his hand. "Kalugal has told me a lot about you."

"Good things, I hope."

"The best." Esag kept staring at him. "I know you are not Khiann's son, but I swear I can see him in you."

Kian just nodded, not wanting to dive into the long explanation about his mother choosing the fathers of her children according to qualities she recognized in them that resembled those of her lost husband.

"Annani is eager to see you all," Syssi said warmly.

What she didn't mention was that Amanda was currently transforming the village green into party central, but that was meant to be a surprise.

"Princess Annani lives." Esag shook his head. "And she's the mother of an entire clan. She was always a force of nature."

Lokan and Carol had made their way over, the various groups converging into one large gathering. The introductions were somewhat chaotic, the ancient immortals meeting younger ones, old friends discovering new connections.

"We brought with us many figurines," Esag said. "Is there enough room in this bus for all the passengers and the cargo?"

"Oh, yes, Master Esag." Okidu rushed to open the storage compartments.

Esag looked like he'd seen a ghost. "Okidu? Is that really you?"

"Yes." The butler bowed. "It is I."

Without waiting a moment longer, Esag rushed to the Odu and embraced him like a long-lost family member, which in a way he was.

"You survived." Esag took a step back. "What about your brothers?"

"They are all well, Master. The Clan Mother escaped with all of us. You will see four of my brothers in the village."

"Where are the other two?"

"In the clan's other locations," Kian said. "Let's get everyone on the bus and I'll tell you about it on the way to the village."

"Of course." Esag motioned for Davuh and Roven to come with him.

What followed was a careful procession as the three retrieved crate after crate from Kalugal's plane, and the others joined in to help them, handling each one like spun glass and passing them from hand to hand in a chain that ended at the bus's storage compartment.

"How many are there?" Camden asked, hefting another crate.

"Many," Roven replied. "Five thousand years is a long time to be carving."

"Each one is a memory," Esag added softly. "A person lost forever."

The solemn moment was broken when Din emerged from the jet's cargo hull struggling with something large and ungainly wrapped in paper and blankets.

"Need help with that?" Max called out.

"I've got it," Din grunted. "It's not heavy. Just diffi-cult to carry."

For some reason, his entire group burst into laughter.

"What's that?" Grant asked as he made room for it in the bus storage compartment.

"It's a lamp," Din said defensively.

"That's being generous," Fenella said.

Even Esag was smiling. "In five thousand years, I've never seen anything quite like it."

"And you won't for another five thousand," Max predicted. "Because there can't be two of those in exis-tence. The universe wouldn't allow it."

"Everyone's a critic," Din muttered, but he was smiling too.

With the cargo taken care of, they began boarding the bus, and as Kian followed Syssi inside he glanced at where Wonder was seated together with Esag, clearly wanting to continue their reunion. Anandur sat across the aisle from them with Brundar, close enough to be present but giving them space to reconnect.

"That can't be easy for him," Syssi whispered.

"Seeing your mate reunite with her first love would test anyone," Kian whispered back.

Lokan and Carol claimed seats near the front, with Grant and the other two Guardians sitting behind them, and the Cairo contingent filling the middle section. The energy in the bus was electric—joy, relief, and anticipation all mixed together.

Kian and Syssi sat across the aisle from Lokan and Carol, and as Okidu started the engine, Kian leaned forward to look at his cousin. "Ready to settle down in the village?"

Lokan nodded, but there were shadows in his eyes.

It couldn't be easy for him. He'd been forced to leave behind everything he'd worked for and sever his contact with the island and its people.

His dream of liberating the island seemed farther away than ever.

ANNANI

Annani stood next to the floor-to-ceiling windows in Kian's office, surveying the transformation Amanda and her army of volunteers had wrought. Strings of lights crisscrossed between tree limbs and poles that had been installed just for that purpose. Tables were dressed in white cloth and stood ready for the feast, and a stage had been erected at the far end. The two banners stretched overhead made her heart swell. *Welcome Home, Carol & Lokan,* and *Welcome to the Clan Esag, Davuh & Roven.*

"The lettering is perfect," she murmured to Ogidu, who stood attentively at her side.

"Mistress Amanda bought a special printer so she could print banners on demand. It seems like there is always a need for new ones."

Annani laughed. "Indeed. I hope this printer will get a lot of work. The more newcomers, the better."

After five thousand years, more survivors had been

found. The threads of fate were weaving together in mysterious and hard-to-follow ways, but Annani trusted that the Fates had a plan and were working toward finding her Khiann and ensuring the clan's survival.

Those were her goals, though, and she had a feeling that the Fates had a much grander plan in mind, but they were not sharing it with her.

Toppling the Eternal King could be one of their goals, but he seemed too powerful even for them. Besides, if the lore was correct about the Fates and what they were allowed and not allowed to do, they were restricted to assisting in individual growth and matchmaking, but they were using their limited roles as a means to shape the destinies of entire societies, instead of just helping individuals find fulfillment.

No wonder they had to work in such roundabout ways.

Amanda entered the office. "So, what do you think? Lovely, isn't it?"

"Yes," Annani said as Amanda leaned to kiss her cheek. "You get better with every party you organize."

Amanda grinned. "I had a secret weapon this time, or rather four. Kyra's sisters are incredible. They cooked the entire feast, and they are going to serve it."

"That is wonderful. Are they being properly compensated?" Knowing Soraya, she had volunteered not only the labor but also the supplies.

"Of course." Amanda leaned a hand on her hip. "Soraya tried to argue, but she is no match for me. I told her that if she wanted to get more catering jobs in the future, she would need to issue an invoice for an amount that I deemed fair. If it came out short, I wouldn't give her any more jobs."

"You are a tough negotiator, daughter of mine."

"What can I say, they don't make them like me anymore. I broke the mold."

She was teasing, but Annani thought it was apt. Amanda was one of a kind, and since she was her last child, the mold was indeed broken.

The soothsayer had promised Annani seven children, but since she was not taking on human lovers anymore, that prophecy was not going to materialize unless Khiann was found.

"Has Ingrid finished preparing the house?" she asked to divert her thoughts elsewhere.

"A three-bedroom house is waiting for the new members of our community, and Kalugal instructed his men to make room in his storage area for Esag's stuff."

That left only one concern—finding Esag a suitable workspace. He needed to begin carving Khiann's figurine as soon as possible. Annani had hoped that Esag had prophetic dreams about Khiann like the one he had about Wonder, and she had been very disappointed to find out that his dreams did not reveal any clues as to Khiann's whereabouts. Still, her gut was telling her that they were close to finding him, but the Fates seemed to be taking a circuitous route toward that goal.

Why the delays, though?

Why bring together all these pieces unless something larger was at play?

The answer whispered at the edges of her consciousness. It was as if they were assembling an army in preparation for Khiann's arrival.

Her heart sped up as the implications crystallized. The battle between her and Mortdh's line had begun with Khiann's assassination, so it made poetic sense that it would end with his resurrection.

"Mother?" Amanda's voice pulled her from her reverie. "Are you okay?"

"Yes," she said softly. "Just thinking about patterns and purpose."

Her phone chimed with Kian's ringtone, and she pulled it from her pocket to answer. "Yes, darling?"

"We're in the underground tunnel. Is everything ready, or do I need to stall?"

"Everything is perfect. Bring them to the green."

After ending the call, she turned to Amanda. "It is time."

They made their way down the stairs and walked toward the green, which was already packed.

"Quite the turnout," Alena said, approaching with E.T. in her arms.

"It is a joyous occasion." Annani kissed her eldest daughter's cheek and then her youngest grandson's before shrouding herself and her Odus in invisibility.

As she made her way to the stage with Ogidu and Oridu flanking her, no one saw them approaching. She liked to make a dramatic entrance—not for her own ego, but to give the proper weight to the event. She climbed the steps and waited for the right moment to drop the shroud.

She saw Kian leading the group out of the pavilion and toward the green. Carol and Lokan looked tired but happy, and Carol's hair was brown instead of blond. Behind them came the Egyptian contingent, with Kalugal gesticulating wildly as he no doubt regaled everyone with tales about the artifacts they had just passed in the pavilion.

But it was the three warriors who captured her attention. Esag walked between his companions, his tall frame and flame-red hair impossible to miss. His eyes darted everywhere, taking in the crowd, the decorations, the sheer number of immortals gathered in one place.

When they were close enough to the stage, Annani dropped her shroud.

The effect was immediate. Esag, Davuh, and Roven dropped to their knees as one, heads bowed in the ancient gesture of fealty. The crowd murmured at the sight, as such formality was no longer practiced in their modern world.

"Rise, my friends," Annani said, her voice carrying clearly across the green. "We do not kneel here. We stand together as family."

Esag looked up, his eyes glowing from within. "Princess Annani... I never thought..."

"Rise," she said again, more gently. "Come up here and join me so I may properly introduce you to your new family."

Kian helped guide the overwhelmed warriors to the stage, Carol and Lokan following.

"My beloved family," Annani addressed the crowd, her voice carrying without the need for amplification. "Today, we celebrate two homecomings. First, my nephew Lokan and our brave Carol, who risked everything to keep us informed of our enemies' plans."

The crowd erupted in applause. Carol performed a perfect curtsy and smiled at her crowd of admirers, while Lokan waved like the prince he was.

Annani waited for the applause to die down before continuing. "We are also welcoming three newcomers, who have carried the flame of memory through five thousand years of solitude. Esag, who was my Khiann's best friend, has turned into a master artist and keeper of our history. Davuh and Roven, both Guardians and loyal friends. They believed they were the last of our kind, yet they persevered. They honored our memory in stone and in their hearts."

The applause was thunderous, and Annani waited for it to subside before turning to Lokan. "Would you speak?"

He stepped forward. "Carol and I are just glad to be home. Thank you for the warm welcome."

"Home," Annani repeated. "Such a simple word for such a profound gift. Esag, Davuh, Roven—this is your home now. You need never be alone again."

"Thank you." Esag bowed, and his companions followed.

"Do you want to say a few words?" Annani asked softly.

He nodded and stepped forward, clearly over-whelmed. "I... we thought everyone was gone. For five thousand years, we lived among humans as ghosts. I carved figurines to remember the faces of those we believed we'd never see again. To stand here, to see this..." His voice broke. "Our people survived thanks to you. You built a community. A family. You carried the torch that had almost been extinguished." He paused, collecting himself. "I carved figurines of the dead while you created life. You preserved not just memories but our entire culture. You gave our people a future when we thought there was only the past. Light in the dark-ness, hope against despair."

"We all did our part," Annani said. "You preserved our history in stone. I preserved it in flesh and hope."

She turned back to the crowd. "Let me introduce you to some of those who make our future possible. My daughter Amanda, who organized this beautiful celebration."

Amanda waved, smiling brightly.

"My daughter Alena, whom I call the true Clan Mother, for blessing us with fourteen children."

Laughter rippled through the crowd as Alena lifted her baby. "And perhaps more to come."

"Fates willing," Annani agreed. "We are not merely surviving. We are thriving. Each child born, each Dormant discovered, each refugee given sanctuary—they all add threads to the tapestry of our future."

She raised her arms. "Family found, hope sustained, future secured. These are not just words—they are promises we make to each other. We are all family."

She paused, letting her words sink in. "Now it is time to enjoy the feast prepared by four incredible sisters who are newcomers themselves. Soraya, Rana, Yasmin, and Parisa. Thank you."

The crowd surged forward as music began to play. Annani watched with satisfaction as clan members approached the newcomers, introducing themselves, offering welcome.

Esag stood slightly apart, still looking overwhelmed. Annani made her way to him.

"It is a lot to take in," she said.

"I keep expecting to wake up," he admitted. "To find myself back in my workshop, alone except for stone faces and these two." He smiled at his friends. "I would have gone insane without them."

"You are not dreaming, my dear Esag, but I hope you will soon dream prophetically, once you begin carving again."

He nodded. "As soon as I'm settled, I will start working on Khiann's figurine. I couldn't do it before. Every time I thought of him, I saw him...dead." He shivered. "You have given me hope, Princess Annani. I no longer feel like a huge weight is crushing my chest every waking hour."

"I know what you mean. That is how I felt until recently, when clues started to emerge that changed the narrative I believed in. Now I know Khiann is alive." She put a hand over her chest. "I feel it in here. I hope that carving his image will trigger visions of him in your dreams." She hesitated before continuing. "The Fates seem to be preparing us for something big ahead of Khiann's discovery. It seems like they are assembling the chess pieces, gathering forces."

Esag frowned. "For what?"

"This conflict began with what we believed was Khiann's murder. It seems fitting it should end with his return."

FENELLA

*C*offee mug in hand, Fenella leaned against the kitchen counter of their new house, trying not to laugh as she surveyed the corner of the living room that Din had dedicated as his reading nook.

The brass octopus lamp held pride of place beside his leather recliner, its multiple arms reaching out in all directions like a mythical sea creature suffering an emotional breakdown.

But it was the newest addition that he'd just finished hanging on the wall that really completed the aesthetic disaster.

"Scottish Terriers playing poker." She shook her head. "Where did you even find this newest monstrosity?"

"The internet, where else?" He took a step back to observe his work, and a look of smug satisfaction spread over his face. "It's whimsical, and it makes me smile every time I look at it." He turned to look at her, and his grin widened. "Just like every time I look at you."

She snorted, spluttering coffee, and wiped her mouth with the back of her hand. "Did you just compare me to this abomination?"

"It is not an abomination. It's art."

"It's what happens when art has too much whiskey and makes poor life choices."

He walked up to her and kissed her on the lips. "You love it. Admit it."

"I hate it." She was barely managing to keep a straight face.

"I saw you smiling at it."

"I was grimacing." When he made a sad puppy face, she finally conceded. "Fine, it's charming in its ridiculousness, and the most important thing is that it makes you happy."

The truth was that she felt a little guilty about him giving up his university position to live with her in the village because she was not too keen on going back to Scotland with him. He'd assured her that he wasn't doing it because of her and that it was only a sabbatical, and if she got tired of the village and wanted a change of atmosphere, they could move to Edinburgh, and he could resume his teaching. Still, he was leaving the decision up to her.

It was a sensible approach, and given her history, she probably would get tired of living in this tiny community, but right now she liked it too much to ever want to leave. After half a century of being on her own, she had safety, family, friends, and a job she loved. Why would she want to give it up?

She'd had enough adventures to last her at least a few centuries.

Din reached for her hand and led her to his recliner. "Come sit with me. See for yourself how cozy it is in my reading nook."

"I know it is." She settled against him, careful not to spill her coffee.

The electric recliner was ridiculously comfortable, she had to admit. Din had spent an absurd amount of time testing chairs before selecting this one, which was big enough for the two of them to cuddle on together.

She loved this corner of their home precisely because it was so perfectly Din—intellectual pretensions mixed with absolutely terrible taste, all wrapped up in endearing optimism and enthusiasm.

Their house was a two-bedroom Italian villa in what was considered the 'old' section of the village, though 'old' was relative when the entire village was new. It had come fully furnished, but they'd managed to make it theirs with some minor redecorating in the week since they'd moved in.

Frankly, it had looked better before the application of Din's eclectic style, but it now felt more like home.

"What are you reading?" she asked, when he reached for the book he'd left open on the side table.

"Robert Burns," he said, then added with an exaggerated Scottish accent, "Would ye like me to read ye some proper Scottish verse, lassie?"

"I don't know who he is, but as long as it is not in

Gaelic, I'm willing to listen." She settled more comfortably against his chest.

He cleared his throat dramatically. "Here's a classic — 'A Red, Red Rose.'"

He began to read. "'O my Love is like a red, red rose,'" he began properly enough, then continued, "'That's newly sprung in June, O my Love is like a melody, That's sung by a Highland coo.'"

Fenella was no expert on poetry, but that didn't sound right. "Highland coo?" She twisted to look at him. "Did Robert Burns write love poems about Highland cows?"

"Oh, aye," he said, returning to the exaggerated accent. "Burns loved a good Highland coo. Very poetic, coos."

"You're making this up."

"I would never." He continued with a straight face, "'As fair art thou, my bonnie lass, So deep in love am I, And I will love thee still, my dear, Till all the seas gang dry. And also till the coos come home at teatime no less.'"

Fenella laughed. "You're terrible."

"'Till a' the seas gang dry, my dear,'" he continued, ignoring her protests, "'And the rocks melt wi' the sun, And the Highland coos learn to dance, In kilts sized extra-large for their bums.'"

"Stop," she gasped between giggles. "You're being disrespectful to Scottish literature."

"On the contrary. I'm enhancing it, and Burns would approve. He was very fond of coos."

"He was not!"

"He was. There's an entire chapter about it in his biography. *Burns and Bovines: A Story of Deep Appreciation.*"

She swatted his chest. "There is no such book."

"There could be." He set the poetry aside and wrapped both arms around her. "Should I write it? I think I have a calling."

"Your calling is to stop desecrating our culture."

"Never." He pressed a kiss to her temple. "I just love hearing you laugh, and nothing is too sacred to be sacrificed on the altar of your happiness."

"Now, that was poetic." She put her coffee cup on the side table and cupped his cheeks. "And deserving of a proper kiss."

He dropped the poetry book, wrapped his arms around her, and kissed her deeply, pouring all of his love for her into the kiss.

"I should probably get ready for work," she said when they came up for air, though she made no move to get up.

"You have time." He gestured to the octopus lamp. "Harold doesn't think you need to leave for another twenty minutes."

"You named your lamp Harold?"

"He looks like a Harold. Very distinguished."

"That lamp is the least distinguished thing I've ever seen."

"Which is precisely why he needs a distinguished name. For balance."

She shook her head but couldn't stop smiling. "And the painting? Does it have a name too?"

"That's obviously 'Dogs Playing Poker: The Scottish Edition.' It's self-naming."

"Obviously." She rested her head against his chest. "I love our home. I just want you to know that."

"Even Harold?"

"He's growing on me."

Din laughed, the sound rumbling through his chest. "That's the nicest thing you've said about my decorating choices."

"Don't get used to it." She glanced at the clock, a nice one that she'd selected. "I really do need to get ready now."

"Five more minutes?"

"Atzil will have my head if I'm late. He's still grumpy about me taking the whole week off."

"You deserved a week off. You deserved a month off. A year, even."

"A year off would drive me crazy. I like working at the Hobbit." She finally, reluctantly, extracted herself from his lap. "What will you do while I'm gone?"

"Read actual Burns poetry. Go over paper submittal. Contemplate buying a matching painting for the other wall."

"Don't you dare."

"Scottish Terriers Playing Golf?"

"Din..."

"Highland Cows Playing Backgammon?"

"I'm leaving now." She bent to kiss him, intending it to be quick but lingering when he cupped her face.

"I'll walk you to the bar," he murmured against her lips.

"You don't have to. Harold will get lonely."

"I want to." He smiled. "Harold will survive without me for a few minutes. Besides, it will be good for him to develop some independence."

Fenella laughed as she headed to their bedroom.

As she changed into her work clothes, she caught sight of herself in the mirror. She looked settled. Happy. There were still bad nights, still moments when shadows made her heart race, but they were becoming less frequent.

She was healing.

"You are beautiful," Din said from the doorway.

"I'm just wearing my bar uniform."

"You look beautiful in your uniform." He crossed to her, turning her to face him. "Beautiful anywhere, in anything."

She wrapped her arms around his neck. "I love you."

"I love you, too." He kissed her forehead. "We should go, or Atzil really will have both of our heads."

As they stepped outside, the evening air was perfect —warm but not oppressive, with a breeze carrying the scents of various flowers from their neighbors' gardens.

They walked hand in hand toward the Hobbit, passing familiar faces, exchanging greetings. The pub came into view, its round door partially open.

"Have a grand time tonight and call me when you are ready to come home. I'll come to get you."

"I will," she promised, stretching up to kiss him goodbye.

That was the compromise they'd reached. Din

would no longer sit at the back of the bar every night she worked, but he would escort her to and from the Hobbit, even though the village was probably the safest place on the planet.

As she pushed through the door into the familiar chaos, Fenella felt that warm sense of belonging wash over her again.

"You're smiling," Atzil said as she joined him behind the bar. "Had enough rest?"

"Yes, sir. I'm more than ready to get to work." She put on her apron and tied it in the back. "And I'm not going anywhere anytime soon. I'm here to stay."

After fifty years of roving and never quite fitting anywhere, she finally had a home, with throw pillows that she'd selected herself and an ugly lamp selected by Din, a job where she was valued, and a community that had become family.

And Din, wonderful Din.

She wouldn't change a single thing.

Well, maybe the painting. The painting could go.

But even as she thought it, Fenella knew she'd never let him get rid of it. That horrible Scottish Terrier poker game was part of their story now, part of what made their house a home.

ANNANI

nnani had Ogidu prepare the living room for her young visitor, like she usually did in preparation for her grandchildren's visits. A couple of soft cushions on the floor, a low table with paper and crayons, and a selection of toys that might appeal to a child who was far older in soul than her physical years suggested.

When the doorbell chimed, Ogidu walked over to open the way for Yasmin and Cyra, and Annani rose from her chair to welcome them.

Yasmin dipped her head. "Thank you for inviting us, Clan Mother."

The child partially hid behind her mother's skirts, but her dark eyes were fixed on Annani with an intensity that belied her shy posture. There was a little wariness in that gaze, but mostly curiosity and excitement.

The girl knew by now that they were going to have fun together.

"Hello, sweet girl." Annani crouched down to Cyra's

level. "I see you brought a friend." She looked at the rabbit the child was clutching under her arm. "What is his name?"

"Mr. Ears," Cyra said proudly.

"Would Mr. Ears like some tea? I have an extra cup for him." She motioned toward the child-sized tea set. "And he can sit on the floor pillow next to you."

That earned her a smile, and Cyra stepped out from behind her mother's skirt.

"I'll return in an hour as usual, Clan Mother." Yasmin looked reluctant to leave.

"Cyra and I will have a lot of fun together," Annani said for the mother's benefit as well as the child's. "Right, sweetness?"

The girl nodded and offered her little hand to Annani.

She had gradually built trust with the girl, so she was no longer fearful to see her mother go.

Annani had not given the child the transfusion yet, even though she was older than most other girls were when they received it from her, for the simple reason that appearances needed to be maintained. It would have seemed as if Cyra's transition to immortality happened too fast.

After all, it was supposed to be a gradual process, induced by Annani's mere proximity. Today would not be that day either. Weeks needed to pass before the time was right, but in the meantime, she enjoyed spending time with the young child who seemed to house an old soul.

After Yasmin departed, Annani led Cyra to the

cushioned area she had prepared. "Would you like to color while we have our tea?" She gestured at the art supplies.

Cyra nodded, settling cross-legged on a cushion with Mr. Ears placed carefully beside her. She selected a blue crayon with the deliberation of an artist choosing a brush.

Annani busied herself with the miniature tea set, filling tiny porcelain cups with apple juice while observing the child from the corner of her eye. Cyra was a curious mixture of a child who had seen too much and was still processing her trauma, and the resilience that only children seemed to possess—the ability to get fully absorbed in whatever they were doing because it was all new and exciting to them.

"Maman says that you are very old." Cyra did not look up from her drawing. "But she said it's not nice to tell you that she said that, but I don't know why. You are so very beautiful." The girl looked at her from under lowered lashes. "You don't look like other old ladies."

"That is true." Annani settled across from her and offered her a cup. "Does that confuse you?"

"No." Cyra accepted the tiny cup with both hands. "You are not like those other old ladies. You are different." She took a small sip of the apple juice. "Our neighbor, Mrs. Darvish, had good stories to tell. But then she went to sleep and didn't wake up and took her stories to heaven."

The matter-of-fact way in which she spoke of death was both heartbreaking and mature for a child that young, but perhaps she was just repeating what her mother had told her.

"What kinds of stories did Mrs. Darvish tell you?" Annani asked.

Cyra sipped her juice-tea thoughtfully. "All kinds of stories. Sometimes they were things that didn't happen yet, like a storm about to come, or someone having a baby." She paused. "I have stories like that, too, sometimes."

Annani's pulse quickened, but she kept her voice calm. "What are they about?"

Instead of answering directly, Cyra returned to her drawing. Annani waited patiently, understanding that children often communicated better through action than words. The scratch of a crayon on paper was soothing, almost meditative.

After several minutes, Cyra pushed the paper toward her. "For you."

Annani studied the drawing, her breath catching. It showed a horizontal stick figure surrounded by golden swirls that seemed to indicate either waves or sand dunes.

"Is this the doll man you have dreamt about?" Annani asked.

Cyra nodded. "But I drew it wrong." She pulled the paper back and added more stick figures around the first. "I don't know how to make him look pretty, and he is not alone. I forgot to draw the others."

Khiann had had immortal guards with him, escorting the caravan. If he was buried in the sand in stasis, perhaps they were as well.

"Are they also doll men?" Annani asked.

Cyra nodded. "They are all sleeping in the golden sand. Like Sleeping Beauty."

"Do you know the story of Sleeping Beauty?"

The girl nodded. "I saw the movie." She looked up from her drawing and smiled. "The prince gave Sleeping Beauty a kiss, and she woke up. It was nice." Cyra selected a yellow crayon and began adding more swirls. "Sometimes the sleeping men flicker."

"Flicker?" Annani kept her voice gentle. "What do you mean, sweetheart?"

Cyra's small face scrunched in concentration. "Like... like candles when there is wind. I worry when they do that."

"Why does it worry you?"

"Because I don't know what's happening." Cyra looked up, her dark eyes troubled. "Are they trying to wake up? Are they trying to tell me something, but I'm too little to understand?"

Annani reached across the low table and took the child's small hand. The fingers were so tiny, so delicate, but she could feel the potential thrumming beneath the skin. This child was special.

"You understand more than you know. These dreams are gifts, even when they are confusing."

"Maman says I shouldn't talk about them. She says people will think I'm strange."

"Your mother wants to protect you, which is what good mothers do. But here, with me, you can speak of anything you see. I will never think you are strange."

Cyra studied her with that too-wise gaze of hers. "Do you have dreams too?"

Annani nodded. "Different kinds of dreams, but yes. Sometimes I can close my eyes and see what someone I care about is doing, or where they are, just like you do."

Annani had a gift of far viewing, but it was limited.

"Can you see the pretty man?"

Annani swallowed the lump in her throat. "I lost a very pretty man a long time ago, a man I loved more than life itself. But I was not blessed with dreams of him. I only have a deep yearning to find him."

Cyra nodded. "If he's sleeping, like Sleeping Beauty, you can wake him up with a kiss. You are a princess, so you can do that."

Annani smiled, though it carried millennia of sadness. "I guess I could, but I need to find him first. I do not know where he sleeps."

Cyra returned to her drawing, adding black and orange shapes above the sand that made no sense. They were probably decorations.

"What are these?" Annani pointed.

"Dragons," Cyra said in a tone that indicated she thought Annani should have known that.

"What are they doing in the desert?"

Cyra shrugged. "I don't know. I just thought it would be cool. Maybe the dragons can help wake up the sleeping men. There are four more in the sand."

"Dragons or men?"

Cyra gave Annani an incredulous look. "Men." She pointed at the dragons she drew. "There are only three dragons. Two black and one gold."

"I see." Annani pretended to examine the drawing more closely. "Do all the men look the same?"

Cyra shook her head. "No, but they are all waiting." She paused, crayon hovering over the paper. "The sand sings to them."

"What does it sing?"

Cyra hummed a few notes, a melody that seemed hauntingly familiar, though Annani could not place it.

"That is beautiful," she said when the child stopped. "Where did you hear it?"

"In the dream. The sand sings where they are sleeping." Cyra selected a brown crayon and started to draw what looked like big rocks.

"Do you see these rocks in your dreams?"

The girl shook her head. "No, but maybe there are big rocks. I just see sand." She sounded despondent.

"That is alright, dear one. You have already helped me more than you know."

Cyra nodded, looking relieved, and went on adding details to her drawing. "They want to join the party."

She was probably talking about the welcoming party for Esag and the others, wishing for a brighter topic to talk about. She was just a little girl, and it was time to lighten the mood.

"When we find them, we will have an even bigger party than what we had last week. Do you like parties?"

The girl nodded eagerly. "I like the music and the dancing." She squirmed on her cushion. "I like to dance."

Evidently, Cyra had reached her limit of sitting in one place.

"Would you like to take a walk in my garden?" Annani offered.

The child brightened immediately. "Yes, please!"

They walked hand in hand through Annani's backyard, with Cyra exclaiming over flowers and then dropping Annani's hand to chase butterflies. She seemed more childlike here, giggling when the butterflies evaded her reach.

It warmed Annani's heart.

"The pretty man dreams too," Cyra suddenly said. "He dreams of you."

Annani's throat tightened. "Does he?"

Cyra nodded enthusiastically, and Annani appreciated the child's effort to lift her mood.

"He wants to wake up, but the sand song is too strong."

"Perhaps," Annani said.

"Can I take one flower for Maman?" Cyra asked.

"Of course." Annani walked over to the flower bed. "Let me get it for you so you do not hurt your fingers."

They were interrupted by Ogidu stepping out through the sliding doors onto the back porch. "Mistress Yasmin has arrived, Clan Mother."

"Maman!" Cyra ran to her, the rose clutched carefully in her small fist. "Look what the Clan Mother let me pick!"

"It's beautiful," Yasmin said, but her eyes were on Annani, questioning.

"She was a delight as usual," Annani assured her.

After they left, Annani returned to her living room and studied Cyra's drawing more carefully. Five figures in the sand, flickering between existence and void, waiting to be found.

"Ogidu," she called her butler. "I wish to visit Esag. Have the golf cart ready."

He bowed. "Yes, Clan Mother."

For the past week, Esag had been deflecting all of her inquiries about his carvings of Khiann, saying that he had nothing to show her because they were all subpar.

Annani was tired of waiting.

Twenty minutes later, the golf cart stopped outside the house Esag shared with Davuh and Roven. The sound of a chisel on stone drifted from an open window, probably the skylight the males had installed in the walk-in closet they had converted into a workshop.

"Esag?" Annani called out. "May I come in?"

The chiseling stopped. After a moment, Esag appeared at the door, stone dust in his hair and shadows under his eyes.

"Princess Annani." He bowed. "I don't have anything to show you yet. None of them is right. None of them capture Khiann's essence."

"I came to see the others you have carved over the millennia. I assume you had enough time to put them on display?"

The shelving units had been delivered to the residence two days after the three had moved in. Surely they had enough time to unpack at least some of them.

Reluctantly, Esag led her into the house, and as she entered, Annani's steps slowed. The living room had been transformed into a gallery. Simple shelving units lined the walls, and on them, arranged with loving care, were dozens of figurines from Esag's collection.

Her father's imperial face gazed down at her from the highest shelf, captured perfectly in pale marble. Beside him stood her mother, serene and beautiful, her stone lips curved in the gentle smile Annani remembered. The detail was extraordinary—every fold of fabric, every strand of hair rendered with seemingly impossible precision.

"We've only unpacked about a third of them," Esag said apologetically, misreading her silence. "We are still in the process of setting them up."

Annani moved closer, her trained composure the only thing keeping her features smooth. There was her Uncle Ekin, who had taught her most everything she knew. Her cousin Toven, who was in the village, alive and well. Her Aunt Athor, who had tried to explain genetics to her.

If only she had listened.

Khiann's parents. Gulan's. All gone, yet there they stood, preserved in stone with such life that she almost expected them to move, to speak.

"They are magnificent," she managed, her voice steady despite the storm of emotion within.

On a lower shelf, she spotted more familiar faces—courtiers she had known, guards whom she had played stones with, even the old tutor who had been fired so Khiann could replace him and court her in secret.

Her fingers itched to touch them, and she wished she had Fenella's gift so she could see what memories

Esag had embedded in each piece. But that would mean feeling their loss all over again, and she could not endure that.

Not today.

"You have honored them all. I am amazed at how well you remembered them. You must have possessed an artist's eye for detail even before you became one."

"I did my best." Esag wiped his hands on a rag that was dirtier than his palms. "I did it so I wouldn't forget." His gaze shifted to the figurines on the upper shelf. "Do you want to hear something really crazy?"

She tilted her head to look up at him. "Always."

"I have dreams of the gods all being alive. I know they are wishful thoughts just as my dreams about Khiann are, but they are so vivid." He chuckled. "Do you remember the slaves from the north that Mortdh brought as a present for you?"

She grimaced. "The poor primitive tribesmen that Mortdh somehow caught in the northern lands and brought to me as a novelty because they were all blond and pale." Later, when she had escaped, Annani had gone to their lands and found refuge there. "They are all probably dead, murdered when the assembly and the palace were bombed."

Esag nodded. "They talked of auroras, and back then, I didn't know what they were and thought that they were making them up. Now I know that auroras are a real phenomenon, and that's what I see in my dreams. I see the gods living in a place where auroras are constantly in the sky." He chuckled. "Maybe that's my idea of paradise."

"I lived among those northern tribes," she said. "That is where I escaped to avoid capture by Mortdh when the council deliberated endlessly about how to bring him to justice. The auroras are indeed beautiful, but it is a harsh land, and as far from paradise as you can imagine. Sumer was the real paradise before it was destroyed."

"I know," Esag said quietly. "Mortdh destroyed more than a beautiful land. He eradicated the gods and by doing so doomed humanity."

Annani had not told Esag about the Eternal King and Anumati yet, not because she wanted to keep it from him, but because he had been busy setting up his workshop, and they had not had the opportunity to talk.

"It might not have been Mortdh who did that."

Esag frowned. "Then who?"

"I have so much I need to tell you, but I do not want to distract you from your work. I need you to make a figurine of Khiann that will make you dream of him and help me find him. We are running out of time."

She thought about the flickering Cyra had talked about, and her gut clenched.

Esag swallowed. "I'm doing the best I can." He motioned for her to follow him.

They continued through the house to Esag's makeshift workshop—the closet had been transformed, the skylight flooding the small space with natural light, and the shelves lining the walls holding tools and materials instead of clothing. But the figurines were what drew Annani's attention.

Khiann's face gazed back at her from multiple angles, carved in different stones. Each was exquisite, capturing some aspect of the man she still loved with every fiber of her being—his strength, his kindness, the way his eyes crinkled when he smiled. But Esag was right about something missing from each one of them.

"They're technically perfect," Esag said miserably. "But they're dead stone. No spirit, no spark. Nothing like how I remember him."

"I have a portrait of Khiann in my bedroom." Annani lifted one of the figurines. "The clan works with an artist who can draw eerily accurate portraits of people just from their descriptions. Would you like to see it?"

"I would love to." Esag reached for a clean rag and resumed wiping his hands as if their cleanliness would provide him with the answers he was seeking.

"Come to think of it." Annani put the unfinished figurine back on the shelf. "Perhaps I should ask Andrew to arrange a meeting between you and the artist. If he draws a portrait of Khiann from your memory, it might help you with the carving."

Esag looked doubtful. "I don't really see how it could help, but at this point, I'm willing to try anything."

"Then it is settled. I will have Andrew arrange a meeting as soon as possible. In the meantime, you should come to my house, so I can show you Khiann's portrait."

He dipped his head. "I would be honored, Princess."

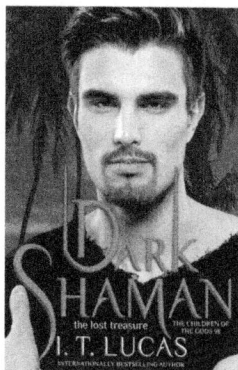

Eluheed believed he was the only immortal on Earth, carrying the weight of a sacred duty—to protect and recover the sacred treasures buried beneath Mount Ararat. But when a catastrophic mistake lands him in the clutches of a Russian mobster and then sold to a mysterious warlord, Eluheed discovers he's not as alone as he thought.

Now imprisoned on a remote island, forced to serve a ruthless master who is not fully human, Eluheed must use his shamanic skills to survive. In this luxurious cage filled with broken souls, he finds an unexpected ally—a female whose spirit refuses to be crushed. As Eluheed plans his escape, he faces an impossible choice: return to his duty or risk everything for a chance at something he's never had before.

JOIN THE VIP CLUB

To find out what's included in your free membership, flip to the last page.

NOTE

Dear reader,

I hope my stories have added a little joy to your day. If you have a moment to add some to mine, you can help spread the word about the Children Of The Gods series by telling your friends and penning a review. Your recommendations are the most powerful way to inspire new readers to explore the series.

Thank you,

Isabell

THE CHILDREN OF THE GODS ORIGINS

1: GODDESS'S CHOICE

When gods and immortals still ruled the ancient world, one young goddess risked everything for love.

2: GODDESS'S HOPE

Hungry for power and infatuated with the beautiful Areana, Navuh plots his father's demise. After all, by getting rid of the insane god he would be doing the world a favor. Except, when gods and immortals conspire against each other, humanity pays the price.

But things are not what they seem, and prophecies should not to be trusted...

THE CHILDREN OF THE GODS

THE DARK STRANGER TRILOGY

1: DARK STRANGER THE DREAM

2: DARK STRANGER REVEALED

3: DARK STRANGER IMMORTAL

Syssi's paranormal foresight lands her a job at Dr. Amanda Dokani's neuroscience lab, but it fails to predict the thrilling yet terrifying turn her life will take. Syssi has no clue that her boss is an immortal who'll drag her into a secret, millennia-old battle over humanity's future. Nor does she realize that the professor's imposing brother is the mysterious stranger who's been starring in her dreams.

Since the dawn of human civilization, two warring factions of immortals—the descendants of the gods of old—have been secretly shaping its destiny. Leading the clandestine battle from his luxurious Los Angeles high-rise, Kian is surrounded by his clan, yet alone. Descending from a single goddess, clan members are forbidden to each other. And as the only other immortals are their hated enemies, Kian and his kin have been long resigned to a lonely existence of fleeting trysts with human partners. That is, until his sister makes a game-changing discovery—a mortal seeress who she believes is a dormant carrier of their genes. Ever the realist, Kian is skeptical and refuses Amanda's plea to attempt Syssi's activation. But when his enemies learn of the Dormant's existence, he's forced to rush her to the safety of his keep. Inexorably drawn to Syssi, Kian wrestles with his conscience as he is tempted to explore her budding interest in the darker shades of sensuality.

THE DARK ENEMY TRILOGY

4: DARK ENEMY TAKEN

5: DARK ENEMY CAPTIVE

6: DARK ENEMY REDEEMED

Dalhu can't believe his luck when he stumbles upon the beautiful immortal professor. Presented with a once-in-a-lifetime opportunity to grab an immortal female for himself, he kidnaps her and runs. If he ever gets caught, either by her people or his, his life is forfeit. But for a chance of a loving mate and a family of his own, Dalhu is prepared to do everything in his power to win Amanda's heart, and that includes leaving the Doom brotherhood and his old life behind.

Amanda soon discovers that there is more to the handsome Doomer than his dark past and a hulking, sexy body. But succumbing to her enemy's seduction, or worse, developing feelings for a ruthless killer is out of the question. No man is worth life on the run, not even the one and only immortal male she could claim as her own.

Her clan and her research must come first.

6.5: MY DARK AMAZON

When Michael and Kri fend off a gang of humans, Michael is stabbed. Though his immortal body recovers quickly, the injury to his ego takes longer to heal, putting a strain on his relationship with Kri.

THE DARK WARRIOR TETRALOGY

7: DARK WARRIOR MINE

8: DARK WARRIOR'S PROMISE

9: DARK WARRIOR'S DESTINY

10: DARK WARRIOR'S LEGACY

When Andrew is forced to retire from active duty, he believes that all he has to look forward to is a boring desk job. His glory days in special ops are over. But as it turns out, his thrill ride has just begun. Andrew discovers not only that immortals exist and have been manipulating global affairs since antiquity, but that he and his sister are rare possessors of the immortal genes.

Problem is, Andrew might be too old to attempt the activation process. His sister, who is fourteen years his junior, barely made it through the transition, so the odds of him coming out of it alive, let alone immortal, are slim.

But fate may force his hand.

Helping a friend find his long-lost daughter, Andrew finds a woman who's worth taking the risk for. Nathalie might be a Dormant, but the only way to find out for sure requires fangs and venom.

DARK GUARDIAN TRILOGY

11: DARK GUARDIAN FOUND

12: DARK GUARDIAN CRAVED

13: DARK GUARDIAN'S MATE

What would you do if you stopped aging?

Eva runs. The ex-DEA agent doesn't know what caused her strange mutation, only that if discovered, she'll be dissected like a lab rat. What Eva doesn't know, though, is that she's a descendant of the gods, and that she is not alone. The man who rocked her world in one life-changing encounter over thirty years ago is an immortal as well.

To keep his people's existence secret, Bhathian was forced to turn his back on the only woman who ever captured his heart, but he's never forgotten and never stopped looking for her.

DARK ANGEL TRILOGY

14: DARK ANGEL'S OBSESSION

15: DARK ANGEL'S SEDUCTION

16: DARK ANGEL'S SURRENDER

The cold and stoic warrior is an enigma even to those closest to him. His secrets are about to unravel...

Brundar is fighting a losing battle. Calypso is slowly chipping away his icy armor from the outside, while his need for her is melting it from the inside.

He can't allow it to happen. Calypso is a human with none of the Dormant indicators. There is no way he can keep her for more than a few weeks.

DARK OPERATIVE TRILOGY

As a brilliant strategist and the only human entrusted with the secret of immortals' existence, Turner is both an asset and a liability to the clan. His request to attempt transition into immortality as an alternative to cancer treatments cannot be denied without risking the clan's exposure. On the other hand, approving it means risking his premature death. In both scenarios, the clan will lose a valuable ally.

When the decision is left to the clan's physician, Turner makes plans to manipulate her by taking advantage of her interest in him.

Will Bridget fall for the cold, calculated operative? Or will Turner fall into his own trap?

DARK SURVIVOR TRILOGY

This was a strange new world she had awakened to.

Her memory loss must have been catastrophic because almost nothing was familiar. The language was foreign to her, with only a few words bearing some similarity to the language she thought in. Still, a full moon cycle had passed since her awakening, and little by little, she was gaining basic understanding of it--only a few words and phrases, but she was learning more each day.

A week or so ago, a little girl on the street had tugged on her mother's sleeve and pointed at her. "Look, Mama, Wonder Woman!"

The mother smiled apologetically, saying something in the language these people spoke, then scurried away with the child looking behind her shoulder and grinning.

When it happened again with another child on the same day, it was settled.

Wonder Woman must have been the name of someone important in this strange world she had awoken to, and since both times it had been said with a smile it must have been a good one.

Wonder had a nice ring to it.

She just wished she knew what it meant.

DARK WIDOW TRILOGY

23: DARK WIDOW'S SECRET

24: DARK WIDOW'S CURSE

25: DARK WIDOW'S BLESSING

Vivian and her daughter share a powerful telepathic connection, so when Ella can't be reached by conventional or psychic means, her mother fears the worst.

Help arrives from an unexpected source when Vivian gets a call from the young doctor she met at a psychic convention. Turns out Julian belongs to a private organization specializing in retrieving missing girls.

As Julian's clan mobilizes its considerable resources to rescue the daughter, Magnus is charged with keeping the gorgeous young mother safe.

Worry for Ella and the secrets Vivian and Magnus keep from each other should be enough to prevent the sparks of attraction from kindling a blaze of desire. Except, these pesky sparks have a mind of their own.

DARK DREAM TRILOGY

26: DARK DREAM'S TEMPTATION

27: DARK DREAM'S UNRAVELING

28: DARK DREAM'S TRAP

Julian has known Ella is the one for him from the moment he saw her picture, but when he finally frees her from captivity, she seems indifferent to him. Could he have been mistaken?

Ella's rescue should've ended that chapter in her life, but it seems like the road back to normalcy has just begun, and it's full of obstacles. Between the pitying looks she gets and her mother's attempts to get her into therapy, Ella feels like she's typecast as a victim when nothing could be further from the truth. She's a tough survivor, and she's going to prove it.

Strangely, the only one who seems to understand is Logan, who keeps popping up in her dreams. But then, he's a figment of her imagination—or is he?

DARK PRINCE TRILOGY

As the son of the most dangerous male on the planet, Lokan lives by three rules:

Don't trust a soul.

Don't show emotions.

And don't get attached.

Will one extraordinary woman make him break all three?

DARK QUEEN TRILOGY

A former beauty queen, a retired undercover agent, and a successful model, Mey is not the typical damsel in distress. But when her sister drops off the radar and then someone starts following her around, she panics.

Following a vague clue that Kalugal might be in New York, Kian sends a team headed by Yamanu to search for him.

As Mey and Yamanu's paths cross, he offers her his help and protection, but will that be all?

DARK SPY TRILOGY

Jin possesses a unique paranormal ability. Just by touching someone, she can insert a mental hook into their psyche and tie a string of her consciousness to it, creating a tether. That doesn't make her a spy, though, not unless her talent is discovered by those seeking to exploit it.

DARK OVERLORD TRILOGY

38: DARK OVERLORD NEW HORIZON

39: DARK OVERLORD'S WIFE

40: DARK OVERLORD'S CLAN

Jacki has two talents that set her apart from the rest of the human race.

She has unpredictable glimpses of other people's futures, and she is immune to mind manipulation.

Unfortunately, both talents are pretty useless for finding a job other than the one she had in the government's paranormal division.

It seemed like a sweet deal until she found out that the director planned on producing super babies by compelling the recruits into pairing up. When an opportunity to escape the program presented itself, she took it, only to find out that humans are not at the top of the food chain.

Immortals are real, and at the very top of the hierarchy is Kalugal, the most powerful, arrogant, and sexiest male she has ever met.

With one look, he sets her blood on fire, but Jacki is not a fool. A man like him will never think of her as anything more than a tasty snack, while she will never settle for anything less than his heart.

DARK CHOICES TRILOGY

When Rufsur and Edna meet, the attraction is as unexpected as it is undeniable. Except, she's the clan's judge and councilwoman, and he's Kalugal's second-in-command.

Will loyalty and duty to their people keep them apart?

DARK SECRETS TRILOGY

On a sabbatical from his Stanford teaching position, Professor David Levinson finally has time to write the sci-fi novel he's been thinking about for years.

The phenomena of past life memories and near-death experiences are too controversial to include in his formal psychiatric research, while fiction is the perfect outlet for his esoteric ideas.

Hoping that a change of pace will provide the inspiration he needs, David accepts a friend's invitation to an old Scottish castle.

DARK HAVEN TRILOGY

Welcome to Safe Haven, where not everything is what it seems.

On a quest to process personal pain, Anastasia joins the Safe Haven Spiritual Retreat.

Through meditation, self-reflection, and hard work, she hopes to make peace with the voices in her head.

This is where she belongs.

Except, membership comes with a hefty price, doubts are sacrilege, and leaving is not as easy as walking out the front gate.

Is living in utopia worth the sacrifice?

Anastasia believes so until the arrival of a new acolyte changes everything.

Apparently, the gods of old were not a myth, their immortal descendants share the planet with humans, and she might be a carrier of their genes.

DARK POWER TRILOGY

Attending a charity gala as the clan's figurehead, Onegus is ready for the pesky socialites he'll have a hard time keeping away. Instead, he encounters an intriguing beauty who won't give him the time of day.

Bad things happen when Cassandra gets all worked up, and given her fiery temper, the destructive power is difficult to tame. When she meets a gorgeous, cocky billionaire at a charity event, things just might start blowing up again.

DARK MEMORIES TRILOGY

53: DARK MEMORIES SUBMERGED

54: DARK MEMORIES EMERGE

55: DARK MEMORIES RESTORED

Geraldine's memories are spotty at best, and many of them are pure fiction. While her family attempts to solve the puzzle with far too many pieces missing, she's forced to confront a past life that she can't remember, a present that's more fantastic than her wildest made-up stories, and a future that might be better than her most heartfelt fantasies. But as more clues are uncovered, the picture starting to emerge is beyond anything she or her family could have ever imagined.

DARK HUNTER TRILOGY

56: DARK HUNTER'S QUERY

57: DARK HUNTER'S PREY

58: DARK HUNTER'S BOON

For most of his five centuries of existence, Orion has walked the earth alone, searching for answers.

Why is he immortal?

Where did his powers come from?

Is he the only one of his kind?

When fate puts Orion face to face with the god who sired him, he learns the secret behind his immortality and that he might not be the only one.

As the goddess's eldest daughter and a mother of thirteen, Alena deserves the title of Clan Mother just as much as Annani, but she's not interested in honorifics. Being her mother's companion and keeping the mischievous goddess out of trouble is a rewarding, full-time job. Lately, though, Alena's love for her mother and the clan's gratitude is not enough.

She craves adventure, excitement, and perhaps a true-love mate of her own.

When Alena and Orion meet, sparks fly, but they both resist the pull. Alena could never bring herself to trust the powerful compeller, and Orion could never allow himself to fall in love again.

DARK GOD TRILOGY

59: DARK GOD'S AVATAR

60: DARK GOD'S REVIVISCENCE

61: DARK GOD DESTINIES CONVERGE

Unaware of the time bomb ticking inside her, Mia had lived the perfect life until it all came to a screeching halt, but despite the difficulties she faces, she doggedly pursues her dreams.

Once known as the god of knowledge and wisdom, Toven has grown cold and indifferent. Disillusioned with humanity, he travels the world and pens novels about the love he can no longer feel.

Seeking to escape his ever-present ennui, Toven gives a cutting-edge virtual experience a try. When his avatar meets Mia's, their sizzling virtual romance unexpectedly turns into something deeper and more meaningful.

Will it endure in the real world?

DARK WHISPERS TRILOGY

62: DARK WHISPERS FROM THE PAST

63: Dark Whispers From Afar

64: Dark Whispers From Beyond

A brilliant scientist and programmer, William lives for his work, but when he recruits a young bioinformatician to help him decipher the gods' genetic blueprints, he finds himself smitten with more than just her brain.

With a Ph.D. at nineteen, Kaia is considered a prodigy and expects a bright future in academia. But when William invites her to join his secret research team, she accepts for reasons that have nothing to do with her career objectives. Wiliam's promise to look into her best friend's disappearance is an offer she just can't refuse.

DARK GAMBIT TRILOGY

65: Dark Gambit The Pawn

66: Dark Gambit The Play

67: Dark Gambit Reliance

Temporarily assigned to supervise a team of bioinformaticians, Marcel expects to spend a couple of weeks in the peaceful retreat of Safe Haven, enjoying Oregon Coast's cool weather and rugged beauty.

Things quickly turn chaotic when the retreat's director receives an email with an encoded message about a potential new threat to the clan.

While those in charge of security debate what to do next, Safe Haven's first ever paranormal retreat is about to begin, and one of the attendees is a mysterious woman who makes Marcel's heart beat faster whenever she's near.

Is the beautiful mortal his one truelove?

Or is she the harbinger of more bad news?

DARK ALLIANCE TRILOGY

A daring operation half a world away devolves into a full-scale crisis that escalates rapidly, requiring the clan's full might and technological wizardry to manage and survive.

Hardened by duty and tragedy, Jade is driven by a burning desire for revenge. When Phinas saves her second-in-command, Jade's gratitude quickly becomes something more.

DARK HEALING TRILOGY

The sanctuary is Vanessa's life project. The monumental task of rehabilitating the traumatized victims of trafficking doesn't leave much time for personal life, let alone dating or finding her one and only.

When Kian asks her to help the Kra-ell, she's torn between her duty to the sanctuary and a group of emotionally wounded aliens who no other psychologist can treat.

She's the only immortal with the necessary training to get it done.

The Kra-ell culture and the purebloods' nearly androgynous alien looks shouldn't appeal to her, and yet, she finds one of them disturbingly attractive.

Is it the dangerous vibe he emits?

Does it speak to her on a subconscious level?

Or is it her need to put the broken pieces of him back together?

And why is he interested in her?

She cannot offer him a fight for dominance like a Kra-ell female would, but some strange and unfamiliar part of her wishes she could.

DARK ENCOUNTERS TRILOGY

Convinced that her family is hiding a terrible secret from her, Gabi decides to pay them a surprise visit.

Something is very fishy about the stories her brothers have been telling her lately. Her niece, a nineteen-year-old prodigy with a Ph.D. in bioinformatics, has gotten engaged to a much older guy she met while working on some top-secret project, and if Gabi's older, overprotective brother's approval of the engagement wasn't suspicious enough, he also uprooted his family and moved to be closer to the couple.

What Gabi discovers when she gets to L.A. is wilder than anything she could have imagined. Her entire family possesses godly genes, her brothers and her niece have already turned immortal, and she could transition as soon as she finds an immortal male to induce her. Finding a suitable candidate in a village full of handsome immortals shouldn't be a problem, but Gabi's thoughts keep wandering to the gorgeous guy she met on her flight over.

Could Uriel be a lost descendant of the gods?

He certainly looks like them, but that doesn't mean that he's a good guy or that he's even immortal. He could be a descendant of a different god—a member of an enemy faction of immortals who seek to eradicate her family's adoptive clan, or what is more likely, he's just an extraordinarily good-looking human.

DARK VOYAGE TRILOGY

77: DARK VOYAGE MATTERS OF THE HEART
78: DARK VOYAGE MATTERS OF THE MIND
79: DARK VOYAGE MATTERS OF THE SOUL

As Annani and Syssi set out to unravel the mysteries of Syssi's visions about the gods' home world, the long-awaited wedding cruise sets sail with Aru, Gabi, and Aru's teammates on board.

While the gods find themselves surrounded by immortal clan ladies eager for their affections, they soon discover that destiny has a different plan for them.

DARK HORIZON TRILOGY

80: DARK HORIZON NEW DAWN
81: DARK HORIZON ECLIPSE OF THE HEART
82: DARK HORIZON THE WITCHING HOUR

What begins as a carefree vacation quickly spirals into a heart-pounding adventure when a chance encounter with a mysterious woman entangles Margo in a shadowy world of deceit and danger.

Meanwhile, aboard the Silver Swan, the Fates weave their intricate web. Armed with Margo's photograph, Frankie is on a mission to match her with the last unmated god. Despite his initial disinterest, the image consumes Negal, and when

Margo's situation becomes dire, the once indifferent god is compelled to join the frantic rescue mission.

DARK WITCH TRILOGY

Jasmine's quest for her Prince Charming takes an unexpected turn when she finds herself on a luxurious cruise ship steeped in secrets. Navigating a tangled maze of destiny, intrigue, and desire, she discovers that the key to unlocking her future may lie in the very cards she's been dealt.

DARK AWAKENING TRILOGY

"Your destiny awaits across the stars," Ell-rom's mother told him. "The seer foretold your future. You will live, and you will thrive, and you will be safe."

The seer's prophecy has come true. Ell-rom and his sister are safe, surrounded by people who care for them and want to help them heal, which is in stark contrast to where they came from. On Anumati, they were considered abominations because of their mixed heritage. As half gods and half Kra-ell, they would have been eradicated if ever discovered.

But even as he clings to that thought like a talisman against the darkness, he can't shake the lingering sense of unease, the feeling that something lurked in the shadows of his past, something dark and dangerous that is much worse than his inability to tolerate the taste of blood.

What is it about him and his sister that he is not supposed to let anyone see?

After millennia in stasis, Morelle is lured out of her slumber by a seductive storyteller with a velvet voice. As she awakens to twenty-first-century Earth instead of the primitive planet she's been expecting, she struggles to adapt, but thankfully she does not have to do it alone. She has her twin brother to guide her, and a charming stranger who refuses to leave her side.

Some warriors are born. Others are chosen by fate and forged by circumstances. In the mountains of Kurdistan, a mysterious woman fights for freedom while her own past remains locked away.

Stay tuned as the truth about Kyra's disappearance begins to unravel.

95: DARK **R**OVER'S **L**UCK

96: DARK **R**OVER'S **G**IFT

97: DARK **R**OVER'S **S**HIRE

For five decades, Fenella has led the life of a ghost, wandering from place to place and relying solely on herself. Now, while seeking refuge in the immortals' hidden village, she uncovers an unexpected connection that may inspire her to stay longer than she planned.

Din has held a torch for Fenella for half a century. Yet, instead of the spirited bartender he fell for, he encounters a hardened, disillusioned nomad who struggles to remain in one place for long.

Some secrets are meant to remain buried, while others are destined to be revealed, and sometimes, luck is simply a matter of being in the right place at the right time.

DARK **S**HAMAN

*98: D*ARK *S*HAMAN: T*HE* L*OST* T*REASURE*

Eluheed believed he was the only immortal on Earth, carrying the weight of a sacred duty—to protect and recover the sacred treasures buried beneath Mount Ararat. But when a catastrophic mistake lands him in the clutches of a Russian mobster and then sold to a mysterious warlord, Eluheed discovers he's not as alone as he thought.

Now imprisoned on a remote island, forced to serve a ruthless master who is not fully human, Eluheed must use his shamanic skills to survive. In this luxurious cage filled with broken souls, he finds an unexpected ally—a female whose spirit refuses to be crushed. As Eluheed plans his escape, he faces an impossible choice: return to his duty or risk everything for a chance at something he's never had before.

The Children of The Gods Series Sets

Dark Stranger Trilogy
Includes a bonus short story:
The Fates Take a Vacation

Dark Enemy Trilogy
Includes a bonus short story:
The Fates' Post-Wedding Celebration

Dark Warrior Tetralogy

Dark Guardian Trilogy

Dark Angel Trilogy

Dark Operative Trilogy

Dark Survivor Trilogy

Dark Widow Trilogy

Dark Dream Trilogy

Dark Prince Trilogy

Dark Queen Trilogy

Dark Spy Trilogy

Dark Overlord Trilogy

Dark Choices Trilogy

Dark Secrets Trilogy

Dark Haven Trilogy

Dark Power Trilogy

Dark Memories Trilogy

Dark Hunter Trilogy

Dark God Trilogy

Dark Whispers Trilogy

Dark Gambit Trilogy

Dark Alliance Trilogy

Dark Healing Trilogy

Dark Encounters Trilogy

Dark Voyage Trilogy

Dark Horizon Trilogy

Dark Witch Trilogy

Dark Awakening Trilogy

Dark Princess Trilogy

MEGA SETS

The Children of the Gods: Books 1-6

INCLUDES CHARACTER LISTS

The Children of the Gods: Books 6.5-10

TRANSLATIONS

DIE ERBEN DER GÖTTER

Dark Stranger

1- Dark Stranger Der Traum

2- Dark Stranger Die Offenbarung

3- Dark Stranger Unsterblich

Dark Enemy

4- Dark Enemy Entführt

5- Dark Enemy Gefangen

For a **FREE** Audiobook, Preview chapters, And other

PERFECT MATCH SERIES

Vampire's Consort

When Gabriel's company is ready to start beta testing, he invites his old crush to inspect its medical safety protocol.

Curious about the revolutionary technology of the *Perfect Match Virtual Fantasy-Fulfillment studios*, Brenna agrees.

Neither expects to end up partnering for its first fully immersive test run.

King's Chosen

When Lisa's nutty friends get her a gift certificate to *Perfect Match Virtual Fantasy Studios*, she has no intentions of using it. But since the only way to get a refund is if no partner can be found for her, she makes sure to request a fantasy so girly and over the top that no sane guy will pick it up.

Except, someone does.

Warning: This fantasy contains a hot, domineering crown prince, sweet insta-love, steamy love scenes painted with light shades of gray, a wedding, and a HEA in both the virtual and real worlds.

Intended for mature audience.

Working as a Starbucks barista, Alicia fends off flirting all day long, but none of the guys are as charming and sexy as Gregg. His frequent visits are the highlight of her day, but since he's never asked her out, she assumes he's taken. Besides, between a day job and a budding music career, she has no time to start a new relationship.

That is until Gregg makes her an offer she can't refuse—a gift certificate to the virtual fantasy fulfillment service everyone is talking about. As a huge Star Trek fan, Alicia has a perfect match in mind—the captain of the Starship Enterprise.

THE THIEF WHO LOVED ME

When Marian splurges on a Perfect Match Virtual adventure as a world-infamous jewel thief, she expects high-wire fun with a hot partner who she will never have to see again in real life.

A virtual encounter seems like the perfect answer to Marcus's string of dating disasters. No strings attached, no drama, and definitely no love. As a die-hard James Bond fan, he chooses as his avatar a dashing MI6 operative and to complement his adventure, a dangerously seductive partner.

Neither expects to find their forever Perfect Match.

MY MERMAN PRINCE

The beautiful architect working late on the twelfth floor of my building thinks that I'm just the maintenance guy. She's also under the impression that I'm not interested.

Nothing could be further from the truth.

I want her like I've never wanted a woman before, but I don't play where I work.

I don't need the complications.

When she tells me about living out her mermaid fantasy with a stranger in a Perfect Match virtual adventure, I decide to do everything possible to ensure that the stranger is me.

THE DRAGON KING

To save his beloved kingdom from a devastating war, the Crown Prince of Trieste makes a deal with a witch that costs him half of his humanity and dooms him to an eternity of loneliness.

Now king, he's a fearsome cobalt-winged dragon by day and a short-tempered monarch by night. Not many are brave enough to serve in the palace of the brooding and volatile ruler, but Charlotte ignores the rumors and accepts a scribe position in court.

As the young scribe reawakens Bruce's frozen heart, all that stands in the way of their happiness is the witch's bargain. Outsmarting the evil hag will take cunning and courage, and Charlotte is just the right woman for the job.

MY WEREWOLF ROMEO

The father of my star student is a big-shot screen-writer and the patron of the drama department who thinks he can dictate what production I should put on. The principal makes it very clear that I need to coop-erate with the opinionated asshat or walk away from my dream job at the exclusive private high school.

It doesn't help matters that the guy is single, hot, charming, creative, and seems to like me despite my thinly-veiled hostility.

When he invites me to a custom-tailored Perfect Match virtual adventure to prove that his screenplay is perfect for my production, I accept, intending to have fun while proving that messing with the classics is a foolish idea.

I don't expect to be wowed by his werewolf adapta-tion of Red Riding Hood mesh-up with Romeo and Juliet, and I certainly don't expect to fall in love with the virtual fantasy's leading man.

THE CHANNELER'S COMPANION

A treat for fans of *The Wheel of Time*.

When Erika hires Rand to assist in her pediatric clinic, she does so despite his good looks and irresistible charm, not because of them.

He's empathic, adores children, and has the patience of a saint.

He's also all she can think about, but he's off-limits.

What's a doctor to do to scratch that irresistible itch without risking workplace complications?

A shared adventure in the Perfect Match Virtual Studios seems like the solution, but instead of letting the algorithm choose a partner for her, Erika can try to influence it to select the one she wants. Awarding Rand a gift certificate to the service will get him into their database, but unless Erika can tip the odds in her favor, getting paired with him is a long shot.

Hopefully, a virtual adventure based on her and Rand's favorite series will do the trick.

The Valkyrie & The Witch

After breaking up with my boyfriend, I vow never to date a physician again and avoid workplace romances like the plague. Seeking an escape from bad memories and hospital politics, I apply for a job at the Perfect Match Virtual Fantasy Studios, where I hope to explore fantastical scenarios and beta-test new experiences.

I have no intention of entering a new relationship anytime soon, but it is difficult to ignore Kayden, a fellow trainee who's good-looking and charming but regrettably has aspirations of becoming a physician.

Hoping never to get paired with him to beta test an experience, I choose the Valkyrie adventure. It seems like a safe bet to avoid a guy like him, who would never select an experience where the female is the kick-ass heroine and the man only gets a supporting role. However, the algorithm has other plans in store for us. It seems to think that we are a perfect match.

In this post-apocalyptic virtual reimagining of Aladdin, James, the enigmatic prince, and Adina, the fearless thief, navigate the treacherous streets of Londabad, a city that echoes London and Ahmedabad and fuses magic and technology. In the face of danger, the chemistry between them ignites, and the lines between prince and thief, royalty and commoner blur.

FOR EXCLUSIVE PEEKS AT UPCOMING RELEASES & A FREE I. T. LUCAS COMPANION BOOK

Join my *VIP Club* and gain access to the VIP portal at itlucas.com
To Join, go to:
http://eepurl.com/blMTpD

INCLUDED IN YOUR FREE MEMBERSHIP:

YOUR VIP PORTAL

- Read preview chapters of upcoming releases.
- Listen to Goddess's Choice narration by Charles Lawrence
- Exclusive content offered only to my VIPs.

FREE I.T. LUCAS COMPANION INCLUDES:

- Goddess's Choice Part 1
- Perfect Match: Vampire's Consort (A standalone Novella)
- Interview Q & A
- Character Charts

If you're already a subscriber and you are not getting my emails, your provider is sending them

TO YOUR JUNK FOLDER, AND YOU ARE MISSING OUT ON IMPORTANT UPDATES. TO FIX THAT, ADD isabell@itlucas.com TO YOUR EMAIL CONTACTS OR YOUR EMAIL VIP LIST.

Check out the specials at
https://www.itlucas.com/specials

Printed in Dunstable, United Kingdom